Blood of the Father
The Children of Cain
Book 1

I0629940

ISBN: 979-8-9899068-5-7

First Printing, 2023

My Little Island in the Ether Publishing
PO Box 419
Lewistown, MT 59457

Also by David R Bishop

The Children of Cain
Blood of the Father

Standalone
No Good Deed

Also by J Scott Cordero

The Children of Cain
Blood of the Father

Standalone
No Good Deed

Also by David R Bishop & J Scott Cordero

No Good Deed
Blood of the Fallen

David & Scott thank Janet Cordero, Kimberlee Decker, Joshua Garrick, Ginger Jackson, Danyeil Luna, Jared Segers, Chelsea Stutz, and Don Wilson for their feedback and support.

David & Scott would like to offer special thanks to Trevor Rose.

David dedicates this novel to Gary.

Scott dedicates this novel to his loving bride.

Prologue

38 A.D., Vienne, Isère

Pontius pulled his cloak tighter about himself in protection from the sharp, icy wind coming off the river. He followed Gaius, his bodyguard, down the main public road leading from the docks on the bank of the Gère to the town of Vienne proper.

In the quickly gathering dusk, he could see the lights of torches and small cooking fires ahead in the main square where vendors roasted and hawked lamb, rabbit, boar, and badger. The odors of cooked meat were already wafting down the road to greet him. His stomach grumbled its lust. He'd not eaten anything all day.

Gaius must have a grumbling stomach too, Pontius thought, for Gaius's already brisk pace had quickened across the polished stones of the Roman road.

This road, which, he hoped, would be renamed after him once he'd finished with the improvements, at local landowner expense, of course, had occupied his every waking hour this past year. It would be his instrument for gaining the favor of the local people and, ultimately, the emperor. His exile would finally come to an end, and he would be welcomed back to Rome.

"Make way for Curator Pilatus," Gaius shouted as he pushed through the main square, thick with people.

Curator.

Pontius's face soured with bitterness. He bit down on a curse, silencing it in his throat. Not even twelve months ago, his title had been Prefect. The Chief Magistrate of Judea. Now it was the Curator, the Road Commissioner.

The people closest to Gaius and Pontius only sneered at the declaration. No one stepped, let alone rushed, out of Pontius's way. The locals held as little regard for the Curator as Pontius did, perhaps even less.

Pontius put a hand on Gaius's shoulder to silence him.

Gaius nodded his understanding and set his jaw. If verbal requests to make a path weren't heeded, Gaius would do so by force. Tall and powerfully

1

built, corded muscles moving like a den of snakes under his leathery skin, Gaius made an easy way.

"Hey," a fat man shouted through grease-drenched lips. After looking into Gaius's 'dead' eyes, the fat man immediately searched the ground for something he'd obviously just dropped and moved further out of the way.

Pontius snickered. He remembered the first time he'd met Gaius and remarked about his dead eyes. Gaius had asked what Pontius had meant. Pontius replied, "Dead eyes. Eyes that tell the world this is a man who has killed."

The man had briefly considered Pontius's words before responding, "Exceedingly dead eyes, my Lord."

Gaius continued to push and toss people aside. Ordinarily, Pontius would have objected to such behavior from Gaius, his secondhand since before his Prefecture of Judea. Manhandling the Locals didn't sit well with anyone, especially one exiled for the massacre of more than a thousand Samaritans.

Pontius wouldn't let himself think about that. It'd been a mistake, he realized now, but at the time—

ENOUGH!

He gave himself a mental shove. It's just nerves, he told himself. They were frayed. His mind and muscles were weary. Every day was spent haranguing the local landowners, merchants, and ship owners. Bullying dock workers and laborers. Cajoling that the roads are the responsibility of Rome, and the maintenance is the responsibility of its citizens.

The day's politicking was complete. Now it was time to relax. Wash his feet. Enjoy a goblet of wine. Perhaps two. Maybe even a third, and after a third, especially on an empty stomach, he might even enjoy the company of Claudia.

Pontius felt his heart and stomach contract as if they'd just been doused with the winter waters of the Gère at that thought.

He knew their marriage had been troubled since before they were exiled. No. That was not correct.

Their marriage had been wondrous, especially by Roman standards. He and Claudia had been in love. Truly in love. They'd enjoyed the same interests, the same passions. They enjoyed discussing the day's topics together.

And they'd been the perfect political couple. Each party. Each event. They'd decide on whom the other needed to get to know. They'd plot how best to gain an audience. They'd keep their ears and eyes open and work together to further their place in the Roman hierarchy. He always listened to Claudia's advice. Until...

Until she'd come to him and told him she'd suffered because of this man, this King of the Jews, this Jesus of Nazareth. She'd begged him not to have anything to do with him, to find some way to be rid of him. Instead, he'd washed his hands of the affair and put Jesus to death.

What had flashed in her eyes when he'd told her had almost made a believer of him in what the mystics had called demon possession. She did not speak to him until he sat on his throne, brooding over the news he'd just been told of the disappearance of Jesus' body, brooding over what this entire...fiasco...would cost him.

Claudia entered the audience chamber, a slack-jawed smile on her face.

"So, my Lord, the body of the King of the Jews no longer lies in a tomb." She crossed in front of him.

Pontius grunted.

She continued walking, passing behind his chair.

"And a detachment of guards," she bent to his ear, "Roman guards slept while how many men? Six? Rolled the stone away."

Pontius's hands balled into fists.

Claudia circled Pontius' chair. "Meanwhile, a man, a known traitor to Caesar, is allowed to go free to plot against Caesar. With your approval."

"I'm well aware of the implications—"

But Claudia cut across him. "I had advised you to have nothing to do with him," she spat. "To release him. And now he is the risen King in the eyes of his followers. And you are the benefactor of traitors."

She stopped before him, and a cruel smile split her face into a grotesque mask of hatred and mental agony. "But you washed your hands." She mimed an exaggerated, comical hand-washing. "All of our work." She was shrieking now. "All of our planning." She continued to wash her hands. "All of our dreams. Our triumphant return to Rome." Pontius never saw her hand, but he felt the sting on his cheek. Saw stars for a moment.

His mind processed what had just happened. Claudia had struck him. Him. Pontius Pilate. The Magistrate of Judea.

Pontius was out of his chair. The back of his hand connected with Claudia's jaw, spinning her around. His left hand grasped her hair, twisting and snapping hard downward. The motion jerked her around to face him and drew her head back, exposing her throat. His other hand grasped the ceremonial dagger always on his belt, his knuckles white, the point of the blade pressed to the hollow of her throat.

He might have sheathed the blade in his wife's neck, but as his muscles flexed to push the dagger home, his brain registered he was staring into his wife's wide, horror-stricken eyes, her mouth in the frozen rictus of a soundless scream.

Pontius let the blade fall from her throat and from his hand. It clanged on the stone floor, resounding in his ears like a death knell. He suddenly felt bone-weary. His stomach roiled. Pain speared his brain from his right eye to his nape. Releasing Claudia's hair, he stared at his open palm. Strands of her mane, strings of burnished onyx, clung to the rings on his fingers.

Claudia gasped, spluttering a cough.

Pontius looked down into Claudia's eyes, still wide with horror. Spittle dripped from her chin down her dress. She hadn't moved. She'd stood frozen as if the knife were still at her throat, her life in her husband's hands. He opened his mouth to speak, but his tongue was dry. He closed his mouth and tried swallowing, but couldn't. Turning on his heel, he fled the room.

They shared the bedchamber that night, neither saying a word. Neither ever acknowledged what had happened. He never asked her forgiveness, nor did she ever offer absolution. It stayed between them like some dank, festering chasm that slowly deepened.

It was why he'd been distracted and angry; he knew now and slaughtered more than a thousand innocent souls. It was why he'd been banished. And even as Claudia had begun to show signs of sickness, a cough which ended in Claudia spitting blood, and bed-drenching night sweats, they still did not speak of reconciliation.

As Claudia's illness seemed to consume her from the inside out, the strain between them had reached a breaking point. Pontius no longer slept in the same chamber as his wife; he no longer took meals with her. He treated her more as a memory than an actual presence within the walls of his home.

Pontius bounced off the stationary frame of Gaius. "What—?"

His words froze on his tongue as he looked past Gaius at his home. No torches had been lit. The house was dark. Cold. There were no sounds of the servants preparing for their master's imminent return, no smell of meat roasting or bread baking.

Gaius looked over his shoulder and fixed Pontius with a gaze that said, You stay right here. Don't. Move.

Pontius knew better than to protest. He nodded.

Gaius walked to the front door and pulled down one of the torches. Retrieving a flint from a small bag tied to his belt, he lit the torch, pushed the front door open, and stepped inside. He swore.

"Gaius," Pontius shouted as he sprang to the door and stepped across the threshold. Hot bile burned the reprimand in his throat.

Shards of bone protruded from the blood-spackled wall as if hammered there. Blood, bone, and clumps of gray matter formed a trail down the wall to a body, the head of which was now flat and square. What gray matter was left inside the skull oozed out of the ears and eye sockets. The scent of metal floated in the air.

Gaius darted into the main room.

Pontius stared at the skull and heard Gaius retch in the main room. He wanted to run screaming from the house. Instead, he found his feet moving toward the main room, his heart thrumming in his chest.

He entered the darkened main room, his left sandal slipping and his right sticking to the floor. The room was rancid with the odors of a slaughterhouse and a metal smith's forge. His stomach lurched, doubling him over, dropping him to his knees. He dry-heaved again and again until his abdomen cramped. His brow slick with sweat, he panted heavily through his mouth, wanting to spit but finding his mouth too dry. Pontius rose to his feet, his legs threatening to buckle.

"Gaius?"

Gaius only grunted.

Night had now fallen, and the moonlight fell in a watery swath through the skylight, bathing the room in shadows.

Pontius squinted hard and thought he made out the form of Gaius on his knees, his head over the pool in the center of the room. He heard Gaius retch again.

"Master," Gaius spat. "Don't come in here."

"Where's the torch, Gaius?" Taking shallow breaths through his mouth, Pontius moved with legs threatening to collapse. His sandals stuck to the floor, sounding like he was walking across spilled honey.

"You need to leave this room, Master," Gaius's voice rasped in the darkness. "This is a room of...of death."

"I've seen death before, Gaius."

"Not like this, my Lord," Gaius responded. "No one has. This is-...perverse. Evil."

Pontius reached Gaius and placed a hand on the scruff of the man's neck. It was as icy cold as the winds coming off the Gère. "Where's the torch? Why isn't it burning?"

"I extinguished it. I never want to gaze upon this room again."

"Light the torch," Pontius ordered.

"No." Gaius's voice sounded stronger.

Pontius felt a wave of irritation pass through him. Gaius was a seasoned warrior and a Roman who'd seen battle. He'd witnessed death. He'd delivered death. The Romans had perfected torture, the elongation of death to its most beautifully agonizing and exquisitely painful end, and dreamed up the most violent ways to watch a man die. This room could not compare.

"Give me the torch and some flint." Pontius held out his hand to the shadow of Gaius's prostrate figure.

Passing the torch and flint, Gaius gripped Pontius's wrist hard with a trembling hand. "Please, my Lord. Leave this room, this house." His voice quavered.

Pontius stared at the man's shadow. "Let me go, Gaius."

Gaius did as he was told.

Pontius relit the torch. As its light illuminated the room, Pontius heard his screams echo throughout the space.

The walls, ceiling, and floor had been splashed with buckets of blood. Bits of flesh stuck to the ceilings and walls. Fragments of bone lay scattered about like shards of a broken vase. Chunks of bodies and pieces of body parts were strewn about the room.

Pontius looked back towards the entrance and saw what he'd slipped on: the entrails of one of his servants. Nothing remained of any human form.

Lions, Pontius thought. It had to be. At least two. Maybe three. There was no other explanation. Lions have come into my house and devoured my servants.

He would've believed it if not for the skulls sitting on the pool's ledge stripped of their skin, the muscle and fatty tissue exposed.

Pontius gagged again and looked up. Chills swept through his body, and he felt his stomach muscles clench. Draped across the head of each bust depicting his family were the faces of his servants. Some were whole. Others were just the tattered remains of the face.

"What kind of evil did this?" Gaius's voice whined.

Pontius had no answer. He only stared at the skin masks, thinking of one thing.

"Claudia." His voice was nothing more than a choked whisper.

Pontius staggered towards the bed chamber. He felt drunk. He wished he were. It would explain how the floor seemed to lurch right then left, how the walls caught him hard in the shoulders to right him, how his legs trembled, his stomach roiled, and his head swam. He finally reached the open doorway of Claudia's bedchamber and froze.

Lying on the bed, still in her nightclothes, was the form of Claudia. She looked more waxen than human under the soft glow of the candles and harsh shadows created by the crackling torches. Unlike the other rooms, the bed chamber was clean. Pristine. Unlike the others in the house, her olive skin was unmarred except for the lines of age and illness. Her hair, once the sheen of polished onyx, was now streaked with silver and still fell past her shoulders. And the bed showed no signs of the violence littering the rest of the house.

In an instant, Pontius was at the bedside. He collapsed onto it, gathering her hands into his. Moisture blurred his vision as he registered how cold her hands were. Cold. Not like the waters of the Gère in winter, but the cold of the dead. He began to sob. "Claudia, Claudia, Claudia, Claudia."

"She no longer suffers, Roman."

The voice was flavored with an accent Pontius had never heard before. He spun to find a man like no other man he'd ever seen before leaning against the jamb of the terrace entrance.

The man's tunic, cloak, and sandals were as ordinary as any other peasant's in the main square. His wavy black hair hung unkempt past his broad shoulders. His skin was the texture of oak. His arms, heavy muscles knotted from years working the land, hung at his side. One muscular leg bent at the knee, the foot pressing against the jamb. But what caused Pontius to slide to the other side of the bed, to place the bed between himself and this stranger, was the man's eyes. His eyes were not the dead eyes of Gaius. They were something beyond.

Drawing the sword from his belt, Gaius screamed a battle cry and advanced into the room.

Pontius watched the stranger disappear and then reappear behind Gaius. He heard the sickening thunk as he watched the stranger remove Gaius's head from his body. The stranger dropped Gaius's head. It rolled across the floor, coming to rest at his feet. Dropping to his knees as if bowing, Gaius's body crumpled to the floor.

"Why do you grieve for her, Roman?"

The voice came from behind Pontius. It bore no strain from just parting a head from a body.

Pontius turned and found the stranger sitting in a chair on the opposite side of the room. He watched as twenty years vanished from the man's appearance. His wavy, unkempt hair was now brushed out, its sheen reflecting the light from the candles and torches in the room. His skin no longer resembled oak, but was now a creamy hue. And his eyes... Pontius took several more steps backward.

Pontius's mouth opened and closed several times, but he said nothing. He tried to swallow but heard only a dry click in his throat.

"Why do you grieve?" The stranger repeated. The accent was neither Roman nor any of the dialects used by conquered nations within the empire. "She was in great pain. Dying little by agonizing little each day." The stranger smiled. "In your heart of hearts, you've wished for this day. When she could no longer utter whimpers of agony or barbs of antagonism." The stranger stood. "You are free, Roman."

Pontius stared at the stranger. He'd been ready to grapple with this...this...whatever it was. It was by no means human. He'd wanted to grab it by the throat and choke its life from it. But...It had been right. He'd watched his beloved Claudia waste away. Felt his heart rip open with each cry of pain, wanting to rip her heart out with each accusation she uttered when she wasn't crying.

Her accusation that the illness was his fault. If not for his exile, she wouldn't be in Vienne. She wouldn't be sick. If not for his growing disregard for human life, even Samaritan life, he wouldn't have massacred all those innocent women and children. If not for his stubbornness in not listening to her when she told him of her dream and how he shouldn't have anything to do with this Jesus.

But he'd washed his hands of him. Of the Sadducees and Pharisees. Of the crowds screaming, "Give us Barabbas. Crucify Jesus." His fear of the repercussions had cost him the very thing he'd been trying to save, his political career. And then he'd turned...cruel. First, disregarding the Jews, then goading their religious leaders, and finally murdering hundreds of Samaritans to win back the favor of both the Jews and Rome.

Sometimes she said it. Sometimes she didn't. But it was always in her eyes. The accusations. The anger. The hate. The disappointment that he was no longer the man she loved. The dare for him to wash his hands of her.

"Well, Roman," The stranger said. "I'm waiting."

Pontius stared at the stranger, no longer feeling fear. At that moment, that memory of a dare in her eyes, he'd realized Claudia had been right. She'd told him the gods would turn against them if he allowed the man accused of calling himself the King of the Jews to be harmed. That's what this stranger was, the executioner of the gods. He was here to dole out the wrath of the gods upon him and his family.

Well, Pontius thought to himself, that didn't mean he was a rodent to be toyed with by its predator. He was still a man. If this "thing" wanted some satisfaction by playing games, Pontius would have none of that, and that bit of defiance, not willing to be toyed with, straightened his back, squared his shoulders, and set his jaw. "Do what you came here to do, Stranger."

The stranger smiled. "What do you think I came here to do, Roman?"

"To kill me." Pontius hated the tremor he heard in his voice, but he gritted his teeth and stared defiantly at the stranger.

"I came here," the stranger stood, "to offer you what you are hungering for."

A long, silent moment passed between them before Pontius tried to process what he'd heard. "I...don't understand."

The stranger took a step towards Pontius. "Every part of you has lived for only one purpose: To regain power. Regain prestige. To again win the hearts and minds of Rome.

"Rome is the center of the universe," Pontius retorted.

"Spare me the idle words, Roman. I've lived far too long." The stranger's skin rippled and suddenly looked as frail as aged parchment. His hair turned as brittle as straw. He took another step forward, and his skin and hair gleamed again. "You see Rome as unstoppable. Immovable. But I see Rome as morning mist in a meadow. It may be thick at first light, but by the time the sun is high, it will have burned away.

"I've seen empires rise and fall. The Babylonians. Macedonians. Egyptians. They are gone. I am still here. As I will be when Rome falls."

"What are you?" Pontius heard the question come out of his mouth and was surprised. That hadn't been what he'd planned on saying.

"My name is Cain. I am the Firstborn. The firstborn of Eve. The firstborn of Sin. The firstborn of the Fallen One. His blood courses through my veins. Freely, it was offered. Willingly, it was accepted. I've made eleven like me before you. You will be my twelfth. My last.

"I offer you, Roman, power like no human can understand. You will continue after the Roman Empire and all the empires that follow. There will be no pain. No death. No decay. You will have wealth and power. You will be my son. My child." The stranger took another step forward. "So what say you, Roman?"

10

Pontius didn't need to think about it. This Cain offered him everything he'd striven for in life. He nodded acceptance. He looked into the stranger's eyes and shrieked.

Cain's eyes weren't dead but dancing with fire. The smile on his face widened with malice. Wickedness. And sharp, gleaming fangs behind his smile.

Pontius opened his mouth to scream again.

1

Present Day, Washington, D.C.

Senator Walter Copeland couldn't rein in his toothy grin as he walked through the door into the lobby of his office. It'd taken him twenty years, but he'd finally gotten an education bill with bipartisan support to the floor that would raise teacher salaries, increase the number of teachers in the schools, and improve the curriculum nationwide. He was also very close to brokering another healthcare reform bill.

Copeland savored the moment as he watched his staff members freeze in whatever they'd been doing right before he walked in, eyes wide, breath held.

"Break out the sparkling grape juice," Copeland announced, thrusting a fist of victory into the air.

At fifty-seven, Copeland was not only in the prime of his political career, enjoying bipartisan popularity at home in Florida and on the Hill, but he was also in the prime of health. He didn't eat junk food or sweets. Didn't drink anything more potent than cough syrup. Didn't smoke. He swam forty laps every morning.

Back in college, he could swim sixty laps easily every morning. He was proud he'd only lost twenty laps in thirty-seven years. He figured he'd still be lapping double digits in another thirty-seven years. Just that morning, he'd had a long laugh in the shower, imagining his ninety-four-year-old speedo-clad body emerging from the pool after twenty laps.

Though his hair was all salt now, the last of the pepper fading the previous year, he had the spring in his step of a man half his age. He was a senior member of Congress with a reputation for getting things done. He was happily married to his high school sweetheart. His three children were the poster children for success. Walter Jr. was a decorated Infantry Captain in the Army. Richard had just graduated from Yale Law. His daughter, Karen, will graduate from Annapolis next year.

Thunderous applause greeted his words. His staff was the best group of young people he'd ever seen. They were hungry for change, eager to roll up their sleeves, and determined to fix the system.

Copeland was on top of the world and at the top of his game as he took the glass his secretary, Rebecca, offered him. He raised his glass. "To you." He looked each person in the room in the eye. "The citizens of this great nation may not know your names just yet or what you've done for them today, but thanks to you, their future will be a little bit better." He raised his glass higher and then downed its contents in one swallow.

Cat calls, wolf whistles, cheers, and backslaps followed around the room. Rebecca refilled his glass.

"Thank you, Dear." Copeland took another gulp, savoring the juice's taste as it danced on his tongue.

Rebecca smiled as she took a sip.

Copeland looked at Rebecca and frowned a little inside. She reminded him so much of his daughter, Karen. Smart. Ambitious. Not in the 'people are just stepping-stones' kind of way. Sassy. But with the heart of a servant. If Rebecca had had a few opportunities growing up, she'd be the one walking in and making the announcement. It would be her name on the outside door. She'd be the Senator instead of working for the Senator. Or maybe she'd have gone to Annapolis like Karen. Who knew? That was the problem Copeland realized. In this land of opportunity, too many people were getting too few opportunities.

Copeland nodded to Rebecca, quietly vowing to change that. For Rebecca. For all the others. This was the greatest nation in the history of the world. Surely that meant each citizen deserved the best education and healthcare in the world. And one day, God willing, he'd run Rebecca's campaign for Senate.

A thought struck him as he finished the glass. "I haven't called the H.O.H. yet." He scurried to his private office.

One of the newer staff members shot Rebecca a quizzical glance. "H.O.H?"

"Head of House," Rebecca explained, smiling. "His wife."

Rebecca watched Copeland disappear into his office. He was a good man, she thought to herself; a very good man working for his state and his country. And a good man to work for.

When she'd first started making the rounds, trying to get a staff job, she'd met politicians with wandering eyes and others with wandering hands. Some believed she should be on her knees, thanking them for the opportunity. Copeland was different. He always looked her in the eye, and sometimes, she thought, straight into her brain, watching the gears in motion. She was proud to work for him.

She was proud of him as she watched his office door close. He deserved it today. She hoped for many more days like today with him. Maybe, just maybe, he'd help her have a few of her own.

2

"Roman." Copeland's voice was delighted at his unexpected but always welcome guest, a surprised but genuine smile on his face, his hand extended for a hearty handshake. "Great to see you. I'm sorry, but nobody told me you were here."

He seized Dvanaesti's hand, willing himself not to flinch as Dvanaesti's fingers enclosed his own in a cold iron vice. Summer or winter, the man's hands felt like he'd been handling ice cream or a cold drink. And he had a grip Copeland had never felt from a man of Roman's age. Roman appeared to be in his late fifties, with short, curly gray hair, tanned skin radiating vigor and vitality, and hazel eyes that shone brightly. As always, he wore a thousand-dollar suit.

This time, though, as Dvanaesti took his hand, Copeland felt a jolt run through it, up his arm, and into the rest of his body, like the shock someone gets when grabbing the spark plug of a running lawnmower. His heart fluttered.

Roman released Copeland's hand.

Copeland took a few awkward steps backward, bumping into the corner of his desk. He felt disoriented and decided to rest his backside on the corner of the desk so as not to broadcast his unsteadiness to his biggest benefactor.

"D-did you happen to catch C-c-SPAN...an hour ago? We...we had a...b-big day."

Copeland rubbed at the tingle growing in his fingers as if they were falling asleep.

Roman sat on the sofa.

Copeland raised a hand to his chest, tightening with indigestion or heartburn. Perhaps the sparkling grape juice didn't agree with him, he thought.

Sweat dampened his brow and the collar of his shirt. He pulled at his tie, his fingers not responding as his chest tightened. Copeland looked to Roman, who only looked back as if waiting for the punchline to a long-winded joke.

"Roman. I think...I think I might be...having...a heart...attack." Copeland winced as his chest constricted. Sweat drenched his shirt and face.

Roman continued to sit watching. Waiting.

Copeland wasn't too sure why Roman couldn't see what was happening. The man was oblivious to Copeland's presence in the room with him. He gave up on Roman's help and staggered behind the desk to get to the phone.

But moving only made it worse. Copeland felt intense pain as he'd never felt before. It radiated out from his chest into both arms down to the fingertips. He shrieked or would have if he could've sucked any air into his lungs. He looked again at Roman.

Roman only sat there.

It hit Copeland with the same force as the heart attack he was now having. Roman knew it was a heart attack and was content for some reason only known to Roman to wait and watch him die.

A wave of horror swept through Copeland as he tried again to move to the phone, but things were starting to get fuzzy. Blurry around the edges. The room tilted like that old Batman TV show he loved as a child. It kept him off balance, preventing him from reaching the phone.

Copeland reached out with one last rush of energy but missed the phone, knocking the small-framed photographs of him with his wife, the kids, and his whole family off the desk.

The frames crashed to the floor, breaking the glass. Copeland heard the sickening *thwack* as his head hit the table, but couldn't feel it. He felt his legs give out and his entire body slide to the floor behind the desk. He turned his head to see Roman still sitting calmly on the sofa.

Then he felt nothing as the light in the room slowly extinguished, leaving it dark.

Rebecca heard a muffled crash in Senator Copeland's office and went to investigate. Her fellow staff members, still caught up in the reverie of the day's victory, heard nothing. Opening the door, she saw the empty office and Senator Copeland lying on his back, eyes open. Vacant.

Rebecca screamed.

3

James Peterson, the executive assistant to Senator Weathers, walked through his boss's Georgetown brownstone filled with party guests. Smiling and waving, he greeted congresspeople, their spouses, and celebrities as he kept an ear out for his boss's booming baritone voice.

He's telling one of his *Bubba and Goober* stories, Peterson thought to himself, and grimaced. The senator hated being interrupted, especially when regaling an audience of contributors, their fat wallets ready to be thinned, with the adventures of Bubba and Goober, but he would want to know this. Peterson pushed himself into the room.

"...So Goober yells up, 'It's only ankle-deep.'" The senator's voice was in rare form tonight. "So Bubba jumps into the pile of manure, and it's clean up to his neck. And Goober shrugs and says, 'Well, I,'" Weathers saw Peterson gesturing, "dove.'"

Weathers excused himself amidst the laughter that quickly turned to cries of 'boo.' He flashed a tooth-filled smile, gestured surrender, and moved to Peterson.

"This better be good." Weathers fixed the young man with a steely gaze.

Peterson couldn't help but be in awe of Weathers. He was a tall, broad-shouldered, African American man in his late forties, in better shape than men half his age. And that voice, Peterson thought. It could be as sweet as molasses or as acidic as heartburn when he wanted it to be.

"Uh, yes, Sir." He cleared his throat. He looked around before exclaiming in a whisper barely loud enough for his boss to hear, "Senator Walter Copeland was found in his office dead. From an apparent heart attack." Peterson paused for effect. "He's gone, Sir."

Weathers turned away from Jamie, but not before his executive assistant heard an expletive escape the senator's mouth. It was the closest he'd ever come to publicly seeing his boss lose his composure. He was impressed. Again.

Weathers turned back to Peterson. "Get everybody together in my office." His face and tone looked as nonchalant as if he were saying he wanted a tuna on rye for lunch today.

"Yes, Sir," Peterson responded, sounding officious.

The senator turned on his heel and marched back into the study. "Sorry folks, but I've got a phone call I've got to take." His wife, Johanna, shot him a reproving glance that said *You better not leave me alone with these people.* Weathers's responding glare screamed, *Don't test me right now.* Her eyes dropped to the floor. "I'll be back in a country minute."

The crowd laughed as Peterson heard Johanna Weathers's voice exclaiming, "Did you hear the one about Bubba and Goober..." as he followed Weathers from the room.

4

"Top off your drinks, Gentlemen." Senator Weathers said from the bar as Peterson closed the heavy mahogany door to the study. "We're going to need it."

Peterson grabbed a brass handle above the brass doorknob and pushed it hard. A faint *wffft* could be heard as the sound dampeners around the door engaged. Without ultra-sensitive sound-detecting equipment, no one on the other side of the door would hear anything. Weathers had virtually soundproofed the room with dampeners, double-paned windows, and double insulation between the joists.

He'd installed one other soundproofing device no one, even Peterson, knew about. The senator didn't think it would be necessary. If he did, all he had to do was flip a switch. No sound would be detected in or out.

Weathers topped off his scotch and moved to his favorite chair, a plush leather wingback. He settled into the chair, listening to the soft crackles of the leather. He indulged in the fantasy of lighting a cigar, pressing the remote of the plasma screen hidden within the paneled wall, and watching tennis or a film.

It was good to indulge a little, he told himself. Internally, it gave him time to settle. Externally, it gave the men assembled in the room, now staring at him, the impression that he was calm amid the coming storm. It also fed into Weathers's flair for the dramatic. The *Pinter Pause* is what his Introduction to Theatre professor would call this moment of silence.

The men filled drinks, lit cigars or cigarettes, or swallowed pills according to their habit. The room now waited in silence for Weathers, the host of tonight's Democratic National Fundraiser and Majority Leader (and the next presidential hopeful), to announce the reason for their assemblage. One thing Weathers was not known for was a flippant nature.

Weathers took a sip of scotch, swallowed, and silently cursed Senator Walter Copeland. It was time to talk.

"Senator Walter Copeland of Florida died of a heart attack this afternoon."

There was a collective intake of breath.

Weathers sipped at his scotch. "Which means we have a problem."

The collective continued to hold its breath—all except one man.

Brent Albee, the junior Senator from Texas, guffawed. "A problem? How could that be a problem?"

Weathers bit his lip and exhaled as if Albee was an eight-year-old who couldn't understand at that age that a girl punching you meant she liked you. "The Distinguished Gentleman from Texas wonders why Copeland's dying at this juncture is problematic. After all, he was most likely the Republican presidential nominee. A nominee we were already strategizing against. A nominee with a track record we could attack. And that new education legislation," he chuckled, "we were going to destroy that with PAC and super PAC advertising. It's much better with some unknown entity we have no time to prepare for than a known entity." His face slid into that Georgia red clay grin he was famous for as he drawled, "Ain't that right?"

Albee nodded, though not as confidently as when he'd guffawed. It dawned on him that no one else had joined him in thinking this was good news. He looked around the room at the grave faces tinged with incredulity at his ignorance and realized perhaps the best thing he could've done for himself would've been to keep his mouth shut. His thoughts were interrupted by Weathers.

"As you look upon the grand horizon of politics, does anyone stand out as the future of the Republican Party?" Weathers sipped his scotch and waited for an answer.

"You mean *besides* Copeland?" Albee regretted opening his mouth as the men around him chuckled in derision.

Weathers waved a dismissive hand at Albee. "Copeland is—...was the Republican Party. But behind him," Weathers looked around the room, "we hoped several more years down the road, is not just the future of the Republican Party, but of American politics." Weathers sipped as he locked eyes with Albee. "What do you know of Governor Cain Dvanaesti?"

Albee looked as if he'd been asked to provide the chemical breakdown of *Tide* laundry detergent. "Governor Cain...?"

"Deh-Van-Es-Tee," Weathers admonished. "Kid, if you're going to survive in D.C., you better learn to pay attention to every other state in this Union. Not just the Longhorn State." Weathers looked at Peterson.

Peterson stepped forward, setting his glasses firmly on the bridge of his nose. "Governor Cain Dvanaesti, the youngest governor in American history, was expected to announce his intention to run for a second term as governor of Florida. But he'll certainly now pursue the vacant Senate seat."

Albee seized upon a thought like a child grabbing a prized piece of candy behind his mother's back. He could barely suppress a triumphant smile. "Correct me if I'm wrong, but isn't Florida one of the states that doesn't hold a special election when a congressional seat is vacated?" He was growing more confident. "In which case, as I understand it, the governor of that state appoints someone to the seat. He wouldn't be able to appoint himself."

Peterson cleared his throat. Albee and the rest of the men in the room set their eyes upon him. "Florida is one of thirteen states that do *not* hold a special election, and Governor Dvanaesti has already reached out to no less than twelve potential candidates."

"And?" Weathers prompted. He knew the answer to this question, but it was all part of his flair for the dramatic.

Peterson pushed his glasses back up his nose. "Almost every person he asked said they would agree to take the vacant seat on one condition, that Dvanaesti runs for president."

"Of the United States?" Albee's voice squeaked, and he hated himself for it.

"Yes." Weathers agreed. "You have an astutely obvious eye, Albee."

The other men in the room chuckled at Albee's expense.

Weathers nodded for Peterson to continue.

"One person. Former Senator Diana Vancore and Florida's current Secretary of State agreed to step down from the cabinet and complete Copeland's term on the condition that Dvanaesti does not run for a second term as governor but for the Senate seat."

"And if he does," Weathers interjected, "he'll be unstoppable."

Albee looked around the room, waiting for someone to scream *Gotcha!* Nobody did. "But he's just a governor." Albee's protest sounded more like a whine.

Senator Perlman of New Jersey took a step towards Albee. He was a large man who believed in Grecian Formula and pomade. His hair was unusually dark for a man his age, parted on the side and slicked back. "Right now, he's *just* a governor. A big actor on a small stage, even if it's Florida. And he knows that not even forty percent of the governors who have run for president in the history of this country have sat in the Oval Office.

"As a United States Senator, he becomes a smaller actor on a bigger stage. It won't take him long to move into the spotlight. And his father is Roman Dvanaesti."

"Who's Roman Dvanaesti?" Albee looked around the room.

Weathers pounded back the last of his scotch. He needed more, but didn't think his legs could support his weight. So he held the glass up to Peterson, who retrieved the glass from Weathers and slinked to the bar. "Probably one of the richest guys on the planet, practically nobody's heard of, with his hands in every major campaign over the past two decades."

Albee's face was a comic mixture of awe and greed.

"Finally, something this kid can understand." Jack Lemay's voice rang out. Lemay, the D.N.C. National Chairman, and the complete antithesis of Perlman, young, trim, and generally soft-spoken, wiped his glasses with the back of his tie.

"Why isn't he on the Forbes list of richest people?" Albee wasn't challenging, more reaching out for something to grasp. "I've never seen his name in any newspaper or financial magazine."

"And you won't," Weathers said. "Roman Dvanaesti is the man *behind* the man behind the scenes. He comes with money, affluence, and connections. There are unlimited dollars and resources available. It's not just his money."

"It's believed that through his company, The Javelin Group, which is worldwide and multi-faceted," Jamie said as he brought the refilled glass to Weathers, "no one has been elected in any country that his prints aren't all over it. Except that, no one can prove it."

Weathers accepted the glass. "You should know from personal experience." He took a hearty swig. "Nobody gets to this stage of their political career without money. Lots of money. And when you're elected, you become beholden to the money."

"Just think of a politician who didn't need to kowtow to financial backers." Lemay walked to the bar.

"Cain Dvanaesti already doesn't answer to anybody because he doesn't need to answer to anybody," Weathers added.

"And he can do no wrong." Another voice sang out.

"Of course, he can do wrong." Now it was Albee's turn to freshen his drink. "He's *human*, after all."

Weathers scoffed. "No, he's not. He's John Kennedy on crack."

"What does that mean?" Albee was becoming alarmed.

"Mr. Albee—"

"Senator Albee," Albee corrected.

Jamie smiled with a veiled sheepishness. "My apologies. Senator Albee." Jamie moved to stand in front of Albee. "Cain Dvanaesti was the valedictorian of his high school in Miami. He was also a first-team All-American in football. He lettered in football, track, baseball, and academics. He graduated Summa Cum Laude from the University of Miami with a degree in political science. He graduated Summa Cum Laude from the University of Florida with an M.B.A. and passed on a full ride to Harvard Law to keep it in the state. He received his Juris Doctorate from Florida State University. Again, Summa Cum Laude.

"After school, he became an assistant state attorney in the Eleventh Circuit. Not only did he have a better than ninety percent conviction rate, but he was also an integral part of the state attorney's human trafficking task force and elder and vulnerable adult task force. On weekends, he worked in soup kitchens in the barrios and dispensed legal advice. In purely hypothetical terms, of course.

"When he ran for Governor, he swept every county in Florida, including Leon, where the capital is located. Usually a Democratic stronghold. He received seventy-eight percent of the Democratic Party vote. Every piece of legislation with his name on it has passed. He gives hundreds of thousands of dollars of his wealth to all the Florida colleges and universities. He loves the state and is the best P.R. guy a state could ever hope for, free of charge."

Perlman was all caught up in the fervor now. "This guy will do on a national level just what he's done in Florida. It will be the ruin of politics in this country. Actual, genuine bipartisanship."

"That sounds a little melodramatic, Senator Perlman." Albee looked like he was on a merry-go-round that was getting faster and faster.

Perlman shot back. "No, it isn't. I've met this guy." Perlman's eyes glazed over. "He makes you feel like you're the only person he's ever wanted to talk to. He makes you feel like your ideas, no matter how stupid or off the wall, are the most riveting he's ever heard and worthy of discussion. Even if he disagrees with you, he treats you with respect. You can't help but love the jerk. Or worse. Respect him." Perlman chuffed. "I walked away questioning my entire platform."

"He had Obama wondering why he wasn't a Republican when they met," Jamie added.

"And after he finishes his first term as the distinguished gentleman from Florida, he'll have the political clout and name recognition to run for president." Lemay's voice and face filled with admiration. "His presence will dominate the American political landscape for the next twenty years."

Perlman added, "Democrats and Republicans alike will be seeking his endorsement for everything from candidacy to bills on the floor. All he'll have to do is show up at a rally or a photo op and," he snapped his fingers, "a sure thing ain't so sure anymore."

Weathers stood up to regain control of the room. "I can have Jamie run out and make up some We Heart Dvanaesti T-shirts if y'all want."

Peterson took a confused half-step towards the door.

Weathers held up a hand to Peterson. "I was being facetious."

Peterson's face reddened.

"Okay. This guy is our single biggest threat." Albee seemed focused now. "What are we going to do about it?"

"Well." Weathers began to pace around the room. "That's the rub. When he first appeared on our radar, he was already governor. We hoped he'd want a second term, then take a few years off. Maybe he'd work for the R.N.C. before going for the Senate seat or stay on the Florida political stage. We figured we had at least six years to work on a strategy to deal with him. Now..."

"Now," Lemay took a long drag on his cigarette. "Now it's time to give him a call."

Weathers walked back to the bar. He poured himself another drink, held it to his lips as he decided, then downed the scotch to stiffen his resolve. He turned back to face the men in the room. "Jamie. Give Hawthorne a call."

5

"We need you to go to Florida," Weathers said through exhaled cigar smoke.

"What's in Florida?" Gabriel Hawthorne knew what was in Florida, or who, more accurately. He wasn't stupid. He'd listened to N.P.R. that morning as he made breakfast and cleaned the Beretta tucked in his jacket. He'd heard about Senator Copeland's sudden coronary. There was only one serious contender for the seat. Governor Cain Dvanaesti.

Gabriel knew why he was here. His specialty was dirt. Not the kind you till in the soil, but the dangerous kind. The nasty kind. It ruined careers, destroyed marriages, and drove their children to drugs and alcohol. There was always dirt. Nobody had a bare closet or a well-swept house. Nobody's life could pass a white-glove test. Gabriel had a knack for digging dirt.

He was good at it. Much better than he'd ever been as a cop. That wasn't true, Gabriel thought with a pang as he waited for the answer. He'd been a good cop with a great future. What was that saying? The Blues ain't nothing but a good man feeling bad. He liked that one. He also liked the one that said sometimes bad things happen to good people. Sometimes, the circumstances are beyond your control. You don't see it because they're so small they don't seem like circumstances. Like baby steps, they still move you to where you never thought you'd go. Before you know it, you're in a bad place. You're turning in your badge and your gun. You're a disgrace.

That had never sat well with Gabriel. It was a jagged pill he wasn't willing to swallow. He had a skill set and intended to use it well. He would shut down those unfortunate events and the men who planned them. In that respect, he was better at the job than being a cop.

He had a reputation in this town. He was so good he'd been dubbed *The Gardener*. When he first heard of this moniker, he was slightly offended. The Gardener, he thought, was a little too prosaic, like he was Mr. Greenjeans, or maybe he should be hallowing the benefits of Miracle-Gro to little old ladies lamenting the droopiness of their pansies and petunias. *The Gardener* had stuck, however, and had grown on him, and now, when his type of "gardening" was called for, he made a lot more money than Mr. Greenjeans and all the Miracle-Gro Spokespeople combined.

The one thing Gabriel didn't do was fabricate dirt. He hadn't done that when he was a cop. He hadn't planted it either. He'd covered it up, looked the other way, and protected the producers and consumers. But he'd never created it. The way he saw it, if he did that now, he'd prove the people who said he wasn't just a crooked cop but a dirty one correct. Besides, the one thing he'd learned first as a cop and now as a gardener is that he didn't have to. Look hard enough and long enough, and you'll always find dirt.

"We need you to do a bit of gardening," Weathers said, sounding like a wise guy from a bad Noir flick.

"And do a bit of fill-in where you need to," Lemay interjected.

Gabriel looked between the men. Weathers was a decent guy. He could be forgiven for his flamboyant love of his alma mater, Georgia, and cornpone Bubba and Goober jokes. He paid for his season tickets and airline tickets to all the Georgia home games, not the taxpayers. But he was a politician. They were always looking for a way to discredit the other guy. Not the ideas, but the guy. As soon as Weathers announced he was running for President, Gabriel knew he'd be receiving a call from the Republicans looking for a bit of gardening. Gabriel would take that job. Republican or Democrat. They were all the same to Gabriel. Dirt was dirt. It just came down to who handed him the shovel first.

And Lamay? Well, he and Gabriel went way back.

Gabriel stood. "You've got the wrong guy." At just over six feet tall, Gabriel had an inch on Weathers and four on Lemay.

Weathers looked at the man, noting the wavy, dark hair lightly dusted with gray, the weathered face with two-day stubble over a square jaw, and the crooked nose from multiple breaks, and stepped back. The distance felt like a smart move.

Lemay, however, had never been accused of being perceptive. He held up a hand like a bouncer denying entry. "Now hold on there—"

"I find dirt. I don't put it there. I don't fabricate." Gabriel started for the door.

"But it's just...well, you've got a reputation," Lemay interjected. "No one can just *find* dirt that easily. Some of it has to be...put there."

"There's *always* dirt." Gabriel looked Lemay in the eye. "Always." A perverse smirk eased across his face. "Let's take you, for example, Mr.

Chairman. There isn't a more doting husband and father on the political landscape, nor a stronger advocate for the Pro-Choice position. I'm sure your wife and daughters would be surprised to learn of that "niece" of yours in Biloxi, and everyone might be surprised just how much you've paid, in cash, for those abortions for your "niece" in Hattiesburg. Not to mention that hooker who O.D.'d in Georgetown."

Lemay took a step towards Gabriel, visibly shaking with rage. "You Sonuva."

Gabriel stepped towards Lemay.

Weathers grabbed Lemay by the arm. "You're looking a little peaked, Lemay. Why don't you get yourself something to eat?"

Lemay spun to face Weathers, but Weathers only gripped him harder. "Jamie. Take Mr. Lemay to the kitchen, please."

Peterson stepped up. "Right this way, Mr. Lemay." Grabbing Lemay by the elbow, he ushered him from the room.

Weathers moved to the table by his wingback chair, picked up the glass, drained it in one swallow, and refilled it from the decanter. He sipped silently for a minute before pulling a Visa card from his jacket pocket and handing it to Gabriel. "Debit. The PIN's two-zero-two-four. Expenses are sixteen hundred a day."

Gabriel stood and accepted the card. "Twenty-twenty-four, huh? A little wishful thinking?"

Weathers ignored the last question. "Your garden is Cain Dvanaesti."

6

Ajaka "Stefan" Owusu answered his phone on the second ring. "I'm on a date," Stefan said in his deep baritone voice. After ten years in the States, six of those working for Gabriel, Stefan's English was better, but his Sudanese accent was still thick.

Gabriel looked at the clock hanging on the wall across from his desk.

7:45 pm.

"With *Jeopardy!*"

"What do you want, Gabe?"

Gabriel smiled. Stefan didn't suffer cuteness or small talk, or chit-chat. He liked the simplicity of facts. It's what made him so good at his job and why Gabriel had taken him under his wing six years ago.

Ten years ago, when Gabriel had still been a cop, his last day to be exact, he'd responded to a 9-1-1 call about three men who'd jumped some poor black kid. The black kid was down, but so were two of his attackers. Stefan had been twenty-one at the time, and when Gabriel interviewed him, he looked like an ordinary kid, except for his eyes. They weren't the eyes of a serial murderer or gangbanger. These eyes had witnessed murders, violence, and horrors that people three times his age had never seen.

Gabriel soon learned Stefan was famous, at least within the group to which Stefan belonged. Stefan was one of the Lost Boys of Sudan. At twelve, he'd returned to his village after spending the day tending his family's cattle to find his family murdered and soldiers waiting for him and the other returning boys. They were conscripted into the rebel army and forced to become soldiers. For days, civilians were lined up against a wall before him as a soldier put a machine gun in his hands and a pistol to his head. He was told to kill the people or be killed.

He killed the people. This continued until he no longer needed to be ordered or threatened. He just killed. He served in the rebel army until he was sixteen. His patrol was ambushed. Stefan was hit and left for dead. Discovered by Catholic Charities workers among the corpses, he was moved to Kenya, where his mind and body could heal.

As part of the joint American government and UNICEF program, Stefan (a nickname given to him by an elderly Sister) immigrated to the U.S., first settling in Omaha, Nebraska. But Stefan had spent too many years roaming and making camp under the stars. He wandered across America, savoring freedom, onto the streets of Washington, D.C., and into the path of three young men who didn't have the common sense to recognize whom to mess with and whom to leave alone.

When Gabriel looked into those eyes at the hospital, seeing the wisdom, the hollowness, he knew he wanted to help this young man. So he'd paid for his attorney out of his pocket and offered him a job once he was cleared.

Now, Stefan worked for Gabriel. He also had a knack for gardening. And planting. At night, when other men his age were in bars or at parties, Stefan preferred to plant himself alone in his recliner, his TV tray on his lap, and his television tuned to *Jeopardy!*

"I need you to go to Tallahassee," Gabriel said.

"Tallahassee?" Stefan sounded out the word.

"The capital of Florida," Gabriel explained. "I need you to start a jacket. I want you to go tomorrow."

"Tomorrow," Stefan repeated. Who is the subject?"

"Cain Dvanaesti."

"Spell, please."

Gabriel did, hearing Stefan scratch the name on a piece of paper as he repeated each letter.

"I will leave as soon as *Jeopardy!* is over." Stefan hung up the phone.

Gabriel couldn't help but laugh at Stefan's bluntness as he pressed the digits to another number.

7

I hate Miami in August!

Gabriel felt the summer heat slam into him like a safety tackling a wide receiver as he stepped out of Miami International Airport. Sweat immediately bloomed on his forehead and armpits as he waited for the bus to take him to the rental car lot.

It's the dirty little secret that cities in South Florida leave out of their brochures and off their websites. The heat. They show you pictures of sugary-white beaches, Caribbean-blue waters, Art Deco buildings, and plenty of young, nubile people. Sun-bleached hair, sunglasses, and bronze bodies. But they never mention the heat.

Gabriel was not happy. But he didn't have a choice, he reminded himself, not after his previous conversation with Gutierrez.

Miguel Gutierrez had been a fellow cop. They'd worked together on several dicey situations during their tenure with the Washington D.C. Police Department. Gutierrez had quit the Force a few months before Gabriel and moved to Miami to start a private security and investigations firm. He'd done quite well for himself. When Gabriel began gardening, they found they could use each other's services. That was until yesterday.

Gabriel had called his old friend, Miguel, about a young Cain Dvanaesti in South Florida. Miguel had had no compunctions before discussing much more famous and infamous names. Not anymore.

"What could I possibly find on the governor of Florida when no one found anything when he was running for office?" Miguel sounded like Gabriel had asked him to prove the Shroud of Turin to be authentic.

"Come on, Miguel," Gabriel had persisted, surprised by his friend's resistance to the idea. "There's got to be something. Maybe someone was paid to keep quiet."

"Cain Dvanaesti is the hometown boy done good." Miguel retorted.

"You sound like a fan, Miguel."

"Maybe I am, Gabe. I've got good reason. This guy's legit."

"What does that even mean?"

"It means even his detractors can't find a single indiscretion. He wants what's best for this state and its citizens, and he doesn't think only his party has all the answers. It means he doesn't kiss the babies while stealing their lollypops." Miguel sounded like he was lecturing a three-year-old on why not to put a grilled cheese sandwich in the DVD player.

"Nobody's that clean, Miguel. Especially if they're in politics." Gabriel turned up the disbelief in his tone. "And especially in Florida politics, from what I've heard."

"I've got better uses for my time than investigating the ultimate Boy Scout." Miguel sounded like he was gripping the telephone as if it were Gabriel's neck.

"I'm not asking you to do this for free, Miguel. I'll pay you. Does that make it worth your while?"

There was a long silence. So long, Gabriel thought, maybe Miguel had hung up on him. "Hello?"

Miguel heaved a sigh. "All right. I'll see what I can do."

"Thanks, Miguel." Gabriel was not convinced.

"I still think you're wasting your money, but if you insist on wasting it, it might as well be on me, huh?" Miguel forced a snicker.

"Yeah, might as well be," Gabriel replied, looking at the phone like he'd never seen one before. That's when he'd decided he needed to go to Miami.

"Give me a couple of days, okay?" Miguel sounded relieved.

"Yeah." Gabriel had hung up, sure that Miguel was hiding something. Something Cain Dvanaesti was hiding. He'd booked a seat on the first flight to Miami the following day. The last thing he wanted was to travel to Florida. That's why God had given him an employee and friends who owed him favors.

I hate Miami in August!

Gabriel thumbed the speed dial for Stefan's number on his cell phone. Stefan answered again on the second ring.

"I'm in Atlanta." His tone was bland.

"I thought I told you to go to Tallahassee," Gabriel chided.

The chiding was lost on Stefan. "I have a two-hour layover in Atlanta waiting for a plane to Tallahassee, which no airline travels to nonstop," Stefan said. "No. Airline." Stefan repeated, his tone dripping with incredulity. "Are you sure Tallahassee is the capital?"

Gabriel couldn't help but laugh. Stefan was not a fan of flying, even less of layovers. "Have you been productive in Atlanta, or have you just been sitting around reading the latest Danielle Steele novel?"

"Who?"

"Never mind. Have you found anything out yet?"

There was a pause, and Gabriel could hear Stefan thumbing through the pages of the little notebook he always carried.

"Governor Dvanaesti will be leaving Tallahassee this afternoon."

Gabriel pulled out his little notebook and a pen. "Where will he be?"

"Miami. He is flying there this afternoon for a Republican national fundraising dinner."

"Do you know where?"

"At his private residence."

Gabriel pocketed his pen and notebook and picked up his bag. "I gotta go." He thumbed the End Call button on his cell phone, dropped it into his pocket, and got on the bus. "This is fortuitous," he said to himself as he sat.

As the bus moved him to the rental lot, he got out his cell phone and dialed Miguel's number.

Miguel answered with an irritated tone he didn't try to hide. "I told you I needed a couple of days, Gabe."

Gabriel ignored Miguel's irritated tone and replied with a pleasant one. "I just thought maybe you'd gotten lucky."

"I haven't even started looking yet. Look, I have to go, okay? I'll call you tomorrow."

And with that, Miguel hung up on Gabriel.

Gabriel swore. There was no way Gabriel was going to let this go now. Miguel was acting too strangely.

The bus stopped at the end of the row where his rental car was parked. Gabriel pocketed his phone as he picked up his bag and exited the bus.

Gabriel spotted his rental car, a Toyota Yaris, and started walking toward it. Miguel was hiding something. Gabriel knew it. If Miguel had just taken the job and said he'd found nothing, Gabriel would've written this Dvanaesti guy off as legit. But Miguel was acting like a guilty man. Worse. Like a cop on the take.

To someone watching, it would've looked like Gabriel walked into a brick wall. He winced as if he had. He'd known Miguel a long time, and the one thing he knew about the man was that he'd never been a dirty cop. Not like...

Gabriel shrugged, sloughing off the rumination. Don't lose focus, he told himself. Dvanaesti is hiding something. Dvanaesti is a guilty man.

8

Gabriel switched on his left blinker, waiting for a break in traffic. In the car, he'd used his phone to go online, find a tux shop, get a reservation for a fitting, reserve a room at a hotel, and look at Miguel's website, all without killing himself as he headed toward South Beach and South Beach Security Agency, Miguel's firm.

The name was a little misleading, Gabriel thought. They offered home and office monitoring systems. They also provided bodyguards willing to take a bullet for a fee and chauffeurs with evasive driver training. There was an investigations branch that handled everything from the banal situation of a wife trying to catch her cheating husband in the act to an F.B.I.-type investigation of a cold case or background check of an employee for a small business or large corporation.

The building housing South Beach Security Agency was typical high-end South Beach - beige and white Art Deco. Miguel liked to bill his company as a mom-and-pop operation. "And Jeff Bezos runs a little country store," Gabriel snickered.

As he sweltered, Gabriel scanned the entrance. The door opened, and Miguel Gutierrez stepped out. Gabriel could tell Miguel's suit was in the thousand-dollar range, even at this distance. It was charcoal gray, and he wore a dark red shirt and a matching tie. He moved with an elegance that betrayed his street-kid and then street-cop past. He walked like a man worth a million bucks. Gabriel laughed as he realized he probably was, but his laughter faltered when another thought crossed his mind. Miguel seemed unfazed by the August sun.

Cool customer.

Miguel moved to a Lexus SUV parked in front of the building, unlocked the door with a key fob, and climbed inside.

"Nice car," Gabriel said out loud to the car's interior. "Maybe I should ask Miguel if he wants a partner." Mopping sweat from his face, he said, "No."

Miguel pulled the Lexus out of the parking spot, whipped it around, and moved into traffic a few cars ahead of Gabriel.

Gabriel switched off his blinker and proceeded straight ahead, maintaining sight of the Lexus but staying three or four cars back.

"Let's see what you're up to, Miguel," Gabriel said to himself as he cranked the A/C up fully.

I hate Miami in August!

Miguel didn't seem to be in a hurry, keeping with the flow of South Beach traffic.

Gabriel never let himself get closer than three cars to Miguel, not changing lanes. Though that simple little ploy almost backfired. As the light turned yellow, two of the three vehicles ahead of Gabriel sped up to make the light. Gabriel ended up caddy-corner to Miguel's Lexus. He tried to exploit Miguel's blind spot. The problem was that the blind spot worked both ways. Gabriel couldn't see what Miguel was doing.

He could be loading a pistol or calling his office to put a tail on me.

The guy in front of Gabriel was one of those drivers who believed that if you kept creeping forward, the light would change, or you'd eventually be across the intersection. Gabriel stayed put. The guy behind Gabriel was a fellow believer. He started honking.

Gabriel's eyes twitched between the light, Miguel's vehicle, and the car behind him. The light and Miguel seemed steady. The car in front of him kept creeping. The guy behind him kept honking. Gabriel white-knuckled the steering wheel to resist the urge to exit his vehicle, pull the guy behind him out of his window, and stuff his horn in a most uncomfortable place. He knew it was just the heat, so he turned on the radio, hoping to find something to drown out the guy behind him.

Finally, the light turned green. The guy ahead of Gabriel gestured at the light as he passed underneath it. Miguel's Lexus lumbered forward. The guy behind Gabriel hammered his horn. Gabriel waited another two seconds for spite before accelerating. It earned him a gesture from the guy behind him. Gabriel gestured back and put his eyes back on his quarry.

Miguel was five cars up in the left-hand lane.

Gabriel forgot all about the guy behind him as Miguel signaled a left turn. Gabriel moved into the left lane and signaled as well. He made the turn.

Miguel was again three cars ahead of him. Gabriel kept that distance as they traveled from South Beach to a rundown area. Now there were no cars between him and Miguel, just a few blocks of space. Miguel pulled in at an abandoned parking garage.

"What are you up to, Miguel?" Gabriel said out loud as he glanced around. Broken down vehicles, weeds in the cracks of the sidewalks, and gang graffiti on the walls. Gabriel knew he would regret it, but he had to know. He turned into the garage as he thumbed off the safety on his sidearm holstered underneath his button-down. He scanned the area.

No Miguel.

He moved to the next level.

Still no Miguel.

Gabriel moved to the third level and found Miguel's vehicle parked, lights on, idling. He looked around but couldn't see anything.

Gabriel stopped behind the Lexus, cut the engine, unholstered his Glock, and exited his car. As soon as he did, he felt cool steel press against the base of his skull.

9

"Gabriel Hawthorne." Miguel's voice rang through the deserted garage. It was not happy. "I ought to shoot you for being a pinhead." Miguel lowered the weapon.

Gabriel turned. "Hey, Miguel. Fancy meeting you here. Great to see you."

Miguel holstered his weapon. "I wish I could say the same."

"How'd you know it was me tailing you?" Gabriel asked as he put the safety on his weapon and holstered it.

"I didn't. Not until I put my pistol to your fat head."

"But you still knew you were being tailed?"

Miguel nodded. "Of course, I should've realized it was you. Tailing was never one of your strong suits, I remember."

"I'm that bad?" Gabriel felt his cheeks pink.

"No. I'm that good." Miguel said with a grin, revealing white, straight teeth.

Gabriel looked at that grin. *You've got more money in your mouth than my rental car's worth.*

"You're pretty good, Miguel." Gabriel gestured to the weapon in Miguel's holster. "Becoming a fat cat hasn't slowed your reflexes."

"Don't try to butter me up, Gabe." Miguel dropped the smile and buttoned his suit jacket. "Just tell me why you're here in Miami tailing me."

Gabriel shrugged. "You know me. I just *love* Miami in August. And then I saw you and thought playing a little cat and mouse would be fun."

"So you're Tom, and I'm Jerry?"

"Well, since I was the one caught with a barrel to the back of his head, I'd say that was about right." Gabriel leaned against his rental.

"I told you on the phone, Gabe, I'd look into it. Just give me a couple of days." The tension was now in Miguel's voice.

Gabriel could hear the bells ringing and decided to press it. "Well. It's been a couple of days, hasn't it?"

"You called me yesterday," Miguel snapped.

"Yesterday and today. Two days." Gabriel could feel his hip throb from the pressure point created as it rested on the door handle, but he resisted moving. He suspected Miguel might take any movement on his part as an act of aggression. One thing Gabriel knew about a guy with Miguel's skill set: you didn't give him a reason to move first and ask questions later. "Have you got anything for me?"

Miguel cursed as he spun on his heel, facing directly away from Gabriel.

Gabriel felt his hand flinch, wanting to put his Beretta between the two of them. Again, he resisted moving. He was sure Miguel would be just a tad bit quicker and would be just a tad bit deader. Even with Miguel facing away from him, Gabriel still didn't let himself shift his weight or move a muscle. Instead, he waited another minute before saying. "You found something, didn't you?"

Miguel turned around. "It's just like I told you, Gabe. There's nothing to find. Absolutely nothing. He was clean going into the governor's mansion and still is."

"Oh, come on, Miguel. You don't expect me to buy that, do you?"

Miguel nodded. "You need to go back and tell your client this guy's a waste of time. No dirty laundry on the line. No skeletons in the closet." He smiled. "No weeds in the garden."

Gabriel shook his head. "I just can't believe that. *Nobody's* that clean, Miguel. Nobody."

"It doesn't matter if you believe it or not, Gabe. It doesn't matter if your client believes it. It's the truth." Miguel slipped his hands into his pockets.

Gabriel couldn't decide if that made Miguel look more or less dangerous. At least with his hands in his pockets, the odds might be even.

Gabriel started pacing and thinking. "Okay...Okay...So maybe this guy's not a tweaker or into strippers. He's not married. Is it because he's gay?"

"There's no evidence, stereotypical or otherwise, to indicate."

"Well. Maybe he's a mama's boy." Gabriel looked at Miguel.

Miguel shook his head. "His mother died in childbirth."

"She wasn't a legal citizen?" Gabriel sounded hopeful.

Pulling his hands from his pockets, Miguel crossed his arms and cocked an eyebrow.

"Okay. Sorry. She was a natural-born citizen. I just thought with a name like Dvanaesti...What is that anyway?"

"Slavic. Look, Gabe, do yourself a favor and let it go. Take your client's money. Or don't. But walk away."

Now Gabriel was getting irritated. It was hot in this parking garage. He was sweating so much that he looked like he'd dressed in the shower. His stomach was growling. Miguel wanted him to believe that Cain Dvanaesti had walked on water his entire life and had never gotten his feet wet. And most interesting. He'd just been told, warned, that the best and safest course of action was to continue to believe that.

With this last thought, Gabriel felt his anger flare. He punched the cement pillar beside him. Pain shot through his arm as his knuckles immediately began to swell. The pain, however, cleared his mind for one more thought, and he turned to Miguel, his face splitting into a smirk.

"So if Cain Dvanaesti is the best thing since Jesus or Muhammad, Miguel, why do I need to walk away? If he has nothing to hide, why am I being told to *act* like he's got nothing to hide? Doesn't that mean he's not as clean as you're making him out to be? And if that's true, why are you covering for him? Does he know something about you? Are you into strippers or meth? Maybe small boys?"

Miguel's face contorted with rage at Gabriel's taunt, and Gabriel wondered if he might have gone too far and should be reaching for his weapon. But Miguel's face became placid again. "You have no idea who you're dealing with."

"Okay, maybe I went a little too far there—"

"Not me," Miguel interrupted. "Not even Cain Dvanaesti."

"Who then?" Gabriel demanded.

Miguel pulled his key fob out of his pocket. "Follow me." He punched the unlock button. The lights on the Lexus blinked.

"Where are we going?" Gabriel didn't move.

"To lunch. You like Cuban?"

10

Miguel gestured to an outside table.

Gabriel looked toward the indoor eating area, imagining the cool air blowing down on him from a vent. He pointed towards the glass. "You sure you don't want to eat inside?"

Miguel only shook his head and started walking to the table. He slipped off his suit jacket, folded it, and laid it carefully across the back of a vacant chair. Sitting down, he loosened his tie and unbuttoned his collar. "The food is excellent here. The place is packed inside, especially on a day like today."

Gabriel gave the restaurant interior one last glance, shrugged, and walked in resignation over to the table where Miguel was sitting. A roll of paper towels stood on the table, and he ripped a few off, wadded them up, and mopped his face as he sat. "How do you people stand this?"

Miguel's eyebrows narrowed. "You people?"

"The locals." Gabriel ripped a few more towels and mopped at his neck. "I don't know what you call people who live in Miami. Miamians? South Beachers? Insane?"

A wry smile tugged at the corner of Miguel's mouth. "I thought you meant Latinos or Hispanics." Miguel leaned forward. His tone sharpened. "Or if you were lumping us all together in the "Spic" category."

Gabriel's eyes shot wide. "Whoa, whoa. Back the racist train up, Miguel." He looked around to see if Miguel had attracted anyone's attention. "Where's this coming from?"

"I want you to understand I don't take that crap from anyone. Even my friends."

Now that the shock was over, Gabriel's eyes narrowed as well. He hadn't meant to offend Miguel, nor was he interested in fighting the man. He wasn't afraid of Miguel; he was pretty sure Miguel could beat him, knife, hand-to-hand, or firearm. How could you fear certainty? But now that he realized Miguel was trying to prove a point, Gabriel was too hot for beating around the bush.

"We are still friends, aren't we? Miguel?" Gabriel wiped his face, removing the sweat from his brow and lashes threatening to seep into his eyes. He didn't want his eyes to look anything but fierce at this moment as he leaned in toward Miguel, not blinking. "We've known each other a long time. And in that time, I have never uttered a racial epithet in your presence. Have I? So I'm not sure why you think you need to make me understand what crap you will and won't take. But if you're going somewhere with this, you better get there quick."

This last statement was a bluff, and Gabriel knew it. Miguel knew it also, and his face widened into a genuine grin. He leaned back and laughed.

The waitress bustled up to the table as if she'd been watching the two men waiting for the ice forming between them to thaw in the South Beach summer afternoon.

"Buenos Dios, Señores. My name is Angel. I'll be your server today. Can I start you off with something to drink?"

Miguel said. "I'd like a cup of French Roast."

Angel nodded to Miguel and turned to Gabriel.

"Iced tea, please," Gabriel said. "Heavy on the ice."

She smiled and left.

"I wish you had a wife, Gabe. Maybe that would motivate you to follow the advice I'm about to give you."

Gabriel snorted. "Advice?"

Miguel nodded. "By way of a story." Miguel tugged at his collar, but Gabriel could tell it wasn't because of the heat. "A few years ago, we were hired to investigate a company. It was one of those corporate buyouts. The company being acquired wanted to know who the shark in the water was. They also wanted a security detail for the C.E.O. We thought they were missing the point. *Who* didn't matter. They were being acquired. But they were willing to pay. So we took the job. I put my two best guys on it. They were both ex-Special Forces, black ops."

Angel came with coffee and iced tea. Miguel nodded his thanks and then waved her off. Her smile faltered a little, but she turned and left.

Gabriel looked at the steam rising from the cup. "The day's just not hot enough for you?"

Miguel ignored the question. He grabbed the mug and gulped down a stiff belt as if trying to steady himself. "I figured I'd be killing two birds with one stone."

"While increasing the profit margin," Gabriel interjected as he squeezed the lemon wedge, flooding his tea. He gulped down half the glass and wished he'd asked for a pitcher of iced tea.

"Anyway, they called one night. Said the shark was a corporation called the Javelin Group run by a guy named Roman Dvanaesti. They said he was clean. They said the takeover was not only legit but a win-win for both parties. They said everything was above board and requested a new assignment. So I reassign them. Tell the client what my guys told me."

Sweat coated Gabriel; his clothes clung to him. His tea was gone. He wanted more, but Angel was nowhere around. He found himself irritated with Miguel. "Why are you telling me this?" Gabriel snapped.

"I started asking questions about Roman Dvanaesti. I mean, Dvanaesti. That isn't a common name. He had to be related to Cain Dvanaesti. A couple of days later, I was at dinner with Roma. We were celebrating. We'd found out that morning, Roma was pregnant."

Gabriel stopped thinking about the heat. "You've got a child?"

Miguel nodded. "Eva. She's two now. So. We're at dinner when a man sits down at our table uninvited. I'm about to ask him what his problem is when he says to me, 'I'd like to congratulate you and your lovely wife on the news of her pregnancy.'"

"So a guy congratulates you for your good news. What's the big deal?" Gabriel had moved back from stunned to irritated.

"The big deal is, Gabe, we'd just found out that morning and hadn't told anyone. Not even our parents, because we wanted to tell them in person."

"But surely you told someone. You must've forgotten." Gabriel didn't like where this was going. A mysterious man with private information he shouldn't have. Right out of a thriller.

Miguel shook his head. "I told no one. Not a soul. Parents first. Not even my secretary knew why I wasn't in the office that morning."

"So what'd you do?" Gabriel prompted.

"Well. I wanted to throttle him. But the man sat there. Pale. Lifeless. And yet...so full of energy. He smiled as if he knew what I wanted to do, and it amused him." Miguel blanched.

"What happened then?" Gabriel prodded.

Miguel turned green and then white, then green again. He gulped down the last of his coffee and signaled with his cup for more, which Angel refilled as she dropped off a pitcher of iced tea and then evaporated.

Miguel took a long swig. "I reached for my cell phone and found it wasn't in my pocket. The man smiled again and held it up to me. He kept his eyes on me but sniffed my wife. Don't ask me how I know, but that's what he was doing. Finally, he told me my wife was pregnant with a girl, and it would be a shame for them to suffer. Even worse for me to watch."

Miguel shivered. "And that's when I noticed. The man talked. He smiled. He seemed to breathe. But there was no light in his eyes...no life in his eyes."

Gabriel was on the edge of his seat now. Even if Miguel was trying for intimidation, the man could spin a good yarn. Except...Miguel looked genuinely shaken. He was sweating, but his skin looked clammy. "What do you mean, no life in his eyes? You mean dead? Like a...zombie? Are you sure he didn't have cataracts?"

Miguel only sat transfixed by the memory of the man's eyes. Gabriel had to slap Miguel's shoulder to break the macabre revelry. "Who did this guy work for?" Gabriel asked when Miguel's eyes finally focused on him.

Miguel swallowed hard. "Dvanaesti."

"Cain Dvanaesti?" Gabriel's voice thrummed with excitement. This was it. He'd found his dirt.

"Will you keep your voice down?" Miguel hissed, his eyes darting around to see if anyone had heard. He picked up his coffee cup and brought it to his lips, speaking quietly through the steam. "I wish you had a wife. And a child or two."

"What? If I had a wife and a child, maybe I'd be less likely to rush in where angels fear to tread?"

"There's a reason why the angels fear to tread, my friend."

"Oh," Gabriel motioned between the two of them. "So we're friends again?"

Miguel finished his coffee and stared at Gabriel for a long minute. "We've been friends for a very long time, Gabe. Maybe not the best of friends. But friends nonetheless." Miguel leaned forward. "Gabe, the man-...the man with the dead eyes worked for *Roman* Dvanaesti. You may know that name, you may not, but trust me when I say I know him better than you. The best thing for you is to fly back to D.C. tonight, tell your client you have nothing, and then go away on vacation."

"Roman Dvanaesti," Gabriel said. He looked at Miguel. "Cain's father?"

Miguel nodded with relief as if he'd finally gotten through to Gabriel.

Gabriel sat back in his chair, picked up his glass, and took a throat-cooling swig. "So Roman Dvanaesti is a scary guy who hires thugs. So what? We've both dealt with our share of thugs over the years."

Miguel gave Gabriel a reproving look. "You're not going to let this go, are you?"

Gabriel stared at Miguel. They'd both been cops. Good cops. They'd been good because they didn't let things go. They pursued them with dogged determination. This was no different. Of course, he wasn't going to let this go. Sure, Miguel had told a pretty good tale about a zombie-eyed guy who'd spooked him. He'd been enthralled, which still hadn't covered over his irritation, but he hadn't been intimidated.

The tale had done just the opposite. Gabriel didn't like being intimidated or threatened. He usually did what he was being intimidated or threatened not to do. This time was no different. Miguel could talk till he was blue in the face. Gabriel Hawthorne had at least one piece of dirt now on Cain Dvanaesti: his old man had threatened the life of a mother and her child.

"You're right, Miguel. I'm not going to let it go. I was hired to find out what dirt there was on Cain Dvanaesti. Maybe you're right. Maybe he's cleaner than a baby's freshly pampered bottom. But it sounds like his old man could be what's in the diaper."

Miguel had been in the middle of lighting a cigar when he heard this last statement. As it registered in his brain, he forgot the cigar, which dropped into the lap of his thousand-dollar suit. He gaped open-mouthed at Gabriel.

The look reminded Gabriel of the frog in the video game Zuma he'd seen once. He wanted to duck in case a large marble spewed from Miguel's mouth. In another situation, Gabriel would laugh until he cried, but not this time. Miguel was his friend, and he knew why his friend was giving him that look.

"Your cigar." He nodded towards Miguel's lap.

Miguel felt the cigar burning a hole in his lap. He yelped as he swatted at his slacks. He let the cigar fall to the ground.

"Don't worry, Miguel. I'll pay you for the information."

"Oh no, you won't." Miguel's face was a grotesque mixture of rage and incredulity. His mouth was screwed up; his eyes open wide, his brows high on his forehead. "I didn't tell you that story so I could get paid or so you could do your job. I told you so you'd do the same thing I'm about to do."

"What's that?"

Miguel got up, pulled out his wallet, fingered two twenty-dollar bills, and laid them on the table. He picked up his jacket and slid it on.

"I thought we were eating," Gabriel protested.

"I'm no longer hungry." As Miguel tugged at his cuffs, he looked Gabriel in the eyes.

"Are you going to let this go?"

"You know I can't," Gabriel answered.

"Then do me a favor," Miguel said.

"What?"

"Forget you ever knew me." Miguel fled. He never looked back at Gabriel as he got into his Lexus and drove away.

11

Gabriel turned the A/C up to max and then turned the knob a little more, hoping to coax another degree of coolness out of the car's atmosphere.

I hate Miami in August!

He now understood why there was so much road rage in Florida in the summer. People weren't evil in this state, just perpetually ticked off because of the sun.

Then there was Miguel. Gabriel cursed at the thought of Miguel's parting words a half hour ago.

Forget you ever knew me. Forget I ever knew who?

Miguel was not a man with a wild imagination; he was as easy to intimidate as a rock and didn't turn his back on his friends. Not until now.

"What *really* happened between you and Roman Dvanaesti?" Gabriel said to no one. Gabriel had felt Miguel had spun him a good yarn, but that's all. Though he remembered a high school English teacher saying that every good story had an element of truth, Gabriel couldn't believe there was any truth to this one. Miguel just wasn't the type. Still, something had happened. Roman Dvanaesti had something on Miguel.

Gabriel didn't know Roman Dvanaesti, but he knew the type. He'd crossed paths with them more than his share in his line of work. They had shady dealings. Employed muscle. But not all of their actions were necessarily illegal. Immoral. But not illegal. They'd gotten their hands dirty. How did you get that much money without getting them dirty getting it or keeping it? Then they finally had enough money to keep their hands clean and pay others to do the dirty work.

His phone chirped with a new text. At the next red light, he opened it. It was Stefan:

Prelims on Dvanaesti's family.
He's an only child. His dad is from Europe.
He comes and goes U.S. as he pleases.
When in the U.S., he calls Miami home.
Dad met Cain's mom while setting up
offices in Miami. She died in childbirth.

A search on Mom has turned up nothing.
Attached is a photo of Cain Dvanaesti.
Not so much as a parking ticket.
I couldn't find photos of Mom or Dad.
Stefan.

Gabriel pondered Stefan's text as he navigated the August Miami traffic to the tux shop. There was political fodder here. The fact that his dad could enter and exit the U.S. as easily as anyone else enters or leaves their house alone should be sending up signal flares.

Cain Dvanaesti is dirt-free.

Gabriel thought about the politicians whose careers didn't necessarily end because of their shortcomings but of their family members. Even when those relatives' antics didn't hurt their careers, they were a thorn in their side. Jimmy Carter's brother, Billy. F.D.R.'s son Jimmy. Teddy Roosevelt's daughter Alice. Brother, son, daughter. What about a father?

Cain Dvanaesti is dirt-free.

Gabriel found a spot just past the tux shop and pulled in. He sat there, foot still on the brake, hands on the wheel, thumbs tapping an absentminded beat. The air was still blowing full in his face, but with the engine idling, the air wasn't as cool. Beads of sweat formed on his forehead and hands. He didn't notice.

Cain Dvanaesti is dirt-free.

He had an image in his head of Cain Dvanaesti, dressed in a black Armani tux, with a gloss on his shoes, walking through a pigsty and coming out just as clean and fresh-smelling as when he entered. He eats spinach quiche and smiles, but there's nothing green wedged between the molars. It's a hundred degrees, but he looks like it couldn't be a degree over seventy-two. M&Ms don't melt in his mouth or his hands.

This last thought struck Gabriel's funny bone, and he barked with laughter. Placing the car in park, he cracked the windows and shut off the engine. As he climbed out of the car, he thought again about Miguel's reaction to his statement, 'Sounds like his dad might be what's in the diaper.' Miguel was scared. He'd refused any payment. He didn't want anything that linked him to Gabriel or an investigation of Roman Dvanaesti.

Gabriel pulled out his cell phone and sent Stefan a text.

Dig deeper into the father.

12

The guard eyed Gabriel's driver's license. "You said you're a reporter?"

Gabriel nodded up at the guard from the front seat of his Yaris. "Washington Times. Here to cover the Republican fundraiser Governor Dvanaesti is hosting tonight."

Gabriel sized up the man and his little shack. It didn't seem like much, Gabriel thought, not enough to take seriously given the residents of this private island: Two ridiculously wealthy businessmen, a rock star, a movie star, and the private residence of the governor of the state.

A small nondescript cinderblock building sat some twenty yards off the road behind the guard shack. Gabriel wondered if it'd been built as a bomb shelter by some survivalist during the Bay of Pigs when Castro had Russian missiles pointed in this direction. It was more impressive than this little shack. Gabriel wondered how long it'd been abandoned.

At that moment, light spilled from the cinderblock building as the door opened.

Gabriel saw two men in black fatigues sitting at a table playing cards. The silhouetted figure stepping from the building, with what Gabriel surmised was a compact assault rifle hanging from a tactical sling and a sidearm holster on his hip, slammed the door and marched around to the back of the building.

Gabriel heard a vehicle start. A black pickup pulled around the building and onto the blacktop, heading towards the island.

The actual security.

The guard ignored the pickup but returned Gabriel's license. "Do you know where you're going?"

Gabriel took his license, pocketed it, and nodded.

The guard motioned for Gabriel to proceed. "Have a nice night."

Gabriel strode through the open wrought iron gate and up the driveway to the two-story Mediterranean-style home, light blazing from every window. Unlike the other dwellings on this road, the Dvanaesti mansion sat back only thirty yards from the street, where it could be easily seen. The drive followed a straight line from the gate to the home and ended in a roundabout at the foot of two stairways. The stairways, to the left and right, led to a front landing. From there, a single stairway up to the front door.

As Gabriel cut across the roundabout, he glanced in both directions. Off to the left was a six-vehicle garage. To the right was a beautifully manicured lawn and a slim glance of the waterway running behind the house in this private island neighborhood.

Gabriel bounded up the left stairway two steps at a time and then up the main stairway to the front door as if he'd just stepped from a stretch limo in his personally tailored Armani or Hugo Boss tuxedo. The tux was neither, though the kid at the tux shop did a pretty good job of hemming the slacks as Gabriel stood in them; an extra hundred twenty-five in cash was quite a motivator.

He strode to the door and was about to let himself in when two tuxedoed gentlemen blocked his path.

"Your invitation, Sir," the man on the left said.

Gabriel reached for his wallet as he considered the man. He was six-one, maybe six-two, with short-cropped hair and a Florida flag lapel pin. So he was part of the Florida Department of Law Enforcement security detail. The man on his right, also wearing a Florida flag lapel pin, was shorter but no smaller.

"Gabriel Hawthorne. Washington Times." Gabriel pulled out his driver's license and presented it to the agent. I forgot my press card back in D.C."

The man on the left pulled a clipboard out of thin air and began flipping through the pages. "What was your name?"

"Hawthorne." He smiled as broadly as he could. "Gabriel Hawthorne. Washington Times."

It had sort of a James Bond vibe in his ears when he said it like that, dressed in a tuxedo, and he winced at the realization. Whether it was the wince or the vibe, Gabriel didn't know or care, but the man on the right had picked up on it as he stepped towards Gabriel.

The man on the left thumbed through the papers without looking up. "Not on the list."

The man on the right twisted his body, protecting his firing arm from Gabriel and giving him more room for close-quarter maneuvering.

"Ah, man, I knew this was going to happen. As soon as I realized I'd forgotten my press card, I thought, I bet the paper forgot to call and get me on the list." Gabriel whined, trying to change the vibe.

"I can't allow you to enter." The man on the left dropped the clipboard and looked at Gabriel steadily. "I'm sorry, Sir. His tone indicated he wasn't.

Gabriel decided to change tack. He lifted his arms as if in surrender. "Okay. I'm not on the list, but if you call the Times, they can tell you I'm supposed to be on it."

The two men in front of him stared stone-faced at him.

Gabriel pressed on. "I'm a reporter here to cover the fundraiser." Gabriel added, "The Washington Times. The conservative voice in Washington, D.C."

The two men remained motionless in front of him as if waiting for the next guest to approach and present their invitation or name.

"Look. I'm just trying to do my job here. Isn't there someone I can talk to?"

"You can contact the communications office tomorrow to request a press packet. As for tonight, I'll have to ask you to leave."

"But I need to get in tonight. I could lose my job if I don't," Gabriel whined.

"Gabriel?" The female voice came from behind him. It was soft. Surprised. It was a voice he hadn't heard in a long time.

Gabriel spun around. "Claudia—" His voice stuck in his throat.

Claudia Bennett wore an off-the-shoulder emerald-green evening dress. Gabriel looked at those bare shoulders, still the color of fresh cream, and remembered the last time he'd touched them, kissed them.

It was ten years ago. He was a detective with the Washington D.C. Police Department. She was a young reporter at the Washington Post. He'd come off duty and stopped by the Post headquarters. She was sitting in her cubicle, staring at the computer. After silencing her colleagues with an index finger to his lips, he sneaked up behind her. Placing his hands on her shoulders, he began kneading. He expected to hear her purr after he brushed a kiss along her nape.

But she didn't purr. She didn't relax. Instead, the muscles in her neck had tightened; her back stiffened. He kissed her again, but he might as well be kissing the sidewalk for all the warmth he was feeling. Something was wrong.

"Babe?" He'd said as he'd spun her around to face him. "Are you okay?"

Gabriel had been a cop for over ten years. He'd looked into the eyes of murderers and rapists, jilted husbands and abandoned wives, the accusing eyes of a mother because his testimony hadn't put the molester or killer of her baby boy away as the District Attorney had promised.

But nothing had prepared him for the look in her eyes. Betrayal. Anguish. Love. Hate. Disgust. Pain. Loathing.

Her make-up was smudged around her bloodshot eyes, her cheeks still damp with tears. But she had stopped crying. Her eyes were cold. Distant. She looked at him not as a lover nor as a friend. Not even as a stranger. But as something repulsive. Odious.

"How long have you been in Senator Downing's pocket?" Her voice was hollow.

Gabriel felt like he'd been doused in ice water. But he forced a weak smile. "What're you talking about?"

Her eyes narrowed to dangerous slits. "How long have you been accepting money from Senator Downing, and what services are you providing for the Senator?" She bit off every word.

Gabriel didn't want to lie, but he had for a long time. To her. To himself. It just didn't seem right to come clean now. Not this way. He'd planned to, over dinner in their favorite little booth at their favorite Chinese restaurant. That'd been his idea. So he forced his smile bigger and threw a little 'aw, shucks' into a shoulder shrug. "I think you've been working a little too hard, Babe. You're starting to see conspiracies that aren't there."

As soon as he'd said it, he wished he hadn't.

Her eyes had sharpened. Her lips pursed into a thin line. He watched as the last light of love towards him faded from her eyes. "I was there today. I saw the Senator slide an envelope into your coat pocket." She pointed toward his jacket as if the envelope were pinned to his lapel.

Gabriel felt the ice water again. "Babe, I—"

"Don't." She held up a hand showing him the memory card of a digital camera. "Don't tell me it's not what I think. Don't tell me you didn't meet

Downing today. And don't call me Babe." Her hand dropped into her lap. "How long have you been on the take?"

"What does it matter?"

"It matters to me, Gabe. It matters to me. And not just because I've been working on this story for a year. Not because I've been discussing the details with you. Asking you about corrupt cops." Tears began to flow down her face again. "What a fool I've been. Telling a dirty cop, I was investigating dirty cops. And. You. Lied. To. Me."

"I never lied to you about dirty cops or—"

"I'm not talking about that. And for the record, yes, you did. It's called the sin of omission. You took an oath to serve and protect the public. You didn't fulfill that oath."

"But I was always honest about us."

Now Claudia laughed a sad, sardonic laugh. "Us? You weren't honest about yourself. *We* were never in an honest relationship because *you've* misrepresented yourself. I don't know you. I don't know us."

Gabriel felt his heart pang. He loved this woman as he'd never loved any other woman in his life. He'd become a better man as a result. She didn't know it, but as she talked to him about the investigation, how she was hot on the trail of Downing, focusing on the corrupt cops working for him, Gabriel had decided he wanted off the Senator's payroll. He wasn't afraid of being caught, but because he realized just how far he'd gone astray from why he'd become a cop in the first place. He had to change. Find that young, idealistic Gabriel Hawthorne again.

So he'd called Downing and told him he was through. Downing didn't want to hear it over the phone. He told Gabriel to have the intestinal fortitude to say it to his face. Gabriel took the bait. They'd met. Gabriel said he was out. Downing had laughed as he slipped an envelope into his pocket. "I get it," he said, "You want to get your girl something special. So here's your Christmas bonus a little early." Then he climbed back into his limo and drove away. Gabriel had dropped the envelope into a donation box at a homeless shelter. He felt good. Free. He hadn't felt that way in a long time.

Now, he cursed himself for not confessing his sins to her sooner. Not letting her know he'd help in her investigation. Losing his job and going to prison was a small penance. Claudia was one of those truly good people. One of those people who lived what they believed. Who lived a life worth living. When you were around those kinds of people, you couldn't help but want to make your life a little more worthwhile.

But now he couldn't say anything. He couldn't tell her the truth. It would be a day late and a dollar short. But he decided to try anyway.

"I was going to tell you tonight. Over dinner."

The words sounded hollow, like answering the phone and telling the caller you were just about to call him. No matter how true it was, you still cringed at the patronizing convenience.

"I'm sure you were." Claudia wiped her eyes with fury. "I'm sure you were going to take me out for Chinese, look me in the eye, and confess everything over your sesame chicken."

Gabriel's gaze dropped to the floor. "So what are you going to do?"

"I'm going to run the story."

Gabriel's eyes shot back up. "With the pictures?"

Claudia flung the memory card at Gabriel. "Is that what you're worried about? Not getting caught? No. I'm not going to use the pictures. I've got enough on Downing so that when it hits the fan, Downing will roll on his little troop of dirty soldiers."

And with that, Claudia spun around and pressed the Enter key. "Goodbye, Gabe."

Gabriel ran a hand over her long auburn hair. "Claudia—"

"I said goodbye."

Gabriel had gone to the precinct the following morning and turned in his badge and sidearm. He'd counted up all the money he'd taken over the years as a corrupt cop and written a check to a charity. He was going to serve and protect the public. But not as a cop. Never again as a cop. He'd tarnished a respectable profession. Now he'd search for the truth in an occupation most felt was less than reputable: a private investigator. And he'd do his best to keep politicians on the straight and narrow from here on out.

When he arrived home that evening, Claudia was gone. Gabriel felt it was best to let her go. She was one of the good people, after all.

He hadn't seen her in ten years. His chest tightened. Her auburn hair was still long, but pulled up tonight.

Gabriel's mouth dropped open. Claudia smiled at the compliment, not just Gabriel's impression of a large-mouthed bass. "Wow," she said, looking him up and down. "You look great. Is that a rental?"

She could still spot a hack job a mile away.

Gabriel nodded. "You look...there's no other word for it. Breathtaking."

She smiled again and reddened deeper, making her eyes blaze like emeralds in a firelight. She was mesmerizing. Gabriel used to love embarrassing her so he could stare into those emeralds. "Thanks. So what're you doing here?" She asked. "Last I heard, you were a private investigator in D.C."

Gabriel nodded. She hadn't said 'private investigator' like most people did with that derogatory lilt to their voice. Something else that hadn't changed about her, Gabriel thought. She never made anyone feel less about themselves or their condition. She was still one of the good people. "And I understand you're on television now."

"I host the morning show here in Miami."

"That's great." Gabriel meant it. She was the best of every television journalist or personality all rolled into one person. When she got to the network level, and she would, he knew she would make a difference. "Are you here for an interview?"

Her lips curved upward into an ironic smile. "More like an interrogation. What about you?"

"I'm working," he said, stealing a glance over his shoulder at the two officers at the door and dropping his voice, "It just so happens I'm trying to," he decided to tell the truth, or a half-truth, "crash the party."

"Crash my party?"

Gabriel turned to see Governor Cain Dvanaesti standing at the open door. The warm, golden light of the interior cast him in an ethereal posture as it washed over him and down the steps of the home. Gabriel was struck by how young the man looked, how healthy and vital. Gabriel was sure that if you closed the door behind him, he would still exude that golden glow. He stood six-two, with wavy, sandy-blonde hair and steel-gray eyes that radiated health and vitality. His tailored tux clung to his swimmer's physique.

"There you are," Dvanaesti exclaimed as his preternatural gaze fell on Claudia.

Gabriel watched dumbfounded as Cain bounded down the steps to Claudia, kissing her cheek and wrapping an arm around her waist. "I was afraid you'd changed your mind." He only had eyes for her. "You look gorgeous. Was the car late?"

Claudia gestured to herself. "This doesn't just happen. It takes a lot of time and preparation."

"Perhaps I can forgive a stunning woman who arrives fashionably late." Cain teased.

Gabriel stared at the two people in front of him, his mouth agape in disbelief. Claudia. The woman who abhorred dishonesty and deceit was dating a *politician*. Claudia. Whose career had been made by exposing politicians and their lies and misdeeds. Dating a politician? And not just any politician, but the one he was investigating.

Gabriel could understand the physical attraction. He'd had half a wish he'd been born a female when he first saw Cain standing in the doorway. But surely someone as street smart and savvy as Claudia Bennett couldn't be so taken in with this guy as to be seen on his arm like some trophy. Gabriel seethed. Right or wrong, he had to warn Claudia about her date and his father.

Gabriel opened his mouth to speak, but Claudia cleared her throat and gestured to Gabriel. Dvanaesti looked in Gabriel's direction and smiled. "I'm sorry." He extended his hand. "I'm Cain Dvanaesti."

Gabriel shook Dvanaesti's hand automatically. "Gabriel Hawthorne." It no longer held the James Bond vibe.

"So, Mr. Hawthorne, you're trying to crash my party?" Dvanaesti's voice was sultry.

Gabriel stared wide-eyed as if the Sports Illustrated Swimsuit Issue cover model had just asked him the question, not Cain Dvanaesti. He nodded without saying a word.

"It's a thousand dollars a plate." Dvanaesti shot Gabriel a conspiratorial grin as he leaned toward him. "But I might be able to get you in for seven-fifty. I've got some connections."

Claudia giggled and punched Dvanaesti on the shoulder.

"Ouch." He faked a crestfallen look at her, then smiled as she giggled more. "Listen, I have some people I want you to meet." He looked at Gabriel.

"Mr. Hawthorne, it was a pleasure to meet you." Taking Claudia's arm and placing his hand on the small of her back, Dvanaesti guided her up the steps and into the home. His home.

"The pleasure's all mine," Gabriel said to a slamming door. The agents stood there looking through him. Gabriel nodded and waved. "Yeah, I know," he said, pointing over his shoulder, "I can call the communications department tomorrow."

He turned and walked back the way he came to his car.

13

Gabriel sat in his rental, thinking about his run-in with Claudia and Cain Dvanaesti. He knew what Dvanaesti had been doing when he told him the entrance price and the discount he was willing to give him. Dvanaesti was a politician. He never used a last name because that was too formal. Each hand he shook belonged to a friend, a vote. No. Dvanaesti knew Gabriel was no voter wanting to be turned into a friend on a first-name basis. Gabriel knew what Dvanaesti was doing, but he was too much of a professional to take the bait. He'd been fishing way too long.

He hated to admit it, but Dvanaesti had it, whatever it was, that made everyone who met him fall for him. He now fully understood the phrase 'man crush.' It was unnerving how put-together the guy was. Gabriel preferred to refer to Dvanaesti as the guy. It made him more human, or more to the point, more like everybody else.

"That had to be planned," Gabriel said aloud as he stared through the front windshield at the Governor's mansion. Thinking of how the light enveloped the guy as he stood at the door, Gabriel snickered as he reached into the back seat for two cases. "Spielberg couldn't have done a better job lighting that sucker." He opened one and pulled out a camera. From the second case, he extracted a telephoto lens. He attached the lens to the camera body and looked through the eyepiece.

The two officers came into sharp focus at the door. He repositioned himself so that the lens body rested on the steering wheel. His lower back sighed with relief as he stretched it. He reached around to the back seat, pulled the lid off a cooler, pulled out a diet soda, popped the top, and guzzled half of it in one swallow, then settled in for the wait. Eventually, the guests would start trickling out. Gabriel figured he could get their mug shots and plate numbers. Somebody was bound to be dishing dirt somewhere. "These are Republicans, after all," he sipped at his soda. "Like Democrats are the bastions of purity and virtue," he chuckled with derision. "Republican. Democrat. Potato. Potahto."

The door opened, and the first of the guests, an elderly couple, exited. The man wore a tuxedo thirty years out of fashion, and the woman was in a ball gown thirty years past her prime. A limo pulled up, and the couple got in. Gabriel snapped photos of each, smiling as he watched the man cop a feel of the woman's bottom while helping her in.

"You go, Grandpa." Gabriel snapped a picture of the plate on the limo as the headlights of an approaching vehicle filled the rearview mirror.

Gabriel quickly placed the camera on the floorboard between his feet, pulled out his cell phone, and started the Yaris as the vehicle stopped beside him. Gabriel recognized the guard from the gate. He rolled down his driver-side window as the guard rolled down his passenger-side window. Gabriel gestured to the phone. "Just me. Sorry. Got a phone call and lost all track of time."

"There's no loitering on the island," the guard responded.

"No problem." Gabriel drove the car and headed out the way he came in. The guard's vehicle followed him.

Gabriel pressed One on his speed dial. Stefan answered on the third ring.

"Stefan, I need some info quick. What vehicles are registered to Cain Dvanaesti in Miami?"

"Public or private?" Stefan sounded bored.

"I don't know."

"Well," Stefan said through a mouth full of food, "he has several high-end sports cars, and there's a government Suburban available to him. Usually, he uses a limo, a black Lincoln Town Car."

Gabriel scribbled down the plate number. "Thanks." He thumbed the End Call button and tossed the cellular on the passenger seat. Time to find a hidey-hole, he thought to himself as he left the bridge for the mainland.

He found what he was looking for, two-tenths of a mile from the bridge, a small public picnic area. Gabriel pulled in, angling the Yaris to face out toward the road.

For the next hour, limos and cars streamed by. Gabriel snapped photos of the plates on the backs of the vehicles with the telephoto lens. Finally, Cain's limo drove past.

Gabriel tossed the camera onto the passenger seat and started the car. He waited until the limo's taillights were small in the distance before pulling out onto the road.

He made mental notes of landmarks and street names as he tailed the limo. It finally pulled to a stop in front of a brownstone. Gabriel pulled to the curb and cut the lights and engine.

He picked up the camera and looked through the eyepiece as the door opened, and out jumped Cain Dvanaesti sans security detail. He turned and offered his hand. Claudia stepped from the limo and allowed Cain to again put one hand on the small of her back and the other on her upper arm and guide her to the front door.

This had to be Claudia's house, he mused. His stomach rolled over as he wondered if Dvanaesti would join her on the other side of the door. He watched Claudia reach into her purse, pull out a key, unlock the door, then turn and plant a kiss on Dvanaesti's lips. Without thinking, Gabriel snapped a picture.

Cain's head snapped up and looked directly into the lens.

Gabriel yanked his head away from the eyepiece and scrunched behind the dashboard. He chided himself. There was no way Cain knew he'd just taken a picture; no way he could've heard the soft click of the camera shutter closing and opening. It was just a coincidence. He laughed nervously as he picked up the camera and looked through the eyepiece, still scrunched behind the dashboard. He saw Cain and Claudia smile at each other just before Claudia closed the door on Dvanaesti.

"Good Girl," Gabriel said aloud as he watched Dvanaesti bound down the steps to the sidewalk like a sixteen-year-old boy floating with the exhilaration of his first kiss and then into the limo. Gabriel snapped a picture of the plate as the limo sped away.

14

Gabriel directed the Yaris into a hotel parking garage and cut the engine. He opened the door and stepped out. The garage felt cool compared to the street, and Gabriel was glad for it, but...

I hate Miami in August!

A drink sounds good, Gabriel thought, as he reached into the car and pulled out his duffel bag. As he made sure the doors on the rental were locked, he noticed a tall, slender man in a dark suit, no tie, leaning up against a silver Crown Victoria, smoking a cigarette. He marveled at the man's attire in this heat, even at night, he thought as he swiped at his forehead. The two made eye contact.

The man's eyes dropped quickly, just like the kids did during his cop days when you'd ask them if they'd seen anything that night. They always found their shoes very interesting. His hackles rose, but he dropped his eyes and walked to the elevator.

As he punched the call button for the elevator, he turned and surveyed the garage as if he had no care or concern. The man was taking a long drag on his cigarette, dropping it to the floor, stepping on it, and popping the trunk without a glance in Gabriel's direction.

The elevator chimed, and the doors opened. Gabriel glanced behind him. No one was in the elevator. Gabriel glanced casually over the garage. The man was bent over, rummaging through his open trunk. Gabriel stepped onto the elevator and pushed the button for his floor, never taking his eyes off the man. As the doors closed and he felt the elevator rising, he chided himself. He was acting like an undercover newbie on his first day.

Still, Gabriel didn't feel his hackles relax until he was in his room with the door locked. Feeling the chill on his forehead as the last beads of sweat evaporated, he sucked the cool conditioned air deep into his lungs. Cooler, he decided he didn't hate Miami so much. Now all he needed was that drink. He turned and smiled.

The minibar.

He selected a Coke and two bottles of Crown, picked up the ice bucket, and went in search of ice.

The ice machine was at the other end of the hall. As he walked, feeling his clothes begin to dry for the first time that day, he noticed the tall, slender man from the garage. He was walking down the hall towards him. Gabriel's hackles rose again. The man wasn't carrying a suitcase or an ice bucket. He was still wearing his suit jacket and shoes.

When their eyes met this time, the man's gaze didn't drop to the floor. Instead, he inclined his head slightly as they passed. Gabriel nodded back. The man continued walking. Reaching the ice machine, Gabriel dropped the bucket under the slot and pushed the button. He turned back. The man had stopped and was stretching, knuckling his back as he pulled a mag card from his pocket and entered a guest room.

Gabriel's hackles relaxed. The guy's been driving all day and was stretching his legs. Gabriel admonished himself for his paranoia. First, Dvanaesti and the camera lens. Now this guy. Gabriel wondered when he'd start seeing a conspiracy. Once back in the room, he locked the door, threw the deadbolt, and slid the security latch into place. Okay, paranoia wasn't a bad thing in his line of work.

Gabriel fixed himself a drink, then plopped down on the loveseat, thumbed the remote, and surfed until he found CNN. Pulling out his phone, he dialed Stefan's number and waited.

Stefan answered. "There was no reason for you to call me yet."

"And it's that winning personality that helps you blend in with the locals no matter where you go." Gabriel retorted. He smiled as he crunched on a piece of crushed ice. "What'd you find out?"

Gabriel could hear Stefan thumbing through the pages of his small notebook. "Not much to say. Everything is quite convoluted. There are dummy corporations that belong to associations that are part of organizations that are divisions of conglomerates that end nowhere."

"Go on," Gabriel prompted.

"Roman Dvanaesti has homes and offices in Miami, New York City, San Francisco, and New Orleans."

"That's interesting," Gabriel sipped his drink. "All port cities."

"He has homes and offices on every continent. His primary business appears to be a company called The Javelin Group."

"So where's the Javelin Group headquartered?" Gabriel asked.

"Your guess is as good as mine," Stefan responded.

"All right." Gabriel finished his drink in one long gulp. "Dvanaesti's not that common a name. Have you thought about looking up historical documents? Deeds? Contracts? Marriage licenses? Lawsuits?"

"No. That never crossed my mind." Stefan's voice was monotone. "I just happened to get lucky with what I have uncovered so far. It just happened to be in the first book I opened today before the library closed."

"Okay, okay." Gabriel couldn't help but smile. "You made your point."

"What point would that be?" Stefan asked.

"That you know your job." Gabriel moved to the bar and mixed another drink.

"I discovered a surprising amount of information in a short period, but it is in appearance only. Scratch below the surface, and you find there is no surface.

Gabriel felt his hackles rising again. What had he said to himself earlier about a conspiracy? "What're you saying, Stefan?"

"Roman Dvanaesti is so on the radar, he is off the grid."

"Off the grid?" Gabriel was incredulous.

"This is the age of the internet. Everyone has a digital footprint. Yet you cannot Google this man. There are no pictures of him on the web or in newspaper articles. Even with a son in the governor's chair, there are no photos of him and Cain Dvanaesti. He was at his son's inauguration. Yet there isn't a single picture of the proud father looking on, hugging him or posing with him."

Gabriel threw a fist into the air. Roman Dvanaesti was definitely where the dirt was. "Good work. Call me when you've got more. And Stefan? Be careful."

"Careful?" Now it was Stefan's turn to sound incredulous.

"Miguel is scared of this guy."

The silence was palpable. Stefan knew Miguel. He knew Miguel wasn't afraid of anyone. Finally, Stefan's sober voice responded. "I will be careful, Gabe. I will call you in a couple of days."

Gabriel thumbed the end button and dropped his phone on the loveseat beside him.

Not a single picture on the internet or in a newspaper of this guy.

Gabriel pondered that for a long time. How does a wealthy guy like Roman Dvanaesti effectively not exist? Gabriel realized the answer was in the question. Money talked and walked and did whatever it wanted. The more money you had, the more it did for you. How else could you have a son who's the governor of the third most populous state in the union, who's announcing he's running for the Senate, not to mention his own homes and businesses around the world, and still no one has even a picture to post in the National Enquirer?

That was another thing. There weren't photographs of a guy claiming to be Roman Dvanaesti. No pictures of a guy that a photographer claimed was Roman Dvanaesti. He wasn't listed on any of the rich or powerful people lists. He wasn't on the New York Stock Exchange. This guy had to be bad news. He had something to hide, and anyone connected to the Dvanaesti name was in trouble. Sooner or later, what was done in the dark came to light. True, Dvanaesti had been able to keep it in the dark for a long time, but that just meant the odds were running out. Anyone connected to the Dvanaesti name would be guilty by association.

That last thought brought to the silver screen in his head the freeze-frame image of Claudia tonight on the arm of Cain Dvanaesti. Gabriel wasn't feeling the pangs of rekindled love or jealousy. He had no illusions that he might still be in love with Claudia or that she might be in love with him. They'd had their chance, and he'd blown it. She was happy now, and he was glad about that. But...she had to be warned.

He looked at his watch.

11:30 P.M.

Hopefully, she's still a night owl, he thought as he pulled her up on his contacts list. A bemused snort escaped his nostrils. It had been ten years, but she was still in his contacts. And he'd thumbed right to her without hesitation. He hit the dial button.

"Hello?"

"Hey, Claudia. It's me, Gabe. Can we meet for coffee? Now?"

15

The silver Crown Victoria pulled out of the hotel's parking garage and headed west. Spotting a payphone in front of an Exxon service station, the driver angled into the parking lot and the spot in front of the phone. He cut the engine and exited the Crown Vic.

As he approached the phone, his slender fingers pulled a prepaid calling card from his jacket pocket. He picked up the receiver, dialed the number on the back of the card, entered his PIN, and waited.

"It's Marcus." His voice was flat. "Mr. Hawthorne and his assistant are on the path to illumination." His expression was unreadable as he listened. "I think we should keep eyes on his assistant." He listened. "I will instruct them not to interfere." He hung up, climbed back into the Crown Vic, and left.

16

Gabriel handed over a twenty to the young blonde barista.

She took it, gave it a cursory glance, and then shoved it into the drawer. She yanked his change out and handed it to him, her eyes already on the guy behind him.

Gabriel moved over to the queue of people waiting for their triple-decaf lattes and iced macchiatos and wondered whatever happened to the simple good ole American cup of Joe.

After a few minutes, a young man called out, "Two Kenyan Classic Grandes," but his tone asked, "What kind of Philistine orders regular coffee?" He picked the cups up and headed to the table where Claudia waited.

"Here you go," he said as he sat down. He deposited a cup in front of her.

Claudia popped the lid off to cool the coffee.

Gabriel pulled the lid from his cup and deposited six sweetener packets. Popping the top back on, he said. "I was surprised you were willing to meet with me."

"Journalistic curiosity," Claudia answered. "So what brings you to Miami, Gabe? And why were you trying to crash Cain's party?"

Gabriel sipped his coffee, burning his tongue. He winced but pretended he had a coffee grain stuck to the tip of his tongue.

Claudia caught the wince and smiled. "I would've thought nothing could burn your acid tongue."

"Cute," Gabriel replied.

"So. Why are you here?" Claudia asked.

Gabriel set down his cup. "I've been hired to find dirt on your boyfriend."

Claudia's back straightened as her eyes narrowed.

Gabriel held up supplicating hands. "I just wanted to warn you. The burros are at the door, and they're paying me a lot of money to find a way to unlock it. I don't want to see you hurt when the stampede starts."

Claudia sat there for a moment, fixing him hard with a glare. She looked like she believed him, or at least wanted to believe him. After a few more seconds, she spoke. "There's nothing to find on Cain. You're wasting your time."

"What about his father?" Gabriel asked.

"What about his father?"

"I think he's bad news."

Claudia's eyebrows rose. "What proof do you have?"

"I don't," Gabriel admitted. "Not yet, anyway."

Claudia's lips turned upward in a knowing smile.

"It's not like that, Claudia," Gabriel said. "I don't have feelings for you, but I do think of you as a friend. And I don't want to see you hurt."

"I'm not going to get hurt because there's nothing to uncover. Cain is a good man. A great man. And I can't believe his father is any less. So go back to whoever hired you and tell them they're wasting your time and their money."

"That's just what Miguel said." Gabriel decided on a little more truth. "I saw you last night, after the party. I followed you home. I saw Cain escort you to the front door and kiss you. I think the two of you are more than just casual."

Claudia stared at him for a long minute before standing up. "Goodbye, Gabriel."

She walked away without hesitation in her step or a glance over her shoulder.

17

Cain let his body fade into the plush seat of the limo as Isabella Reese, his assistant, droned on about his schedule for the day. Isabella loved routines, and you didn't deviate from them. Everything was on the calendar as an event or an appointment. She carried two smartphones and a tablet with her at all times. Cain looked askance at her and saw she had a phone in each hand, her practiced fingers navigating the screens with a speed that would make a teenager envious.

He sighed and held up a hand. "Isabella. Please."

Isabella gave him a reproving look as if she were a teacher interrupted by a student making a rude noise.

"Can't I just enjoy a little peace this morning? I'm not going to get another chance today."

Isabella opened her mouth to say something, but stopped herself. She closed her mouth and set the phones down. "You may have a moment."

Cain laughed. "Thanks, Mom."

Dell, the Florida Capitol Police Officer riding in the limo, chuckled.

Cain closed his eyes as he heard Isabella huff with disapproval, but he didn't care. This morning, he would make the most significant announcement of his life to date. Everyone knew it was coming, or should, Cain felt, but that didn't make it any easier. He couldn't believe he was going to do it. His stomach didn't need butterflies; it had sprouted wings and was busy fluttering around. He loved this feeling of excitement and fear, which he so rarely experienced. He didn't want to enjoy it; he wanted to savor it. There'd be no time to savor, enjoy, or even remember afterward.

Isabella interrupted his musings. "It's seven-twenty-eight. You'll be on the air at eight- oh-three making your announcement. When they take their commercial break, we'll leave directly from the set to the limo and head to the airport. You can call your father on the way. You have a one o'clock lunch appointment with the Republican leadership at the Governor's Club."

The limo pulled to a stop. Dell spoke into his wrist, "The Governor's exiting the limo." He opened the door and jumped out.

As Cain moved to the door, Isabella grabbed his arm. He turned to face her. She gestured towards the open door. "Why does he have to ride with us?"

Cain smiled. "Appearances." Cain scooted out the door.

Isabella rolled her eyes as she followed him out the door. She said over her shoulder to the driver, "We'll be back in forty-five minutes."

Dell stood beside the Governor as the rest of the security detail surrounded the two. One member had already arrived at the studio earlier. Once Isabella joined Cain, the entire party entered the building.

Samantha, a twenty-year-old communications student at the University of Miami, thanked God she'd had to put her internship off until this semester because of that nasty little incident at the fraternity last summer as she held out a trembling hand toward Cain.

"Good morning, Governor Dvanaesti. Welcome to M.D.T.V. My name's Samantha Riddell, and I'm here to service you."

That got double-takes from the security detail and chuckles.

Cain raised an eyebrow.

Samantha turned six shades of red. "I-I... I mean..."

"We know what you meant," Isabella responded curtly.

Samantha looked from Cain to Isabella and nodded weakly.

"Perhaps you could take us to the Green Room." Isabella prompted.

"What? Oh, yeah—I mean, yes." Samantha didn't move.

"You might start by giving the Governor his hand back," Isabella added firmly.

Samantha now reflected the color of a radish. She dropped Cain's hand and turned on her heel. "If you'll follow me." She started walking, not looking back to see if they were following.

As they approached the Green Room, Dell raised his wrist as if to check whether the cologne he had just spritzed there was still detectable. "Jim? What's your twenty?"

"Problem?" Cain wasn't worried. He knew that Jim, the newest detail member, didn't realize that when Isabella said seven thirty-three, she meant it.

"Jim should be at the door," Dell responded. For his part, he liked the fact that he could trust when Isabella said seven thirty-three that she meant it. It made his life easier. He called Jim's name again into his wrist. Still nothing.

Upon reaching the Green Room door, Dell discovered where Jim was and why he wasn't responding. The curly wire running up from underneath his jacket did not end in his ear as it should, but lay on his shoulder. In one hand was a cup of coffee; in the other, a bagel. His attention was all on the pretty young production assistant responsible for the craft services table in the Green Room.

Before the detail could react, Isabella was in the room and at Jim's side. "*BANG,*" she shouted.

Jim, who'd just been lifting the hot cup of java to his mouth, showered his face, shirt, necktie, and trousers with hot, steaming coffee. "Crap," he yelled as he turned to face Isabella.

Jim stood six-three, nearly a foot taller than Isabella, with a neck larger than Isabella's bust line measurement. It was like watching a Chihuahua pick a fight with a Rottweiler, Dell thought.

"The Governor's dead."

Jim's eyes went wide, as much from the look on Isabella's face, which reminded him of the look on the chick from that horror flick *The Ring,* only scarier, as from the knowledge that something had happened to Governor Dvanaesti.

Isabella took a step toward Jim. He took a step back. "Shot just now while you were flirting." Isabella took another step toward Jim, and he took another back.

Dell watched the blood drain from Jim's face and realized which was the Chihuahua and the Rottweiler.

Isabella didn't take another step toward Jim, but he stepped back again. Isabella looked at him for a long beat. "We won't speak of this again." Her voice was a soft hiss, but Jim heard it clearly, heard the frosty danger in her voice. He nodded weakly.

"I'm sorry, Ma'am." The young production assistant said in a small voice. Isabella's head snapped in her direction.

The girl's mouth gaped in a silent scream, and she stepped back.

Isabella reached out a hand and placed it on the girl's shoulder. "You have nothing to apologize for, young lady." Her voice was smooth and soothing. Her hand caressed the girl's shoulder as a mother might caress her daughter.

The girl relaxed and smiled. "Thank you."

Isabella turned to Jim. "Perhaps you could offer the Governor a cup of coffee? Maybe a bagel? I understand they are to die for." Her voice was firm but pleasant.

Jim looked as if he were trying to shake off a well-placed but very effective cheap shot to his jaw. "Yes, Ma'am."

18

Cain watched from the wings as Claudia and her co-host, Luke, a guy more shellac than polish, welcomed the audience at home back to the show. Their facial expressions and body language were coy or as coy as two cats that had just eaten the proverbial canary as they prepared to announce their next guest, their special surprise guest. Isabella flitted around Cain like a hummingbird, checking the knot in his necktie, brushing his shoulders for dandruff (something he'd never had), and adjusting his jacket. Cain rolled his eyes like an eight-year-old as his mother prepared him for his first day of Parochial school.

"Well, Claudia," Luke was saying with that smile.

"I guess it's time, Luke," Claudia responded with a like smile.

They turned to the camera in unison. Luke thought, *E! News here I come,* as he said, "Ladies and Gentlemen, may we introduce to you…"

Claudia thought, *CNN, this time next year,* as she said, "…The Governor of the Great State of Florida. Miami's own Cain Dvanaesti."

The studio audience erupted, as did the people in their living rooms, kitchens, and bedrooms watching or listening to the morning show, moving closer to their television sets to watch Cain walk out to Luke and Claudia, waving as he went. Cain took Claudia by both hands and kissed her cheek, then shook Luke's hand. He sat down in the chair provided. He looked at the camera and flashed his Florida-famous smile. His hand combed through his hair. Women in the viewing area suddenly felt the need for a cold shower.

Luke started. "So, Governor Dvanaesti. Thank you for coming on the show today."

"I'm glad to be here, Luke. This is my favorite morning show."

"Really?" The word was out of Luke's mouth before he realized, with all the tone of *you watch this podunk fluff of a show?*

Cain smiled and stole a not-so-furtive glance toward Claudia. "Of course. This is the best-looking morning show in all of Florida." He looked at the audience. "Don't you think?"

The audience applauded, cat-called, and wolf-whistled.

Even though Cain had looked at the audience, the viewers at home swore he'd looked right at each of them. They applauded just as wildly as the studio audience.

Cain seemed to hear them. He nodded his acknowledgment. "I thought so."

"And it doesn't hurt you're dating one of the hosts of the show." Luke cursed himself under his breath. He'd meant it to sound playful. Instead, it had come out as jealous and patronizing. E! News was signing off.

"Ah, Luke," Cain said with a sheepish smile, "you told me you'd keep our relationship a secret."

At home, viewers heard the snickers and laughter from the studio audience and watched Luke turn the color of a red onion.

Claudia decided it was time to get back on track. "All kidding aside, Governor, why don't you tell us why you're here?"

Cain stood up and cleared his throat. "Ladies and Gentlemen, I asked to come onto the show this morning so I could make an important announcement. I wanted you to be the first to hear it." In one movement, Cain took Claudia by the hand, dropped to one knee, produced a three-carat diamond engagement ring, looked into Claudia's eyes, and asked, "Will you marry me?"

The studio and home audiences went wild.

Claudia looked from Cain to the ring and back to Cain. She opened her mouth and heard herself say, "Huh?"

"Will you be my wife?" Cain asked.

The audience watched as Claudia's mouth fell open, and she stared at the man on his knee as if he'd just spoken Latin in Pig Latin, trying to work it all out.

A full twenty seconds of silence passed before Luke finally said, "Claudia?"

"Well?" Cain prompted. "Are you going to keep me and, more importantly, the people of Miami-Dade waiting?"

She just kept staring at him, mouth agape.

Cain smiled. "Claudia Bennett? Will you do me the honor of being Mrs. Cain Dvanaesti?"

Claudia snapped out of her stupor. She nodded. Tears began to flow down her cheeks. "Yes," she said, smiling and crying and shaking. She nodded more emphatically. "Yes."

People in the studio and at home yawped, screamed, and applauded as Cain slipped the ring onto Claudia's finger. Cain stood, and the two embraced and kissed.

"Well, Miami, you heard it here first. The Governor's taken a wife." Luke cursed himself. *Not even TMZ is returning my calls.*

19

Isabella stared down at the LCD screen of her phone. She'd entered Roman's number and was ready to hit the Send button as soon as Cain had made his announcement. But he hadn't. She stood there, frozen in disbelief. Nothing had gotten past her in a very, very long time.

She knew when Cain awoke and when he went to bed. She knew what he was having for breakfast, lunch, and dinner. She knew how often he brushed his teeth and what he would wear every day. She planned and scheduled his days, his weeks, his months.

In the Sixties, a commercial asked, *It's ten o'clock. Do you know where your kids are?* She was better than any parent; you ask her any hour of the day or night, and she could tell you where the governor was and who he was with. Now she looked at the rock on Claudia's finger and realized she'd had no idea when he'd stopped to shop for a ring, let alone that he was planning to propose.

Claudia and Cain walked into the wings past Isabella, oblivious of her presence. Her eyes, a soft green, now blazed the color of jade on fire. Turning on her heel, she marched straight up to Cain.

Claudia was gushing, "I can't...I just thought-...I mean-...You-. Wow."

"Now I can see why you chose television over print. You are so eloquent with words." Cain teased as he held her hand up to admire the diamond sparkling in the studio lights.

Isabella opened her mouth without taking his eyes off Claudia. Cain held up his index finger to her. Isabella's teeth made an audible clink as she closed her mouth.

"You be nice." Claudia tried to pout, but the bottom lip couldn't outdo her beaming smile. "I thought you were going to announce your candidacy for the Senate."

Cain smiled. "Would you rather I'd done that?"

Claudia rolled her eyes. "No. I'm just...I just thought that's what you were going to do." Now she stared hard at her shoes. "I just don't want to be a campaign tactic."

Cain took Claudia's face into his hands.

Claudia's eyes looked up at his, searching, hoping he was going to tell her differently.

Cain moved his lips to hers and kissed her tenderly, then pulled back and looked into her eyes for a long beat before saying, "I want you by my side when I make that announcement."

Now Claudia kissed Cain.

A voice behind them yelled, "We're back in twenty."

Claudia pulled away. "Oh. I need to go." She started moving back to the set. "Will you still be here?"

Cain shook his head. "I've got to head back to Tallahassee. But I'll call you from the plane."

Claudia looked disappointed, but she nodded. Waving, she sprinted back onto the set as the voice yelled, "We're back in five."

"May I speak with you, please?" Isabella's tone wasn't a question.

Cain turned to watch Isabella, turning on her heel and heading to the Green Room. He sighed and followed, removing the lapel mike they'd attached to him. He handed it to a production assistant as he heard Isabella from the Green Room.

"The Governor and I need a moment." It was not delivered as a demand or even a request. But the production assistant in charge of the Craft Services table shot from the room as if avoiding being hit by flying objects.

Cain smiled at the young lady, but she was too freaked out. She burst through the Ladies' Room door.

And into tears, I imagine, Cain thought as he entered the Green Room.

Isabella pointed towards the set. "That won't happen again."

Cain moved to the Craft Services table and poured a cup of coffee. "What?"

"Don't play coy with me, Cain—"

"I wasn't," Cain interrupted, sipping coffee. "Boy. That is good. I should try a bagel." He moved towards the bagels. "Besides, you should've seen that coming."

"What?" Her tone was both incredulous and scandalized.

"Don't play coy with me, Isabella. I've been dating Claudia for the past eighteen months. I've never dated a woman for more than a few weeks when

I have dated, and I'm about to move into the true, big time. You can't do that without a wife."

"And what am I supposed to tell your father?" Her voice was deadly calm. "This wasn't part of the plan."

A smile curled in one corner of Cain's mouth. "That's why it's called a surprise."

"Your father doesn't like surprises," Isabella said, her voice growing colder.

"Perhaps he should get used to them," Cain responded, even colder.

Isabella took a step towards Cain. "Governor, I know that you and your constituents think you're just about the brightest thing in the universe—"

Isabella's voice, icy with sarcasm, stuck in her throat as Cain turned his back on her, picked up a bagel, and started to slather it with cream cheese.

Isabella's eyes went to slits as a hiss like a King Cobra escaped her lips. She had a hold of him in less than a heartbeat. She spun him around, the bagel and plastic knife flying out of his hands. "Do not ignore me when I'm talking to you," she spat as she drove Cain's head into the wall. His skull made a loud, satisfying _Thunk_ for Isabella as it hit.

White starburst fireworks flashed before his eyes. Cain placed his hand over hers as it wrapped around his throat, lifting him off the ground, his feet dangling. "You forget your place, Cain Dvanaesti." She let him go.

He slumped to the carpet, looking up at Isabella.

She stood above him, looking down at him.

"Are you through?" Cain asked as if Isabella had done nothing more than throw a temper tantrum. "Get it all out of your system?"

Isabella nodded, then stepped back.

Cain stood up, straightened his tie, turned to the table, and picked up a fresh bagel. Smearing it with cream cheese, he took a bite before saying, "I'll be waiting for you in the limo." With that, he opened the door and exited, closing it calmly behind him.

20

"Welcome aboard, Governor," the lone flight attendant for the Bombardier Global 5000 jet chirped as Cain stepped from the stairway into the plane and past the two FDLE officers standing guard at the door.

The jet, a gift from Cain's father upon winning the Florida governorship, boasted a stateroom and seating for sixteen passengers. Roman had also installed a desk and chair for Isabella just before the cockpit.

Cain smiled at the young blond woman, melting her heart, before moving to the stateroom, ignoring the two men seated on either side of the door.

The young flight attendant's welcome did not carry the same enthusiasm for Isabella as she stepped into the cabin. Instead, the smile faltered, and her heart shivered in her chest. As Isabella sat in her usual seat just outside the cockpit, the FDLE security detail climbed aboard.

The cabin door closed, and the flight attendant asked all aboard to prepare for take-off.

The FDLE detail looked at the two men seated in the back. They didn't like these two men. The men never spoke or acknowledged anyone's presence. They had never been introduced to them or even been told their names. They'd been told only that they were private security hired by Roman Dvanaesti. Also, these men never moved. They could sit or stand for hours and never shift weight, scratch their noses, or sneeze, like two statues. Lastly...the FDLE officers had been around long enough to know that no matter how big and bad you thought you were, there was always someone bigger and badder. These two guys were the baddest.

The FDLE officers took their seats and buckled themselves in. Isabella opened up her laptop. Cain poured himself a cup of coffee and sat in the plush stateroom command chair. He swiveled right and left as he waited for the flight attendant to let him know it was okay to use electronic equipment.

Isabella didn't wait but went to work on her two smartphones, tablet, and laptop. The flight attendant, accustomed to Isabella's disregard for FAA rules concerning electronics and take-off, waited for the last agent to adjust his seatbelt, then said, "I'll be around in the next few minutes with your beverage service." She checked the door to ensure it was securely closed, then took her seat.

The jet moved onto the runway tarmac as the pilot let everyone know, to no one's surprise, they were clear for immediate departure. The jet was airborne within minutes, flying across the Florida skies back to Tallahassee.

Cain picked up the phone on his stateroom desk and punched in Claudia's cell phone number. As he listened to the ring, he looked out the door past the security detail to the back of Isabella's head at the front of the plane. She hadn't yet acknowledged him, but she would. He smiled as he heard the click of the answer.

"Hey, Stranger." Claudia's voice carried no post-show exhaustion.

Cain smiled. "And how is the future Mrs. Dvanaesti?"

"Awesome. But I miss you." She sounded as if the wind were leaving her sails rapidly.

Cain watched Isabella stand up and press the end call button on the smartphone she always used for his business. Her other hand thumbed the smartphone she used for his father's business. She'd kept it pressed to her hip. Perhaps everyone else on the plane missed what she was doing, but Cain didn't. She looked towards him, nodded, then sat back down.

"How'd you like to join me for the weekend?" There was silence at the end of the line. Cain continued. "You could fly up to Tally today and be back on Monday evening."

"Oh, I don't know."

"What's the problem?" Cain kept his eyes on Isabella's posture, sure she was still texting.

"I've got to work on Monday morning."

"No, you don't."

"Cain—"

"I've already cleared it with your boss." Cain interrupted.

"What'd you promise him?" She sounded both offended and flattered.

"Just an exclusive interview."

"When you announce your candidacy for the Senate?" Now she sounded hopeful.

"That will have already taken place."

"Oh." Now she sounded hurt.

"I plan on doing that Monday. With you by my side."

"Oh." Now she sounded like she'd just been told she'd won the Publisher's Clearing House sweepstakes.

"So what do you say? I'll have my assistant make all the arrangements." He emphasized the word 'assistant' as if the word were an indiscretion left on the area rug by the family pet.

Isabella's head shot up.

Cain grinned, knowing she could hear everything.

"No, don't do that." Claudia sounded embarrassed. "She's busy enough."

"Nonsense." He laughed. "She lives to do my bidding. I'll have her email you later with your flight information."

"You sure?"

"Of course, I'm sure. Honey, I've got to go." He said.

"Okay. I'll see you later." She said.

"I'll see you later." He hung up and sipped his coffee. "You heard all that, I'm sure."

Isabella stared straight ahead for a moment before finally frowning and pulling out her smartphone.

21

The Mercedes SL350 made a right off of North Monroe Street into the parking lot of the Hotel Duval, pulled up to the covered area, and stopped. The driver, a serious and capable young man, jumped quickly from the vehicle and moved around to open the door for Claudia before the Valet could reach the car.

"Ms. Bennett," he said, offering her a thin, long-fingered hand.

Claudia was impressed. This guy was worth his salary and then some. He'd been waiting at the gate, which no one was allowed to do anymore, and only said her name as she exited the jet bridge. No sign with her name on it or an expectant expression on his face. He knew exactly who he was waiting for. They'd walked to baggage claim, where he asked, "May I?" and then withdrew her luggage from the conveyor belt without asking her to identify her bags.

They'd walked to the idling Mercedes under the scrutiny of a Tallahassee Police Officer. Claudia couldn't believe the guy had left the vehicle unattended and expected the officer to hand the driver, who'd only identified himself as "your driver" when she'd asked him for his name, a ticket. Instead, the officer only nodded to the driver and walked off to let someone else know it was time to move their vehicle.

The Mercedes moved through the light Friday evening traffic, though Claudia noticed heavy traffic leaving the city. She laughed at that thought. The city. She remembered her first visit to Tallahassee seven years ago.

She was there before to interview the previous governor, and she'd had time to kill. She went to the Governor's Square Mall to do some Christmas shopping. As she threaded her way through the throngs, Bing Crosby dreaming of a "White Christmas" over the PA system, Claudia was brought to a halt by a large woman in flip flops, khaki shorts, and a red Santa Claus t-shirt exclaiming in a loud Southern twang to the woman she was hugging, "It's just amazing who you run into when you come into the city."

Until that moment, she'd never thought of Tallahassee as a city. Not like New York or Miami were cities. Tallahassee was just a town. It might be a big town with two universities and the seat of state government, but a town nonetheless. She'd learned a lot at that moment about perspective.

"Thank you," Claudia said as she took her driver's hand. He lifted her gently from the vehicle as the valet muttered something under his breath. She moved towards the door without looking back. Her driver had taken issue with what the young man had said in the presence of a lady. Well, she thought as she caught the reflection in the glass of the men behind her, I'm glad I'm not that guy.

Claudia opened the lobby door to find a young blonde in a black dress waiting. She watched the girl's face bubble into a smile as she recognized Claudia. "Ms. Bennett," the young woman beamed, her body vibrating with excitement, "if you'd follow me, I'll take you to your room."

Claudia returned the smile and nodded.

The woman escorted Claudia to the top floor, where she produced a mag card from Claudia knew not where, and presented it to Claudia outside the room door. "Enjoy your stay in the capital city, Ms. Bennett. Your bags will be right up."

Claudia accepted the card, and the young woman was off without a look back. Claudia opened the door and stepped inside the room. On the table was a vase filled with a dozen red long-stemmed roses, a bottle of champagne on ice, and a platter of strawberries. She moved to the roses and inhaled deeply. They smelled wonderful. She picked up a strawberry and sniffed. It smelled fresh. She popped it into her mouth and smiled. The strawberries couldn't have been left in the room more than a minute before she'd entered. She noticed a card in the roses. Her heart lifted with the thought of what sweet nothing Cain had written in it. As she read it, her heart sank. The card was typed.

Congratulations on your engagement.

Hotel Duval.

Oh well.

She turned, admiring the room, and noticed a white box on the bed, with an envelope and a single long-stemmed white rose resting across it. After an inhale, this time of the white rose, she picked up the envelope and opened it. Inside was a small one-page letter in Cain's elegant penmanship.

Claudia,

Meet me at Shula's 347 Grill in the hotel at 7:30. I hope to see you wearing what's in the box.

Love, your future husband,

Cain

Claudia smiled. She dropped the note onto the bed, opened the box, and squealed. She lifted out a Donna Karan little black dress, in her size, with matching Manolo Blahnik heels.

She held the dress to her frame and spun around, giggling like a teenage girl. Catching her reflection in the mirror, she stopped and asked, "So? Are you ready to be the future Mrs. Cain Dvanaesti?" She frowned. "Or is it the future Mrs. Governor Cain Dvanaesti?"

She spun on the balls of her feet and smiled. "Who cares?" she trilled as she held the dress to her again and pretended to be at a party. "This ol' thing? I only wear it when I don't care what I look like. No offense to Donna. Why Donna Karen, of course. Oh yes, she's a close personal friend of the family."

This last little part of the pretend conversation stopped her in her tracks. It was a lie. Just a pretend conversation as she stood alone in her hotel room, alone for the first time since becoming the future Mrs. Cain Dvanaesti. Donna Karen hadn't picked out the dress and wasn't her friend. She cared very much about how she looked and would care more when she was Mrs. Cain Dvanaesti. She hadn't had a pretend party conversation since she was a girl. She marveled at how easily she'd slipped back into it. Easier than slipping into the little black dress. Would it be that easy once they were married? Would she wear it as comfortably as her fashionable clothing?

Now her mind was spinning faster than she'd been a minute ago. Would she be willing to turn the lies on and off like a light switch? Would something she said at a dinner party in Tallahassee bite her on her show in Miami?

And what about her show in Miami? What about her work? Her career? How would she be able to continue working in Miami when Cain's work was here in Tallahassee? Sure, she could probably get a job in TV here in Tallahassee, but she'd be starting over. She'd never know if she was getting the job based on the strength of her resume or her husband's name. What happened to the difference she was making and hoped to continue? Would she lose that if she came to Tallahassee? Did Cain expect her to leave that all behind? Did he expect her to become less of herself and more of what she was expected to be: the strong woman standing behind the great man?

That last thought made her laugh. Cain was a great man. Nobody needed to be standing behind him to make that happen. She was being silly. Of course, Cain wouldn't want her to give up on her dreams, her career. Most politicians may be looking for the best trophy to slip a ring on to help their career, but Cain wasn't one of those.

She giggled again as she twirled back to the bed and fell on it. Letting go of the dress, she picked up Cain's note again. She smiled as she read, 'Love, your future husband.' She sighed as her eyes fell on the words, *future husband.* "Right back at you, Babe."

22

Stefan guided the Cadillac DTS to the curb of the passenger pick-up and a waiting Gabriel.

Gabriel took in the DTS and rolled his eyes. He opened the back door to throw his bag in next to Stefan's. "Going somewhere?" He asked.

Stefan didn't answer until Gabriel was seated in the front passenger seat, seatbelt securely in place, and he was pulling away from the curb. "I am catching an afternoon flight to New Orleans. That's why I thought we should have this conversation in the privacy of a moving vehicle."

With all Stefan had seen and been through in his short life, Gabriel knew the guy didn't spook easily. Stefan was a stickler for doing things "by the book," like not having discreet conversations in indiscreet places. Most of their conversations never fell into the discreet category, and certainly not at the start. This was early. Especially for Stefan. "What's going on?"

Stefan reached up, snagged a manila folder tucked between the glass and dash, and handed it over to Gabriel.

Gabriel opened the folder. "What am I looking at?" There were photos of Cain Dvanaesti surrounded by different people at different events, Stefan's handwritten notes, and several photocopied documents.

"What I have so far," Stefan said. "The Dvanaesti family has only been in Florida for a short period, just Cain Dvanaesti's lifetime. There isn't much here beyond Cain. Like I said before, until Cain, the Dvanaesti family didn't seem to have any footprint. Even the personal homes of Roman and Cain in Miami are owned by companies owned by corporations. Across the country, those companies and corporations have been tied to commercial properties and investments for years. But in New Orleans, that presence goes back to what I assume is Roman's grandfather. If there's anything to find on the Dvanaestis."

Gabriel thumbed through the photos. They were taken at different events. In one, Cain was in slacks and a sport shirt in the skybox at a football game. Cain is dressed in a tux at night in another. One photo was taken outside, and Gabriel could see on a bright day. The edges of the shadows were sharp, and everyone not wearing sunglasses had their faces screwed up, squinting hard to protect their eyes. Excepting Cain Dvanaesti. He seemed unfazed by the brightness.

Gabriel noticed something else. "Who's this woman?" He held up one of the photos and pointed to a woman in the background. "This one here. She's in all these pictures, but always in the background or on the sidelines. Always has her head turned so you can't see her face outright."

Stefan glanced at the photo, then back at the road. "Isabella Reese," he responded.

"And she is?" Gabriel prompted.

"Cain's assistant. Not on the taxpayer payroll. He pays her salary himself."

"Do you know what she did before she started working for Cain Dvanaesti?"

"Worked for Roman Dvanaesti."

Again, Gabriel's head snapped up. "Did she?"

"Yep," Stefan replied.

"Do you know doing what?"

"Nope," Stefan answered.

Gabriel looked back at the images of Isabella Reese. "Interesting. That's very interesting."

"I thought you might think so," Stefan said.

Gabriel closed the manila folder. He had some things to mull over. But first, "Where are we headed?"

"I reserved you a room at the Hotel Duval," Stefan said as he reached into his pocket and pulled out a hotel key card. "Room four-zero-five. I put the reservation on my card. When you pay for it, make sure you use your card."

Gabriel took the card. Why the Hotel Duval?"

"Because that is where Miss Claudia Bennett is staying," Stefan responded with a matter-of-fact tone.

"She's here?" Gabriel demanded. "In Tallahassee?"

Stefan nodded. "Hotel Duval. Room four-eleven."

Now Gabriel had more to mull over. Claudia was in Tallahassee. Cain was in Tallahassee. How could he see her again? He needed to persuade her that the man of her dreams was either bad news or the son of bad news.

"You can keep the car, but do not forget to turn it back in at the airport when you leave."

Gabriel looked around at the DTS. "Stefan? Why do you always stay at Motel Six, only shop at the Dollar Store, but always rent a Cadillac? And how do they always have one?"

Stefan shrugged. "Membership has its privileges." He maneuvered the vehicle into the Hotel Duval's parking lot and stopped at the valet parking sign.

Gabriel opened his door to get out and said, "I couldn't help noticing you seem a little more cautious than usual."

Stefan hesitated for a second before opening the door and stepping out. Opening the back door, he reached for his bag. "I do not know, Gabriel. I cannot prove it. I have not spotted a tail." He looked around. "But it is the same feeling when I was walking point when we were out on patrol. Like I was being watched." He pulled out his bag and closed the back door.

Gabriel retrieved his bag and came around the car.

Stefan offered his hand to Gabriel. "Be careful, Gabe."

Gabriel took his hand. "You, too." Gabriel watched Stefan walk toward the parking lot exit and out onto Monroe Street. Something didn't feel right.

23

"Can I take that plate out of your way, Ms. Bennett?"

Claudia looked up to see the waiter standing beside her. She still wasn't accustomed to being addressed by the wait staff, but it always happened whenever and wherever she dined with Cain. They could slip into a pizza joint for a slice of pepperoni with onion and a beer, and he was still 'Governor,' and she was still 'Ms. Bennett'. She sighed. Soon it would be 'Mrs. Dvanaesti'.

But what if I didn't want to change my name? I'm already known in the industry as Bennett. What would happen if I were Dvanaesti? Does Cain expect me to change my name? Probably.

The waiter misunderstood the sigh. "I'm sorry, Ms. Bennett. Please forgive me." He stepped away as if he'd been standing on a red ant hill.

"Nothing to apologize for, Drew." Cain's voice was soothing. "My bride-to-be's still uncomfortable with the formal address." He motioned to his plate. "By all means."

Drew's posture lifted with the lightened weight of his shoulders. He bustled back to the table and picked up the plates. "May I show you the dessert menu?"

Claudia put a hand to her stomach and made the universal expression that one more bite of anything might make her puke. Cain laughed. "I think Ms. Bennett and I feel like that excellent meal was dessert enough."

Drew's spine straightened with pride, making him an inch taller.

"And unimpeachable service."

Drew's smile was all teeth and gums. "My pleasure." He was gone.

Claudia stared at Cain in awe. "How do you do that?"

"Do what?" Cain placed his elbows on the table and stared straight into her eyes.

The look made her tingle with excitement. "That. That look. That...tone in your voice. Like me or Drew or whoever just made your life complete."

Cain shrugged. "Because you and Drew do. I was going to wait, but since you brought it up. How do you feel about us adopting Drew? After the honeymoon, of course."

She rolled her eyes. "You're incorrigible." She looked around the room, her eyes stopping on a middle-aged woman whose eyes were already on her and Cain. The woman noticed Claudia looking at her and waved excitedly.

Claudia waved back, albeit with less enthusiasm. "Um... do we know that woman?"

Cain's glance drifted in the direction of Claudia's gaze.

That was all the encouragement the woman needed. She was on her feet and moving towards them.

"Oh gosh." Claudia swallowed, her hand suspended mid-wave. "She's coming this way."

Cain nodded towards the bar that everything was okay. Claudia turned to see the two members of Cain's security detail nod to the Governor and sit back down.

This was something Claudia loved about Cain. He refused to be unapproachable. He never wanted the public to feel threatened. The men who guarded him were all ex-cops or ex-military and were paid to take a bullet for him. But Claudia knew these guys would take a bullet without the paycheck. They were suspicious of everybody. They didn't care if you were a twenty-eight-year-old man or an eighty-two-year-old woman. Every person who approached the Governor was a potential threat.

Cain, though, seemed to know who was benign and who was malignant. It was like a sixth sense, and he was never wrong. There were times when someone behaving strangely would approach Cain. He'd wave his security off. Other times, Cain would be shaking hands and kissing babies and smiling for the camera, and then give his detail a look at a man or woman, and sure enough, when that man or woman was detained and searched, items used to inflict serious bodily harm were found in their possession. Cain's sixth sense told him this woman was harmless.

The woman smiled, revealing teeth smudged with pink lipstick, a shade lighter than her dress. "You're Governor Cain Dvanaesti." It wasn't a question.

Cain nodded.

The woman sucked air through her teeth and smiled again. She closed her eyes to reveal a garish blue eye shadow. "I knew it," she shrieked. "I just knew it. Can I ask you a huge, huge favor?" She pulled out a digital camera and pressed forward, receiving no response from Cain. "Can I get a picture with you?" She glanced at Claudia. "Maybe...?" She waited for an introduction.

"This is Claudia Bennett, my fiancée." Cain was pleasant.

"Maybe your fiancée could take it?" She'd put an unpleasant emphasis on the word fiancée as if the word indicated what the teenagers were caught engaging in on the living room sofa by the girl's parents.

The slight seemed lost on Cain. He raised a questioning eyebrow at Claudia.

Claudia exhaled a bemused sigh. "Sure. Why not?"

Jamming the camera into Claudia's gut like a quarterback handing off to his running back, the woman squatted next to Cain. She draped her pink arm around his neck and moved her pink lipstick and garish eye shadow to within an inch of Cain's face as if she were going to kiss him.

Claudia quickly snapped a couple of photos. "All done. Okay." She pressed the camera back towards the woman. "Here you go."

The woman grabbed it as if it were the Miss America pageant tiara and backed away. "Thank you, Governor Dvanaesti. Thank you."

Claudia said, "Oh, it was no trouble at all. You're welcome." She rolled her eyes.

Cain laughed. "Have you thought about keeping your name or changing it?"

Claudia stared at him, completely taken aback. "Huh?"

"Do you want to stay Claudia Bennett or change your name to Dvanaesti?" He frowned. "Dvanaesti," he said slowly. "Claudia Dvanaesti." He let the name play on his lips like he was tasting wine. "Claudia Bennett Dvanaesti." He grimaced. "That's horrid. One or the other, but no hyphenation."

Claudia couldn't help but laugh out loud.

Cain smiled as he took her hand. "I know we haven't had a chance to discuss living arrangements and name changes, but I want you to know I will support your career no matter what." He kissed her hand. "I'm in love with you. Not your name or your career. Where you lead, I will follow."

And he meant it too. He loved her. He would do anything for her, and if she told him tonight the only way to have her would be to walk away from politics, the money, or his name, or all of it, he'd do it. He'd do it before she finished telling him.

As the son of an extremely wealthy businessman and now a politician, Cain knew his responsibilities to his family and country. He'd grown up knowing people wanted power and prestige, or at least a protector who did. People were motivated by self-interest, by gain. Everyone around him had an agenda. Everyone. He loved his father and Isabella, but even they had an agenda, a plan.

Except for Claudia. Claudia was a giver, not a taker. That came from her father, who'd taught her to remember who you are and whose you are. And he'd told her, if you never collect skeletons, you never have skeletons to hide.

Claudia's voice snapped him out of his reverie. "I'll think about it." She squeezed Cain's hand. "I had a wonderful time tonight."

"So did I," Cain replied as Drew bellied up to the table with the check.

Cain pulled two C notes from his wallet and handed them to Drew. "Keep the change."

Claudia could've sworn Drew's body visibly lifted a few inches off the ground as he stared hungrily at the two bills. "Yes, Sir. Thank you, Sir." He moved away.

Cain stood up and held out a hand to Claudia. Claudia took the hand. Cain escorted her to the bank of elevators. She could feel the weight of all those eyes in the lobby, at the desk, in the restaurant, all staring at them. She couldn't bring herself to turn around.

As the elevator chimed its arrival, Cain leaned in and gave Claudia a long, slow kiss on her lips. "I'll see you tomorrow morning." And with that, Cain Dvanaesti turned on his heel and walked towards his waiting limo.

24

Claudia rode the elevator up with a couple who seemed just seconds away from spontaneously combusting. They kissed and giggled that little giggle lovers share when they think everybody is clueless to what they're about to do, clueless to the fact that everyone knows. Claudia was simultaneously envious and annoyed.

As the couple pawed each other behind her, for the first time in her life, she felt claustrophobic. She wanted off the elevator. Who thought up elevators anyway? That's the problem with America today. Too many elevators. Stairs, she affirmed to herself with a pursing of the lips. From now on, she was a stairs woman. It was healthier, and none of this...this...goings-on behind her. She heard the woman exhale as the man nuzzled her neck. Her foot started to tap impatiently. She *needed* off this elevator.

The floor chime sounded, the doors opened, and Claudia practically jumped into the hallway. She didn't turn around but sulked down the hall to her room.

Once inside, she kicked off the heels and shrugged out of the Donna Karen, a dress she'd thought made her butt look good, and into a pair of Betty Boop sleep pants and a matching Betty Boop T-shirt. She poured a glass of champagne and padded into the bathroom to remove her makeup.

I can get used to this, Claudia thought, pouring a glass of champagne. Crawling into bed, she grabbed the remote off the nightstand. She surfed the channels. *That Touch of Mink* with Cary Grant and Doris Day was on. Cary and Doris were riding an elevator up to their hotel room. Everyone saw an elevator as an elevator. Doris saw the elevator as a bed.

Claudia dropped the remote beside her and picked up her glass of champagne. She smiled at the very self-conscious way Doris was acting and thought of the couple on the elevator just a few minutes ago. How times had changed, she thought. She watched Cary open the door to his and Doris' hotel room.

"Always the gentleman," she said, not to Cary but to the image of Cain tonight walking her to the elevator door and pressing the call button. He always did those things: held the door for her, stood when she walked into the room, and always treated her like a lady. Not just a lady, but a Grand Dame. The most important person in the world. He did that with everyone. Cain treated everyone with respect. He could see the greatness in each person and wanted to help them realize it for themselves. He didn't see people as votes or dollars but as the most precious creatures he had the pleasure of knowing. It was genuine. That's why people loved him. He wasn't a motivational speaker riling people up for a fee or a politician buttering them up for a vote. He lived what he believed. He walked his talk. He made people want to be better people.

She looked at the engagement ring and wondered. What if there was a wedding band already there as well? What if Cain were her husband right now? Then Cain would've come up on the elevator with her, smiled at her as they quietly endured the pawing couple, then laughed about them as they left the elevator.

A thought came into her head, which caused her to bite her bottom lip. If Cain were her husband right now, they wouldn't be here at the Hotel Duval but down the street in the governor's mansion. He'd be coming out of the bathroom in his pajamas, crawling into bed, taking her glass of champagne from her, sipping, then handing it back to her before pulling her to him and cuddling with her to watch this movie. If only...

A quick burst of knocking on her door had her heart jumping in her chest, her eyes as big as a Meerkat's scanning the horizon for predators. There was another quick burst of knocking.

Who in the world?

"Just a minute," she shouted as she scurried out of bed and over to the door. She looked through the peephole and frowned.

Gabriel Hawthorne.

A flood of emotions ran through her. Surprise. *How did he know where she was? And not just the city, but her hotel and room as well?* Anger. *Why was he banging on her door at this time of night?* Frustration. *What could he want?* She frowned. The answer to that last question was simple–Cain Dvanaesti.

Gabriel was doing the job he'd been hired to do: find Cain's indiscretions. His half-truths and falsehoods. His dirt. She could respect that. She was a journalist. She understood the dogged determination needed to uncover the truth. It wasn't personal. The truth was universal. It couldn't be personal. That worked both ways. When it was not what you wanted, you couldn't ignore that. That's when the half-truths and falsehoods, the dirt, were created and fostered with malicious aforethought. If the truth wasn't what you wanted, invent a lie more suitable. Then keep telling it until everyone believes it's the truth.

She'd never fallen for that temptation. She'd been tempted before, especially when you just knew that you knew your hunch was correct. What did it matter? The ends justified the means. Again, it wasn't personal. It was for the greater good. The truth would eventually come out. This time, though, it was different. Cain wasn't just a good man poised to do great things; he was also her man. This time, it was very personal.

She needed to quash this before Gabriel Hawthorne decided to fake the dirt till he could make the dirt. She straightened her back and flung open the door.

Gabriel understood. "I need to talk to you, too."

Claudia waved him in, and as he bustled past her, she stuck her head into the hall and glanced both ways, making sure no one had seen Gabriel enter her room. Satisfied he hadn't been noticed, she closed the door and whipped around on him.

"So. It's been twenty-four hours," she hissed. "What dirt have you dug up, Gabriel? What skeletons have you found in Cain's closet?"

Gabriel walked over and dropped onto the loveseat with enough resignation to make a teenager proud. "Nothing," Gabriel admitted as he slumped. "Not one thing."

"Not one thing," Claudia spat.

"And that's what scares me."

Claudia was caught off guard by this last admission. "Scares you?"

"This guy is perfect. That's not human."

"No. That's not *you*," Claudia said.

Gabriel's smile was thin as he rubbed his forehead with his palm. "I don't know. Maybe you're right. Maybe Cain Dvanaesti is clean. Maybe he is the Boy Scout he claims to be."

"And that's driving you crazy, isn't it?" Claudia moved to the corner of the bed and sat down. "Have you ever considered the possibility that he is?

That the reason why you haven't found anything is because there's nothing to find? He's a good man. He not only stands up for what he believes but lives it. And what about me, Gabe? If anyone can spot dirt, it's me. I've been a journalist for almost half my life. I've been dating Cain for eighteen months. People can hide their spots for only so long. Six months usually. But not eighteen months. I would've heard or seen something. Somebody would've let something slip in that time, but they haven't. And I haven't."

"But your judgment's...compromised, Claudia. You're dating him. Excuse me, *marrying* him. Love can cover a multitude of sins."

"Well, what about you then, Gabe?" Claudia asked, exasperated. "If you won't trust me, what about you? You're good at your job. How long have you been looking into Cain? Forty-eight, Seventy-two hours? Has it ever taken you this long to find something on someone? And the fact that you're not finding anything?" She let that question hang out there for a minute.

So did Gabriel. "Okay," throwing up his hands in supplication, "okay. Maybe you're right. Cain's clean. He's a good man who's lived right and never made a mistake. Always put the good of the people ahead of his own interests. But what about the people around him?"

"Ahh. So that's it." Claudia rolled her eyes. "You didn't come here tonight to gloat over something you found on Cain. You came here tonight looking for dirt on the people around him."

"His father specifically," Gabriel stated. "What do you think about Roman Dvanaesti?"

Claudia looked at Gabriel as if she didn't know him. "Wow. You're going to fake it till you make it."

"Excuse me?"

"You heard me. You can't find any dirt, so you make it up."

"I don't think I've got to make it up where his father's concerned."

"Ah. Guilt by association. His dad's less than perfect, so he must be, too. It's in the blood, right? In the genes? After all, his dad's rich and lives in Rome, so he must be in the mafia. He's got businesses in America. His son lives in Florida. So obviously, the son is corrupt as well. Don't you see what you're doing, Gabe? You're going to create a rumor that is worse than a lie. A lie can at least be proven untrue. But a rumor? If you deny it, everybody knows it's true. If you say it's true, hoping to diffuse the situation, people say, 'I *knew* it.'"

Claudia stood up and walked across the room like she was trying to put distance between them. "Ten years ago, I found out something about you. Something real. Something tangible. I could've ruined you, Gabe. You wouldn't have been able to find work as a security guard, let alone what you do now. Not legitimate anyway. But I didn't. I confronted you. I ended our relationship, but I didn't end your career."

Gabriel opened his mouth to speak, but Claudia held up her hand. "You seem to be a better man for that, Gabe. You're out there looking to keep politicians on the up and up in your own way. You've done some good, Gabe. I've kept tabs on you. If you still think of me as your friend, go to whoever hired you and tell them the truth. There's no dirt to find. And then you'll pick up some case involving some truly awful politician and do your job."

Gabriel looked at Claudia. She was right. He hated to admit it, but she was right. He had found nothing because there was nothing. On Cain Dvanaesti. But his father? That was a different story. She was also right that she could have ruined him, but she hadn't. He was a better person, making his contribution to society, though few people saw it that way. He did owe her.

He nodded. "Okay. I'll stop looking for dirt on Cain Dvanaesti." He held up his index finger. "On one condition. I'm still going to check out Roman Dvanaesti. As long as nothing I find traces back to Cain, it's between Roman and me. Or if it's criminal, between Uncle Sam and Roman."

She nodded as her body relaxed. "Fair enough."

Gabriel stood up. "Okay then." He crossed to the door, opened it, and turned to her. "I never got to say thank you, by the way. For not turning me in."

"You don't have to," Claudia said.

Gabriel looked at her, nodded in appreciation, and left the room.

Claudia collapsed onto the bed.

Gabriel went down to his room, unlocked the door, and, just before entering, glanced down the hall to Claudia's room. Then stepped inside his room and closed the door. He crossed to his cell phone on the charger and checked it. He had a text from Stefan.

*Landed in New Orleans. Checking on
some things. I'll call you in the morning.*

Gabriel set the phone down. He thought about calling the airlines and getting a flight out in the morning, but decided against it. That would wait till morning. He also considered fixing a drink, but decided against it. Right now, he just wanted to lie down and sleep. He suddenly felt exhausted. And very exhilarated. Maybe Claudia was right. He'd been so jaded he'd lost his perspective. When he finally came face to face with the politician he was holding all politicians to, he couldn't handle it. The standard wasn't unattainable. It wasn't impossible. Highly improbable. But not impossible. That was the fault of the individual politician, Gabriel decided as he kicked off his shoes and stretched out on the bed. Improbable. Not impossible.

Gabriel rolled over onto his side. Improbable, he thought, but not impossible. He drifted off to sleep.

25

Isabella offered the red cell phone to Cain. Isabella carried two cell phones, a black one for Cain and a red one for his father, Roman. She also packed a tablet for herself. Cain never ceased to be amazed at how Isabella had one of the two phones, if not both, and her tablet going at all times. She was a super multitasker.

Or maybe the word was hyper multi-tasker, Cain mused to himself, as he thought about what she'd been doing in the limo when he got in, the red one up to her ear, listening quietly as her other hand worked feverishly over the screen of her silver tablet. She'd been Roman's assistant as far back as Cain could remember, until he graduated from law school. Then she'd gone to work for Cain as his assistant. Only, she hadn't stopped working for Roman.

Cain looked at the phone still in Isabella's hand. He knew what this meant. Yesterday morning, all he'd wanted was to surprise his father. That seemed like the single most important thing in his day. For the first time in his life, he'd be able to say "Gotcha!" to Roman Dvanaesti. Today, however, that didn't seem like such a cool thing. He knew when his father didn't call him yesterday that he'd anticipated Cain's on-air proposal. No call also meant he knew Claudia Bennett's personal history and approved of her as a mate. He therefore knew that his father would not be angry. It took a lot to make Roman Dvanaesti angry. Or so he assumed. Cain couldn't remember seeing him angry in his entire lifetime.

But he might be disappointed. Cain hadn't thought about that yesterday. He would take anger over his father's disappointment any day. If there is a poster boy for a son seeking his father's validation, Cain would be in more teenagers' rooms than the current American Idol heartthrob.

Isabella raised an eyebrow.

Cain couldn't put off the moment any longer. He took a deep breath, exhaled, took the phone from her waiting hand, and placed it to his ear.

"Father. How good to hear from you," Cain said.

"My Son," Roman said, his words flecked with just the tiniest hint of an Italian accent, "it always does my heart good to hear your voice."

Cain couldn't help but smile. "Are you on the plane?"

"No. I am afraid my affairs here in Rome have delayed me. But rest assured, my son. I will be with you shortly."

The smile drifted off Cain's face. "I was hoping you'd be here tomorrow."

"The press conference is not until Monday," Roman responded.

"Well, actually, I was hoping you could finally meet Claudia. Without all the press around."

"I see. So you have decided not to announce your candidacy on Miss Bennett's television program but at a proper press conference with your fiancé by your side."

Cain's shoulders shrugged. He glanced at Isabella, whose expressions were always measured stoicism, and this time was no different. "Yes, Father," he said.

"A good idea. I won't be there, but I will watch your announcement on the plane."

Cain smiled weakly. "Yes, Father."

"And now I must chastise you for a moment."

Cain frowned and looked at Isabella. If she knew what was coming, and she always did, her face bore no recognition.

"You have not been taking your supplements properly." It was not a question or an accusation.

"No, Father. I have not."

"See to it that you do." This was not a request.

"Yes, Father."

"Good. I'll see you and your fiancé on Monday, then. We'll have dinner."

"Yes, Father."

Cain heard the click and knew his father was gone. He handed the phone back to Isabella. "I'm sorry, Isabella. I didn't take my supplements on time yesterday."

"I'm sorry," Isabella said without a trace of triumph or shame. "Your father entrusted me with that responsibility the day you were born. I should've been paying better attention."

She reached out, took his hand in a maternal gesture, and patted it. "I'll do better by you in the future." She smiled.

He returned the smile.

"Now," Isabella said, returning to all business, "we'll pick Ms. Bennett up in five minutes. Remember to compliment her on her attire and present her with the corsage she should wear for this morning's brunch."

Cain rolled his eyes. "Yes, Mother Dear," he whined.

26

Roman felt the eyes of his assistant on him as he hung up the receiver. His gaze was on a photograph of Cain being sworn in as governor of Florida. It sat on his desk, replacing the picture of Cain posing for his Assistant State Attorney photo. Before that, the picture had been of Cain graduating from law school.

"Yes, Bianca," Roman answered.

Bianca shifted her weight from her left hip to her right as she bit her bottom lip in embarrassment. She'd been caught eavesdropping.

"You were wondering if you should shred the folder in your hand. Yes." His voice was as cold as the Aosta Valley in December.

Bianca looked down at the folder she was holding. It contained the names and dossiers of the short list of potential mates for Cain she'd put together for Roman, just in case Claudia didn't work out. It wasn't that she doubted her employer. He was an Ancient after all. But he was a man or had been a man. What he'd found to be the best attributes in a mate were not necessarily the same today. Nor did each man value attributes equally. However, Bianca knew that the attributes most men valued in women were physical. Men chose those attributes over and over again. She wasn't old enough to have met Roman's Claudia, but she had to assume the Claudia he'd selected for his son had a lot of the same physical attributes.

She'd only been Roman's assistant for a short while, only since Cain was born. Isabella had not given her any useful words of advice except never to question or second-guess her master. That and not to grow accustomed to the position. It would again belong to Isabella. Shivering from the frost in Roman's voice, Bianca wondered if she would soon be vacating the position and this earth.

"You have nothing to fear." Roman's voice was softer, but Bianca still jerked as if his words had teeth. "However, I would encourage you not to waste your time in the future creating tasks. The assignments I provide should keep you busy. Do you understand?"

Bianca's gaze dropped to the floor as she nodded. "I apologize for my impertinence, Signore. Your choice of Claudia was correct. I should've realized that."

"You should have also realized that I'd already considered the potential mates in your folder and discounted them."

Bianca nodded again.

Roman nodded as well.

"I am confused about something," Bianca said, still looking at the floor. "You told Cain your engagements would keep you from being at his press conference. But your schedule is clear."

Roman smiled. "I'm sure Cain has more...surprises for me."

27

"Claudia," Cain had his hand on the small of her back, "I'd like to introduce you to the Chairman of the Florida Republican Party, John Goodman."

John Goodman took Claudia's hand into his. "No relation to the actor." His voice was reed-thin, and his long, spidery fingers seemed to dance on her skin. "May I introduce you to my wife, Georgia?"

Georgia Goodman's eyes were a little vacant, thanks to the one Mimosa in her hand and the other four coursing through her bloodstream. "My, you are gorgeous," she said in a husky slur. She looked at Cain, genuinely impressed. "I'd say you've outdone yourself with this one."

Cain nodded as he moved her to the next couple. "Claudia, this is Ed Sherwood, the Treasurer of the Florida Republican Party. Ed, this is Ms. Claudia Bennett." Ed's palm was damp with sweat, as was his capacious forehead.

"A pleasure to meet you, Ms. Bennett." He said in a deep voice, light on the twang & heavy on the rasp after years of cigar smoking. He nodded towards a woman who was only slightly shorter and rounder than he was. "This is my wife, Mitzy."

"Hello," Claudia interjected with pleasure. She'd said nothing to John Goodman or his wife and had felt supremely stupid because of it. Not that *hello* sounded very clever.

Mitzy's palm was also damp, but she had a warm smile, a welcoming twinkle in her eye, and a squeaky teenage shrill in her voice. "Hello."

Cain's hand on the small of her back directed Claudia to a severe-looking man holding a cup of coffee. "This is Senator Joe Kincaid of Florida's Sixth District." The man was as wan as his smile. "And this is his wife, Meg."

Her handshake was firm, and her smile broad. "I love your talk show, Ms. Bennett."

"Thank you," Claudia said, and not knowing what else to say, she complimented Meg on her shoes, a lemony satin that went smartly with the yellow pantsuit she wore. "Those are lovely shoes." Then feeling more stupid than when she met the Goodmans (*no relation to the actor*; what a lame joke, she thought), Claudia looked around the room known as the Library

Bar. Mahogany paneling covered the walls from floor to ceiling. Recessed shelving held volumes of Florida law. "I keep waiting for John Adams to stroll in and pluck a book off the shelf."

Georgia Goodman toasted Claudia with her Mimosa.

John Goodman's smile reached ear to ear.

Mitzy Sherwood guffawed. "I think we'd all have a heart attack if John Adams strolled in here today." Her laugh was warm, and Claudia knew the woman was not making fun of her.

"Claudia? Can I offer you a Mimosa?" Cain was at the table in the center of the room. It had been set up with coffee service, juices, and champagne.

"That would be lovely."

Cain nodded and prepared her a Mimosa, a little lighter on the champagne than she would've preferred. He handed her the glass and took a sip of his tomato juice. "Shall we move to the Capital room?"

Mitzi took Claudia's hand. "You're going to love the Capital room. It has the loveliest view of the state capital."

"Really?" Claudia allowed herself to be escorted into the room, where a gentleman was already standing at the window, admiring the view.

"Paul," Cain said, unwilling to hide the pleasant surprise. "I didn't know you were here."

The man turned and smiled. "Governor Dvanaesti. It's always a pleasure." His voice reminded Claudia of a used car salesman with a post-nasal drip and that aw-shucks-I'm-so-excited-to-meet-you tone. He offered his hand, which Cain accepted in a warm grip. "Senator Kincaid had mentioned he'd be here this morning, and I just happened to be in the neighborhood. So I thought you wouldn't mind if I dropped in for a visit." He shot Cain a toothy grin, Claudia noticed, that didn't quite make it to the man's watery blue eyes.

Cain turned and motioned for Claudia to join him. "Claudia, I'd like you to meet Paul Drury, the Chairman of the R.N.C."

Claudia's mouth dropped. "As in the Republican National Committee?"

"The very one." Paul extended his hand.

"Paul, this is my fiancé, Ms. Claudia Bennett."

Claudia accepted Paul's hand.

"My, she is a lovely lady." He gave Claudia's hand a light squeeze and then dropped it. He turned his attention to Cain. "Do you mind if I join you?"

"Not at all, Paul." Cain smiled and motioned to the long table. "Please."

Cain sat at the head of the table. Paul made sure to sidle up next to Cain and sit to Cain's immediate left. Claudia sat on Cain's right. Senator Kincaid and his wife sat next to Claudia. Mr. Goodman and his wife sat next to Paul. Ed sat next to Mrs. Goodman, while his wife sat next to Mrs. Kincaid. Isabella, whom Claudia had forgotten about, sat at the other end of the table facing Cain. If anybody thought it odd that the personal assistant was sitting there, no one said a word.

The waitstaff came in, and the party placed their orders. As they ate, Cain kept the conversation deliberately off politics. He talked of Miami's chances against F.S.U. (not placing any bets), who had the best opportunity to get to the Superbowl, the Bucs, Jaguars, or Dolphins (just as long as it's one of them), and why Universal Studios Orlando is better than Universal Studios Hollywood (location, location, location - Florida), wasn't Claudia the most beautiful woman in the world (she was), isn't Cain the luckiest man in the world (he is), and how many Mimosas could a woman of Georgia Goodman's weight and height handle (as many as she wanted to).

Claudia watched in amazement as he cast his magic on the assembled people. They ignored him when he wanted them to and hung on to his every word when he wanted. Paul Drury was doing as much puckering to Cain's backside as Mrs. Goodman was doing to her glass. She was embarrassed for him. Then there was Cain. In the presence of all these important people, including the National Chairman of the Republican Party, he was as relaxed as if no one else were in the room.

Finally, however, Claudia felt the urging of her bladder. She leaned over to Cain. "Where's the ladies' room?"

Georgia Goodman stood up. "I'll show you, dear," she slurred as she held out a hand.

Mitzi stood up. "I think I could powder my nose."

Georgia, Claudia, and Mitzi moved off. Meg leaned over to her husband. "I'll make sure Georgia doesn't take the Mimosa plunge off the roof." She looked towards Cain. "If you'll excuse me, Governor." She jumped up without waiting for a response and trailed off after the other ladies.

Cain smiled. "And that's why there's always a line to get into the ladies' room. They take it with them."

The gathered men laughed.

Cain continued. "I just wanted you to know how much I've appreciated your support in the past, and I hope I can count on it again as I start my run for the Senate seat."

The gathered men nodded, their expressions sober.

"We've been through a lot over the past few years. And I hope we can say the same for the next six years."

The gathered men thumped the table.

"The next Presidential election's in two years." Paul offered.

The gathered men rolled their eyes.

Cain shook his head. "I run for Senate, and I serve out my entire term. I'll run for the White House in six years."

The gathered men applauded.

28

"**I** hope that wasn't too boring," Cain said to Claudia as the limo pulled away from the Governor's Club. He took her hand in his, rubbing his thumb over the knuckles of her fingers. It was a move that always caused Claudia's toes to curl.

She smiled. "Not at all. I guess I should get used to those kinds of things."

"I haven't yet," Paul responded.

Claudia laughed and glanced at Isabella. Isabella remained stone-faced. She looked back at Cain and nodded. "So what's the plan? Do you have the rest of the day off?"

"The whole rest of the weekend." Cain stretched and put his hands behind his head, looking satisfied.

"Wow." She snuggled up to him. "So what are we going to do?"

"I was thinking Rome."

"*Excuse me?*" It was Isabella. The ferocity in her tone caused Claudia to jump.

Cain, however, didn't even flinch. Ignoring Isabella, he turned to Claudia. "Go up and get into something comfortable and bring an overnight bag with a change of clothes, make-up, and whatever else you might need, and come right back down."

Claudia gaped at Cain, who stared back as if he'd just said they would play golf or tennis based on what she was wearing when she returned. She looked at Isabella, but Isabella had her steely, impassive mask back in place. The only thing suggesting something was wrong with Isabella was her inactivity on her smartphones or tablet.

"But...but," Claudia stammered.

"Is something wrong?" Cain finally asked, thumb caressing her knuckles.

"I can't go to *Rome*. *We* can't go to Rome."

"Why not?" Cain asked.

"Well...," she looked to Isabella for help. This was usually when Isabella reminded Cain of all the reasons why he couldn't deviate from the schedule. But she was silent, though her lips were now pursed into one thin line. "We've got the show Monday morning."

"We'll be there," Cain assured her. "We'll be in Rome for breakfast and come back tomorrow afternoon. I can have you back in Miami tomorrow evening."

"How are you going to do that?" Claudia raised a skeptical eyebrow.

"My jet." Cain's tone was matter-of-fact.

"You know, that sounds a little pretentious when you say that." Claudia chided him.

Cain put a hand to his heart in mock hurt. "I'm sorry. My aircraft." He leaned over and kissed her on the lips. "My father was supposed to be here this weekend to meet you, but he's tied up in Rome. So we're going to go to him."

"But—"

Cain held a finger up to her lips. "I want to take you home, in a manner of speaking, to meet the family. All I've got is my father, and I want to introduce him to his future daughter-in-law, and I don't want to wait."

Claudia looked into Cain's eyes and saw something she'd never seen. Desperation.

"Okay," she said as she stroked his cheek. She looked out the window to see the valet of the Hotel Duval moving towards her door. "Give me ten minutes."

She jumped out of the car and ran through the lobby doors.

Isabella cleared her throat to get Cain's attention.

Cain didn't look at her.

"The jet's waiting on the tarmac. I've filed a flight plan and had your suitcase delivered to the plane."

Cain watched Claudia rush through the lobby.

Isabella stared hard at the man before her. He was taking more action without informing her. Or his father. It was starting to get out of hand. He was acting like a petulant teenager. He had always followed his father like a good boy. But now he was behaving like he knew what was best for himself. She wanted to throttle him, to show him in some way that, despite being governor, he was still an infant in the ways of politics. Except he was governor, and she, on the instruction of Roman, was his assistant. She softened her tone. "I just wish you had informed me."

Cain turned to face Isabella. She could see the same desperation he'd had in his eyes with Claudia and hear it in his voice. "I need to do this, Isabella. I need my father to meet my bride."

Isabella looked at him. Yes, she thought, maybe that's what you need right now. And what Claudia needs. She nodded.

The way Cain relaxed in his seat reminded Isabella of when he was a boy, and she agreed not to tell his father about something he had done wrong.

"Thank you."

"You're welcome." She watched Cain as her fingers worked furiously over the red smartphone.

29

Claudia had to remind herself; she was on an airplane as she stood up from the dinner table to follow Cain to the loveseat. Realizing she'd forgotten her wineglass, she turned back to get it, making what she thought was eye contact with the two guards seated in their usual chairs on either side of the stateroom door. She smiled and said, "Hi."

They sat motionless.

She made an *okay* expression, picked up her wine glass, turned, and sat beside Cain on the loveseat.

Nodding over her shoulder, she asked, "Where'd you get Deaf and Mute?"

Cain stole a glance over his shoulder. "Oh, Flotsam and Jetsam? They were runners-up in the Mr. Bulgarian Congeniality Contest."

Claudia laughed.

"Did you get enough to eat?" Cain asked.

They'd just finished a five-star meal that included their choice of Oysters Rockefeller or shrimp cocktail for appetizers, seafood risotto for the entrée, and baked brie with raspberry sauce for dessert. The food was fresh, warm, and wonderful. It was like dining in a fine Miami Beach restaurant at thirty-five-thousand feet.

Claudia rubbed her belly. "Yes. That was wonderful. My compliments to the chef," she said as she sipped the most delightful red wine she'd ever tasted. What the server had said was 'the house wine.' That'd made Claudia giggle since she could look out the window and see the clouds below them. The bottle must've cost a fortune.

"You can tell Jacqueline when she comes to refresh your glass." Cain picked up a remote and pressed a button. The wood paneling parted to reveal a plasma screen television.

"Jacqueline?" Claudia was incredulous. "Our server? She made dinner?"

Cain nodded as he hit another button. The screen lit up with the menu for *The Ugly Truth*.

"I just thought she kept it warm in the galley."

Cain gave her a wide-mouthed *you did not just say that* look.

She punched him.

"Jacqueline prepares each menu fresh from scratch with every flight."

"So she's a chef? An *actual* chef?"

Cain looked towards the small table where they'd eaten dinner. "What do you think?"

"Wow. Where'd you find her?"

That impish grin slipped across his face. "I discovered her in a restaurant in South Beach. I can't say the name, but let me tell you, Emeril was not happy with me when I stole her away."

He pushed the play button and set the remote down. Claudia pulled her legs onto the loveseat and tucked them under herself as she rested her head on Cain's shoulder. Cain responded by wrapping his arms around her.

Neither noticed Isabella get up and move to the private stateroom. Closing the door behind her, she walked to the wall behind Cain's desk. She slid a panel aside to reveal an alphanumeric keypad with two LED displays. She punched a 'Go' button, which started a thirty-second digital countdown on the smaller display. Isabella gave the clock a bemused eyebrow lift, like Spock from Star Trek, and began typing a twenty-digit alphanumeric code into the keypad, her finger movements a blur.

The countdown clock displayed twenty-six when it stopped counting down. A 12-inch by 18-inch door popped open to Isabella's left.

She reached in and pulled out a stainless steel box. Cain's supplements. She opened the lid to reveal six slots. One slot was empty, which Isabella had expected. The other five slots held a container each, just as they should. The containers were very similar to inhaler canisters, except they were constructed from double-walled, insulated stainless steel.

Isabella selected a canister and plucked it from its resting place.

Empty.

Her green eyes flashed onyx. She pulled out another canister. Also empty. She pulled each one out, feeling the weight of it in her hand. They were all empty. For the first time in a very long time, Isabella felt a wave of panic grip her. She stood motionless for almost five minutes as her mind raced over the implications.

I have been a fool.

She placed the canister back into the box, closed it, and returned it to the safe. She closed the safe door, which blended seamlessly into the paneling, and slid the keypad panel closed. Taking a deep and steadying breath, Isabella pulled the red smartphone from her belt. She eyed it for another moment before pressing the '1' key. She heard it ring twice before a click and then, "Salve."

Isabella's throat clicked dryly as she swallowed hard. "Roman...we have... a problem."

30

Claudia gawked open-mouthed as she looked out the passenger window of the 1960 Rolls-Royce Silver Cloud II at the rolling countryside. As far as her eyes could see, the landscape was wave after crashing waves of vibrant green, rich garnet, and deep purple grapevines. She felt tiny. Like she was no more than a dinghy on an ocean.

"Exactly how much of all this does he own?"

"The entire countryside," Cain answered.

Claudia tore her eyes from the grapes to Cain's face, which beamed back at her.

"I love that look," Cain said. He took her hand in his and caressed her knuckles with his thumb. "We're about ten minutes from his villa. You'll be able to see it when we pass over this ridge."

Claudia followed his finger to see the road cresting a quarter of a mile ahead. She also saw something else that caused her to stare in wonder. They were on a dirt road. She hadn't felt it and hadn't noticed when they'd moved from pavement to dirt.

Her appreciative eyes ran over the interior of the Silver Cloud: the creamy white leather and genuine wood accouterment, the gold-rimmed clock set into the backrest of the front seat. Cain said the car was more than fifty years old when they'd climbed into it. It looked and smelled like it'd been driven straight from the showroom to the airport. "Wow, this car rides smoothly."

Cain smiled. "It isn't the car. Father won't allow asphalt in the vineyard. He says it hurts the grapes. And he doesn't want vehicles getting bumped underneath and possibly rupturing something. So he keeps this road well-maintained."

"Either way, it certainly is impressive." Claudia tried to sound unimpressed. She failed miserably.

"Oh, he doesn't have it to impress people. No, for him, it's like when you put the fine China out for guests. It's a sign of respect. But he doesn't do it for everybody." Cain pointed towards the front of the car. "Look."

Claudia looked through the front windshield as the car crested the ridge and gasped. It was like peering through a looking glass at some master model maker's interpretation of paradise.

They descended into a valley, the road cutting a lazy but gentle path through the undulating rows of grapevines, the garnet, green, and purple of the grapes sparkling like clusters of precious stones. At the other end of the valley, where the ground started to rise again, sat the only swath of land not covered in grapevines. Well-tended cypress trees separated the vineyard from the manicured grounds of the estate. The road ran alongside the cypress trees and continued past the estate, disappearing over another ridge. A cypress tree-lined drive ran straight from the road to a large structure.

That had to be what Cain had called his father's *villa*, Claudia thought with a scoff. More like a cross between a mansion and a castle, with, she squinted, a water feature in front. To the right of the main house was a large warehouse. Several smaller buildings were scattered around the property. There was also a helipad.

Claudia goggled, feeling her eyes bug out of her head. As they reached the bottom of the valley, Claudia's view of the estate was obscured by the six-foot-tall grapevines. She felt a mixture of disappointment and thankfulness and rubbed her eyes.

"So what'd you think?" Cain asked.

Claudia turned to Cain. "Breathtaking," she replied. She couldn't think of a better word and understood why Roman never wanted to leave. Why did Roman always use the excuse that his affairs in Rome were detaining him? If she lived here, she'd never want to go anywhere either. She'd use any reason to stay right where she was.

Claudia looked back out the window as the road turned left. They were now alongside the cypress trees. The trees were uniformly spaced so that Claudia felt like she was passing fence posts. She was reminded of the fences she'd seen in the Midwest as a child, riding in the backseat as her family drove cross-country. She half-expected to see barbed wire between the cypresses now.

The Rolls-Royce slowed and turned right onto the drive. Claudia gasped again as she took in the view before her. The driveway was not dirt. Claudia wasn't sure what it was. She guessed gravel, but that was only a guess at best.

It didn't look like any gravel road Claudia had ever seen. It didn't resemble any driving surface she'd seen before. It looked like marble but didn't feel like a hard surface.

The trees lining the drive had been trimmed to resemble arrowheads, casting crisscrossing shadows. Claudia had a slightly claustrophobic feeling as if she were in a funnel, so she took her eyes off the road and tried to focus beyond the trees. The lawn was a thick carpet of rich, velvety green that melted right into the surrounding grapevines. It was like God had decided to make a second Garden of Eden, but this time with a mansion and a winery.

"Here we are," Cain announced.

Shaken from her reverie, Claudia looked forward, her mouth gaping again.

The villa was three times the size of any building on the property, including the winery. The façade (and here Claudia realized the word was not used in its more contemporary sense) was of natural stone and mortar, three stories high, each window framed in brick. Two marble stairways lead to a front patio and a large oak-and-glass door.

The drive circled what Claudia could now see was not just a water feature but a larger-than-life fountain depicting Christ on the cross. Water flowed from his eyes, hands, feet, and side. Carved in bas-relief, wrapping around the sides of the basin, were images of Roman soldiers casting lots over a pile of clothing, John comforting Mary, people crying, and people jeering. Claudia found the entire piece disturbing.

"My father's not a religious man. But he's very moved by the crucifixion." Cain's voice was little more than a whisper. "It's a motif throughout all his decorating." Then he added, "Not always this unsettling," at the look of horror on Claudia's face.

The Rolls-Royce stopped in front of the villa. Isabella had opened the door and exited the vehicle before Claudia could blink. The driver, Sembello, didn't notice or care about Isabella's departure. Climbing out of the car, he opened Claudia's door and tipped his hat to her as she stepped from the back seat and said, "Signorina," before looking at Cain coming around the back of the car. "Signore." He got back behind the wheel and pulled slowly away.

Claudia looked around but didn't see Isabella. "Where'd she go?"

Cain stretched. "Who cares?" He walked up the steps of the house and pushed open the large door, which, though it looked ancient, swung without squeak or creak on its hinges. "Welcome to Villa Dvanaesti."

They were standing in the foyer, which besides the marble flooring and paintings, many of which Claudia thought she remembered seeing in her high school Humanities textbook, boasted a large fresco cycle depicting Jesus' last days: his entry into Jerusalem on a donkey, the Last Supper (resembling nothing of Di Vinci's), his arrest on the Mount of Olives, Pilate washing his hands, and finally, Jesus hanging on the cross. It covered an entire wall. In addition to the paint, it had been sculpted in places, giving depth and dimension to the images. And emotion. Like the sculpture outside, it was at once breathtakingly beautiful and horrible.

What did it say of her future father-in-law that the first two pieces of art he showed a guest concerned the crucifixion of Jesus Christ? Claudia, like half the world's population, considered herself a Christian. But outside of a gold cross on a gold chain, she didn't own anything religious. Cain had said that his father wasn't religious. Yet he had a larger-than-life statue of the crucifixion, and this...at once wonderful and awful masterpiece. If he wasn't religious, he was obsessed. That thought caused a chill to lick her spine from her gluteal cleft to the base of her skull. Now she knew why Cain had never introduced her to his dad.

Cain interrupted her thoughts. "I'll give you the tour in a minute. Right now, I need to visit the little governor's room." He was gone.

"Okay." Claudia looked around. "I'll just stand here. In the foyer. With the fresco...*that's seriously creeping me out.*"

Claudia walked around the foyer, carefully avoiding the fresco, counting her steps, and realizing half her condo would fit in this space. She looked through the glass panes of the front door and noticed an older man in his late fifties, maybe late sixties, walking out of a stand of trees into the front yard. He was dressed in a wrinkled, worn white button-down shirt, grayed with time, what looked like wool pants held up by suspenders, and a large straw hat. He pulled work gloves off his hands and slapped them against his thigh, knocking off dust.

The man saw her looking at him and smiled, revealing beautiful white teeth. He waved.

She waved back as he walked towards the house. She watched him in amazement. His gait was easy and graceful, and she could imagine how he'd glide across a dance floor. She also noticed that though his clothes were dusty with outdoor work, the man was neither flushed nor sweating.

Claudia moved to open the front door, but the man was already pushing on it. She stepped back as he walked into the grand foyer, which seemed to shrink in his presence.

"Claudia Bennett." Her name flowed off his tongue with a slight tinge of an Italian accent. "You are more beautiful than my son gave you credit."

She stared back at the man. His hair was naturally curly and flavored with salt and pepper. The wrinkles and crow's feet may mark him as a man in his late fifties or early sixties, but his eyes blazed with the fire of youth. And yet, that fire felt ancient.

"I'm sorry. Where are my manners?" He offered his hand.

Claudia realized he wanted to kiss the top of her hand in greeting, so she slipped her hand into his and winced. It was like putting her hand between two blocks of ice.

"Forgive my poor circulation," he said, leaning over and kissing her hand. He released it. "I am Roman Dvanaesti."

31

The breakfast plates were cleared, and Espresso was placed before each person seated at the table. Claudia took a sip and smiled, a delightful ending to a delicious meal.

After her future father-in-law had introduced himself, Cain reappeared from the little governor's room. Hugging his father, Cain reproached him for not taking the morning off from the vineyard.

Roman had commented that grapes behaved the same as beautiful women; they demanded your time and attention without thought to convenience, and as with a beautiful woman, a man whose heart was consumed did not mind. He'd then excused himself to wash up for breakfast.

Cain had only had time to show her the ground floor of the villa, which consisted of a formal living room, an informal living room (still more formal than most American formal living rooms), an outdoor living room where they had breakfasted, a family room, two sitting rooms, a dining room, a kitchen, an office, an indoor lap pool, and three bedrooms. The bedrooms were each the size of a townhouse with king-sized four-poster beds. The furniture was classic Italian, and paintings of Italian rural scenes hung on the walls. Each bedroom featured an ensuite bathroom with a marble shower and mosaic-covered Roman-style tub.

The flooring was marble throughout the house, but some rooms, such as the informal living room and the two sitting rooms, featured mosaic designs. Each room was also decorated with an area rug; each rug, Claudia realized, probably cost more than her annual salary. The paintings hanging on the walls of each room were all by Italian artists and ranged from what looked to Claudia like pre-Renaissance to the present.

Over breakfast, Cain had explained to her that in addition to the other two floors above them, there was also a wine cellar that not only boasted perhaps the most incredible collections of wine ever assembled but also another formal dining room.

"You have a dining room in the cellar?" Claudia asked, unable to hide her disbelief.

Roman nodded.

"And another in the winery," Cain added.

"You really must see the rest of the villa and the grounds," Roman said.

"That'll take the day." Cain was shaking his head. "I'm sorry, Father, but we must get back," Cain said.

"Nonsense." Roman sounded like Cain was refusing another slice of Tiramisu because he was watching his waistline. "The flight is only ten hours, and you'll gain six hours back." He smiled. "You must see the vineyard at sunset from the roof terrace." His eyes were on Claudia. "We call it *Il fuoco di Dio*. The fire of God."

"That will definitely put us behind," Cain protested.

Claudia noticed, though, that his expression at the thought of 'Il fuoco di Dio' betrayed his objection.

Roman waved a dismissive hand. "The press conference isn't until eleven a.m. Eastern. If you're in the air by six-thirty tomorrow morning, you'll be in Tallahassee no later than ten-thirty a.m. I'll have the helicopter pick you up here at six. You'll be at the airport in fifteen minutes. Besides, it will be better for Claudia. She can sleep in a bed for a few hours and then finish resting on the flight back." Roman stood. "Now, Ms. Bennett, if you'd be so gracious as to take an old man's hand, I will show you the rest of the villa and grounds."

Claudia giggled. "Old man," she repeated with humor. "You've got more energy than Cain." She took his hand. It was still ice-cold, but it no longer made her wince. She realized nothing about this man made her flinch anymore. All of her earlier worries about his obsession with the crucifixion had evaporated. She felt completely at ease in his presence. His life force, which wafted from him like fine cologne, had now enveloped her.

Roman smiled as he took her hand. "Come. Let me show you," his smile took on a devilish yet benevolent curl to his lips, "my future grandchildren's inheritance."

He led Claudia to the main staircase in the middle of the villa. It ascended approximately eight feet before ending on a large landing.

Once they'd ascended, Roman said, "The top floor is living quarters and a small kitchen servicing the top terrace, but I thought you might enjoy this." He gestured at two staircases coming off the corners of the landing and angling back to the front of the house.

Claudia ascended the left staircase. Looking up, she could see books on a bookshelf and wondered what could outdo the elegant extravagance she'd already seen on the first floor. As she reached the end of the stairs and turned, she saw the one thing that could.

She was looking at—she could think of no other description for it—what the Library of Congress would look like if it were housed in the Sistine Chapel. The entire second floor was open and filled with rows upon rows of books, glass cases housing scrolls, desks with lamps as you'd find in an attorney's office, and a massive, ornately carved piece of furniture Claudia had to assume was the card catalog for all the manuscripts in this space.

Marble columns framed the walls, each a mural depicting a religious scene: Eve being tempted by the serpent, Cain murdering Abel, and Judas Iscariot accepting thirty pieces of silver from the chief priest. These were the ones she recognized anyway. Others, however, she was pretty sure weren't Bible stories, but they all seemed to share a common theme. What was it, she wondered. She thought she should know.

"Betrayal," Roman said.

Claudia turned. "Excuse me?"

"They're all motifs of betrayal throughout human history."

Claudia nodded in understanding and quickly turned away from Roman. She had the feeling Roman had read her mind. That unsettled her. It was preposterous. She chastised herself. He probably saw her quizzical stare and figured she was wondering the same thing everyone who'd seen those murals wondered. Rather than wait for the question, he answered like he'd done dozens of times.

She looked up at the ceiling. It was covered in one large mural of the Apocalypse, and, like the sculpture in the drive and the fresco in the foyer, it was at once hideous and beautiful to her. She looked at the support columns in the middle of the space and noticed they were covered in frescoes depicting even more religious scenes.

"This...is amazing," Claudia whispered in awe.

"Please," Roman said, "have a look around."

Claudia did. She perused the volumes of books, some bound together with laced leather straps. Other books looked handwritten. Books in English, French, Italian, German, and what seemed to be every known world language. All were categorized by subject and author, and alphabetized by language, Claudia thought. "This is quite a collection. These are all...?" Her voice trailed off.

"First additions," Roman confirmed. "They've been in my family for a very long time."

Claudia stopped at a glass case housing a scroll spread open between two pieces of Plexiglas. She frowned at the writing. "Is that Aramaic?"

Roman laughed. "No. It is Latin. What you would call shorthand today."

"What is it?" Claudia leaned over the case and peered hard at the scroll.

"It is an account of the death of Pontius Pilate's wife. Written in Pilate's hand." Roman watched Claudia peering hard at the scroll. She so resembled his Claudia, studying a scroll, reading between the lines. Strategizing. "You remind me of her."

Claudia's gaze shot up to Roman and found him smiling. An amused grin reached his eyes, but she thought there was something else there as well. Something that dampened the sparkle in his eye just a bit. Tugged at the curve of his lips. Some sadness, she thought.

He pointed at the scroll. "Pilate describes his wife," he leaned in as if he was about to impart some scandalous gossip, "whose name also happened to be Claudia. He writes how intelligent she was. Clever. Brave. And the perfect helpmate. Her strengths covered his weaknesses. His strengths covered hers. His focus was her focus. She aligned her hopes and dreams with his."

"How do you even authenticate something like that? How do you know it isn't a fraud? And if it's genuine, why doesn't the Vatican or the Smithsonian have it?"

Roman shrugged. "It's been in the family a long time." He took Claudia by the arm and guided her away from the case. His grip was gentle, almost frail.

"Why would you even want something like that?" Claudia asked in disgust.

"I keep it for sentimental value. I want to show you something." He led her to another glass case. Inside was—

"A Gutenberg Bible," Claudia exclaimed. "Wow."

"The very first one published," Roman said. "So the family story goes. After all," he gestured around the room, "first editions. Let me show you the winery."

The main floor of the winery was very similar to the pictures Claudia had previously seen of Italian wineries. Presses and processing machines covered the entire floor, but it still seemed to Claudia that it was too small to handle the number of grapes she saw in the countryside.

Roman nodded his understanding. "It may seem rather unimpressive. This part always is. But let me show you something." He led her to a door.

As Roman opened it, Claudia saw a staircase descending into the darkness. This staircase, however, looked as if it were hewn from rock.

Roman started to descend.

"Lights," Claudia shouted in terror. She could imagine Roman missing a step and falling for God knows what distance and breaking a hip or worse. Maybe even killing himself.

"Of course." Roman stepped back up and flipped a switch. "Forgive me. I have walked these steps so many times I could walk them blindfolded." He added. "I almost did." He turned and started descending again.

Claudia followed, feeling the temperature drop with each step.

He waited at a door at the bottom of the stairs, which Claudia could tell was hewn from the rock. Claudia shivered. "How far down are we?"

"Eighteen meters," Roman answered. "Approximately fifty feet." He opened the door and motioned for her to step through. She did. He followed and flipped on a switch.

Claudia heard the buzz of fluorescence as light filled the large room. She gaped. It had to be the size of a football field and filled with row after row of huge wooden barrels.

"At this depth, it is easier to control climate and conditions. This is one of my favorite places." He inhaled deeply. "You can smell the wine maturing." He looked at his hands and smiled. "Perhaps that's why I always feel cold. All the time I spend here."

Claudia laughed, wrapping her arms around herself. Roman, she noticed, didn't show any sign of the cold bothering him.

"Now, let us see the vineyards."

They spent the rest of the day touring the vineyards. Roman insisted on walking.

"Fumes," he said, "are bad for the grapes. Even golf carts contribute their own...*noise* pollution. Also, not good for the grapes. Or my nerves."

Roman stopped occasionally so that Claudia could sample a grape from the vineyard. He would talk about each grape in terms of its personality and character, and discuss how it was influenced by its environment, the lavender growing in the soil, and the pollen in the air. Then he'd have her close her eyes and chew the grape slowly so her palate could discriminate the multiple flavors. Sometimes she could taste the effects of sun and soil immediately; other times, only after Roman explained what she should taste and why.

Claudia described several of her trips to the California wine country and wine-tasting tours she'd participated in, and how they'd never given her even a tenth of the education on the wine he was. Roman's face lit with delight. They pressed on, and it was not until Roman said it was time to head back to the villa that she noticed they'd been out walking all day.

She was surprised to find herself not feeling tired. Not even her feet hurt. Instead, she felt exhilarated. As they stood on the rooftop terrace, Roman opened a bottle of wine and poured generous portions into glasses. She felt like she'd had a full-body massage and the best nap of her life.

"Now you are ready." Roman handed her a glass. "Taste the complexity. The personality. Of the wine."

Following his lead, Claudia swirled the wine, dipped her nose into the glass to inhale the bouquet, closed her eyes, and sipped. Her eyes popped open as she tasted all the flavors and nuances of flavors from each grape she'd eaten earlier in the day. She took another sip, her eyes growing wider.

"Is something wrong?" Roman asked as he took a discerning sip.

Claudia's head shook. "This is the most amazing wine I've ever had."

Roman faced the vineyard as the sun began to set. "Il fuoco di Dio."

Claudia's breath caught in her throat. The vineyard blazed red and orange like the entire countryside had spontaneously caught fire.

32

Gabriel entered his home office on Sunday afternoon feeling anxious. He hadn't heard from Stefan since his text on Friday night. He knew Stefan didn't like to call until he had something important, and if Stefan was on the trail of something substantial, he tended to forget to call in. He hoped that's all it was, though his gut told him that wasn't the case. Stefan hadn't called him all weekend. Nor had he answered or returned Gabriel's calls. There was no reason to expect Stefan would have called his home office. He never did. He always called Gabriel's cell phone. He'd willed himself not to be too concerned until that avenue was closed.

He noticed the message light blinking on his desk phone and hit the replay button.

The automated female voice filled the room. "You have one new message."

"This message is for Mr. Gabriel Hawthorne." The voice was authoritative and carried the distinctive drawl of someone born and raised in New Orleans, Louisiana. "This is Sergeant Paul Boucher of the Nawlins Police Department. I need to speak to you directly regards to a...Ojaka Owusu." He pronounced it Oh-Jake-eh Oh-Wah-soo. "Please return my call at five-oh-four, six-five-eight, four thousand. Extension two, two, two."

The machine beeped. Gabriel stabbed the replay button. Boucher's New Orleans drawl filled the office again as Gabriel snatched a pen and started scribbling down the number, skin prickling with gooseflesh as the room turned cold.

Snatching the phone out of its cradle, Gabriel punched in the numbers and shivered, expecting to see his breath in another minute.

A City Hall operator answered on the third ring. Gabriel practically shouted the extension at her. Sergeant Paul Boucher answered on the second ring.

"This is Gabriel Hawthorne returning your call."

"Ah, yes. Mr. Hawthorne." Gabriel heard shuffling paper. "What is your relation to Mr. Owusu?" Boucher was devoid of all emotion, still mispronouncing Stefan's last name.

"Oh-Woo-Soo," Gabriel corrected. "Business associate. Goes by the name Stefan. What's happened?"

Boucher seemed unfazed by this information. "I'm sorry to be the one to tell you, Mr. Hawthorne, but Mr. Owusu is dead."

33

Cain's Bombardier Global 5000 jet stopped on the tarmac in Tallahassee, Florida, one minute ahead of Roman's projected 10:30 a.m.

Two men hustled out and threw down the wheel blocks as the door lowered.

Cain kissed Claudia's hand as the Florida heat and humidity kissed them on the top step. "You ready?"

Claudia took a deep breath and nodded. She did. Just as Roman had said, she felt refreshed and ready.

Cain smiled and escorted her down the stairs to the waiting limousine. They climbed in, followed by Isabella.

Isabella rolled her eyes as Cain and Claudia made googly eyes at each other and slouched back into her seat as the limo pulled out of the hangar.

Once the limo was on Capital Circle, Isabella pulled out her black smartphone. "Now, Governor, the press conference begins in twenty-five minutes on the steps of the Old Capitol building." She pulled a manila folder from her briefcase and handed it to Cain. "Here is your prepared announcement, talking points, and list of questions. As you can see, I've—"

Cain interrupted her. "I don't think I need these, Isabella. I've been preparing for this moment my whole life."

Isabella's back stiffened. She opened her mouth to reprimand Cain and then caught herself. She relaxed back into her seat and smiled. "As you wish, *Governor.*" She flavored this last word with scorn.

Cain chose to ignore it. "Claudia. I want you by my side."

"Off to the side looking on?" Claudia asked.

"No. Right by my side."

"With your eyes open and your mouth shut," Isabella added.

Cain shot Isabella daggers. "Just be yourself and answer any questions as honestly as you can."

"But maybe Isabella's right, Cain. Maybe I should keep my mouth closed and my eyes open. I don't want to screw this up." Her voice was filled with consternation.

126

Cain rubbed the knuckles of her hands. "You aren't going to screw anything up."

The limo pulled into the parking garage beneath the capital. The limo's interior was plunged into darkness. Claudia felt Cain's lips on hers, kissing her. She kissed back. He pulled away. "We're a team now, you and me. I love you, future Mrs. Cain Dvanaesti."

"And I love you, future Mr. Cain Dvanaesti. Wait-..." The two of them burst into laughter.

"I feel like I'm babysitting children," Isabella said, which caused a fresh round of laughter from Cain and Claudia.

They walked hand in hand from the limo, on the elevator, and up the hall leading to the front of the old capital and its front steps. They could see throngs of reporters and others gathered and hear the gathered chatter as they waited for their appearance.

Cain turned to Claudia. "How do I look?"

She smiled and straightened his tie. "Like a billion bucks."

Cain grinned. "That good?"

"Oh, yeah."

Cain turned and opened the door, held out his arm for Claudia, and the two walked out to the small platform and the microphones.

"Thank you for coming, Ladies and Gentlemen," Cain began. "We all know why I'm here. You've got a lot of questions, some legitimate and some rude. And I want to give each of you the satisfaction of hearing me tell you which one you've asked."

The reporters laughed while the gathered supporters applauded.

Claudia looked on in amazement at how Cain always owned a crowd.

Cain continued, "I love the state of Florida, and it's always been my dream to make Florida the greatest state in the greatest country in the world. I've served the people and state I love as governor. And now I'd like to represent those same people, those same great people, in Washington, D.C. I formally announce my candidacy for the Senate."

The gathered supporters whooped and clapped as cameras flashed.

"Are there any questions?" Cain asked.

Questions were shouted at once, but one question came across like a bullhorn. "Do you support Ms. Bennett's career?"

The crowd, the reporters, and even Cain went silent. He knew this question would come up, but hadn't thought it would be the first. He opened his mouth to voice his support for his fiancée when Claudia stepped to the microphone.

"I'd like to answer that one if you don't mind." She looked at Cain.

The crowd laughed and applauded as Cain relinquished the podium.

Claudia surveyed the crowd for a moment before speaking. "Cain is completely supportive of me continuing in my chosen profession. But he is the best thing to happen to Florida since Claude Pepper." She looked at Cain and smiled. "And so I will continue to work as a journalist until the day we wed. After that day, my job will be being the best helpmate I can be to the next Distinguished Gentleman from the Great State of Florida."

The crowd erupted as if the Seminoles had won the National Championship.

34

After the press conference, Cain and Claudia walked hand-in-hand through the Old Capitol, across the outdoor rotunda, and into the New Capitol building to the governor's ground-floor office. As they walked, people clapped, and a couple of kids ran up and asked for their autographs. Cain and Claudia signed the autographs and allowed an old lady to pinch Cain's cheeks after Claudia offered one condition. Pointing to his face, Claudia told the lady she could only pinch *those* cheeks. The woman giggled like a schoolgirl.

As they entered the Governor's area, Cain informed his staff to hold all his calls. They should also advise everyone else that he would be approximately ten minutes late the rest of the day. He then went into his office with Claudia and closed the door. As he turned, he saw Isabella standing there.

"I'd like a few moments alone with my fiancé," Cain said.

Isabella didn't move.

"Isabella," Cain finally said, "Give me a minute alone with Claudia, please."

Isabella nodded and swept from the room without a glance at Claudia.

"Is everything all right, Cain?" She asked.

Cain's posture relaxed. He smiled. "She sometimes forgets she's my assistant, not my mother." He took Claudia's hand and guided her to the sofa, where he sat her down. He sat down on the coffee table across from her. "But I did want to speak to you."

Claudia smiled. "That came as a shock to you, didn't it? It did to me, too."

"Just a little. I mean…I've always expected you to continue your career as a journalist. I thought that's what you wanted." Cain took her hands in his.

"I thought so too, but…I don't know." She looked around the room, lost in thought. "I met your absolutely terrific dad, and we talked. I just felt this…I don't know, but…it just felt right to me. I'm going to be your helpmate. You're a great man, and you've got great ideas for this country. I want to do all I can to help you." She squeezed his hands and looked into his eyes.

"You sound like my father," Cain said, his brow creasing in apprehension.

Claudia laughed. "I'm asking what I can do for my country, and the best thing I can do is put you first. The country will be the better for it."

Cain's eyes widened in alarm.

"Are you okay?" Claudia's voice was trance-like.

Cain leaned into her and kissed her. "I just... love you. I love you so very much."

Claudia released his hands and caressed his face. "And I love you, Cain Dvanaesti." She stood up suddenly. "Are you hungry? I'm starving. Do you have time to grab a bite?"

"No. Unfortunately, I'm backed up. I doubt I'll get lunch. But... hang on." He moved to the phone on his desk, picked up the receiver, and pressed the '0' button. "Jane. Have my car take Ms. Bennett to the governor's mansion, please. Thanks." He hung up. "I'm sending you over to the governor's mansion. Louie's the head chef. He's originally from New Orleans. He makes the best Po' Boy this side of the Mississippi. You can have some lunch and get acquainted with the grounds and staff. If you can wait till six, I'll fly back to Miami with you, and we can have a late dinner together."

Claudia lit up. "Really? I would love that." She threw her arms around his neck. "You are the most wonderful man."

He hugged her back. "Only because you make me." He pulled her arms from around his neck. "Go on now." He kissed her.

She reached out, caressed his cheek, then left the room, closing the door.

Cain collected himself, staring at the picture on his desk of him and his father. Finally, he whispered, "Okay, Isabella, you can come in."

The door opened. "Governor," Isabella said as she closed the door behind her and moved to the couch.

Cain opened his mouth, but Isabella raised a hand to silence him. "Did you think we'd let you or her jeopardize your father's plans? You were so eager to surprise your father. On subjugating his authority." She sat back and smiled. It was not pleasant. "I've been by your father's side since before you were born, and I will be by his side the day after you die. If you want a long and happy life with Ms. Claudia Bennett, you shall remember your place in the future." She leaned forward. "As for your supplements, I will *personally* supervise their administration from now on."

The ordinary human would not have seen Isabella move from the sofa to the door. But Cain was not ordinary. He tracked her with ease. "I've taken the liberty of ordering lunch for you. One of Louie's Po' Boys should be arriving as we speak. I'll check, shall I?" She looked him over before smiling as she turned, walking from the room with an air of indifference.

Cain stood in the middle of his office, shaking with rage at Isabella and his father. "How dare they," he hissed through clenched teeth. So. They'd discovered his abuse of his 'supplements,' as Isabella put it. That was no big deal. He knew they would eventually, and he knew Isabella would treat him like a child when they did. She'd always treated him like a child. He'd give her a few days and then handle that. But what his father had done to Claudia? That was unforgivable.

Yet, he should've realized his father would not allow him to get away with the surprises. He cursed himself for his foolishness. He'd publicly disobeyed his father and then delivered Claudia into his father's hands, blinded by his exuberance to flaunt his disobedience.

What else have you planted in the back of Claudia's mind, Father?

He would never know. It could be as simple as how many "grandchildren" to give him to as heinous as, 'murder Cain if he disobeys me again.'

Cain could smell the Po' Boy before the door opened. There was a tray of sandwiches, one for each person following Isabella into the office for the noon meeting. Jane followed with a tray of bottled water, sodas, and coffee.

"Great. Thanks, Jane." He eyed Isabella as the attendees exclaimed delight over the sandwiches.

Isabella's smile was cold as she took her usual place at his side.

35

Gabriel shook hands with Sergeant Paul Boucher. "Real sorry about your friend, Mr. Hawthorne," Boucher said. "Real sorry."

"Call me Gabe. And thanks," Gabriel said, his voice as haggard as his insides. After talking to Boucher that morning, Gabriel had called the airlines, packed a bag, and tucked his Beretta with extra magazines into a firearm travel case he'd checked at the counter. He wasn't planning on leaving until he'd found out what had happened to Stefan.

He'd made it to the airport and through security with five minutes to spare. He'd made it through Atlanta with no time to spare; he could hear his name being called over the P.A. as he ran to the gate. He'd landed in New Orleans at twelve twenty-eight p.m. local time.

Boucher was saying something, but Gabriel didn't catch it. "Huh?"

"I said we tried to reach Mr. Owusu's next of kin but couldn't find anybody." Boucher sipped his afternoon coffee.

"He doesn't have any next of kin," Gabriel responded.

"I thought so." Boucher's tone was unemotional. "Nothing came up when we searched his name, driver's license, or social."

"The closest thing he has is me." Gabriel took a sip of the tepid coffee Boucher had offered him. Awful.

"And he had your card in his wallet because...?"

"We work together," Gabriel said. His voice sounded thin in his ears.

"Well," Boucher tapped his desk with his thumbs, "I guess that'll have to do."

"I guess so," Gabriel agreed.

"Do you happen to know whether or not he was here on business or pleasure?" Boucher continued to tap.

"Business." Gabriel picked up the mug for another sip but thought better and set it back down.

"Y'all are P.I.s, right?"

Gabriel knew that Sergeant Boucher was doing his job. The accusatory tone he heard in Boucher's questions was in his head, the defensive mechanism honed over years of being known as the man who dug up the dirt the politicians slung. People had a love/hate relationship with private investigators. They loved the guys in the movies. Bogart in *The Maltese Falcon*, Dick Powell in *Murder, My Sweet*. Tough, no-nonsense guys who brought down the bad guy and got the dame and 'never took nothin' off a nobody.' In real life, private investigators were society's pariahs, just one step up or down from personal injury lawyers. Gabriel couldn't blame them. P.I.s did, after all, make their living exposing the sins of others, from the cheating spouse to the corrupt official.

"What brought him to Nawlins?" Boucher was asking.

"What?"

"What exactly brought Mr. Owusu to Nawlins?"

"To be honest, I don't know. He said he was tracking something and he'd get back to me."

"But he never did."

"No." Gabriel picked up the coffee cup and took a swig. Now it was lukewarm and awful. "Do you have any leads?"

"No, we don't." The apologetic tone was back. "This is Nawlins, you know. French Quarter's got some sharks here that find tourists easy prey. But your friend still had his wallet. All his cash and credit cards. His watch."

"So it wasn't a robbery gone bad?"

Boucher shook his head. "Not as far as we can tell. In fact," Boucher leaned in, "to be honest, we can't tell *what* killed him, let alone *why*."

Gabriel looked at the man, who looked back with a set jaw, pursed lips, and hard, defiant eyes. Gabriel knew the expression. He'd seen it on dozens of other cops throughout his career, both as a cop and a political dirt digger. Knew the feeling behind the expression.

Detectives, the good ones anyway, be they cops or private, didn't like messes. They didn't like unanswered questions. It was hard-wired into them to attack with a pitbull mentality until the who, what, when, and where were answered. *Why* was the least of their concerns. *Why* very rarely made sense.

He decided to feign ignorance. "What do you mean?"

"There are no bullet holes or stab wounds. He's just...dead."

Gabriel leaned in. "So he could've died from natural causes? Like a heart attack or a brain aneurysm?"

"Or drugs. Did Mr. Owusu have a habit?"

"No." Gabriel's eyes had narrowed to slits as his jaw clenched.

Boucher held up his hands. "I've got to ask."

Gabriel relaxed and nodded in understanding. He did the same thing. They were standard questions. Routine to cops and investigators, but novel to the people being asked. Find a kid dead in his bed, frothing at the mouth, with a tourniquet around his arm, a needle in his vein, and you ask his parents if he was a user, and they're scandalized. *How could you be so evil as to insinuate Bobby, my baby boy, is a junkie?* The cop and the investigator already know the answer or have a hunch, but they ask anyway. Someone has to tell you definitively.

"You don't think he died of drugs or natural causes, do you, Sergeant Boucher?"

"No." Boucher was shaking his head. "Just call it a hunch. Where the body was found, how it was left to be found...like someone wanted us to know it *wasn't* an accident." Boucher checked his watch. "Coroner should be done with the autopsy. You up to checking it out?" Boucher stood up.

"Oh yeah." Gabriel was on his feet. "Should I follow in my car?"

"We can walk." Boucher gestured towards the door. "It's just over there a ways. Fifth floor." He set out.

Gabriel followed, a confused frown on his face. *There a ways?*

The redhead behind the counter looked up as Boucher and Gabriel walked through the door of the coroner's office and smiled. "Hey, Paul." Her accent was even thicker than Boucher's. "How're y'all doin' today?"

"Hey, Ruthie," Boucher greeted her with a smile.

Ruthie eyed Gabriel from top to bottom and gave him an approving wink. "Who's your friend?" It sounded like *Hoosier fren?*

"This is Gabriel Hawthorne from D.C." He leaned in over the counter and lowered his voice. "He's here about the young black guy brought in yesterday."

Ruthie's smile soured, and she shot Gabriel a sympathetic look.

"He's here to identify the body," Boucher continued.

"I'm so sorry." She turned a notebook around for the two men to see. "If you could just print and sign your name right here." She pointed to two blank lines.

Boucher picked up the pen and started writing.

Ruthie leaned in and whispered into Boucher's ear loud enough for Gabriel to hear. "Izzy single?"

Boucher continued writing. "I don't know, Ruthie. I ain't interested in dating him." He dropped the pen onto the notebook and scooted to the side.

Gabriel stepped up to the counter, politely ignoring Ruthie's flirtatious grin, scribbled down his name and signature, then dropped the pen and stepped back.

Boucher looked at Ruthie and rolled his eyes. "Come on, Mr. Hawthorne." He motioned for Gabriel to follow with his finger.

As Gabriel did, Ruthie called out. "If you need anything, Gabriel. A tissue, a shoulder to cry on. *Anything at all.* You just let me know."

Gabriel waved over his shoulder in acknowledgment and followed Boucher through the double doors.

"Who were y'all hired to investigate?" Boucher asked as he marched down the hall.

"Cain Dvanaesti," Gabriel replied.

Boucher stopped mid-step. He turned towards Gabriel. "What for?"

"I'm not at liberty to say," Gabriel watched the last bit of warmth in Boucher's expression ice over.

"Cain Dvanaesti's the governor of Florida."

"Yes, he is." Gabriel agreed, not sure where this was going.

"So, what're you doing here in Nawlins?"

"Looking into his father, Roman Dvanaesti."

Boucher took a step forward. "So you lied to me. Back in my office, you said you didn't know what lead your friend was pursuing."

Gabriel resisted the urge to step back. He wasn't intimidated by Boucher, but he did like to keep his personal space personal. "Roman's not the lead. Stefan came out here to see if there were any leads, and he found one."

Boucher stared hard at Gabriel for a long minute. Gabriel tensed, ready to lock horns with the man if he needed to.

Finally, Boucher turned on his heel and started walking. "I would've expected a little more professional courtesy, Mr. Hawthorne."

Gabriel let him get five steps ahead before he followed. "I answered all your questions to the best of my ability."

Boucher grunted something, but Gabriel couldn't catch it as he burst through a door.

Gabriel followed.

A man in scrubs and a white lab coat stood over Stefan's body.

"Who are you?" Boucher's voice boomed.

The man turned around to face Boucher with an annoyed expression plastered across his face. "Dr. Andrews," he said in a *do-I-have-to-tell-you-one-more-time* tone, "Dr. Betton's *intern*, Sergeant Boucher."

"Of course," Boucher said, sounding embarrassed. "Sorry, Dr. Andrews. We're here about the Ajaka Owusu autopsy." He pointed a thumb over his shoulder at Gabriel. "Mr. Gabriel Hawthorne is here to identify the body."

Dr. Andrews and Gabriel nodded at each other. Their eyes met briefly, but Dr. Andrews' eyes dropped quickly to Stefan's body. Gabriel had the immediate impression that Dr. Andrews was hiding something. In Gabriel's experience as a cop and then as an investigator, most people instinctively knew they couldn't look someone in the eye and lie. From the kids who found their shoes interesting to the tough guy in the interrogation room who's finally breaking down, they all had one thing in common: When it came to telling the truth, it was in the eyes.

"Of course," Dr. Andrews said. "I beg your pardon." He started moving towards the door. "I'll run fetch Dr. Betton. He went to the soda machine. You know how he loves his Diet Coke." Dr. Andrews was out the door.

Boucher laughed and nodded. "The man drinks his weight in them every day." Boucher walked over to Stefan's body and stopped laughing. "I'm not a stupid man, Mr. Hawthorne. You guys are P.I.s in Washington. Cain Dvanaesti is going to run for Senate."

Gabriel said nothing but moved to Stefan's body.

Boucher continued. "You were hired to find dirt on Cain Dvanaesti, but you haven't found any. So now you're here looking for dirt on his father." He turned to face Gabriel. I can't allow you to do that."

Gabriel's face was unreadable, but his mind couldn't believe his ears. Boucher, a cop, had just said he couldn't allow him to find dirt and had handed him some in doing so. Not as theatrical as Miguel, he thought, but still dirt. Stefan had been right to come here. Unfortunately, being right had cost him his life. Gabriel realized he'd been honest but not necessarily forthcoming with Sergeant Boucher, who might have been forthcoming but not necessarily honest with him. Gabriel needed to find out if this guy was a messenger or the executioner. He decided to stay quiet for the moment.

Boucher stepped closer to Gabriel. "Roman Dvanaesti has been a friend to our department. Police and firefighters who've lost their lives, their families have seen debts paid off or received a check for twenty-five grand. Or maybe they've been hospitalized in the line of duty and found their hospital bill paid off.

"And not only that, but Roman Dvanaesti has given millions to this city. *Before* and *after* Hurricane Katrina. Never publicly. He's a good man who's done right by this city."

Gabriel decided to push. "Has he been good to cops and politicians so he can cover things up or so they can cover things up?"

Boucher stared, horrified.

"Maybe for kickbacks or preferential treatment?"

"Now you wait just a god—!"

Gabriel interrupted. "Or maybe all of that, plus the cops and the politicians in his back pocket. A-scratch-my-back-or-I 'll-let-the-public-know-just-how-much-I-scratched-yours law unto himself."

Boucher stood there, his face turning purple, his hands clenching and unclenching.

Gabriel prepared himself for a fight.

At that moment, Dr. Betton sauntered into the exam room, sipping from a bottle of Diet Coke. "Oh. Sergeant Boucher. I'm sorry. I didn't know you were here."

"Your intern didn't find you?" Boucher asked.

Betton looked confused. "Intern?"

Gabriel added helpfully, "Dr. Andrews?"

Betton shook his head. "I don't have an intern."

Boucher cursed and slapped the closest thing he could find. "Fantastic." Now he was moving to the door. "First a dirt monger, and now a necrophiliac. I'll be back." He was gone.

Betton followed him with his eyes, then looked back at Gabriel, his Diet Coke paused at his lips. "What just happened?"

Gabriel opened his mouth to explain, but Betton held up his hand. "Rhetorical question. Who are you?"

"Gabriel Hawthorne. I'm an investigator out of D.C."

Betton shrugged in indifference as he moved to the stainless-steel counter next to Stefan's gurney and set down the Diet Coke. "I told Boucher he should call first." Opening a brown paper bag, he pulled out a sandwich in a small plastic container and a bag of Cheetos. "The weekends always get busy around here."

Gabriel watched as Betton pulled the sandwich out of the container and took a large bite. He chewed, mayonnaise globbed on the corner of his mouth. "I was just taking a lunch break." Betton popped a few Cheetos into his mouth without swallowing the bite of the sandwich. "But since you guys are here, I can make it a working lunch."

Betton took another bite of the sandwich and popped in a couple more Cheetos for good measure, and then walked over to Stefan's body, wiping the mayo, tomato, and Cheetos off his fingers onto his scrub shirt.

"Don't you have to wear gloves?" Gabriel asked as Betton started handling Stefan's body.

"This guy doesn't look like he died of anything catchy." Betton went over the body with his eyes. "In fact...I don't see anything. No puncture wounds or other signs of IV drug use. No bruising. No lacerations. He's got some scars consistent with knife wounds and bullet wounds." Betton looked at one scar. "What would've made that? A machete?" Betton reached behind him and picked up a black light. "I guess he's a gangbanger." He turned on the black light. "Or should I say *was* a gangbanger."

"Stefan was never a gangbanger." Gabriel's voice was acid.

Betton shrugged. "African American with those types of scars—"

"Stefan's a Lost Boy." Gabriel's voice was ice as he locked a dangerous gaze on Betton.

Betton swallowed hard. "Lost Boy? Like Sudan... Lost Boy?" Beads of sweat bloomed on his forehead.

Gabriel nodded, then leaned in just inches from Betton's face. "And he was the closest friend I ever had."

Betton's face glistened with a sheen of sweat. Swallowing hard, he opened his mouth to speak, but nothing came out.

Gabriel reached around Betton, who flinched but then relaxed as Gabriel handed him his Diet Coke.

Betton took a long pull, then opened his mouth to speak again. "I'm..." but he didn't say anything else. The dryness might've been gone, but fear still constricted his vocal cords.

Gabriel brought him back to the moment. "You were about to blacklight him."

"Oh...r-right." Betton turned his attention to the body on the gurney. Picking up Stefan's right arm, he ran the light over the top of it. He found nothing. He turned Stefan's arm over. "Hmm." He stopped over a mark on the inside of the wrist.

"You find something?" Gabriel asked.

Betton's eyes narrowed as he focused on the mark on Stefan's wrist under the light. "I don't recognize this particular stamp, but... it looks like an entry stamp."

Gabriel looked at the stamp glowing faint green on Stefan's wrist, a capital V with what looked like quotation marks around it. "Like for a nightclub?"

Betton grunted.

"Do you mind if I take a picture?" Gabriel pulled out his phone.

"Sure." Betton held the light up to give the best image.

"Thanks," Gabriel said as he looked at the image and pocketed the phone. "Anything else?"

Betton did a quick scan of the rest of Stefan's body. "No. Not on the black light anyway." He put down the black light.

Gabriel fished a business card out of his pocket and handed it to Betton. "Would you do me a favor? A professional courtesy, as it were? If you find anything out of the usual, would you give me a call?"

Betton took the card without looking at it. "Yeah, sure. Do you have some idea of what that might be?"

Gabriel shook his head. "Just a hunch."

Betton nodded as he dropped the card into the brown paper bag. He picked up his sandwich as Boucher stormed back through the door. "Oh, what are you doing, Betton?"

"Eating lunch." Betton bit a hunk of the sandwich as he turned away from Stefan's body and faced the wall.

"I meant you shouldn't be conducting the autopsy in front of the next of kin."

Betton's gaze shot to Gabriel. "I thought you said you were a cop."

Gabriel shook his head. "I said I was an investigator." Then Gabriel added, "Private investigator."

Boucher walked up to Gabriel. "Right now, and for the rest of your stay in Nawlins," he poked Gabriel in the chest, "you are next of kin and a private citizen, Mr. Hawthorne."

Gabriel resisted the urge to twist Boucher's finger off. "I've never been to New Orleans before. I might stay a couple of days and take in the sights." He looked towards Betton. "It'll be a couple of days before I can take the body back to D.C., right?"

Betton nodded towards the wall.

Boucher's eyes darkened. "You don't need to wait for the body. You can make the arrangements to ship it in a couple of hours and head back to D.C. to make final plans."

Gabriel met Boucher's hard look with a pleasant smile. "I think I'd prefer to fly with the body. Make sure the airline doesn't lose it."

Betton spewed Diet Coke across the wall as he guffawed.

36

Gabriel looked up from the picture on his phone of the "V" with what he'd thought were quotation marks to the neon blood red "V" with what he now could see were fangs, with a small drop of blood falling from each one. He stood across the street from the Goth bar, biting the inside of his mouth to keep from laughing. The patrons were all vampire wannabes. And each with an individual take on what it meant to be a vampire. Disposable income had a lot to do with this last observation, accessories anyway. No matter the cut of clothing, the most popular colors present were undertaker black and angelic white.

Gabriel stifled a laugh as an obese young woman walked by in frizzy hair dyed blood red, pasty white make-up applied goth girl style to her face, and a French maid's outfit. She looked like she belonged in a third-rate community house rendition of *Rocky Horror Picture Show*. This wasn't the hard-core vampirism scene. The young woman glared at him as she passed, but the look seemed more of an affectation than an actual menace. Gabriel chuckled. He'd found the place he was looking for.

Slipping his phone into his pocket, Gabriel crossed the street and followed the young, hefty Rocky Horror wannabe to the door. Other young people stood paying their cover charge. Gabriel pulled a bill out of his pocket, but the bouncer at the door put a hand on Gabriel's shoulder.

The bouncer had to follow the same hideous fashion sense as the patrons. He wore a black t-shirt, a size too small for his granite torso, tucked into black leather pants over black motorcycle boots, with a black belt and a silver death's-head belt buckle. His ensemble was garnished with black fingerless motorcycle gloves and bandoliers crisscrossing his chest. He finished it all with a heavily waxed Fu Manchu mustache, mirrored aviator sunglasses, and, of course, very expensive, but still not very real, fangs.

"Only vampires allowed," the bouncer said in a deep, ominous tone, but with a lisp, so that 'vampires' came out, 'vampireth'.

Gabriel sniggered.

He gripped Gabriel's shoulder tighter. "You think I'm funny, Punk?"

"Yeth. Yeth, I do." Gabriel responded.

The bouncer only flashed his faux fangs in a wicked smile and retorted, "Wrong anther."

Gabriel howled with laughter. "As funny as you are, I really don't have time to waste on the long-lost and deranged member of the Village People."

The smile melted from the bouncer's face. He grabbed Gabriel by his shoulders, lining him up for a head-butt.

And then Gabriel throat-punched him.

The bouncer's eyes grew wide as he released Gabriel, his hands moving to the universal choking gesture.

Gabriel clapped him on the shoulder. "Don't worry. You can thtill thwallow even if it doethn't feel like it." He was through the door and into the club.

The air pulsed with techno music and dizzying, hypnotic-colored lights. The air reeked of smoke and alcohol, sweat and perfume, cologne and cannabis. Sweat-glistening bodies writhed and gyrated to the music on the dance floor.

Gabriel stood there, taking it all in: the people dancing with their eyes closed, as if in a trance; those seated, staring glassy-eyed at the dance floor. And he felt the presence of the two beasts before he saw them. His head snapped to his left, where two young men dressed the same way as the bouncer at the door were approaching him.

But these two, Gabriel quickly realized, were not like the clown at the front door. These guys weren't simply for show. Despite their size, they stepped as lithely as dancers, moving quickly but unobtrusively through the crowd, their eyes sizing him up, weighing what measure of a man he might be, not taking for granted that it was two against one. Great, Gabriel thought. *This is going to hurt.*

Gabriel steeled himself to do battle when the two men's heads snapped towards the dance floor as if they were dogs hearing an order. They stopped moving but continued listening.

Listening to what, Gabriel wondered. How could they hear themselves think, let alone someone's voice calling an order? His ears throbbed from the beat, and he'd only been in the room for five minutes. These guys worked here night after night.

Perplexed, Gabriel followed their gaze across the dance floor; the dancers parted like a writhing curtain to reveal a man seated at a circular booth, surrounded by an entourage of young people desperately trying to be Goths and freaks. Only Gabriel wasn't sure if it was a man.

The form staring at him had a slight, diminutive frame and very effeminate features. His hands were long and delicate. The wisps of hair on his chin and upper lip only enhanced that image of a girl trying to pass as a man and failing. His clothing was not the gothic biker garb of the bouncers, but more like a 1960s hippie who doesn't understand drag- A thick black fur coat, no shirt, brown suede pants with matching suede shoes. His hair was buzzed short. He was laughable. And Gabriel laughed, and then he looked into the man's eyes.

Gabriel's laugh caught in his throat, and he felt both frigid and hot at the same time as he shivered.

The man noticed the shiver, heard the click as the laughter stopped, and grinned.

Gabriel felt a fresh shiver run up his spine as he saw the man's canines. They were stained like a smoker's, but a rustier color. Not brown. Gabriel had no idea how he noticed that from across the room, but he did.

The man's grin twisted with cruel effect as if the man had wanted Gabriel to see his teeth and knew he had. Gabriel didn't like feeling intimidated, so he marched to the man's table.

"Sorry to bother you," Gabriel said as he hitched a thumb over his shoulder towards the door, "but your boyfriend said it'd be all right." Gabriel hoped his voice didn't sound as thin to this man as it did to him.

It did as the man flashed Gabriel a bemused yet menacing smile. "Manners, Mister...?" His accent was straight from the bayou.

"Hawthorne," Gabriel replied. "Gabriel Hawthorne."

"Gabriel Hawthorne." The man let the name roll around in his mouth like new wine. "I am LeBlanc."

Gabriel laughed.

LeBlanc smiled. "Do you find my name funny, Mr. Hawthorne?"

"It's a tad bit... theatrical. But it fits in with the ambiance."

LeBlanc's smile broadened. He cast a lazy look around the club. "Yes, this place is a tad bit theatrical." He shooed a young lady dressed in black lace sitting on the edge of the booth seat. She bowed and fled the table. LeBlanc motioned to the vacant seat. "Sit down. Can I get you a drink?"

Gabriel sat down. "No, thank you. But don't let me stop you."

LeBlanc stared at Gabriel. Inhaling and closing his eyes, he sat motionless for a long minute. "You are human. I can smell the blood."

"No, that's my English Leather. Lots of people make that mistake." Gabriel was hoping he sounded a lot less freaked out than he was.

LeBlanc launched a barrage of laughter to the ceiling. "You are very clever, Mr. Hawthorne. I should drain you dry for your insolence, but I like you."

"Well, we are in a vampire bar," Gabriel said. He looked around, took in all the people, and realized the only person who truly made him uneasy was this diminutive, poorly dressed glam rocker. Even David Bowie, at the height of his Ziggy Stardust days, would've been embarrassed by this guy.

"And what do you want, Mr. Hawthorne?"

"Call me Gabriel."

"Oh, we aren't that intimate yet."

"Right. Well, LeBlanc, I'm here to see if you or anyone here might know what happened to a business associate of mine. Mr. Stefan Owusu. He died not too far from here."

LeBlanc stared nonplussed at Gabriel. "I'm not sure how I can help you."

"The coroner found the black light entry stamp from this bar on his wrist."

LeBlanc yawned. "And you think I might remember one black man," he waved his hand across the sea of African Americans, Caucasians, and Asians, "among all this?"

"I didn't tell you he was black," Gabriel said sharply, his police instincts popping on.

"I assumed by the name Owusu," LeBlanc said. "It sounds African. Perhaps... Somali? No. Sudanese."

Gabriel nodded. "He was here in New Orleans on business."

"What type of business?"

Gabriel decided to drop the formalities and go right for the throat. "Roman Dvanaesti." A less experienced investigator might've missed LeBlanc's flinch, but Gabriel saw it. LeBlanc was scared.

LeBlanc recovered quickly, however, and waved his hand above his head. The two biker vampire bouncers appeared at their table. "I'm sorry, I cannot help you, Mr. Hawthorne. Now, if you'll excuse me, these two gentlemen will escort you out."

Gabriel stood up and pulled a card from his wallet. "Sorry to have bothered you." He put the card down in front of LeBlanc. "If something does cross your mind, give me a call." Gabriel turned on his heel. He walked with all the nonchalance he could muster away from LeBlanc, feeling the diminutive man's glare burn into the back of his head.

LeBlanc watched Gabriel until he disappeared through the front door. The young woman in black lace returned to his table, manhandled her way beside him, and began nuzzling his ear. He shrugged her away. She tried again but stopped at his glare and bolted from the table.

LeBlanc picked up Gabriel's card and stared at it for a long time. Finally, as if resolving himself, he raised his hand and waved. The two bouncers were at his table. "Bring the car around."

37

Gabriel watched from a block and a half away as a Black Lincoln Navigator skidded to a halt in front of the club.

"Certainly subtle, I'll give him that," Gabriel mused.

A moment later, LeBlanc, still dressed as a glam rock reject, hurried out of the club with one of the biker vampire bouncers in tow. Gabriel tried but failed to suppress a shiver as LeBlanc climbed into the back seat of the Navigator. The bouncer climbed into the front, and the vehicle pulled into traffic.

Gabriel waited for a break in traffic and then pulled out. He knew he'd been right about the flinch. Hopefully, his hunch would play out with another clue, he told himself, and he wasn't just following them as they made a run to McDonald's or Taco Bell. Now that he thought about it, his stomach growled, and he decided to keep an eye out for Taco Bell.

What was it about this guy that gave Gabriel what his grandmother called the heebee jeebees, he wondered. Gooseflesh covered his sweat-soaked body. It was all an act, like everyone else in the little Goth bar. By day, they were college students, secretaries, and fry cooks. By night, they were creatures of the night. LeBlanc was the same. By day, he was a businessman making sure he had enough liquor behind the bar and toilet paper in the johns. By night, he was a Twisted Sister vampire. Yet... the little guy had unnerved him. As a cop, Gabriel had run up against guys who were small but wiry, who'd glared daggers at him. This was different. It was the eyes, Gabriel thought. And those rust-colored teeth.

The Navigator made a left, and Gabriel followed. They were leaving the glitzy, touristy part of *Nawlins* and heading for what looked to Gabriel a less-than-reputable section. There was still traffic, but not as much.

And the name Roman Dvanaesti shook people up in this town, Gabriel thought as he saw the Navigator pull to the curb. Gabriel turned down the side street and parked. Cutting off the dome light, he exited and moved to the sidewalk just in time to see LeBlanc's silhouette hurry across the sidewalk to a nondescript building with a large iron door.

LeBlanc didn't look around or even over his shoulder as he marched up to the door and banged on it. He waited a few seconds, then beat again. A shaft of light cut across LeBlanc's face in the darkness. LeBlanc spoke into the peephole. Gabriel closed his eyes, straining to hear what he was saying, but couldn't.

The shaft of light was cut off as the peephole door slid shut, and the iron door opened. LeBlanc stepped immediately through. The door slammed shut.

Gabriel stole a glance at the Navigator. The two bouncers sat motionless in the front seat. He looked at the building. There were no windows. No other doors. He scanned the building, looking for a name or street number, but there wasn't one. Nor could he find a name for the cross street he was on. He checked his watch.

Well, he mused to himself, nothing to do now but wait.

LeBlanc heard the iron door slam shut with a finality that caused his knees to quiver. He looked down and tried to cover his flesh by buttoning the coat. He suddenly regretted not changing clothes. The people on the other side of the door, the people he hoped to be invited to join one day, would not take kindly to his appearance. There was no going back now. It was too late. He was here.

He stepped to the other door, where the muffled sounds of conversation and music could be heard. He took a deep breath, raised his hand to knock, hesitated, then knuckled three sharp raps.

The door opened, and the muffled sounds became louder. The door opened onto an elegant hallway, not in keeping with the building or the small chamber he was standing in, with its bare, weathered concrete walls and floor. The hallway, sloping downward, was carpeted in a rich, chocolate-colored plush velvet. Mint green and buttery yellow brocade draped the walls. The hall opened onto a similarly decorated chamber. This time, the door was solid mahogany and carved with images of Satan's temptations of Christ in the desert. LeBlanc remembered them from his Catholic school days, and they always made him uneasy.

LeBlanc took a deep breath and then opened the door. He felt distinctly out of place as he took in the decorations, the people in their tuxedos and evening dresses. There was no smoky haze or stench of sweat here. No pulsating beat or light flash. No gyrating flesh. This was rich. Classy. This was where he wanted to be. LeBlanc knew a long time would pass before he was invited here if he made it out of here alive. He thought if he did, he would change his clothes and hair. But first...

He spotted the bartender watching him as he poured what looked like red currant wine into glasses. LeBlanc moved with as much stealth as he could to the man, but he need not have worried. He was invisible to this class.

"I need to see him."

The bartender looked LeBlanc up and down. "Are you sure?"

LeBlanc bristled at the insult but stood his ground. "Now."

The bartender nodded and pressed a button. An electronic lock disengaged, and a door beside the bar swung open. The bartender gestured with his head that LeBlanc should go through.

Now that the door was open, LeBlanc had second thoughts, but it was too late. The door was open. LeBlanc stole a sidelong glance at the bartender, who stared at him, panic-stricken. Smirking at that realization, he held his head up high and walked through the door.

He stood in an office. LeBlanc calculated his office could easily fit into it four times over. On the same chocolate-colored velvet plush lay a Persian rug that covered three-quarters of the floor. On the walls hung what looked to LeBlanc like original masterpieces painted by French painters such as Monet, Matisse, and Bouguereau. The desk and bookshelves were all mahogany. The chairs and sofas were covered in dark chocolate leather.

Sitting on one of the sofas was the man he'd come to see. Currently, he was preoccupied. Two young women sat on each side of him, holding a third woman. The woman was sitting in his lap, and he was hunched over her, his long black hair pulled back into a ponytail. She was not being held by force, but to ensure she didn't need to worry about falling out of the man's lap. The image reminded LeBlanc of the make-out sessions in his club. This one was more...

The woman let out a soft moan.

"Georges," LeBlanc said, his voice coming out as a horse whisper. The two women heard and turned to him, but Georges did not. "Georges," he repeated a little louder.

Georges's head snapped up from the woman, deep-set eyes glowing like embers, blood dripping from the corners of his mouth, fangs stained a dark crimson. His clean-shaven face was narrow. His nose was a sharp blade. His square jaw was now set in a sneer.

LeBlanc stepped back. The scent of the woman's blood was intoxicating, but the sight of Georges was terrifying.

The woman to the left of Georges quickly wiped the blood away before it dripped on his chocolate brown shirt. The shirt alone, LeBlanc mused, probably cost three-hundred dollars. It complemented the thousand-dollar brown Armani pinstriped suit very well, LeBlanc thought with envy. Yes, he thought to himself as he saw the suit jacket folded elegantly on the back of the sofa. *If I survive, this is how I will dress. This is how I will live.*

The woman moaned in disappointment at the interruption. Georges looked back at the young woman and stroked her hair, the ruby in his pinky ring blazing in the light. "There, there. It's all right. I know you are disappointed. But LeBlanc will make it worth our while." He continued to look at the woman. "For he knows to have a good reason to come to me when he's not called."

Georges's voice was as icy as the grave, but the smile on his face was as pleasant as a spring day.

LeBlanc felt his knees weaken. "I... uh... another man has come into my club. Asking about Roman."

Georges's head moved slowly up. Now his eyes were black as coal. "*Another?*"

LeBlanc wanted to sit down but stood still.

"Tell me. Exactly how many men have come to your club asking about Roman?"

"He's the second, Sir."

Georges eyed LeBlanc, then turned back to the woman in his lap. "They are of no concern. Ignore them."

"But they've asked me about Roman, Sir."

"*Precisely*. If these men knew anything, they'd be coming to me. Tell them you don't know him and leave them be."

He started to sink toward the woman's neck. She sighed in expectation.

LeBlanc cleared his throat. "I already killed one, Georges. That's why the second man came. He was looking for his associate."

Faster than even LeBlanc could track or dream of moving himself, Georges was off the couch. LeBlanc had the most peculiar sensation. Cold water was running down his chest and stomach. He looked down to see crimson fluid running. He tried to scream but couldn't. He reached up to his neck and could feel his backbone.

Georges stood before him, holding LeBlanc's throat and voice box.

LeBlanc searched Georges's face in disbelief as he sank to the floor.

Georges stared down at the dead vampire at his feet, spat, and dropped his throat onto him, noticing a business card in Leblanc's dead hand.

Walking to the sink at the wet bar, Georges elbowed the faucet and rinsed his hands. After toweling them dry, he snapped his fingers.

The woman he'd been feeding upon jumped up and grabbed his suit jacket.

Georges felt the cool weight of the jacket resting on his shoulders as she helped him slip into it. Tugging on his sleeves so that the cuffs just peeked out, he buttoned the top button and then stooped over and picked up the card.

He eyed the card for a silent moment. "Gabriel Hawthorne."

38

Gabriel checked the Navigator. The two bouncers stared straight ahead. The engine idled.

So, he thought, they're not expecting this to last long."

As if on cue, the steel door opened, flooding the sidewalk with light.

Gabriel flattened himself against the wall and watched as a man dressed in a suit, his long dark hair pulled back into a ponytail, exited the building and walked over to the Navigator. The man tapped on the glass, which came down immediately. Gabriel strained to hear the conversation, but it was over before the window could fully retract.

The man turned on his heel and walked back towards the building without a glance back at the Navigator. As the Navigator pulled away from the curb, the man stopped and spun around to face the corner where Gabriel was hiding.

Gabriel pulled his head back around the corner and held his breath. Pressing his body as flat as he could against the wall, he moved his hand as quietly as he could up to the Beretta he had tucked in the back of his pants. He felt the comforting grip and finally took a breath as he heard the steel door slam shut and the scrape of the lock.

Gabriel scanned the darkened street, making sure the man had not stayed outside to linger on a cigarette break, and then moved quickly back to his car. He got in, closed the door gently, and put the key in the ignition. He was about to start the car when he heard a tap on his window.

He looked up to see Dr. Andrews, the intern from the morgue, looking at him. Only Dr. Bennett had informed him that he had no intern. Dr. Andrews pulled out a cigarette and lit it.

Gabriel pulled his Beretta out and pointed it at the man as he rolled the window down.

The man looked unimpressed at the weapon pointed at his chest as he smoked his cigarette. He exhaled. "It would be unwise to follow those men." His voice carried no accent or timbre to betray what part of the country or world he might have been born and raised in.

"Oh yeah?" Gabriel thumbed off the safety. "Why do you think I was going to follow them?"

"Because, Mr. Hawthorne, I've been following you." He dropped his cigarette and stubbed it out with his foot. "Those men are dangerous," Dr. Andrews said.

"I handled them pretty well a half hour ago," Gabriel replied.

"I don't mean their proficiency at hand-to-hand or armed combat, Mr. Hawthorne, but who they work for and where they are going now. Especially if they realized they were being followed. And they would have realized it."

"I'm pretty *proficient* at tailing." Gabriel kept the Beretta trained on the man's chest.

The man smiled. "But not at being tailed."

At that moment, Gabriel heard the metallic tap of steel on the glass coming from the passenger window. He turned and cursed to himself as he saw the hulking silhouette of a man pointing a pistol with a silencer at him.

"We aren't here to hurt you, Mr. Hawthorne," the man said.

"Really," Gabriel said with as much insolence as he could muster. "So this is your way of welcoming me to the neighborhood? What? Were the Welcome Wagon folks all out of gift baskets?"

"With all due respect, Mr. Hawthorne," the man gestured to Gabriel's pistol, "you were the first to draw a weapon. Now. We have no wish to harm you or gain your cooperation by force. But I want to make sure you understand the seriousness of the situation, even if you do not understand the situation itself."

Gabriel shot a glance at the hulking silhouette. The pistol was still pointed at him, and the man's hand wasn't wavering. Gabriel was sure the man could stand there pointing his weapon through the window at him all night without so much as a flinch or a tremble from it getting too heavy. He looked back at the tall man.

"What do you want?" Gabriel asked.

"For you to follow us."

There came another metallic tap at the passenger window. Gabriel turned and watched the man holster the pistol into a shoulder harness. Gabriel kept his weapon pointed at Dr. Andrews. "Why?"

"So that you might be *illumined*."

"And what exactly does that mean?" Gabriel started the car with his free hand. Neither man moved to stop him, but Gabriel didn't think the Beretta in his hand had anything to do with that.

"Come with us, and you will see," the man answered calmly.

"If I don't?" Gabriel challenged.

"We will not stop you, Mr. Hawthorne. But we will not be able to protect you either."

Gabriel looked between the two men. They stood calm and impassive.

"Protect me from what?" Gabriel demanded. "Who are you people?"

Dr. Andrews looked towards the hulking figure on the other side of Gabriel's vehicle, and the two men moved to a Crown Victoria parked at the opposite end of the side street from Gabriel's car. Gabriel cursed again. He hadn't even noticed the Crown Vic. They got in, and now Gabriel recognized the man behind the wheel, the man from Miami, who'd first been at a Crown Vic in the parking garage of the hotel and then walking on his floor. This man started the Crown Vic up and pulled past Gabriel, waiting for him at the stop sign.

"Okay," Gabriel said after a moment. He did a three-point turn and pulled in behind them. "I'll play along."

39

Gabriel looked at the sign above the shop. The Crown Victoria had stopped in front of it, but none of the men had exited the car.

"Poor Willie's Crawfish Café," Gabriel said with a shake of his head. "Why do New Orleans Restaurants all have to have the words 'poor' and 'crawfish' in them?" He pulled into a parking spot, exited, and walked over to the Crown Vic.

The man behind the wheel nodded towards the café and then drove off.

Gabriel watched the taillights as the car pulled onto the main drag. He looked back towards the café, shook his head, and headed for the door.

As he entered, he was greeted by the chill of the air conditioner and a waitress with too much makeup and too little fabric, carrying too many platters filled with crawfish.

"Jes' sit yo'self anywhere, Honey." She flashed him a tooth-filled smile.

"I'm looking for someone," Gabriel said, scanning the café, which looked more like a diner to Gabriel. The floor was black-and-white checkered linoleum. Booths and tables in generic beige vinyl littered the space. Green neon strip lighting formed a pattern along the tops of the walls, and Zydeco music blared from a jukebox.

"Well, take a scoot 'roun' an' have a look-see, Suga'," she drawled over her shoulder as she bustled off to a table.

"Look-see," Gabriel repeated in amusement as he started walking around. "If I only knew what a 'look-see' was and who exactly I was taking a scoot 'roun' for said look-see for."

As Gabriel approached the booth of a man sipping coffee, the man said over his cup, "So good of you to come, Mr. Hawthorne." The accent was educated, British.

Gabriel stopped. The man, Gabriel guessed by the discoloration of the skin on his hands and swelling of his knuckles, had to be pushing seventy, and sat ramrod straight in his seat. The crown of his head was smooth, and what little hair he had left was snow white and cropped very close to the skull. He was clean-shaven and wore a charcoal-gray pinstripe suit with a red silk tie on his slim frame. On his left ring finger was a gold signet ring. The man looked up, and Gabriel saw the most vibrant steel-gray, deep-set eyes he'd ever seen. The man's nose and chin were broad and strong.

"You may call me Caiaphas." He extended his hand, and Gabriel accepted, appreciating the man's firm grip. He gestured to the seat across from him. "Please. Have a seat."

Gabriel sat down.

The two men stared at each other for a long moment. "So. Caiaphas," Gabriel began. "Is that your real name?"

Caiaphas smiled. "It's the only name that matters."

"Uh-huh."

The toothy waitress appeared at their table. "I see you found yer frien'." Her smile revealed every tooth, even the gum line. "What can I getcha, Honey?"

"A cup of coffee, please." Gabriel looked up and noticed she was showing more cleavage. He hoped that wasn't for him.

"Okey-dokey." She flashed him an even bigger smile. Gabriel wondered how her head could hold that many teeth.

She glanced at Caiaphas, and he nodded. She smiled as if nothing could make her happier than bringing him another cup of coffee.

Once she left the table, Gabriel went on the attack. "Okay, Caiaphas. What's with the Three Amigos? And who's the beanpole?"

Caiaphas sipped his coffee. "Marcus."

"And what're the other guys' names? Moe and Curly?"

"They haven't earned one yet."

"Well, what names do they go by?"

The waitress returned with a carafe and another cup, setting them on the table. "Can I get y'all anythin' else right now?"

"Nothing right now. Thank you." Caiaphas poured fresh coffee into his cup.

"You got the funniest accent I e'er heard if you don' mind me sayin'," the waitress said. "Where you from?"

"Elsewhere," Caiaphas answered.

The waitress stood there expectant, but when she finally realized Caiaphas wasn't going to say anything else, she shrugged and walked away.

Caiaphas waited till she was safely out of earshot. "I'm very sorry about what happened to Mr. Owusu. We tried to protect him, but..." his voice trailed off as he stared somewhere beyond the table.

Gabriel studied the man. His face showed what appeared to be genuine pain at failing to protect Stefan. Why? What was Stefan to this guy? Why did this guy feel an obligation to protect Stefan? And what did Stefan need protection from?

"Do you know what happened to Stefan?" Gabriel asked.

Caiaphas's sigh carried heavy weight as he stared at something Gabriel could not see. Somewhere, Gabriel couldn't. He seemed to age ten years in the next few moments of silence. Finally, he looked up and met Gabriel's eyes.

"Your friend was murdered."

"And do you know who murdered him?"

Caiaphas nodded.

"Who?"

Caiaphas locked eyes with Gabriel. "Vampires."

Gabriel stared across the table at Caiaphas for a long time. Reaching out, he grabbed the man's coffee cup, held it under his nose, and sniffed. Just coffee. He set the cup back down. Gabriel smelled his cup. Gabriel repeated the man's last word in a tone suggesting he just wanted to make sure he'd heard him correctly. "Vampires."

Caiaphas's nod was sober.

"And you've personally seen these... vampires? Met them? Other than your dreams or the occasional bad acid trip?" Gabriel's tone oozed mockery.

A patient smile crossed Caiaphas's face. "Vampires are real, Mr. Hawthorne."

"Oh, I'm sure." Gabriel nodded as he reached into his back pocket. "Right along with zombies and the Easter Bunny." He pulled out his wallet and fished out two dollars. "That sounds like the start of a joke. A vampire, a zombie, and the Easter Bunny walk into a bar." He threw the money on the table. "And *you're* the punchline." He stood up. "I'll just be going now." He turned to leave.

"Please sit down," Caiaphas said in the gentle yet firm tone a grandfather might use when he's sharing some life lesson with a grandchild.

Gabriel hesitated.

"I know a lot about you, Mr. Hawthorne," Caiaphas continued pleasantly. "I know you were a police officer before becoming a private investigator. A dirt digger, I believe, is how some people refer to your particular line of investigation. Some call you 'the gardener.' You've seen and heard many strange and fantastic things. How can what I'm saying be any stranger or more fantastic? After all, you deal with politicians daily." After a moment, he added. "Don't you want the truth about your friend's death?"

Gabriel turned back and looked at the older man. In his fitted suit and silk tie, his close-cropped hair, and his clean-shaven face, he didn't look insane. Perhaps if Caiaphas had long, greasy hair and an unkempt beard, reeking of alcohol and urine, wearing soiled and ratty clothing, he would find it easier to believe. Those people were always easier to believe. You just had to know how to sift the truth out of their story. There were more times than not when their blossoming insanity held a kernel of rationality. When their few remaining lucid brain cells were trying to communicate with what few words they had left. Maybe he could do the same with Caiaphas.

He sat back down.

Caiaphas started again. "There are beings that walk this earth that started life as human but are now... something other than human. I use the word 'vampire' because it is the easiest, most efficient word to communicate."

"So there aren't vampires. You were just using the word as a metaphor?" Gabriel poured himself another cup of coffee.

"Oh, there are vampires, but that's not a name they call themselves." Caiaphas also poured himself another cup of coffee.

"What?" Gabriel was incredulous. "They call themselves goblins? Elves? Orcs?"

"What I mean is... these creatures created the word vampire as part of the mythos about themselves."

"Why would they do that? Why would they need to do that?"

A wicked curve pulled at Caiaphas's lips. "I think the answer to that question is in the facial expression you're giving me right now."

Gabriel had to admit the man was right. His expression could easily be translated to, 'You're full of the stuff plants are fertilized with.' But why not? Gabriel enjoyed a good vampire flick. Well, the old school movies anyway, not the 'sparkle in the sun teenage vampire angst' stuff or sex with vampires or schools for vampire kids. Regardless, old-school dark or new-school sparkly, it was all just fiction. If vampires were real, if they were all the fables said they were, or if the myths didn't reveal all their powers, why would they *need* to create words and mythos?

Caiaphas seemed to read Gabriel's mind. "If you want an enemy to think you're more or less than you are, you help create an image. Think of teenagers in school. A boy might want to be considered cool, so he might fabricate or embellish certain facts to make him seem more of a Casanova than he is."

"But why would they need to do that?" Gabriel persisted.

"Because now they can move freely through a society that believes they are nothing more than old wives' tales and superstitions and good ole Hollywood popcorn sellers."

"Uh-huh," Gabriel said, unconvinced.

"Vampires have existed for centuries—"

"Since the dawn of time?" Gabriel interrupted.

"We don't know," Caiaphas responded.

"Then how do you know they've existed for centuries?" Gabriel persisted.

"Because we've been tracking them for centuries." Caiaphas was now beginning to get irritated.

"We?"

"The Illuminati," Caiaphas whispered.

"This keeps getting better and better." Gabriel sat back in his chair. He stared in disbelief at Caiaphas. "I thought the Illuminati was a secret order designed to overthrow the church and establish a one-world government."

"You're thinking of Adam Weishaupt, who founded a movement known as the Order of Illuminati or Perfectibilists movement. It was simply an organization of free thinkers, a continuation of the Enlightenment, and some would argue proponents of far more deluded beliefs than our organization. They sought to end what they saw as Roman Catholicism's hold over government and science. They supported women's education and intellectual equality. The organization was banned in Seventeen Eighty-Five and subsequently disbanded.

"Conspiracy theorists have argued this organization survives and thrives to this day, affecting world events, manipulating and controlling governments. There have been other organizations since Seventeen Eighty-Five, and even into the present, that have claimed a fraternal relationship with this group. But there is no evidence of any link to Weishaupt's organization. No evidence that any of these groups, including Weishaupt's, are affecting, manipulating, or controlling anything."

"But isn't that exactly what a secret society bent on world domination would want the world to believe?" Gabriel's tone oozed with sarcasm. "Aren't we playing semantics right now? Isn't attempting to overthrow the church and ending the church's hold over government the same thing? By the way, that sounds like freedom of religion, which is the basis of this country." Gabriel leaned onto the table. "Speaking of this country, isn't our government's deluded belief that patriotism is not questioning our leadership? Our leadership's obsessive impulse to shove its brand of democracy down the rest of the world's throats is the same thing as establishing a one-world government?" Gabriel threw up his hands. "Now that I think of it, a secret society calling itself the enlightened because it believes in vampires isn't so half-cocked. After all, according to the N.R.A., guns don't kill people, people do." Gabriel waved a hand at Caiaphas, "But according to you, it ain't even people. It's vampires."

Caiaphas stared hard at Gabriel, his mouth slowly working over whatever measure of the situation was happening in his mind. Finally, his face steeled with resolve. He picked up the coffee cup and drained it. "What I'm about to tell you, no one outside of our order has ever heard."

He poured another cup with a trembling hand. "In Seventeen-Hundred and Two in Ingolstadt in Bavaria, a young priest by the name of Johann Widmar answered the door of his cottage to find a filthy, naked young man standing before him. Johann brought the young man into his home, wrapped him in blankets, and placed him before the fire. The young man complained of hunger and thirst but refused to eat the meat and wine placed before him. Instead, he said only human blood could slake him.

"Johann thought the man was simply fevered by thirst, hunger, and exposure to the elements. He made a sleeping pallet on the floor before the fire and laid the young man on it. As the young man lay upon the pallet, he spoke of dark and dreadful powers which had been bestowed upon him after a woman he came across in the Black Forest had bitten him. He claimed he was a vampire and could make people do whatever he wished without telling them. He could gaze at them, and they would do anything he wanted. He talked of biting and drinking the blood of innocent men, women, and children. Whoever crossed his path. He didn't care. He looked no more than sixteen to Johann, but he claimed to be over a hundred years old. He said many vampires were walking the earth.

"The man said he was sickened by what he'd become. He no longer wanted to live, but didn't know how to kill himself. He convinced Johann to help him, but no matter what they tried, the young man's natural sense of preservation could not be thwarted. So Johann and this man created the Illuminati to study and destroy vampires."

"So you guys are the first. Always imitated," Gabriel's sneer was sardonic, "but never duplicated."

Caiaphas watched Gabriel with a blank face, waiting for Gabriel to continue.

So Gabriel did. "Okay. Let's take everything you've said to me at face value. As absolute truth. What do you know about vampires? I mean their origin. Where'd they come from?"

Caiaphas shrugged. His face remained flat.

"Okay." Gabriel thought for a moment. "Who's the head honcho? Are there bigwigs?"

Caiaphas frowned, but not at Gabriel's question. It seemed to Gabriel that Caiaphas was frowning more at his answer. "We refer to the 'big wigs' as the Ancients. We have identified...three definite Ancients, but there may be more. We think so. A total of five. Seven. Maybe more. As far as a...what did you say, a 'head honcho'...? There must be one. We have...definitive evidence from the vampires on that."

"Sounds like a definite maybe to me." Gabriel scratched his chin. "So. For being a worldwide, super-secret organization hunting the same prey for centuries, you don't have much to show for it, do you?"

To Gabriel's surprise, Caiaphas smiled in appreciation of Gabriel's observation as he nodded. "After more than three hundred years, we can tell you how not to kill a vampire and which of the wives' tales, superstitions, and myths are false."

Gabriel stared at Caiaphas for a long moment. Caiaphas stared right back.

Finally, Gabriel looked away. "Okay. Let's get back to the story you just told me. What happened to this Johann character?"

"He left the priesthood and became our first martyr."

"And the young vampire?"

"Hunted down and murdered by his kind."

"But you discovered how to kill a vampire?"

Caiaphas hesitated. "No."

"No?"

"We know that all the conventional ways, garlic or a wooden stake, for example, are useless."

"Why?"

"For the simple reason of, how do you kill a creature which moves faster than you, hears better than you, sees farther than you, smells better than you?"

"The gazelle doesn't hunt the lion." Gabriel stirred his coffee without thinking.

"Precisely. Only recently has the technology existed to create weapons which could kill vampires with specificity."

"What do you mean?"

"Before that, weapons could be created to destroy vampires, but would also destroy humans as well. It wasn't worth the collateral damage. One thousand human souls for a vampire? Unthinkable."

"What about the sun?" Gabriel asked.

"Ah, the sun." Caiaphas swigged a swallow of coffee. "Yes. The sun is the universal constant. The sun kills everything. However. We do know that there are vampires, what we would call day walkers, that are not harmed by the sun."

"Of course."

"We know that all vampires created in the last one-hundred years cannot survive in the sun. Those created before that...we don't know. We have discovered, however, that the term vampires use for themselves is *Akhkharu*."

Gabriel snickered.

Caiaphas agreed. "It sounds made up, doesn't it?"

161

Gabriel nodded.

Caiaphas nodded in understanding. "It's Sumerian. The oldest known language in the world. The earliest written evidence of Sumerian dates back to thirty-two hundred Before Christ- or the Common Era if you are politically correct. It means 'the children of'...something. What that something is, we don't know yet. But if you were to Google the Sumerian language, you would find that the word Akhkharu translates roughly to, the vampire."

"Well, this has all been very...enlightening," Gabriel punned. "Why have you decided to violate the rules of your most sacred order?"

"You are now on their radar," Caiaphas answered.

"*Their*... radar?" Gabriel's tone exuded skepticism. "*Their*... meaning the vampires."

Caiaphas nodded.

"And I'm on the... what, the vampire *bat* radar?"

Caiaphas looked at Gabriel for a long time before answering. "We want to keep you alive, Mr. Hawthorne. We want you to come with us."

"Oh, I think I've gone just as far as I can with you." Gabriel stood up. "See you in the funny papers. Literally." He turned on his heel and made for the exit.

40

Gabriel scanned the parking lot of the café as he tugged the rental car key out of his jeans pocket. Just as he expected, the tall man called Marcus and his partners, who had yet earned names, were in their Crown Victoria tucked away in the darkest parking spot. This gave them a view of the diner and parking lot in one sweep of the eye. Marcus was watching the diner, and the other two men were watching him.

"Good," Gabriel said as he unlocked the car, opened the door, eyes sweeping the back seat, and climbed in. He wanted them to see him drive away. He shut the door, started the engine, and pulled out of the parking space. As he left, he locked eyes with the yet-to-be-named men.

"Why don't you get a name?" Gabriel asked aloud. "Is it because they don't expect you to live long, so there's no reason to get attached?" He pulled out of the parking lot and made a right. He drove a block and hung another right. Another right turn, and he pulled to the side of the road behind the diner. He could see Caiaphas standing, pulling a bill out of his wallet, laying it on the table, then walking towards the exit as a late model dark-colored Ford Taurus pulled up to the café.

"Nothing flashy about this group." Gabriel watched as Caiaphas folded his slender frame into the Taurus. Gabriel chuckled. Nothing flashy at all. These guys were good at blending in. Almost *too* good a job as he watched the Crown Vic slip in behind the Taurus as it left the parking lot. A Taurus and a Crown Vic? Either they were a secret society not necessarily concerned with the finer things in life, or this was the result of today's economy: Secret societies on a budget.

Gabriel made a quick scan for tail cars and then cut through the café parking lot. He pulled out onto the main road. Crazy or not, Caiaphas and Marcus were worthy leads. They knew him and Stefan. And if they didn't kill Stefan, they knew who did. They might even work with them or possibly for them. He picked up the two vehicles' taillights and dropped back.

Gabriel slipped the lid of the small cooler on the backseat floorboard and fished out a can of Diet Pepsi. This might take a while, and though the soda might facilitate the need to pee, he could use the caffeine. He popped the top, swigged, and watched as the two cars traveled precisely at the posted speed limit. He rolled his eyes. Their inconspicuousness was conspicuous. They waited patiently to make a left.

"Looks like they're leaving the city," Gabriel said to the windshield as he checked his map.

Vampires, he thought to himself with another chuckle and a swig of soda. "No, wait. *Akhkharu.*" He pronounced the word with mocking reverence. "I don't care what he says. Sounds made up." He watched the cars ahead of him and sniggered. "They're probably off to an all-night marathon of *Buffy the Vampire Slayer.* Or maybe they were into Live Action Role-Playing and would be donning costumes and running through an abandoned warehouse or even the swamp, playing "I vant to suck your blood." Or maybe—"

The guy stepped out of the darkness and right into the path of Gabriel's car. Gabriel cursed as he swerved to the right, hearing the unmistakable and sickening *thump* of a moving vehicle striking a stationary human body, and the man was gone.

Gabriel cursed again as the car jumped the curb. Tires screeched. He yanked hard on the wheel to avoid a telephone pole and felt the sting of the airbag on his face as it deployed on impact.

Gabriel opened the door and staggered out of the vehicle, expecting to see pavement smeared with flesh. But there was the man, in dirty jeans, cowboy boots, and a long-sleeved dark button-down, untucked, about a hundred feet back, shuffling towards him.

"Are you okay?" Gabriel staggered towards the guy.

The man continued walking, silhouetted by the headlights of an approaching vehicle.

Gabriel shielded his eyes with a hand from the vehicle's high beams. He realized it was traveling fast. Gabriel's stagger turned to a fast walk. "Hey," he yelled. "Get out of the way."

Gabriel could hear the engine revving. Whoever was driving had decided to play chicken with the unsuspecting man and was heading directly for him, picking up speed. "Behind you," Gabriel yelled as he ran towards the man. "BEHIND *YOU.*"

The man turned. The vehicle was less than a car length behind him. It was like watching someone walk into the light, and that's what Gabriel thought was happening, but then the driver slammed on the brakes.

The man was gone.

Tires squealed as the vehicle stopped beside Gabriel, who could now see it was a black Ford E-Series van with extensive modifications. The side doors swung open, and four figures dressed in black, carrying machine guns, jumped from the vehicle.

"Who the—" Gabriel started, but he was interrupted by a man whose face resembled more a chunk of gnarled wood than flesh.

"Get in," he growled at Gabriel as he turned, along with other men in the van, towards the direction they'd come.

"Do you realize you just killed a guy?" Gabriel yelled after the man.

The man's laugh sounded more like the bark of a Rottweiler. "No. But you can bet—"

"There." Another man was pointing down the street. "Approximately two-hundred feet." They all followed the direction of his finger.

The man in the soiled denim and cowboy boots shuffled toward them.

"How...how'd he get there?" Gabriel asked, dumbfounded.

"Maybe he knows how to apparate," the man with the gnarled wooden face growled. "Just disappear and reappear somewhere else like Harry Potter."

"I saw you hit him," Gabriel said. "Run him down."

"Did you?" The man with the gnarled wooden face growled as he raised his assault rifle and pointed it toward the man in denim. In unison, the other men raised their weapons.

"Light it up," The man yelled. The night air was pierced. Bullets struck the road before the man, spitting up little clouds of dust and gravel. Some rounds hit behind the man, but the majority struck him, picking him up and slamming him into the ground.

"*MOVE!*"

Gabriel felt himself lifted off his feet, the air whistling past him, and then the impact of the van's interior wall. The door slammed shut as the tires squealed with the force of acceleration.

"He's coming," One of the men shouted. "He's coming fast."

Gabriel sat up and looked out the back window. The man in the cowboy boots was no longer shuffling. He was running. No. Sprinting. Gabriel watched the blur of pistoning legs, then turned and looked past the driver at the speedometer.

80.

Gabriel looked back.

The man was even closer.

The gnarled man busted out the back window with the butt of his weapon and opened fire.

The man in the boots no longer looked human as he dodged the bullets like they were poorly thrown tennis balls.

"How's he running so fast?" Gabriel asked, feeling stupid. His brain felt as if he'd just guzzled an entire bottle of whisky. He'd *struck* the man. He *knew* he had. The van *should've* hit him, but he'd somehow gotten out of the way. They'd unloaded clips of bullets into him. There was no way this guy could still be coming for them. So either Caiaphas slipped him something in his coffee, and he was experiencing a first-class hallucination, or this was some sort of... what?

"Maybe he's the Six-Million Dollar Man," the gnarled man retorted. "I don't know if you're old enough for that reference. Maybe he's one of the X-Men." He raised his weapon and fired. "He's in the air," he bellowed.

WHAM!

"The roof," another man bellowed.

The men opened fire, filling the van with choking smoke, deafening noise, and hot brass.

Gabriel covered his ears with his hands and looked up to see a hand rip through the steel roof, then peel it back as a soup can. The man's head thrust into the van, the eyes scanning for...

The eyes alighting on Gabriel were like nothing he'd ever seen before. They were wild and alive, but not with the light of life. Burning, but not lustful. They didn't see Gabriel as a human or even as meat. Gabriel sensed that those eyes saw his soul deep within him and wanted to devour it.

The man smiled.

Gabriel saw fangs, but they didn't frighten him. Not like his smile did. It was hideous and gruesome, sending chills of terror through Gabriel.

"*Now,*" the gnarled man barked.

Gabriel felt every bone in his body dislocate. He could smell the fetid odor of burnt flesh, hair, and vinyl. Taste acrid smoke. He couldn't hear or see anything for a few long moments. He lay there in a muffled silence as a million points of light danced in front of him wherever he looked.

Gradually, the lights began to fade. His ears felt like he'd been front row at a heavy metal concert, but he could hear. He coughed and choked.

"You okay?" The gnarled man was in his face.

Gabriel strained his eyes to bring the man into focus. The man's face was covered in soot. His clothes looked and smelled like they'd been on fire, which Gabriel realized they probably had been.

Gabriel fought through the daze. Was he okay? He could see. Smell. His ears were filled with a violent ring, but he'd heard the man ask him a question. He realized he probably looked and smelled the same as the gnarled man. Nothing seemed broken. He nodded his head. The man cuffed him on the shoulder.

"What... what was *that*?" Gabriel felt like his mouth was full of cotton.

The gnarled man smiled. "Well. It might've been Superman. Or maybe an alien. Or even an android. But one thing you know for sure. It wasn't no vampire." He cuffed Gabriel on the shoulder again, his Rottweiler laugh, and the laughter of all the other men, filling the van.

41

The van pulled off the highway onto a gravel road Gabriel would've sworn hadn't been maintained in years. After the laughter had died down, a guy called Spinner checked everyone out for injuries. Spinner then applied a salve to each man's hands and face. Gabriel hadn't realized how badly his skin hurt until it *stopped* hurting. Then everyone hunkered down where they were and kept to their thoughts, except the guy called Husqvarna. He quickly fell into a steady snore.

Gabriel winced as the driver, Gabriel would swear, deliberately found another pothole.

"We spend a lot of money making sure this road looks unmaintained." The gnarled man's voice was a quiet rumble. "It keeps the folks who like to go exploring and the teenagers out. But it does make for a bone-jarring ride." He offered his hand to Gabriel.

Gabriel took the man's hand, feeling the hard calluses and vice-like grip. He remembered being five years old, and his grandfather, a retired cop turned mechanic, teaching him how to shake a man's hand.

"Everything you need to know about a man," his grandfather would say, "is in his handshake, Gabriel. No matter what he says or does or claims he can do. If he doesn't grip your hand, then he's a man with no self-esteem. Don't be intimidated by a man like that. He may look like he can pound you into the ground, but he has no inner strength."

This man had a firm grip, but he didn't try to break the bones in Gabriel's hand, which his grandfather had said was a man compensating for low self-esteem. There were only three types of men, according to Gabriel's grandfather. Men with no self-esteem, low self-esteem, and those esteemed by other men. This man was the last type.

"Name's Rothenberg. But everyone calls me Rotty."

Gabriel looked into the gnarled man's face, blackened with soot, looked at the man's hands, covered in hair, and started to laugh.

Rotty knew what Gabriel was thinking. "Don't worry. My bite is always worse than my bark." He started laughing too.

Gabriel didn't think he'd stop laughing. Not until the laughter died in his throat as suddenly and as surely as the guy in the cowboy boots *should have*. He may still be very much alive for all he knew. That thought had stopped his laughter.

And he'd come for me. No. He'd been...hunting me. Gabriel shivered.

Gabriel thought Caiaphas was right. Someone was aware of him. He was on someone's radar. He wasn't yet ready to call that someone 'vampire.'

"Akhkharu." The word escaped past his lips in a reverential whisper. He shivered again. After what he'd just seen, he decided the word 'vampire' was much less frightening. Regardless, being on their radar was not a safe place to be.

The van stopped in front of a large, rundown antebellum mansion.

"All right, boys," Rotty said, opening the side door. "Up and at 'em. We're here."

The men pulled themselves from the van and trudged into the darkness.

"Hit the rack. You can shower in the morning," Rotty called after them as he helped Gabriel from the van. He gestured towards the house. "Follow me, Hawthorne."

Rotty sprang up the steps of the mansion two at a time. The evening's events hadn't worn him out. Gabriel took each step. Rotty opened the door, spilling light out and down the staircase. A shadow stepped into the doorway.

Caiaphas.

"Mr. Hawthorne," Caiaphas said in a relieved voice. "I'm glad you're all right."

Gabriel walked up the last few steps and stood on the porch, swaying.

"There is much to discuss, but I think it can wait." He called over his shoulder. "Marcus."

Marcus appeared immediately behind him.

"Show Mr. Hawthorne to his room, please." Caiaphas gestured for Gabriel to enter. "Until tomorrow, then." Caiaphas turned and walked into another room, with Rotty close behind him.

Without a word, Marcus led Gabriel to an elevator. They took it to the second floor. Marcus walked down a hallway to a door at the end. He opened the door, flipped on the bedside light, and stepped aside.

Gabriel walked into the room and collapsed onto the bed. He suddenly felt the mental exhaustion of the evening settle over his body like a thousand-pound blanket. Stretching out onto the bed, he reached up and felt for the lamp. Once he found it, he turned it off, plunging the room into darkness. He thought about this evening, about what he'd seen. He saw in the dark those eyes, that smile, and turned the bedside light back on.

42

Georges sat at his desk and stared without blinking at the rack of monitors on the wall across from him. His eyes never wavered from the one focused on the old iron door and sidewalk. A woman stood behind him, still wearing an elegant cocktail dress, caressing his shoulders.

"Come join us on the couch, Georges. The leather's cold without you." She nodded toward the couch, where the other two women sat, watching him. "You haven't had Veronica yet. You know how she gets when she feels left out."

On cue, Veronica put on her best pout. It was for naught.

Georges hadn't taken an eye off that monitor since he'd hung up the phone fifty-six minutes ago. His throat made a loud, dry click as he swallowed hard at this realization. "Fifty-six minutes," his voice was little more than a dull rasp.

The three women stared at each other, nonplussed.

The woman behind Georges finally shrugged and moved over to the couch. She plopped down on the sofa beside Veronica, and the two started thumbing through a Cosmopolitan magazine as the third picked up an emery board and started filing her nails.

Georges had forgotten about the women on the couch. His eyes were still planted on the monitor while his mind's eye replayed the scene that had taken place in his office fifty-seven minutes before. He'd been sitting on the couch, two women making sure the woman he was drinking from didn't fall from his lap, Veronica whining how it was her turn now.

The door had opened, and Philippe walked in carrying a scrap of fabric. "I'm sorry, Georges."

Georges had looked up.

"This is all we could find of Allain. Hawthorne's car was still there, crashed into a telephone pole. There were shell casings everywhere."

Georges looked at the fabric. "That's all?"

Philippe grimaced. "The...pieces...are in a box." His voice sounded as if he were talking about his brother. "This...is all I could...bring myself...to show you."

"And Hawthorne?" Georges asked hopefully.

Philippe had only shaken his head.

Georges nodded, stunned at what he'd heard. "Thank you, Philippe. Attend to Allain's remains."

Philippe nodded weakly and staggered from the room.

Georges had stood, forgetting there'd been a woman in his lap. She'd hissed when her backside hit the floor.

He'd ignored her protests and Veronica's renewed whine as he moved to the phone. For the first time in more than a century, he felt tired. Exhausted. His legs felt like he was trying to walk through the swamp again, lifting a leg with all his effort from the mud, hearing the wet *thwack* as his foot came free, sloshing a step forward, then the wet *thwop* as the slimy, sticky mix swallowed his foot again.

He'd finally made it to his desk and the phone. Picking up the receiver, his hands trembling, he'd dialed her number three times before he got it right. He'd shivered at her silence as she listened to him tell her what had happened. She told him she'd be in his office in an hour. Stillness after she'd disconnected the call.

His eyes shot immediately to the screen monitoring the iron front door. They hadn't blinked from it since. He'd sat down heavily and waited.

Fifty-nine minutes.

The Grandfather clock behind him chimed two times.

She was at the front door.

Isabella hadn't walked into the frame. The space in front of the door had been empty. Then in less than a tenth of a second, she was there.

George felt his heart drop into his intestines. He watched as she knocked on the door. The small viewing door opened, then the door. As she walked through the iron door, Georges' eyes twitched to the next monitor showing the inner room. The door opened. She walked down the hall of chocolate and purple brocade. He watched her on the monitor as she moved into the club. He watched as dancers stopped dancing, drinkers stopped drinking, and servers stopped serving.

He watched as she walked up to the office door. He heard the knock on the door as he looked at her on the monitor. Saw the terrified bartender slowly creep up, the fear of being noticed by her contorting his face, as he hit the button under his bar. The door opened.

Georges's eyes flicked from the monitor to Isabella stepping into the room.

Isabella eyed the women. They bolted for the open door; their mouths tore open in silent screams. Isabella shut the door and turned to face Georges.

"I—"

Isabella lifted a finger to her lips to silence him, then used the same finger to beckon him to her.

He obeyed.

She ran that finger across his forehead, over the bridge of his nose, down over his lips, and to his chin. "You know you've always been my favorite," she purred. "Now, tell me again what happened, and don't forget any details."

Georges felt his heart climb up his spine back to its place in his chest. He told Isabella of LeBlanc and how he'd foolishly killed an investigator and left his body to be discovered by a tourist, how LeBlanc had come to Georges and told him about this after the man's partner, Gabriel Hawthorne, had paid him a visit, how he'd killed LeBlanc for his foolishness and sent Allain, his best tracker, to find Hawthorne and bring him back dead or alive, and how the pieces of Allain's body fit in a shoebox, and Hawthorne had escaped.

Running her hand over his chest, shoulders, and back, Isabella walked around him as he spoke. When she finished, she stopped before him, cupped his face with her hands, and kissed his lips.

"You have been my lover and a loyal and faithful steward. In over a hundred years, you have never failed me. You have nothing to fear."

It happened in an instant. One moment, he was standing, and the next, he was across the room, on his back on his desk, Isabella's fingers digging into his throat.

Her eyes blazed deadly black. "However." Her fangs sprang from her gums razor-sharp. "You must be punished." Her smile was vicious. "This will hurt."

Georges shrieked as she planted her fangs into his right eye.

43

Gabriel's eyes fluttered open. Bright sunshine streamed through the opened blinds. He squinted and rolled heavily onto his back, staring blearily at the ceiling as his brain tried to focus. He'd had the most amazing dreams. Amazing wasn't the right word. Neither was the word dreams. Nightmares. That wasn't the right word either, but it was the closest. Horrible nightmares of a vampire chasing him. Catching him. Devouring him. They were just nightmares, he reminded himself. Nightmares that had played and replayed on the silver screen of his mind's eye after he'd finally fallen asleep.

He looked over at the nightstand. The light was still on. Usually, he couldn't sleep with artificial light burning in the room, but that's not what had kept him awake last night. That lamp was as much a comfort to him as a light is to a child going to bed at night, except that what a child is frightened of is just the dark. What had frightened Gabriel into sleeping with the light on, into having those nightmares, was an *actual* monster.

Had he not experienced the events of last night, he would've thought the person telling him the tale had a good idea for a Hollywood movie. Vampires walked the earth, and a secret organization most people associated with trying to destroy the church was created to destroy them. Last night, an ordinary guy from D.C. appeared on the vampire radar, and the vampires sent an executioner to deal with him.

There was a short knock on the door. Gabriel immediately reached towards his holster and grabbed air. He looked.

Empty.

He hissed an expletive as his eyes scanned the room. This was not the moment to find yourself with your proverbial pants around your ankles. This was one of those moments when that dream of walking into class or the office in your underwear would be welcomed by the reality of being caught without your firearm.

There were only two places Gabriel kept his weapon. His holster or under his pillow. He hadn't done anything with it. Someone else had. He hissed the expletive again. It was like waking up and finding someone had removed your trousers, stolen your boxers, and slipped your pants back on you while you were sleeping. He cursed one more time for good measure.

The door swung open. Marcus stood there. He saw Gabriel, hand still at his holster, gripping air. "You're up. Good." His tone was pleasant. "I always hate waking a person the morning after illumination." He pointed to Gabriel's empty holster. "They're always ready to shoot first and ask questions later."

Gabriel was not amused.

"We took it as a precaution. For our safety, more than yours. Rotty has it locked up."

"And he'll be giving it back to me...?" Gabriel was up and off the bed in one quick, fluid motion; his eyes narrowed to slits, right hand balling into a fist.

"Soon," Marcus said, taking an involuntary step backward. "I assure you, hurting me won't return your firearm to you any quicker." Marcus pointed to a door across the room. "Lavatory is through there. You'll find fresh towels behind the door, but please be quick." He waved at a chair. "Your bag. Everything is there. When you're ready, go down the staircase, U-turn, and the second door on the right. We'll see you in fifteen minutes." Marcus nodded and closed the door.

Gabriel looked at the bag. The last time he'd seen it was in his hotel room in New Orleans. The Illuminati had been hunting him as well.

Grabbing his toiletries bag, Gabriel headed for the shower. Fifteen minutes later, a washed, shaved, and dressed Gabriel pushed open the second door on the right to find Caiaphas and Marcus seated at a breakfast table. They were drinking coffee and reading documents in Manila folders. Caiaphas looked up.

"Ah, Mr. Hawthorne." He closed the manila folder. "I trust you slept well."

"When he finally slept," Rotty growled. He was leaning against the kitchen counter, drinking a cup of coffee. He smiled. "Don't worry. It'll get easier from here on out."

Gabriel looked at Rotty. "My Beretta?"

Rotty flashed a knowing smile. "I feel naked without mine, too. I'll get it back to you after."

"After what?" Gabriel persisted.

Caiaphas gestured to one of the kitchen chairs. "Please have a seat. And some coffee. Are you hungry?"

Gabriel sat down and shook his head. "Just coffee."

Rotty brought the coffee pot and a mug to the table and set them in front of Gabriel. He then sat down in another chair as Marcus pushed a creamer and a sugar bowl to Gabriel.

"We need to have an after-action review with you about last night," Rotty said. "It would've been better last night when it was still fresh. But you weren't in any condition."

"What's to tell?" Gabriel sipped at the coffee. It tasted wonderful. "You were there."

"Yes," Caiaphas responded. "But what we don't know is why. Vampires don't usually hunt humans. They have more subtle and efficient methods. We'd also like your evaluation of Alpha Team's actions during your extraction."

Gabriel summarized the events of the day before, including his run-in with the mysterious Doctor Anderson at the Coroner's office and the discovery of the stamp for "V". Caiaphas frowned at Marcus, but Rotty guffawed.

"As for my extraction evaluation," Gabriel drained the last of his cup. "I'm alive, so I think they did a bang-up job with my...extraction."

Caiaphas was interested in how Gabriel and Stefan came to be on Roman and Cain Dvanaesti's trail. Rotty first probed Gabriel's experience as a D.C. cop and then as a private investigator. Gabriel felt as if he were interviewing for the head of security position. He expressed this observation.

Caiaphas, Marcus, and Rotty looked at each other before Rotty finally said, "Make no mistake about this, Hawthorne. *I'm* Chief of Security and Head of Military Operations."

Marcus added, "You are no longer safe in your life in D.C., Mr. Hawthorne. Surely you realize that."

"No, I don't." Gabriel's defiant stare met each man.

Caiaphas ignored the defiance. "We offer you something you haven't had, Mr. Hawthorne, not since your days as a police officer. A life with real purpose."

"You mean join the Illuminati?" Gabriel asked, not hiding his suspicion.

Caiaphas watched Gabriel for a moment before turning to Rotty. "Show him the compound."

44

Sweat beaded Gabriel's forehead as he and Rotty stood on the mansion's veranda. It was just after nine in the morning, and the heat and humidity already lay across them like a damp sponge. Gabriel mopped his forehead, feeling his shirt stick to his back. It was like Miami, Gabriel reflected, without the beach, tropical breeze, or scantily clad taut bronze bodies. He swatted his neck. They did, however, have mosquitoes the size of pelicans.

"About the after-action review," Rotty pulled a cigar out of his black fatigue blouse, "before that vampire stepped out in front of your vehicle last night, you never saw us, never saw them." He bit off the end, stuck it into his mouth, and offered a second cigar to Gabriel.

Gabriel shook his head.

"Review over." Rotty stuffed the second cigar into his pocket and pulled out a lighter. "The Illuminati has twelve major compounds around the globe, including South America, Asia, and Russia. The compounds house men and munitions twenty-four-seven. More than a hundred cells are spread throughout the world. All cells report to one command cell. The command cell is stationed closest to the center of vampire activity. In this case, that's New Orleans.

"There are six members of the Council, and each is stationed at a different compound to ensure the safety of the Council members. Caiaphas is the Council Chief. Marcus is being groomed to one day take his place as Caiaphas."

"What about you?" Gabriel asked.

Rotty smiled and chewed on the end of his cigar, exhaling a cloud of smoke. "I'm a soldier, Hawthorne—"

"Call me Gabe," Gabriel interrupted.

Rotty shook his head and spat off the back porch. "We're not that close yet."

Gabriel responded, "I think saving my life qualifies."

"I think you saving my life qualifies." Rotty waved a dismissive hand at him. "At this compound, we have research and development facilities, manufacturing facilities, shooting ranges, and barracks." He stepped off the porch.

Gabriel didn't follow. "Research and development? Manufacturing?"

"Let me show you." Rotty walked towards a run-down building. "This particular compound, as you might have guessed, was a plantation built long before the Civil War. We've spent a lot of money making sure the buildings and the grounds all look abandoned." They reached the rusty door. "Inside, however, each building is state-of-the-art." Gabriel had to agree as he looked at the building. He thought a strong wind might bring it down. Wind? Gabriel thought. I could probably knock it over if I just blew hard enough.

Rotty opened the door. It swung with effortless silence despite its rusty hinges. He waved Gabriel in. Gabriel stepped through the door and found himself not actually in the building but in a small room. Rotty stepped through and closed the door. They were plunged into darkness, but then a light flipped on. Gabriel could see they were facing a thick steel door. On the wall next to the door was a digital keypad. Rotty punched in a code. The keypad changed colors, and Gabriel could hear what sounded like someone unscrewing the top of a bottle of soda.

"Vacuum seal?" Gabriel hadn't expected that. These guys took their security seriously.

"For freshness," Rotty answered as he pulled the door open.

Or not, Gabriel thought as he peeked his head through. The room was enormous and looked lit by natural sunlight. Gabriel looked up to see no skylights, only halogen lighting tracks. Twenty-plus men and women in black fatigues like Rotty's, beneath white lab coats, sat at different metal computer and other workstations.

"Welcome to the Geek Squad," Rotty stepped into the room. "Hey, Giblet." He waved at a short, chubby man with a salt-and-pepper buzz cut. "Come over here for a sec."

Giblet rolled his eyes and walked over to Rotty. "The name's Gibble," the man said, not hiding his irritation. "Why must you insist on calling me something as stupid-sounding as Giblet?"

Rotty shot Gabriel a sideways glance. "And Gibble isn't stupid sounding at all."

"No, it's not," the man responded. "*Rotty*," he added in a waspish tone.

Rotty barked, then clamped down one of his massive paws on Giblet's shoulder, causing the man's knees to buckle. "Why don't you show Hawthorne here what you research pukes do while I pay my respects to the latrine?"

Rotty left. Giblet held out a hand to Gabriel. "Pleased to meet you, Mr. Hawthorne."

"Call me Gabe," Gabriel said with a smile, but immediately started frowning. Giblet was shaking his head.

"That just won't do, Mr. Hawthorne." He turned and made a wide-sweeping gesture with his hands. "This is the R and D department. Should you choose to work in our department, you will be tasked with helping to develop the weapons and techniques Rotty and the combat teams can use to dispose of vampires."

"Should I choose?" Gabriel was dumbfounded.

Giblet nodded his head. "We may not be as flashy as the combat teams, but daresay I we're as important. Or we have been in the last ten years anyway."

"Why only in the last ten years?" Gabriel asked.

Giblet reddened. "Well, it's only been in the last ten years that the technology's existed to kill a vampire."

"What about the old standbys of a hammer and a stake?"

"I'm sorry. I thought you were illumined." Giblet's response was flavored with disappointment.

"It's only been about twelve hours. Forgive me."

"Ah, well," Giblet said in relief. "In that case. The old wives' tale about sneaking up on a vampire when it's in stasis is just that, a wives' tale. When vampires are in stasis, that is, they've settled in for the night or day, as the case may be, a vampire's complete attention is on their security. They have no distractions. They're the best home security system around. They can hear you and smell you before you're on the premises, and once you are, they can generally get you to come to them. Plant it inside your head like it's your idea. Once you're gazing upon them...well. Let's just say the only thing as scary as a waking vampire is a" putting his hands up in quotation marks, "sleeping one.

"Even if it didn't get you into believing you want to be there, you might as well try to drive a wooden stake through the sidewalk with a sledgehammer.

Actually, there's no contest. The sidewalk would lose long before the vampire ever did."

"How do you know?" Gabriel asked.

Giblet sighed darkly. "Experience, Mr. Hawthorne. Many unfortunate years of experience."

"Okay. What about garlic?" Gabriel prompted.

"Maybe if you were going to try to breathe on them to death." Giblet may not have meant to sound sarcastic, but it felt that way to Gabriel.

Gabriel mulled over what Caiaphas told him about vampires in the café and what Giblet was saying now. "So are all the myths about k

"Well," Giblet rifled around in his lab coat pocket until he could find a wad of paper towels. He mopped his head. "No reflection. Myth. They are made of a substance that occupies space. Silver is a killer. Myth."

"Myth?" Gabriel asked, an eyebrow raised in incredulity.

Giblet shrugged. "For all intents and purposes. Vampires seem to have an allergy, but it's not silver. What do you know about isotopes?"

"That the word has three syllables," Gabriel answered.

"Cute. Well, it's not silver but an isotope of silver that they're allergic to. It's kind of like poison ivy. Rub silver on a vampire's skin, and he'll break out in a rash where his skin was in contact with the silver. Maybe even boils. It all depends on the silver's purity. So one of the things we do here is to extract the isotope from the silver, reproduce it on a massive scale so we have lots, and then put it into ordnance that the combat teams can use."

"And this has been all in the last ten years?"

Giblet moved to a computer and pressed a few buttons. "Take a look at this."

Gabriel watched as the computer screen illuminated with footage of six men wearing black fatigues and carrying automatic weapons. A second passes, and all six men are lying dead. Giblet punched a few more buttons, and the footage replayed. One second, each man is living. The next, every man is dead.

Gabriel gaped at the computer screen. "Can you turn the volume up?"

"The volume's maxed." Giblet pushed another button. "Here's the footage frame by frame."

The footage reset. Six armed men in black fatigues. The next showed the same image. The next frame revealed two men dead and a blur moving toward a third man. In the next frame, four men were deceased, and the blur moved toward the fifth man. The next frame and the last two men are dead, and the blur is gone.

"That was twenty-four frames per second slowed down to frame by frame, and we can only isolate a fuzzy blur. How do you stake something or lop the head off something moving that fast? Or even set fire to it?"

"So no vampires could be killed up until ten years ago." Gabriel stood transfixed by the image on the computer screen.

"No. There was the occasional fluke accident like today. And then there was the occasional vampire ready to die but not by his own hand."

"Seems hopeless." Gabriel offered.

Giblet shook his head. "All it takes is one success, and then we can try again."

Gabriel tore his gaze away from the screen. "And how do you try again?"

Giblet moved to a table where two women were cutting off tissue samples from a severed arm. "This came in last night. Rotty's on an alpha team. After they finish with an altercation, a second team, called a Bravo team, moves in to collect evidence and make the site look as normal as possible. This arm came from the vampire who attacked you last night."

"So you killed it?" Gabriel asked, feeling his skin crawl as if he were looking at an oversized hairy banana spider.

"We hope so. In truth, we just don't know. Not without eyewitness verification, which can be difficult to come by. So the only way we know is by field testing." He pointed to the arm. "And then field testing." Giblet ran a chubby hand over his buzzcut. "Field testing is the only way. We've lost a lot of good men."

"*I've* lost a lot of good men. And women." It was Rotty.

"We're on the same team," Giblet said in tired resignation as if he'd had this argument with Rotty many times before. "We may not be on the front line with you, but we feel it when someone doesn't return. That's a failure to us."

"And a dead friend to me." Rotty's tone made it clear the topic was closed. He looked at Gabriel. "I'll show you where we practice what they preach."

Rotty took Gabriel into another building that housed shooting ranges. Men and women shot at targets using fully automatic handguns and rifles.

He led Gabriel over to a table. "They're shooting target rounds. But this is what we use in the field. Let me give you a demo." He looked up towards a man supervising the shooters. "Joker."

The man turned towards him.

"Hook me up with a piece of meat, will ya? I want to give Hawthorne here a demonstration."

Joker nodded and turned back to the shooters, shouting, "Ceasefire, ceasefire, ceasefire." He pointed at a young man and woman. "Clear your weapons and place them on the line, then hook up a piece of meat from the locker for Rotty."

The two nodded, cleared their weapons, put them on safety, and dropped them on the line. They hustled toward a small walk-in freezer in the back corner of the building.

The others cleared their weapons, leaving them on the line, then stepped back without a word. Gabriel noticed a tiny grin on each person's face as they fell quietly into parade rest with their arms tucked behind them.

Joker went to the table and began loading rounds into two magazines.

Gabriel stared in horror as the young man and woman returned with the naked torso of a man. "Is that a...?" Gabriel couldn't finish.

"Vampire," Rotty said without looking up. "We don't have many, but what we have...well, let's just say we're like the Native Americans with the buffalo. We don't let any part go to waste. Once we're done testing them, if there's anything left, we put it in the locker. That way, we've got living vampire tissue to work with."

"Living?" Gabriel was skeptical.

"Only real way to kill a vampire, Hawthorne, is burning. Cut the head off. The body is still dangerous if you get too close. Reflex could rip your head right off your body. The locker's got two sections. The first keeps the tissue cold, which slows down the regeneration process. The second contains a vat of liquid nitrogen. Liquid nitro slows the regeneration process down to almost nil. Again, the only way to stop regeneration is to incinerate the tissue."

"But what about winter?" Gabriel asked without thinking and then felt foolish.

"Good question. The truth is, we don't know. Except that a vampire with its head still attached to its body can regenerate fast, and the older it is, the faster it regenerates. All the tissue we have has been separated from the head. We never let tissue sit at room temperature to see how it regenerates for obvious reasons." He watched the young man and woman slap the torso onto two hooks and level it. "That's fine. Make it twenty-five feet."

The young man pressed a button, and the torso moved toward them. Gabriel took an involuntary step back.

"Relax, Hawthorne," Rotty said. "I won't let it get you."

There was some muffled giggling behind them, but Joker turned to the gathered shooters. "Shut it." The group went quiet.

"We use nine-millimeter rounds, Hawthorne." Rotty pulled his Glock from his side holster. "As you know from your days with a badge, it's a cheap and highly versatile round. It can be used in both handguns and submachine guns. It can be made into a subsonic round and used with a suppressor." He held up his Glock. "This is a regular round right out of the box."

Joker handed Gabriel earmuffs to protect his ears, and he quickly put them on as Rotty chambered a round, stepped up to the line, aimed, and fired three shots into the torso.

The torso didn't shudder.

Gabriel would've sworn Rotty missed if he hadn't seen the entry wounds, which had almost sealed themselves before he could turn to Rotty.

"As you can see," Rotty said as he moved back to the table, dropping his magazine and clearing his Glock, "the nine-millimeter, like pretty much any standard out-of-the-box ammo, isn't going to hurt a vampire. You have to throw a lot at it just to slow it down."

Joker handed Rotty one of the magazines he'd prepared. "This is what we call a Phase One round. This was after the Geek Squad learned to synthetically mass-produce the isotope in a solid form." He pointed at the round. "It's the standard nine, but its tip and core are made up of the isotope."

Rotty slapped in the magazine, chambered a round, stepped up to the line, aimed, and fired three times. The torso shuddered a little. Gabriel could see three holes right through the torso.

Rotty turned to him, dropping the magazine and clearing the sidearm with one fluid motion. "As you can see, this causes a hole that does not heal as quickly or easily. The problem with this delivery system is that it punches right through. The round leaves a light residue of the isotope in the wound, so it heals a little more slowly." He pointed back to the torso. "But it does heal."

Gabriel looked, and sure enough, the holes were gradually getting smaller.

Joker handed Rotty another magazine.

Rotty took the magazine and smiled. He looked like a rottweiler about to sink its teeth into a small but tasty animal. "This bad boy is what we call Phase Two. It combines the nine-round with the solid isotope tip. In the center is a cellulose capsule filled with the isotope in liquid form. The tip is split. So it frays and fragments upon impact with the vampire. The cellulose capsule is released and immediately dissolves, releasing the liquid isotope which reacts quickly with the vampire's soft tissues."

He slapped in the magazine, chambered, aimed, and fired three times into the torso without approaching the line. This time, the entire torso rocked back and forth on the hooks.

Gabriel's first thought was that it was like watching a horror movie. The torso gave a violent shudder, as if a man was being hit by the rounds, and continued to shudder as the holes grew. The insides sizzled and popped, sloughing off and falling to the floor in a hot, liquefied form like thick bacon grease. Then the smell hit Gabriel's nostrils, and he retched.

"As you can see," Rotty said as he drew in a deep breath. "The liquid isotope eats the vampire from the inside out. Wolfs it down." He and Joker laughed.

Gabriel retched again.

"That smell," Rotty inhaled, "That vampire rot smell."

Joker took a deep breath. "I love the smell of vampire dying in the morning." He and Rotty laughed again.

Rotty grabbed Gabriel by the shoulders. "Let's get you some fresh air. You're looking green." He loped out of the building.

Gabriel gulped deep inhalations of fresh air, closed his eyes, and looked up. He could see his eyelids through a reddish hue. Nausea passed after a few more breaths. "I've got one question."

"And I know just what it is," Rotty said.

Gabriel opened his eyes and looked at him.

"Why didn't we use Phase Two last night? The answer's simple. We didn't have them." Rotty nodded to the building behind them. "Those were fresh off the assembly line this morning. That's the first batch. But don't worry. By this time next week, every compound and cell around the world will have them, and finally, we won't be bringing knives to a gunfight anymore." He looked around, locked eyes on a building, and Gabriel watched as the smile split his face wide like a kid on Christmas morning. "Come on. You got to see this one."

As he punched the numbers into the digital keypad, he asked, "Remember Giblet and his geeks?"

"Sounds like a punk rock band," Gabriel remarked.

Rotty barked his laugh again. "Good one. Well, these guys make those punkers look like Rambo."

"Who are these guys?" Gabriel took a hesitant step into the building.

"The guys who don't think inside the box. Ever."

Inside the building, eight steel compartments sat in a row, two by two. The compartments all had steel girders holding steel plates around them to protect them from each other.

"Watch your step." Rotty led Gabriel between the plates and the compartments, stepping over and crawling under girders. They looked through windows so thick that the people in the rooms were distorted.

"These guys are researching and developing some very crazy stuff." He pointed at one compartment. "Here lately, they've been playing with different delivery systems. They recently began synthetically reproducing the isotope. They were able to replicate it as a solid first. And then a liquid. Now they're on the cusp of mass-producing it as a gas. Once that happens, if we can safely deliver it in an aerosol or a crop duster, we could spray it odorless and colorless into the atmosphere in the evening and count the dead vampires in the morning." Rotty's smile was almost vulgar at this thought. "Very cool stuff. But we're not even in the testing phase of that. We need to make sure it's completely harmless to every living thing on the planet first."

"Vampires aren't living?" Gabriel asked.

"No," Rotty responded. "They're dead." He popped Gabriel on the shoulder. "Let's get some chow and talk to Caiaphas and Marcus."

45

Gabriel's stomach growled as the odors of food cooking wafted through the house from the kitchen. He and Rotty sat down at the table with Caiaphas and Marcus.

"I do hope you like Cajun and Creole cooking, Mr. Hawthorne," Caiaphas said as he spread his napkin in his lap.

Gabriel inhaled deeply. His stomach growled louder this time.

"I think his stomach's a fan." Rotty snorted.

A woman entered the dining room carrying a serving tray with four bowls.

"Thank you." Caiaphas picked up his spoon.

The woman acknowledged his gratitude with a nod. Once the bowls were down, the woman looked over the table. Satisfied the diners had everything they needed, she left without uttering a word.

Gabriel looked down into the bowl and frowned at the thick, mottled green and brown...stuff was the only word Gabriel could think of.

"Smothered okra, Mr. Hawthorne." Marcus picked up his spoon and scooped some up. "But it may be a bit spicy for your palate."

Gabriel ran his spoon through the smothered okra. It looked like something you should top a fajita with, not eat as an appetizer or soup. The other men were quickly devouring the contents of their bowls, the scraping of silverware on ceramic interrupted only by the satisfied *Mmms* and *Ahhhs*. He spooned some into his mouth. It was wonderful. Gabriel hurried to catch up with the other men.

Caiaphas wiped his chin with his napkin. "So what do you think of our compound, Mr. Hawthorne?"

Gabriel swallowed and set his spoon down. "Well." He hesitated. The men all looked at him with expectation. "You've got quite the setup here. Security. Grow your own food. Make your own weapons. Train your own soldiers. You remind me of those survivalists you see on television preparing for the final race war."

Rotty growled. "You stupid son of—"

Caiaphas held up a hand. "Mr. Hawthorne speaks correctly, Rotty. This is a race war. The race of man against the race of vampires. It is a war we've been fighting for centuries."

"And for the first time, we can win that war," Rotty interjected.

"Perhaps," Marcus said. His voice was soft.

"Perhaps?" Rotty asked. "You've seen what the Phase Twos can do."

"On a range, yes." Caiaphas's voice was calm. "But vampires in the field are a *moving* target. We've yet to discover how many bullets will be needed to take down a vampire. Nor what the impact on the surrounding environment will be."

Rotty waved a dismissive hand. "Whatever the impact, it's worth it. Anything's worth a dead vampire."

"To include a dead innocent?" Caiaphas's eyebrows arched high.

Rotty opened his mouth to speak, but closed his mouth as he stared at Caiaphas.

Gabriel looked between Caiaphas, whose expression looked like a father patiently waiting for his teenage son to understand why he can't have the car on Saturday, and Rotty, who looked like a teenager unable to come to grips with the injustice of it all. "Who exactly are the innocents?"

"Anyone not associated with the vampires." Rotty's tone was cold. Without emotion. He was repeating an answer by rote that no longer held any meaning to him. He didn't take his eyes off Caiaphas.

"Anyone?" Gabriel repeated.

"If you are concerned about Miss Claudia Bennett's well-being, Mr. Hawthorne, your concerns are well-placed. She's not innocent," Caiaphas said.

"How'd you know about—"

"We know everything there is to know about you, Hawthorne." Rotty interrupted. Gabriel opened his mouth to respond, but another woman entered the dining room and collected the bowls, while the previous server entered, carrying plates with sandwiches. She set a plate in front of each man.

Gabriel's mouth watered as he eyed the large, homemade baguette stuffed with...

"Ah," Caiaphas exclaimed in delight. "Portabella mushroom French dips."

189

Gabriel lifted the top piece of bread. What he thought was roast beef, he could now see were mushrooms, not covered in cheese but in caramelized onions, garlic, and what smelled like homemade horseradish sauce. "So you guys are vegans?"

"Not vegans, Mr. Hawthorne," Marcus explained. "We are, as Rotty likes to say, organivores. In that everything we eat is organic."

Rotty spoke through a mouthful of his sandwich. "Food has a direct impact on your body chemistry. In this case, we're talking about blood. You and I can't smell human blood. But a vampire can."

Gabriel picked up the sandwich and took a bite. It wasn't roast beef, but it was good.

"That's one of the few things the movies get right." Rotty took another bite.

"You see," Marcus said, "We think the vampires are smelling the proteins and acids in the blood. Diets high in meat, especially red meat, contain more protein and acid in the bloodstream than diets high in fruits, nuts, and vegetables. The vampires can smell it."

"Kind of like the difference between smelling a salad sitting in a bowl and smelling a steak sizzling on the grill." Rotty had already devoured his sandwich and was waving a finger toward the kitchen.

"So our diet isn't so much a lifestyle choice as a militaristic one," Marcus added.

"Like an olfactory camouflage?" Gabriel offered.

"Exactly," Rotty confirmed. "Like when you were a kid camping and to blend into the environment to keep predators away, you stood in the smoke from the campfire. Same idea."

"So you end up smelling like a tree or a bush to a vampire?" Gabriel popped the last of his sandwich into his mouth.

"More like a deer or some other warm-blooded herbivore," Rotty corrected.

"But don't some vampires choose to live off of the blood of animals?" Gabriel couldn't believe he was asking these questions and discussing vampires with three other grown and well-educated men. Where was the host who popped out of the woodwork to shout 'Gotcha!' in your face and point to where the camera was hiding?

Rotty laughed. "You've been watching too many movies. Just what the vampires want you to do. They're the ones writing the novels and the movie scripts or charming humans to write them. And we start thinking that's the way it's always been. You know, forty years ago, the stories didn't have this notion that there were kinder, gentler vampires. Here lately..." Rotty's voice trailed off to let someone else continue the explanation.

Marcus picked it up. "An injured vampire isolated from its normal food source may drink the blood of a deer or elk, but that would be the only case. Otherwise, all vampires choose to live off the blood of one animal: humans."

"So, Mr. Hawthorne." Caiaphas picked up the conversation. "Each member of the Illuminati is to some degree a vegan."

"What do you mean, some degree?"

Rotty frowned. "Well, since even the rats and wildlife in the Big Apple eat processed...everything, the cells and microcells in New York City need to supplement their organic diet with processed foods to blend in. Otherwise, a vampire would instantly pick one of them out of the crowd. It'd be like a hunter seeing a deer wearing an orange vest in a parking lot full of cars."

"Sort of stands out." Gabriel nodded his head in understanding. He picked up a mushroom slice from his plate, popped it into his mouth, and chewed thoughtfully. Finally, he swallowed. "Microcells?"

Gabriel noticed Joker standing in the doorway. The man's expression was as implacable as it'd been on the range. He moved to Rotty and whispered into his ear.

Rotty's lips pursed, but that was the only sign to let them know what he'd just heard wasn't good. He nodded and stood. "If you'll excuse me." He left without waiting for approval.

Caiaphas gestured around him. "This is a compound. There are eleven others around the globe. Each is a nerve center and, therefore, self-contained. Cells are spread throughout each country or continent. Depending on population density, those cells are further split into microcells. New York City, for example, is comprised of several dozen microcells. Otherwise, they might attract the attention of their fellow inhabitants."

"Wouldn't they think they were just a commune?" Gabriel pointed to the plates. "Especially when they saw what you ate?"

Marcus said, "Even communes in New York City make the news, and if the reporter can get the right angle, that commune may end up on CNN. That's not something we can afford."

Caiaphas added, "Most people believe vampires to be a myth or an old wives' tale. Perhaps it should stay that way. Who knows what vampires might do if their true identity and nature were discovered? Humans may find themselves a race enslaved with no better quality of life than the animals locked up to create food for humans. So the Illuminati, like the vampires, need to stay secret."

"As well as all who have become illumined," Marcus said.

The room went quiet. Gabriel looked from Marcus to Caiaphas, a thought slowly germinating in his brain. "I've become one of the illumined."

Caiaphas nodded to Marcus, who stood and left the room without a word. "Mr. Hawthorne. I offer you fellowship with the Illuminati."

"And if I refuse?"

"Then I will hold you here against your will to protect you." Caiaphas sat across from Gabriel, allowing his last words to sink in as his teeth sank into his sandwich.

Gabriel considered his options. This wasn't a commune. It was a compound. These were not hippies or religious extremists. And though they were armed and dangerous, they weren't terrorists. He couldn't say they all suffered from mass insanity or hypnosis, not after what he'd seen the night before or just an hour ago on their range. There was no hidden camera. No one to laugh and tell him he'd just been punked. Instead, he was a prisoner. For his protection, but a prisoner all the same.

The one thing Gabriel did have in his corner was the knowledge that he wasn't a fool. He wasn't Bruce Willis or Will Smith, and he wasn't on a movie set. Although he mused to himself, he should be. He was one unarmed man in a compound crawling with armed and potentially jumpy people. He was sure they'd kill him as easily as protect him to preserve their anonymity.

So he'd have to wait until a viable option presented itself. Until that option did, the one thing he could do was educate himself. He cleared his throat.

"Well, Caiaphas, before I can say yea or nay to your offer, I need to be completely illumined."

Caiaphas sat back in his chair, interlaced his fingers, and set his elbows on the armrests of his chair.

Gabriel continued. "I'm going to throw a few assumptions out there, and you can bat them back at me if I'm on the right track."

He looked to Caiaphas, who gazed unblinking back at him. Gabriel took that to mean Caiaphas was willing. "I'll work my way backward. I'm being protected from vampires. Vampires want me dead because I know of their existence and the identity of one of their head honchos. Roman Dvanaesti. Except I wouldn't know that if said vampires hadn't killed my partner."

Caiaphas nodded. "A mistake made by one of the lower-level vampires. It may make you feel better to know that the vampire was punished with the loss of his life last night."

"How do you know that?"

"One of the Illumined witnessed the execution."

"How?"

"That isn't a concern right now. Suffice it to say a mistake was made, and the attempt on your life last night was to rectify that issue."

Gabriel stared at Caiaphas. "That doesn't sound like you think Stefan's murder was the mistake."

Caiaphas shook his head. "The murder happened without authorization, and it was sloppy."

"Sloppy?" Gabriel was feeling heat rush through his body.

"Vampires don't leave a corpse lying around to be discovered." Caiaphas's voice was calm. "It leads to too many questions. Too many needless risks of exposure. Not to say vampires don't sometimes kill needlessly. They just usually do a better job of disposal."

"You sound disappointed." Gabriel tried to overcome the urge to throttle the man.

"I am," Caiaphas answered in a smug tone. "Pleasantly."

Gabriel white-knuckled the napkin in his lap. Caiaphas sensed what was happening in Gabriel's lap. "I'm not at all happy an innocent died, Mr. Hawthorne. I wish Mr. Owusu could've come up against an older vampire rather than one so young."

"He would've been eaten in a more humanitarian fashion?" Gabriel chided.

"No, Mr. Hawthorne. He'd most likely still be alive. An older vampire would most likely have charmed him into believing there were no leads and that he should return to where he came from. That would've been the end of it." Caiaphas rubbed his forehead as if he were feeling very weary. "The older vampires...to them, we are just so many gnats flitting across their path, and the Ancients? Well, we are still like gnats, but then we're flitting across the path of battleships, Mr. Hawthorne."

Gabriel released his death grip on his napkin. He felt the urge to reach out and grab the shoulder of Caiaphas, the man just seconds ago he wanted to throttle, but the man looked so different now, as if the weight of his world had just come down upon his shoulders. Instead, Gabriel looked at him. "And Roman Dvanaesti? Which is he? An older vampire? An ancient?"

Caiaphas's laugh was soured with despondency. "Like you, Mr. Hawthorne, we have assumptions. We, however, are still waiting for someone to bat those back to us. We keep detailed records of all our assumptions and observations. When we identify what we think is a vampire, we meticulously record and pass down descriptions of the body, mannerisms, facial expressions, and so on. Those records are continuously updated. No scrap of paper is ever tossed out.

"We have a branch whose only purpose is to comb through ancient texts around the globe searching for evidence or even the faintest whisper of evidence. When that evidence is discovered, if possible, it is acquired."

"Stolen?"

"Borrowed," Caiaphas answered.

"And how far back does your record of Roman Dvanaesti go?" Gabriel asked.

"More than a thousand years." Caiaphas let that number sink into Gabriel's brain.

"A thousand years?" Gabriel repeated in awe.

"We suspect that may be half or two-thirds of his lifetime. Records on births and deaths have not always been kept. Only in recent history has it become difficult to live anonymously. As you can guess, even if he were only a thousand years old, we think that qualifies him as an Ancient."

Gabriel let the words roll around on his tongue again. "A thousand years?" It just didn't seem possible. Or even plausible. A thousand years? He was having a hard time wrapping his mind around the idea.

Caiaphas interrupted his musing. "Again, all of this is one of those pitches we're waiting to get batted back to us."

"Is he the first vampire?"

"We don't know, but we don't think so. As for the origins of vampires, was it an infection like the flu or a bite from an animal like rabies?" Caiaphas shrugged. "Even the term vampire, as I've already explained, is a classification we've assigned. Charmed is a word *we* use, our own... interpretation or description of their ability to influence and manipulate humans.

"How deeply enmeshed vampires are in society and culture, we cannot honestly answer. We have our suspicions. And they are as varied and as far-fetched as they are unsubstantiated. That's why I'm reluctant to join Rotty in his celebration. An immature vampire, a vampire less than one hundred years old," Caiaphas added, seeing the look of confusion on Gabriel's face, "is hard enough to kill, and we're not always one-hundred percent sure we've been successful. How do you kill a creature over a thousand years old? Two thousand? Would it move fast? Or would it not even have to move at all? Rotty calls it a war. I don't see how a gnat flying at a warship can be defined as war. Especially when that gnat has no idea of what it's heading towards and how many others like it or greater than it there might be."

"Okay." Gabriel drew the word out as if stalling for time as he worked through the next question he was about to ask. "What about Cain Dvanaesti? Is he a vampire? Can vampires reproduce?"

Caiaphas's brows creased, but not as if he were annoyed by the question, but as if he were picking up an idea he'd had earlier but set aside to pick up again later. "No," Caiaphas answered. "As far as we can tell, vampires cannot reproduce offspring. Based on our research, we feel confident they cannot."

Gabriel snickered. "You don't sound too confident."

"Perhaps confident is the wrong word. We feel...comfortable with the assertion they cannot."

"And Cain Dvanaesti? What do you feel confident with as far as assertions about him?"

"I would call him..." Caiaphas chose his words with care. "I would call him...a...vampirically...enhanced...human. We believe that Cain was abducted from an orphanage the day after he was placed there—"

"Why do you believe that?" Gabriel interrupted.

"A preponderance of facts. Approximately thirty-seven years ago, Roman Dvanaesti purchased a home in Miami. Before that, he'd resided in New Orleans when he was in the States. Though he had offices in Miami, he never spent more than a day or two there every few months. Even when residing in Miami, he still frequently returned to New Orleans. Approximately thirty-four years ago, a small orphanage in Boca Raton burned to the ground. There were no survivors. But a week later, a birth announcement appeared in the Miami Herald for Cain Dvanaesti to the proud parents of Roman and Claudia. Claudia, the announcement said, had—"

"Wait," Gabriel interjected. "Claudia? His wife's name was Claudia?"

Caiaphas nodded. "She'd died in childbirth. There would be a private family service for her, and donations should be made to the March of Dimes instead of flowers. We have, of course, tried to track down a birth certificate, death certificate, and final resting place for Claudia Dvanaesti." Caiaphas shook his head. "We've looked for a marriage certificate for Roman and Claudia in America, Europe, and Asia, or any announcement of their nuptials." Caiaphas shook his head again. "Cain Dvanaesti's life, however, is perfectly recorded. The paper trail is not only complete but public."

Gabriel took a moment to think this all through. It just didn't make any sense to him. Why would a vampire who's successfully kept his one-thousand-plus-year existence a secret risk discovery to have a son? And why Miami? One of the sunniest and hottest cities in the country? That had to be vampiric suicide.

He looked up to see Caiaphas waiting for Gabriel to realize he'd just asked all these questions out loud and not in his head. He ran his tongue over his teeth. "So you think Roman Dvanaesti bought a home in Miami, torched an orphanage, abducted a baby, and faked its birth for...what?"

Caiaphas answered. "I believe the answer to that question has been revealed in the last few days."

"What? Cain Dvanaesti's run for the Senate?"

"Run for the White House, Mr. Hawthorne."

"And how do you know that?" For a guy who didn't know the vampire mind very well, that seemed presumptuous to Gabriel's thinking.

"Let me try an analogy with you. Have you ever played *Chess*?"

Gabriel shrugged. "Yeah." Wondering where this was going.

"And how many moves ahead do you think?" Caiaphas asked.

"Huh?"

"A beginning player will think of the move he is making presently. A more experienced player may think two, three, maybe even five moves forward. 'If I move my bishop here, my opponent will respond with their knight there, and then I can use my rook to...' you understand. A master, however, will plan the entire game, move by move, even before his hand touches the first pawn. How does the beginner even begin to understand the mind of the master?"

Caiaphas leaned forward, gesturing. "In your lifetime, you will make plans for a career. Marriage. Children. Retirement. Yet I'm sure you didn't plan your life at the beginning. Even the plans you have made, you haven't exactly followed. But as you've matured, your planning has been more astute. You've learned from past mistakes. You recognize what you can control and what you cannot. And you wish to exert greater control over what you can.

"Now imagine a creature that lives ten lifetimes. How many lifetimes pass before that creature, even from sheer boredom, doesn't begin planning? Strategizing? Controlling?"

"You think thirty-five years ago, Roman Dvanaesti moved to Miami, kidnapped a child, burned down an orphanage, made up a wife, and then killed her in childbirth just so he could capture the Presidency? Why would he do that?" Gabriel was skeptical.

"How does the beginner even begin to understand the mind of the master?" Caiaphas repeated. "Even without vampiric influence, history is filled with events whose consequences weren't felt for years. Having watched for centuries, the Illuminati has witnessed events come to pass that we can trace back years, sometimes decades, to an original act. We've been able to recognize acts that were not committed by a vampire but by someone charmed by one.

"So yes, Mr. Hawthorne, I believe Roman Dvanaesti, as well as any other ancients, see this world as their chess/board and humans, perhaps even each other, as the pieces upon that board. Is Cain Dvanaesti in the White House, his father's end? A means to some other end? I don't know. But I do not doubt that any event in which Roman Dvanaesti is a part has occurred simply by accident."

Gabriel felt like he'd swallowed a fifth of Jack Daniels in one gulp. His head was spinning. His mouth was suddenly dry. Sweat bloomed on the back of his neck and forehead despite the coolness in the room. He felt bile climbing the back of his throat. He had to change the subject before he passed out.

"Okay. Let's set that aside for a minute. Why do you think Cain's vampirically enhanced?"

A wry smile crept across Caiaphas's face like a spider. "Have you ever met Cain Dvanaesti, Mr. Hawthorne?"

Gabriel had. He remembered Cain standing in the entryway of the house during the fundraising party, framed like an angel; remembered feeling like he was the only person Cain wanted to talk to in the whole world, and how good and special he felt. He nodded.

"And I can tell by the nod of your head you were and perhaps still are, in some degree, completely charmed by the man." Caiaphas fixed Gabriel hard with his stare. "This will sound the most insane of all I've said." He paused to frame his words and then continued. "We believe, and we have an eyewitness, that Roman Dvanaesti has been giving Cain one drop of his blood every day of his life since the day he was abducted."

A knock could be heard on the door. It opened, and Marcus stuck his head in. "Please excuse the interruption, Sir, but Rotty needs a moment.

46

Cain looked out the window as his limo eased through the downtown Miami traffic, more to avoid Claudia's gaze than to sightsee. His trembling hands rested on his knees, sweat pouring from his palms. His breathing was slow and shallow. He was sure he looked exactly how he felt: Death warmed over. That gave him a haggard chuckle.

"Cain, Honey?" Claudia brushed his hair. "You're soaked. Are you all right?"

He turned towards her.

"Oh, my God." Her eyes popped. She touched his forehead. "You're clammy. Honey, we need to get you home and into bed."

"You'll try any angle to get me in bed, won't you, you saucy little minx," Cain chided in a playful tone. "I just need a nap. The weekend's caught up with me, that's all."

The limo pulled to the curb. Isabella reached across Cain and opened the door. "Claudia, why don't you go in and get the table while I call his doctor?"

Claudia looked out the open door and then at Cain. "Okay," she said, but hesitated before stepping out of the limo. She leaned back in. "I'll—"

"If the doctor says he should go home to bed, I'll come to get you straight away." She surveyed Cain as if he were an interestingly shaped potato. "I'm sure he's just dehydrated. I'll have him drink a bottle of water while I talk to his doctor."

Claudia nodded slowly, then, looking at Isabella's crooked smile, reached in and kissed Cain hard on the lips. "I love you."

"I love you too." He said, his voice thin.

She beamed at him, glanced worriedly at Isabella, and then hurried into the restaurant.

Isabella rolled her eyes. "Shut the door."

Cain reached out and grasped the door with a trembling hand. Once he closed it, Isabella was ready with a dropper. "Open wide and say ah." She made her tone as patronizing as possible.

He did. She dropped one drop of crimson liquid on his tongue. He closed his mouth and swallowed. Within a minute, his hands were steady, and his color returned. "Thanks, Isabella." He hopped out of the car. "Are you coming in?"

She frowned. "Close the door behind you, please. We'll be waiting here."

Cain threw her a *'Yes, Mom'* salute and closed the door.

Isabella watched as he practically skipped across the sidewalk and into the restaurant. She could feel her phone vibrating in her hand. She answered, "Yes."

"Complete dossier on Gabriel Hawthorne coming your way in the next few seconds." The voice said.

Isabella heard the ding of new mail received. "Got it."

"Anything else?" The voice asked.

"No." Isabella thumbed the End Call button and then pulled up the email. She scanned through it. Thorough as usual. She was about to stop reading when a name under *known associates* caught her eye. She double-clicked on *Claudia Bennett* and read a short synopsis:

Met during a summer internship at *The*
Washington Post. Became involved
after she graduated from Georgetown
until right before he left the Force.

Isabella smiled and dialed Roman's number. He answered on the second ring.

"Salve, my Love." His tone sounded pleased.

"Salve, Roman." She couldn't help but smile. But she pulled the smile from her face and quickly relayed what'd happened in New Orleans. There was a long pause before he spoke.

"Do you know where he is now?"

"I believe he's with the Illuminati."

Roman laughed. "Well, then. I know exactly where he is."

Isabella's mouth dropped. "You do?"

"Yes," Roman replied. "But we will do nothing regarding him at the moment."

"We should eliminate him as soon as possible," Isabella interjected, though now glad the attempt in New Orleans had been unsuccessful.

"We need him alive." Roman continued in a tone not unlike a teacher explaining to a student. "The D.N.C. has hired him to find dirt on the

Dvanaesti family, and if, as they say, he goes missing or turns up dead, then they will surely think he did. They will call for an investigation."

Isabella disagreed. She could make it look like he fell in love with some Miami or New Orleans hooker and ran off to Mexico or Costa Rica. She wanted to tell Roman that in this age of technology, she could make Gabriel Hawthorne live forever. She decided to try another tack.

"There's something else. Cain's abuse was worse than we thought. Instead of enhancing him, he now needs it to survive. I think we have Claudia to blame for that."

"Do we?" Roman asked in bemusement.

"Yes. I think it's best if she goes away. Since Claudia has entered his life, Cain has started disobeying you. He's become easily distracted, forgetting what his priorities are and where his loyalties lie." An idea flashed in her brain. "When Claudia was at Georgetown, and then at *The Washington Post,* she was...physically involved with Gabriel Hawthorne. She is a liability. They both are."

Roman responded, "I like her. She reminds me of my Claudia. She is good for Cain. It's good for him to be young and in love. You remember what it's like to be young and in love, Mi Amore?" He sighed. And when he spoke this time, his tone had a grandfatherly caress. "In my one human lifetime, I learned the consequences of letting my emotions guide my actions. Of how one rash moment can destroy years of careful planning. But you, after hundreds of human lifetimes, still have not learned the art of patience."

Isabella hadn't heard anything Roman had said after Mi Amore.

Mi Amore? Isabella's hand holding the phone to her ear remained relaxed, but the other, holding her tablet, clenched into a fist, crushing it.

"Yes, Roman," she seethed. "I remember what it is to be young and in love. I remember when you were in love with me. I remember a time when your voice carried a lover's caress when you called me Mi Amore. Not the manipulative lilt you used just now. I've known what it is to be young and in love not for one human lifetime, but every minute of every day of more than a hundred human lifetimes."

She wanted to scream all of this at Roman. This and a hundred other things. Instead, she said with calm, collection, and control, "Of course, you're right, My Love."

She heard the click of Roman disconnecting the call. She let the phone drop from her ear. She stared at it. "Mi Amore."

47

Gabriel's eyes shot open. A hand lay cold and hard across his mouth. Another hand lay across his wrist, tucked under the pillow where a pistol would be; a habit started during his days as a cop. Except his Beretta wasn't under the pillow. He didn't have it back. He hadn't seen Rotty since Rotty had left the dining room at lunch earlier. Until...

A voice snarled into his ear. "Come with me." The hand over his wrist, and his mouth lifted.

Gabriel could see the shadow of Rotty backing slowly away from the bed. His eyes darted quickly to the digital clock on the nightstand. 2:01 glowed dim green.

Rotty slung a bag onto the bed. "These should be your size. Don't turn on the light."

Gabriel pulled back the sheets and jumped from the bed. He opened the bag. It contained a pair of jeans, a long-sleeved T-shirt, socks, and running shoes. Gabriel dressed quickly as Rotty kept an ear to the door. Once Gabriel was dressed, he whispered, "Ready."

Rotty's shadow nodded, then moved to the dark and ominous wardrobe.

Gabriel winced at the creaking doors as they opened, confident a rock concert would be quieter.

A dim red light appeared, and Gabriel could see Rotty, dressed like himself, holding a small Maglite flashlight. Rotty put the Maglite between his teeth, parted the clothes hanging, and started running his fingers along the back of the wardrobe. Gabriel remembered *The Lion, the Witch, and the Wardrobe* and was just about to ask Rotty if he was looking for a way into Narnia when he heard a click. The back of the wardrobe opened into darkness.

Rotty's head swung around to Gabriel, illuminating him in red light. "Through here." Rotty reached into his pocket, pulled out another Maglite, and handed it to Gabriel.

Gabriel accepted the Maglite. "You forgetting something?"

Rotty grinned. "Don't worry. You won't be naked much longer." He gestured for Gabriel to enter the wardrobe.

Gabriel, rolling his eyes, twisted on the flashlight. Dim red light spilled out. Gabriel nodded, stepped into the wardrobe, and then through the secret doorway and found himself on a staircase leading down. He started down the steps as he heard Rotty first close the wardrobe doors and then the door to this passageway.

"Leads to the cellar," Rotty's voice whispered.

Gabriel said nothing but continued to follow the stairs. Not only did some of the steps look rotted through, but the passageway was so narrow as to cause both Gabriel and Rotty to hold their bodies diagonally to the steps. They descended three flights before ending at a dirt landing. Gabriel ran the red light around the small room, no bigger than a broom closet, and saw a small block-and-tackle counterweight system hanging on his right. He could see no exit.

"Joist to your left," Rotty's snore of a whisper rumbled in Gabriel's ear.

Gabriel aimed the beam of light at the far side of the wood and saw an indentation in the wood about three feet from the ground.

"Stick your thumb in it and push."

Gabriel obeyed and heard a soft click. The door opened slightly in front of him. He pushed lightly, hearing the block-and-tackle system engage. The door swung open. He stepped into the cellar.

Rotty followed him through.

Gabriel turned to watch Rotty with just the lightest touch close the door. On this side, the wall was weighed down with casks of aging whiskey. Empty or not, the wood hanging on the wall had to weigh a couple of hundred pounds.

"The man who built this plantation had three small children. He built the same secret passageway out of each child's room and the master bedroom. It had to be easy enough for each child to open." Rotty explained, motioning for Gabriel to follow him. "He lived in constant fear for his family's safety."

"Why?" Gabriel could not fathom why a plantation owner, the proverbial king of his castle and master of his domain, would need to create secret passageways to the cellar. After exploring the space, he saw no way a small child could lift the cellar doors. Judging by the hinges, each door would have weighed more than the child trying to open them. How in the world were the children supposed to escape? The passageways led to a deathtrap if the old mansion were, for example, burning.

Rotty reached the backside of the cellar, a wall covered in wine racks filled with dusty bottles. He squatted onto his haunches, pulled out a cobwebbed bottle, and reached in.

Gabriel heard another soft click as a door that had not been seen before swung open.

Rotty set the wine bottle back, stood, and opened the door. He shone his flashlight into the opening. "He was a member of the underground railroad," Rotty said as he looked at the tunnel leading away from the house.

Rotty stepped into the tunnel, and Gabriel followed, closing the door behind him and marveling at the ingenuity of the man who'd built this home. The tunnel was dank and smelled strongly of earth and rotting wood.

Rotty started walking. "We've replaced the timbers that had rotted, but other than that, we've left it alone. Like the house and the passageways, the tunnels were well built."

Gabriel could hear the admiration in Rotty's voice. Another word took a few seconds to register. "Did you say tunnels?"

"A whole network of them," Rotty replied. "You could get lost if you didn't know where you were going. He could hide slaves down here for weeks, maybe months, and then send them out in more than a dozen directions when the time came."

Gabriel felt a shiver not in keeping with the chill in the subterranean air. Slaves. Men, women, and children. Flesh and blood. But nothing more than property to the white men who dared to think they had the right to buy and sell humans like any other commodity, simply because of the color of their skin. These people had lived in these tunnels and trodden the same soil he was now walking on their journey to freedom.

And what had Caiaphas said? What would happen to the human race if the race of vampires decided to enslave them? Would humans be bought and sold again? Would plantations spring up again? But this time, the humans wouldn't be working the crop. They'd be the crop. And there'd be no plantation owners who saw it as unjust, wrong, or inhumane. Because, after all, they, the plantation owners, the harvesters, the vampires, would be inhuman.

Gabriel was startled out of his revelry when he walked into the back of the stationary Rotty. "We're here." Rotty's light illuminated a wooden ladder leading up to a trap door.

Rotty punched the wooden ceiling three times in rapid succession.

Gabriel winced again as he stood in the cellar, waiting to climb the ladder. If even one guard was patrolling the compound, those knocks were bound to draw attention in the still, country night.

Rotty laughed as if he could read this thought in Gabriel's mind. "Relax, Hawthorne. I could fire a round into this ceiling, and nobody on the grounds would ever hear it." Rotty looked up. "I'm not sure they heard that." Rotty lifted his arm and was just about to hit the ceiling again when the scream of metal-on-metal reverberated overhead. Dust and dirt fell onto Gabriel as a two-foot by two-foot square lifted away, flooding the tunnel with harsh fluorescent light.

Gabriel squinted into the light and watched the shadow of two people pull Rotty up through the hole into a building. "Whenever you're ready, Mr. Hawthorne," a young man shouted to Gabriel. Gabriel grabbed the rung above him and scampered quickly up the ladder. As he reached the top, two sets of hands grabbed hold of him under each armpit and hoisted him effortlessly onto a concrete floor.

The trap door he'd just come through was three-inch thick steel, lined in felt, and swung on metal hinges. The young men who'd pulled him out of the tunnel strained to put the door softly back into place, flush with the gunmetal gray concrete floor, free from scuff marks, grease spots, or dirt.

Gabriel looked around, his mouth agape. He was standing in the middle of not just an auto shop but the cleanest, best-equipped auto shop he'd ever seen. Gabriel was sure that just as his maleness could respect such a shop, NASCAR mechanics and pit crews would quite possibly need a cigarette. There were four hydraulic lifts, racks of tires, stations for welding, cutting, and shaping sheet metal, for assembling and disassembling engines, for installing windshields, banks of computers humming with images of vehicles in varying degrees of repair, no less than two bays housing what looked to be plasma or laser cutters as well as shelves of parts and row after row of every tool man had ever imagined for working on all things mechanical.

Thwunk!

Gabriel turned to see a young Hispanic woman, who couldn't be five and a half feet tall, in black boots, black fatigue pants, and a black wifebeater shirt, rubbing the hood of a Ford Econoline Van with a rag.

"Pretty sweet, huh?" The young woman said to Gabriel, looking over the shop as if she were eyeing her lover coming to bed.

"All right, Wrench," Rotty shoved the woman to get her moving, "you can brag about your boyfriend on the way out."

"Yeah." Wrench's smile was glassy as she moved with the purposeful intent of a sloth over to the workbench to retrieve her fatigue top.

"Boyfriend?" Gabriel asked.

"If you ever need to find Wrench on a Saturday night," one of the young men who'd helped Gabriel into the garage said, "just look here."

"She's right, though," Rotty said with appreciation as he surveyed the shop, "this place is pretty sweet. We can modify all our vehicles right here. If you can't find the tool or part in this room, it doesn't exist. And it's completely soundproof and lightproof. It's also shielded against thermal imaging. So whatever we need to do, whenever we need to do it, doesn't bother or alert anyone."

Rotty and the other two were joined by a fourth man who said nothing, climbed into the driver's seat, and started the engine.

"Let's go." Rotty climbed into the front passenger seat. Gabriel and the others climbed into the back of the van. The driver hit a button. All the lights in the garage were immediately extinguished. He slipped on a pair of night vision goggles, then punched a second button. Part of the wall opened like a garage door but made only the slightest, softest of hums.

The driver dropped the gearshift into drive and pulled slowly through the open door, punching the button again. The door came down.

Gabriel noticed no headlights and, glancing over his shoulder, no taillights either.

The van moved slowly up to a gate at the back of the compound. A guard held a hand up to the approaching vehicle as he moved toward the driver's side window.

The driver stopped and rolled down his window. But as the guard opened his mouth, Rotty's hand shot forward; a tranquilizer gun pointed squarely at the man's chest. As the guard's eyes grew wide with realization, Rotty fired the high-powered tranquilizer dart into the guard. The fast-acting tranquilizer pumped into the man's bloodstream instantaneously, and almost as instantaneously, the guard dropped to his knees and then to his side.

Wrench jumped out of the van and opened the gate as one of the other Illuminati jumped out and dragged the unconscious guard back to his shack. The van pulled through, and Wrench and the other man closed and locked the gate.

Gabriel finally decided to ask the first question he had wanted to ask when Rotty woke him. "Where are we going?" At the time, the more prudent move was to keep quiet and escape. Now that he had...

"Where are we headed?"

"Miami, Florida." Rotty growled, "By way of New Orleans."

48

Gabriel sat in the passenger seat of the 1999 GMC Suburban that Rotty was now buying from a used-car lot. Gabriel looked at his watch. It was four in the morning. Gabriel could not hear Rotty and the owner's conversation, but he could see the smiles and the thick envelope handed from Rotty to the owner.

Wrench had the hood up, looking over the engine. The other two Illuminati, who'd yet to earn names, moved the gear from the back of the Econoline into the back of the Suburban. Gabriel had been ordered to sit in the passenger seat.

The hood of the engine slammed shut, and Gabriel could see Wrench wiping filthy hands on a rag, a satisfied grin on her face. She climbed in behind the wheel.

"So, how do you guys normally do this...type of thing? Operation?" Now that they were on their way, Gabriel wanted to know what the plan was and what his part was in it.

"Well," Wrench answered. "Normally, we have an Alpha team. That's the strike team made up of six members. And then we have a Bravo team. Also made up of six members. They're usually the clean-up crew if Alpha's done its job, but they can also double as an extraction team."

Gabriel looked around, counting the people present in turn.

Wrench watched him run the numbers twice before she said, "That's right. There's only five of us." She giggled. "We don't even make up a complete Alpha."

Gabriel didn't share in the humor. "But why are there only five of us? What about the other two members of Rotty's team?"

Wrench frowned. "They're a little too green for this kind of an operation. And Rotty wasn't sure he could trust them to keep their mouths shut. Not spill the beans to Caiaphas or Marcus."

Gabriel checked that the other two were in the van, and Rotty was still talking to the dealer. "I assume this uh...operation is taking place without Caiaphas' knowledge or authorization."

Wrench looked at him with a blank expression.

"And," Gabriel prodded, "I assume something happened yesterday to change Rotty's mind about keeping me against my will."

Wrench's face hardened. "Nothing *changed* Rotty's mind." Her tone was as hard as her stare. "Rotty's always felt the same way since day one. The more people know the truth, illumined as we call it, the happier Rotty is. If Rotty had his way, we'd take out ads in every newspaper on the planet, put it on billboards, make commercials, and buy TV time for infomercials. But Caiaphas and Marcus want to wait. They always want to wait. Run more tests. No operation until you're absolutely sure you have a one-hundred percent chance of success. But that's not going to happen. There's no such thing as a one-hundred percent chance of success. Never going to be a war without collateral damage. Rotty understands that. He hates it, but he understands it. He's willing to do what needs to be done; whatever needs to be done."

"But Rotty backed down yesterday when Caiaphas mentioned the killing of even one innocent." Gabriel admired Wrench's loyalty to Rotty and could believe Rotty would be willing to do anything. Still, Rotty was a soldier, and like it or not, soldiers still took orders from politicians. "So what happened? What made Rotty willing to leave in the middle of the night against his superior's orders to do this rescue operation?"

Wrench looked nonplussed at him. "Rescue operation? You think this is about rescuing your girlfriend?"

Gabriel looked at her. "One. She's not my girlfriend. And two. Yeah. Rotty said we're going to Miami. Why else would we go? She's innocent."

Wrench stared at Gabriel as if he were a child who'd reasonably yet illogically explained why it was preferable to defecate in his pants than in the toilet. Finally, she took a deep breath. "Okay. Try to get this through your skull. You're a means to an end. There's no reason to take you with us, especially if this is a rescue operation, which it isn't. Rotty's going to Miami to pick a fight. If you want to get your girlfriend out of harm's way, great. If not, great. From what I understand, she's willingly attached herself to—"

"She has not willingly attached herself," Gabriel barked. "She has no idea what she's gotten herself into."

Now, Wrench looked alarmed. "Okay, okay," Wrench said in a placating tone. "Let's keep our voices down. We don't need to attract any unnecessary attention." When she said 'unnecessary,' she shot an unconscious, instinctive glance toward Rotty.

Gabriel looked towards Rotty. He was still talking to the dealer. The other two had finished loading the Suburban minutes ago and were now hovering around Rotty, looking every bit like two pet dogs waiting with bated breath for their master's next order.

Gabriel was feeling panic rise in his chest. He strained to tamp it down. "What do you mean?" Gabriel seethed through clenched teeth. "I'm just a means to an end? Rotty's looking to pick a fight? Why's he going to Miami? Can't he just pick a fight with the local New Orleans vampire population?"

Wrench's brow creased with consternation. She stole glances at Rotty, the two soldiers, and Rotty again before leaning in close to Gabriel.

"What I'm about to tell you, according to our laws, I could die for telling you. Do you understand that?"

Gabriel could hear the tremble in her voice.

She continued. "Yesterday, we received word that our entire cell in St. Petersburg, Russia, was wiped out. Annihilated. We don't know how. Or why. Or who ordered it. But over one hundred Illuminati were slaughtered yesterday.

"Rotty demanded Caiaphas authorize a retaliatory strike against the vampires, but Caiaphas said no. Marcus agreed. They said we need to wait. Wait and find out who did it, and why. Then he forbade Rotty from telling anyone."

"So why are we going to Miami?" Gabriel felt the sick thrill rise in his stomach. He knew the answer. He just wanted Wrench to confirm it.

After a moment of what looked like a conflict of emotions warring across her face, Wrench finally did. "Because Rotty wants to go after what we believe is the heart of the vampires. Roman Dvanaesti. And he wants to hurt him the way he hurt us. By taking as many vampires, as well as his son, away from him."

Not for the first time this evening did Gabriel shiver from something other than cold.

At that moment, the back driver's side door opened, and in climbed Rotty. "How's she running, Wrench?"

Wrench shot Gabriel a quick warning glance before glancing at Rotty with a smile. "She's burning a little oil, and the intake manifold's leaking a little coolant. And there's a ticking noise between the dash and the engine. Other than that, she's running square."

Rotty nodded and closed his eyes. The other two, who'd climbed into the back seat with Rotty and who Gabriel now realized would not get to earn names, followed suit. "If anyone's got to use the latrine, now's the time. Office is still open."

"I'll be right back." Gabriel jumped out of the Suburban and made a beeline for the office.

Claudia unsuccessfully stifled a yawn as she poured coffee into her travel mug. She was running late. Cain's fault, she mused to herself. But like the American Express card, she never left home in the morning without her coffee. A sheepish grin crept across her face as the thought of last night played out in her brain.

Cain had dropped her off at her condo, given her a quick kiss, and then bolted back to the limo for the drive to the airport. As she watched the taillights of the limo, her cell phone started ringing. It was Cain. They talked on his way to the airport and boarding. Once the jet was airborne, he'd called her again. They'd talked like a couple of teenagers. "I love you... I love you more... No, I love you more... You didn't hang up... You didn't either... I miss you... I miss you more..."

She dropped cream and Equal into the mug when the landline started ringing. She smiled and rolled her eyes. "*Cain.*"

Claudia reached for the phone but noticed the number on the display. She didn't recognize it and decided to let the answering machine pick it up. Her happiness deflated as she grabbed her mug and car keys and headed out the door. She could hear her quick greeting as she opened the door, and then...

"Claudia. It's me. Gabriel. I'm sorry to be calling so—"

She stopped listening. Claudia's eyes rolled again, this time out of irritation, as she stepped through the door and closed and locked it behind her.

The second set of knocks on his door awakened Caiaphas. The first set had worked its way into his dream. It was a recurring favorite of his: sitting in a meadow, drinking tea, watching children chase dragonflies, as a woman in a white-and-red gingham summer dress prepared plates of fried chicken and coleslaw. Caiaphas had never eaten fried chicken. No chicken in any form. Not even an egg. He'd been born into the Illuminati and never known anything but the strict Illuminati dietary laws.

Caiaphas had no wife. No children. So the woman in his dream, like the children and the fried chicken, was all a figment of his imagination. He sometimes wondered, but only after having this dream, if he'd made a mistake not taking a wife and bearing children. It'd been nearly two-hundred years since a bachelor served as Caiaphas. Marcus was like a son and would make an excellent Caiaphas, but he wasn't blood.

These were the thoughts, Caiaphas thought to himself as he turned on the bedside lamp, of an old man. An old man, nearing the end of his journey, realizes he has no one to see him off on his next great adventure. He slipped on his glasses and sat up. "Enter," he said as if he'd been awake for hours.

It was Marcus. "I'm sorry to disturb you," his tone was both apologetic and slightly frenzied, "but Rotty has taken Wrench and two other team members and left the compound. A guard was discovered incapacitated, and a van is missing."

"And Mr. Hawthorne?" Caiaphas asked, neither the tone of his voice nor the expression on his face suggesting anything other than benign interest.

Marcus's eyes dropped to his feet. "He's also missing. We have no idea where they are or what they're doing."

"Yes, we do," Caiaphas corrected.

Marcus looked at Caiaphas, nonplussed.

Caiaphas sighed. This was why a Caiaphas chose a Marcus early and groomed him (or her) for decades. Emotion stymied the thought process. "Call Augustine in Orlando. Have him send a team to Tallahassee and another to Miami. I want eyes on Governor Cain Dvanaesti and his fiancée, Miss Claudia Bennett."

Marcus nodded and left the room.

Caiaphas looked at the clock. It read four-thirty. He removed his glasses, set them gingerly on the nightstand, and shut off the light. The alarm wouldn't go off for another hour. Perhaps he could have that dream again. This time, he'd eat the fried chicken and kiss the woman.

49

Claudia sat with her co-host, Luke, the show's producer, John Estevez, the director, Elizabeth Dutton, and sundry other personnel at the post-show meeting in the station conference room.

"You keep giving us shows like you did today," John teased Claudia, "and I'll have to find ways to thwart your marriage."

The gathered applauded in approval of John's words. "That was quite a show, Claudia," Elizabeth chimed in. "You even made Luke look like he had more than the thought of, 'Does this tie make my butt look fat?' flying through his head."

"Hey," Luke said with mock offense. "I'll have you know I highly resemble that remark."

Those around the table laughed. The door opened, and a production assistant stuck her head in.

"We're in a meeting, Julie," John reproved.

"I'm sorry," Julie said in a low voice. She glanced at Claudia before saying, "There's a call for Ms. Bennett. He says it's urgent."

Claudia sat bolt upright. "He? Cain? Has something happened?" Dread filled her body as if she'd inhaled noxious fumes. She felt a dizzying thrill.

A voice with a light Italian accent had been whispering in the back of her mind ever since Sunday, when she'd met her father-in-law-to-be, "I am only for Cain. He is all that I breathe. I live only to love, honor, and obey him. Without him, there is no life. No reason to continue." It was irrational, she knew, but there it was. Since Sunday, when it all became real to her in a way she'd never quite imagined, her only fear was something happening to Cain.

Now that voice said, "Silly girl. Could Cain be calling you if something happened to him?" Roman then. She answered the voice in her head. Roman could be calling me.

The voice laughed. "Don't worry, Child. If something ever happens to Cain, you'll know. You won't have to wait to be told. You'll know in your marrow. There'll be no doubt."

"No, Ma'am," Julie said, a look of horror on her face.

"Who is it then?" John bit out.

214

"A Mr. Gabriel Hawthorne."

Claudia sloughed off the dread like a cheap dress and waved a dismissive hand in Julie's direction. "Take a message."

Julie nodded and snatched her head from the room, closing the door with a bang.

"Gabriel Hawthorne." Luke eyed Claudia in mock accusation. "Another fox at the henhouse?"

Claudia eyed Luke right back. "Yes, Luke. And by the way, that tie does make your butt look fat."

Luke sucked air through his teeth as if that last comment had stung.

"He's..." Claudia started, but didn't know how to continue.

"An old flame having trouble accepting he's just an ash of a memory?" Elizabeth offered helpfully.

Claudia considered that for a moment. It was clear, concise, and to the point; it ended a discussion before it could start. She smiled at Elizabeth. "You really should finish that novel. You have a wonderful way with words."

Elizabeth blushed.

Claudia looked around the room. "He's forgotten, so let's forget it."

At that moment, her cell phone rang. "I'm sorry." She pulled it out of its holster on her belt. "I thought I'd silenced it." She looked at the ID but didn't recognize the number. Though she was pretty sure who it was: Gabriel. She pressed the Ignore button and then turned the phone off.

Claudia finished the meeting, filmed a couple of promos, recorded a radio commercial, and prepped for the next day's show without ever thinking of Gabriel. Finally, as Elizabeth asked if she wanted to grab a bite for lunch with the other girls, Claudia remembered she'd turned off her phone.

"Let me just check to see if I've heard from my Honey," she said, turning on her phone.

Elizabeth giggled. "That's funny. And now, Ladies and Gentlemen, I give you the Governor from the Great State of Florida. Honey."

Claudia smiled. Her phone chimed with new voicemails. She thumbed the playback button, expecting to hear Cain's voice.

"Claudia? What's wrong?" Elizabeth asked as she watched Claudia's smile slacken into a frown.

Claudia was listening to the message. "Claudia, it's me, Gabe. Look, I don't have a lot of time. Your life is in danger. Whatever you do, don't contact Cain Dvanaesti or anyone associated with him. I can't tell you why. You'll have to trust me. I'm on my way to get you. Just-...stay away from Cain Dvanaesti or any of his cronies. I'm sorry. I've got to go. I'll explain it all when I get you."

She couldn't believe it. Gabriel had gone insane. He'd become the jealous ex-boyfriend. "Nothing." She looked up to Elizabeth. "You guys go on ahead. I'll catch up. I have to deal with... I have to make a phone call. Won't take long."

Elizabeth offered her a skeptical eye. "You sure?"

"Oh yeah. Be right behind you."

"Okay." Elizabeth finally acquiesced. Turning on her heel, she headed for the gaggle of ladies waiting.

Claudia waved at the girls as they left, then pressed the '1' button. The phone automatically dialed a number. She listened to the ring, which competed with the beat of her heart. On the fourth ring, she heard a familiar voice.

"Hey, Beautiful."

She felt herself melt. "Cain, Honey. Do you remember meeting Gabriel Hawthorne? At the fundraiser at your house last Thursday?"

She heard him click his tongue against the back of his teeth as he thought about it. "Yeah. The two of you were outside talking."

She collapsed into a chair. "Well, I just got the strangest message from him. He said my life was in danger. He said he was on his way to pick me up. He said not to tell you."

"Did he now?" Cain sounded amused. "I've heard of guys realizing what they lost once it was gone, but this is taking it to a new level."

"Stop screwing around," she snapped. This was the first time she'd ever taken Cain's head off. It was a testament to how freaked out she was, she realized. "I'm sorry. It's just...you didn't hear his voice. He sounded...insane."

There was a brief silence as Cain considered her words. "Sorry. Okay. Are you at the station?"

"Yes."

"Stay there with people. Don't leave. I'm sending people to get you. They'll take you to your condo, stay with you while you pack a bag, and then take you to my house. "You'll be safe there. Okay?"

"Okay," Claudia breathed and realized she did feel okay.

"Any idea where he might be?"

"Not a clue," she said. If she could tell him that, especially if he were in Florida, Cain could probably have the police or F.D.L.E. pick him up.

"That's all right," Cain soothed. "We'll find him. Just stay where you are. I'll see you this evening."

"See me?" Claudia asked, excited and afraid. "Oh, don't, Cain. Don't come here. You're too busy."

"I'm never too busy for you, My Love," Cain responded. "I'll see you tonight." He hung up.

Claudia thumbed the End Call button, immediately texted Elizabeth she wasn't going to make lunch, and cursed the day she met Gabriel Hawthorne.

50

"Suburban pulling into the parking lot," the man to Augustine's left in the driver's seat said. "Southeast entrance. Rotty's at the wheel."

Augustine's head snapped to the right, looking out the passenger window of the white Time Warner Cable Econoline van. Sure enough. He could see Rotty's rugged face behind the wheel. He watched as Rotty maneuvered the SUV into a parking spot and counted heads. Five. At that moment, a man jumped from the back passenger side door and ran to the building. The man to Augustine's left laughed as he watched the man push frantically on the glass door before finally realizing to pull. He slung the door open and launched himself into the building.

Augustine checked the SUV. Rotty and the others were crawling out of the Suburban, stretching and flexing tired and cramped muscles. He said over his shoulder, "Give me thirty seconds, then get Marcus on the line."

The man to his left nodded.

Augustine opened the van door, climbed out, and crossed the busy street and into the parking lot of the television studio.

Though Augustine hadn't uttered a sound, Rotty's head whipped around as if he were locating the voice that had just called to him. He spotted Augustine and frowned.

Augustine continued walking to Rotty without hurry, not saying a word. Rotty started walking towards him. As they approached within five feet, they stopped and stared at each other stone-faced.

Rotty watched as another member of the Illuminati crossed the street, a cell phone up to his ear, and came up beside Augustine. The man eyed Rotty with neither recognition nor uncertainty. Rotty might've been just another parked car for all the interest he showed him. He handed the phone over to Augustine.

Augustine pressed the phone to his ear, never taking his eyes off Rotty. He watched but did not acknowledge the others as they walked up and stood silently behind Rotty.

"Marcus. It's Augustine. Cain's people, a driver, and two guards collected Miss Bennett. I have a man tailing them." His face hardened as his eyes locked with Rotty's. "Still no sign of Rotty or his team." He listened to Marcus before finally answering, looking Rotty in the eye. Rotty stood there, his face impassive. "I presume Miss Bennett was taken to Cain Dvanaesti's mansion here in Miami, but I should have confirmation soon. I received intel from our team in Tallahassee that Dvanaesti's jet is being prepped. The flight plan is to Miami." He listened to Marcus, again not taking his eyes off of Rotty. "I will report back to you in one hour." Augustine disconnected the call and handed the phone to the man standing to his left.

Rotty raised his hands. Augustine raised his. The two men embraced. As they released each other, Augustine slipped a phone out of his pocket and placed it in Rotty's hand. Turning on his heel, he walked away, not looking back. Augustine's man fell in step behind him.

The sound of Gabriel's curses echoed through the parking lot. Rotty and the others turned as Gabriel ran up to them. "She's not here. She's not freaking here."

Rotty powered up the phone Augustine had handed him. "Of course, she's not here," he said as he looked at the phone's screen, which flashed one new voicemail message. "You called and told her you were on your way to rescue her. You told her not to tell Cain." He thumbed the recall button and put the phone to his ear, raising a hand to silence Gabriel's protests before they could start. He listened to the message, erased it, powered the cell phone off, then snapped it in two. "Augustine's waiting at the warehouse six blocks to the Northeast."

51

Cain answered his cell phone on the first ring. "You're at the mansion." It was more of a demand than a statement, with just a hint of desperation.

"Yes." Claudia's voice sounded sober.

His body slumped with relief. "I've got this little dinner thing I've got to go to, but I'm going to cut out early. Then we'll be on our way."

"We?" Cain could hear a bemused tone in Claudia's voice.

"Myself. Isabella. And a small detail of my father's bodyguards."

Isabella, who'd been working her smartphones as usual, looked askance at Cain, her face a mixture of aggravation and disdain.

"You think the extra bodyguards are necessary?" Now, Cain could hear a growing panic in Claudia's voice.

Cain thought of the guards at the mansion. No, he thought to himself, the detail he was bringing with him was probably superfluous. Judging by the look on Isabella's face, she agreed. The mansion staff alone could handle a military assault, let alone one man. Then there were the guards. His Miami home was better protected than the White House.

But this was Claudia we were talking about, he reminded himself, and she was more important to him than anything else on the planet. Even, he now realized as he looked at the framed photograph of him and Roman on his desk, more important than his father. His father's eyes reflected Roman's plans for his son. When he looked into Claudia's eyes, he could see the future. Not his future or even hers. But of their children.

He had put fear into her. He cursed himself inwardly, then smiled outwardly. "No," Cain said with confidence. "Sometimes a show of force helps to quell a man's emotions before he does something stupid. That's all."

"Oh." She didn't sound convinced, but she wasn't as panicked either.

"I'll be there tonight. You just make yourself at home till then."

"Okay." Cain listened to the silence for a few seconds before Claudia finally said, with the slightest hint of desperation. "I love you."

Cain felt a wave of warmth in his chest. He would never grow tired of hearing those three words spoken by that one woman. "I love you too." He pressed the End Call button. Without looking at Isabella, he knew she was frowning at him. "What?"

"You are the governor of Florida."

"Thank you for your statement of the obvious," Cain barbed.

Isabella ignored him. "And your," she held up fingers in quotes, "little dinner thing is for the Republican nominee for President of the United States next year.

"So?"

"You're hosting it," Isabella exclaimed in exasperation. "It was your idea."

"It's not like Father wants the guy to win anyway," Cain responded.

"Still. You have duties and obligations you cannot put aside or ignore every time your *girlfriend* breaks a nail." There was a derisive inflection on the word girlfriend.

Cain felt an acute heat rising in his chest, spreading through his body, pumping with every beat of his heart. Felt it surge into his hands, which now felt strong enough to crush the life even out of Isabella. His hands clenched at that thought as if confirming their readiness, their willingness to wrap around her throat.

Isabella noticed his hands, as if reading his mind, and flashed a wicked smile. "No matter how strong you think you are, Cain, you could never defeat me. You aren't iniquitous enough. Sordid enough." The smile on her face turned evil. "Or man enough."

Cain felt the heat intensify, saw his knuckles turn white, and realized she was probably...wrong. But this was not the time to test her statement or his theory. He had to be smarter than that. To act now would be playing right into her hands. It would mean she had something more important than strength, power, or wickedness. She had control.

Cain turned slowly to face Isabella, his eyes locking onto hers. He watched the smile slip from her face. "She isn't my girlfriend. She's my fiancée. Soon to be my wife and one day the mother of my children. And this isn't a broken nail."

Isabella waved a dismissive hand. "Regardless. There are seven vampires and three highly trained humans guarding her. He's just one human—"

"That doesn't matter." Cain interrupted.

"No," Isabella responded in a flat tone. "It doesn't. It could be one-hundred humans, and it still wouldn't matter."

Cain exhaled slowly. "Let me put it this way. If I cannot help but run to the aid of the woman I love every time she breaks a nail," his voice was as bitter as cheap whiskey, "perhaps I shouldn't be governor." His eyes didn't waver as he added, "Or senator. Or president."

The phone intercom on his desk buzzed. "The Secret Service liaison is here to meet with you, Governor," Jane said.

His eyes stayed on Isabella. "Send him in. We're done here."

The door opened, and in walked a very severe-looking gentleman. "Governor."

"Pardon me one moment. Isabella, please see to my travel arrangements. As I've instructed."

Isabella nodded and swept from the room. Cain followed her to the door. "No interruptions, Jane." His eyes were still on the back of Isabella's head. "None."

Jane looked in the direction of his gaze and then nodded her understanding. She gulped. "Yes, Sir."

Cain flashed her a small smile and a nod and closed the door.

52

The Suburban pulled through the garage door and into the darkened warehouse. Three parking spaces, the center space already filled with a white Econoline van emblazoned with the Time Warner Cable logo, were immediately to the right. Wrench pulled the SUV into a spot and cut the engine.

As they stepped from the truck, the garage door slammed shut, and fluorescent lights snapped on. Gabriel heard the hum as they warmed up and watched two men and two women step from their defensive positions and walk toward them. The four each took turns embracing all the new arrivals. All the new arrivals, except for him, he noticed.

Gabriel didn't mind. He wasn't one of them. He was just along for the ride. Instead, they offered their hands, and Gabriel had the distinct impression they knew who he was already. "Nice van," he said, pointing a thumb at the Time Warner vehicle. "Somebody's day job?"

"It's called urban camouflage," Wrench explained. Time Warner's the biggest cable company around. So what's one more T.W. van on the road?" She slapped one of the back doors. "They can outfit it to suit any mission."

"This isn't one of theirs?" Gabriel asked, feeling stupid as he heard snickers from around him.

"Uh, no, Mr. Hawthorne." She looked at the van. "But they've done such a good job even a T.W. geek would be fooled at first glance."

Gabriel nodded and turned away from the van. He scanned the warehouse as the lights grew brighter. On the outside, it looked like any downtown Miami warehouse, perhaps a little unkempt but not nearly as rundown or dilapidated as the compound outside Baton Rouge. Inside, however, again, NASCAR crew chiefs and Gabriel realized that Navy SEALs would be salivating.

The warehouse, which occupied more than half a city block, was configured into four distinct areas. One area was like the garage at the Louisiana compound, with hydraulic vehicle lifts, racks of tires on the wall, welding stations, a sheet-metal fabrication bay, two engine assembly bays, a bank of computers, and a bay housing a plasma cutter. This area also housed a small parking lot with a black Econoline van, a tan Ford Explorer, and a space for another vehicle.

This area melded smoothly into an area set up for the care and maintenance of weaponry and the equipment necessary to manufacture munitions. The wall was covered with grill work from which hung sidearms, rifles, submachine guns, and grenade launchers. The next area was a concrete-and-steel-plate-reinforced indoor firing range. The fourth area was living quarters, with bunks, footlockers, latrines, and shower stations. Also in this area was a cubicle with four-foot walls. The top of a head could be seen, and Augustine stood leaning over it. He looked up and waved.

He came out of the cubicle. "Miss Bennett was taken to her condo, where she packed a bag, and then she was escorted to the Dvanaesti Mansion."

"Assets?" Rotty asked.

"Security system on the house and surrounding perimeter. Cameras on the gate. House staff of four. Six guards, including the two who escorted Miss Bennett. We presume the house staff is all vampires. Three of the guards are assumed to be vampires. The rest are all ex-Special Forces. Regardless, when Cain Dvanaesti's in town, at least eight vampires are watching over the estate."

Gabriel felt his heart begin to pound. "So we need to go right now."

It was as if no one had heard Gabriel.

Augustine tried to suppress a grin but failed. "You were right, Rotty." Augustine continued. "They'll be on their way as soon as his dinner with the president-wannabe is over."

Rotty nodded.

Gabriel knew who 'they' were, but judging by the puzzled expressions, nobody else had a clue.

"That's when we go," Rotty said.

"Oh," Wrench said with dawning realization and a grin.

Gabriel looked around. Outside of Augustine, Rotty, and now Wrench, everyone else was still in the dark, but no one was asking. Gabriel looked at Wrench. "What?"

"We're Daniel going into the lion's den," Wrench said with an appreciative glance at Rotty.

"No, we're not," Rotty said.

"We're not?" Wrench looked crestfallen.

"No. In our case, God isn't closing the mouths of the lions." Rotty clapped a paw on Wrench's shoulder. Rather than wince, she radiated with energy, as if he'd injected her with a stimulant.

Gabriel looked between Rotty and Augustine. He could feel bile rising slowly up his throat. "So, we're going to go now? Right? To get Claudia?"

Augustine frowned at Gabriel.

Gabriel persisted. "This is a rescue mission. We need to go get Claudia before," he looked between Augustine and Rotty, and now Wrench, since she'd cottoned on to what was happening. "Before Cain...knows. Before they..." He continued looking, now at everyone. "...they get here." He knew the truth before Rotty could open his mouth. "This isn't a rescue mission, is it?"

"Yes. It is Hawthorne. It just isn't following the timetable you expected it to. And Cain Dvanaesti knows. You made sure of that."

"I didn't—"

Rotty cut through him. "You called Claudia Bennett when you went to the latrine before we left New Orleans. And again on the road. It's okay," Rotty added, seeing the guilty look on Gabriel's face. "I wanted you to."

"What?" Gabriel felt the bile begin to pinch his tonsils.

"I wanted you to," Rotty repeated. "You see, Hawthorne. The Illuminati, we've come to an impasse. You'll pardon the football analogy. We've sat on the sidelines for centuries, gathering statistics and highlight reels, but have always lacked the equipment to play the game.

"Until today, the gridiron's been a bit one-sided. Until today, the players could only sit on the bench, dressed in whatever makeshift equipment we could muster, and wait for the coaches to say it was time to play. And now that the players are properly dressed and equipped, the coaches still want to gather more statistics. More highlight reels. They fear they're sending a squad of high schoolers out onto the field against a professional team."

Gabriel looked around the room at the sets of eyes watching Rotty pace, faces glowing fiercely.

"You see, Hawthorne. We are the first generation of Illuminati who can confidently strike at the vampires. We no longer have to hope for the best if we run afoul of a vampire. We no longer have to worry about running afoul.

We want to fight." He stopped and pointed to each person in the warehouse. "Every man and woman in the room wants to fight."

They all barked their agreement.

"We are the soldiers." He started pacing. "But our leaders...our leaders are the politicians. They want to watch and wait. And watch and wait." He fell silent.

Gabriel was sure Rotty would pace back and forth for an hour without speaking. Pace for hours in silence, waiting to utter a thought he'd wanted to scream his whole life but was too well-trained a soldier to say out loud. He needed prompting. "Wait for what?"

Rotty stopped pacing. He stared at the wall. "The perfect solution. And what they don't understand is, there will never be a perfect solution. There will never come a day when humans can wake up and find the world rid of vampires like termites after a house has been gassed."

He started pacing again. "I knew when I told Caiaphas what happened to our compound in Saint Petersburg and how we needed to act, he would say we should wait. And he did. So I formulated a plan of my own. I knew if I offered you the opportunity to rescue your old flame, you'd take it. I knew if I left you alone with Wrench and her – no offense, Wrench – diarrhea of the mouth, she'd tell you my plan."

Gabriel expected Wrench to protest, but when he looked at her, she only nodded in resigned agreement.

"I was pretty sure once she'd told you, if you were allowed to say, go to the restroom unattended, you would try to contact Miss Bennett. And I was counting on Miss Bennett calling Cain Dvanaesti because, after all, what woman wouldn't call the love of her life after she'd received a call from an estranged ex-lover she hadn't talked to in ten years telling her he was coming to rescue her from the love of her life? Who, by the way, is evil? And sure enough, he's coming to her rescue."

Gabriel had been listening to Rotty, feeling bile rise to his tonsils and then slide down his throat, burning his stomach. Now his body shook with rage. "So Claudia's just bait to you?" Gabriel launched at Rotty, landing one solid punch to his chin before two team members dragged him away. Wrench pulled the Beretta from Gabriel's waistband. He cursed himself for forgetting Rotty had given him the pistol back just before he'd jumped out of the Suburban at the TV studio.

Gabriel knew he had a jab like Tyson. As a cop, he'd been in several tussles with less-than-upstanding citizens and knew he'd only survive if he could KO the guy, which he'd done. But Rotty? Gabriel seethed as he watched Rotty react to his punch as if it'd been nothing more than a fly, not even so much as a half-step backward.

"You used me," Gabriel roared.

Rotty smiled. "Yes, Hawthorne. I used you." He gestured around the room. "Just like you were using all of us."

"So this isn't a rescue mission, is it?"

Rotty motioned for the men holding Gabriel to release him. Their grips slackened, and Gabriel threw them off.

Rotty took the pistol from Wrench and offered its handle out to Gabriel. "Yes, Hawthorne. It is."

Gabriel reached out, expecting his hand to be slapped away. It wasn't. He took the weapon and tucked it back into his waistband.

"You'll be doing the rescuing. We'll be creating the diversion."

"Speaking of diversions, Rotty," Augustine stepped up. "We're anxious to see it."

"Oh, Hey." Wrench jumped towards the back of the Suburban. "We brought a box for y'all to test fire." The others barked their approval as she opened the back door.

Rotty walked over to the back of the Suburban. "UV spots squared away?" He pulled out a box.

"Affirmative," Augustine answered. He pointed to the box in Rotty's hands. "What's that?"

"A new toy Giblet created." Rotty opened the box and pulled out a pair of night-vision goggles.

"That dude's scary smart," Wrench said as she removed an ammunition crate.

Rotty offered the goggles to Augustine. "He combined night vision with motion sensors."

Augustine looked at him, nonplussed.

"I don't understand either. I just know they work. Something moves, and you can see it." He pointed at one of his men. "Pass them out and make sure they know how to use them before chow."

Wrench handed a box of rounds to one of Augustine's men. "Wait till you see what these babies can do. Do you have any vampire meat to use as targets?"

Augustine answered in the affirmative.

"You guys practice while I load the van." Wrench moved over to the black Econoline van and threw open the back doors. "Hello."

Everyone turned to see Wrench staring into the interior of the cable van.

A young man sat hogtied and gagged with a strip of duct tape.

Rotty looked at Augustine, who only shrugged. "Newbie. Transferred in yesterday morning. Didn't know if I could trust him."

"Then you should've found an excuse to leave him in Orlando." Rotty marched over to the young man. "Since you brought him." Rotty ripped the duct tape off the young man's face. "He's got a right to choose." Rotty looked at him. "Does your mommy know you're playing Vampire Killer?"

The young man only stared at Rotty, awed and terrified.

"I can use another man. If you want to fight, I'll untie you, and you can get ready with the rest of them. If you don't, there won't be any hard feelings. No one will think any less of you. But I will have to leave you tied up and gagged in a corner until we get back, or someone comes looking for you. Won't be personal, so there won't be any hard feelings either way."

The young man continued to stare.

"I need an answer, Son."

At the word, son, the young man reacted as if he'd been slapped out of a stupor. He looked at Rotty, and now the eyes were no longer wide and glassy but fierce and glowing. He cleared his throat. "I want to fight."

Rotty unsheathed his knife and cut the ropes binding him in one slash. "Get suited up. It's almost game time."

The young man nodded as he rubbed his wrists. He trotted off to the table, grabbed a magazine, and filled it with Phase Two rounds.

Rotty watched as both teams prepped their gear, took target practice, and ate chow.

A green light flashed. "Hawk's back," one of Augustine's men said, looking at a monitor.

"Let him in," Augustine ordered.

The man pushed a button. A buzzer shrilled for three seconds throughout the warehouse. Everyone stopped what they were doing and froze. The lights snapped off, plunging the room into total darkness. Then a bay door opened, and a truck came in. As it cleared the entrance, the bay door closed, and after a few seconds, the lights snapped back on.

Gabriel could see a white Ford F-150 truck loaded with two mowers on the bed and weed eaters, edgers, blowers, and rakes hanging from racks. On the door was the silhouette of two birds in flight. Below it read *Bird Bros. Lawn Service.*

The driver pulled in next to the tan Explorer, cut the engine, and stepped out.

"Hawk," Wrench exclaimed as she ran to him.

Gabriel realized his nickname was spot on. Tall and lanky with a sharp nose and narrow chin. His hair was slicked straight back from a severe widow's peak. His eyes were dark, deep-set, and bulging, and he was dressed in a brown mechanic's jumpsuit.

Wrench and Hawk hugged. "Where's Eagle?" Wrench asked.

"Back at the Governor's mansion. He's our eyes on the ground." He pointed to the firing range. "That them?" He unzipped and stepped out of the jumpsuit. A man walked up with a Time Warner work shirt and pants on a hanger.

"Uh-huh. You want to fire off a couple of rounds?" She asked.

Hawk shook his head. "Need to get back. We'll have to field test them." He looked at her as he slipped on the pants.

Wrench nodded, a devilish grin creeping across her face.

"That's all I need to know." Hawk started moving towards the cable van, yanking on the shirt and buttoning it as he went. "Crate already in there?"

"Yep," Wrench responded. "See you guys later."

"See you." Hawk climbed into the cable van and started it up. Again, the warehouse was filled with the buzzing alarm. Then the lights went out, and the bay door opened. Hawk guided the van out. The bay door closed, and everyone went back to work.

The phone rang.

Augustine answered and listened. "Okay." He placed the phone back in its cradle. "Governor Dvanaesti's plane has just landed."

"Detail?" Rotty asked.

Augustine looked at Rotty for a silent beat.

"Let's have a word." Rotty took Augustine's arm and led him away from the group. "What's wrong?"

Augustine looked back at the young men and women finishing preparations, then to Rotty. "I think we should abort," he said through his teeth.

Rotty's brow creased. "Reasons?"

Augustine looked Rotty in the eye. "Isabella's with him."

Rotty eyed Augustine for a long minute. "Are you afraid of her?"

"Personally? Yes." He gestured at the waiting men and women. "Professionally, I'm terrified of what might happen to them."

Rotty only nodded and then turned back to the group. "Let's load up."

53

Wrench pulled the Econoline van into the scenic outlook parking area just before the bridge, stopped, and let the engine idle.

Rotty's laptop chirped. He opened the lid, hit the enter key, and smiled. Pressing the talk button on his throat mic, he said. "All right, Ladies and Gentlemen." He tapped a few buttons on his laptop and hit the enter key. "I've just sent you each a copy of the pics of Cain Dvanaesti's neighborhood, courtesy of Hawk and Eagle. It's on a small island. Familiarize yourself. Memorize it. We've only got a few minutes."

Gabriel looked over the shoulder of the man sitting next to him. He was opening the pictures on his iPad. Gabriel surveyed the images. He'd been on the island and at Dvanaesti's mansion. It didn't qualify as a neighborhood.

That was the difference between the middle class, the wealthy, and the truly wealthy. In a middle-class neighborhood, houses were built on quarter-acre or smaller lots, regardless of house size. Wealthy people might have a little more land, but they still had neighbors they could see, and they could watch people use their street as a cut-through to someplace else. The truly wealthy, like those here in Miami, live on private island communities with ocean views and restricted beaches, in gated homes the size of small gated communities. Cain Dvanaesti was no exception.

The Dvanaesti family mansion sat on the corner lot of one of these private islands, affording a view of the ocean or downtown Miami across the bay, depending on which way you faced. In addition to the view, the backyard boasted a private beach, a boat dock capable of handling vessels up to sixteen thousand pounds, and a covered grill area attached to a pool with recessed barstools in the water.

Protecting the two-story Mediterranean-style mansion was a stone-and-wrought-iron fence approximately eight feet high, with a wrought-iron gate across the drive. Unlike the other homes on this road, the Dvanaesti mansion sat back only thirty yards from the street, where it could be easily seen. The drive followed a straight line from the gate to the home and ended in a roundabout at the foot of two stairways. These stairways, one to the left and one to the right, led to the front landing. From there, a single stairway up to the front door. Off to the left of the roundabout was a six-vehicle garage.

Though he hadn't secured blueprints for the property, Rotty had obtained enough details from a local realtor to sketch out a rough floor plan of the home, which appeared after the real-time photos. The schematic showed a large foyer containing a double staircase to the second floor. The ground floor housed the most rooms. On the right were the living room, dining room, rec room, home theatre, and bathroom. To the left was the kitchen, another dining room, another bathroom, a library, and a music room. Upstairs were six bedrooms, each with an attached bathroom.

On each side of the Dvanaesti property sat another home, but the tree lines deliberately constructed insulated each home from the other and the outside world. Across the street from the house was an eighteen-hole golf course with a beautifully sculpted tree line affording the home a level of privacy from the golfers on the links.

Hawk's voice crackled in each person's ear. "Limo's past the guard gate."

Rotty, Wrench, Gabriel, and two others sat in the van. Rotty let a smile slide across his face. He pressed the talk button on his throat mic. "Two, you in position?"

"Affirmative," Augustine answered.

Rotty nodded into the darkness. He pressed the talk button. "Eagle, this is One. Do you have eyes on the prize?"

"One. Limo's through the front gate." Eagle responded.

"Eagle. If your way is clear, you are free to go." Rotty looked at Wrench and nodded.

Wrench smiled broadly in response, put the van in gear, and pulled onto the road heading towards the bridge.

Eagle sat perched on the branch of a Magnolia tree in the tree line across from the Dvanaesti mansion and watched the limo's brake lights through his scope. "Understood." He didn't say, understood, but tapped his talk button three times in rapid succession as he watched the front door open. A man in a grey pin-striped three-piece suit stepped through the door, the butler. Eagle reminded himself he wasn't a man in any sense of the word. He may have been, but he wasn't now. A woman followed. Eagle recognized her. Claudia Bennett.

The passenger-side door opened. Eagle watched as what no one would mistake for a man stepped from the limo and moved to the back door. In form, it looked like a man, but in countenance, even a child would know this was an evil, unnatural presence.

The driver was also out of the limo, moving back to open the back door on his side. Eagle had a millisecond's view of the back of Cain Dvanaesti's head before the driver, and then Isabella Reese, Eagle recognized her as well, stepped into his crosshairs.

Eagle was patient, however, as he watched the gathered procession move to the stairs. The vampires surrounding Cain were taller than he, but not on the steps. Eagle could feel the grooves of the trigger press lightly into his finger as his patience paid off.

The procession had stopped on the landing, but Cain had continued to walk up the stairs, Isabella beside him, to greet Claudia. The back of Cain Dvanaesti's head appeared in the center of his crosshairs. Eagle pulled the trigger.

Isabella heard the metallic *thunk* and knew. There was no way she could mistake that sound. She'd listened to the evolution of that sound; she had made a point of creating aural memory for that sound. Grabbing Cain by the scruff of his neck and forcing him to the steps, she screamed, "Down," at the others around her.

The bullet intended for the back of Cain Dvanaesti's head sailed over it and into the butler's stomach. He looked from the hole in his suit to Isabella and Cain with bemused surprise. Then his eyes widened, this time with horror. He grabbed his chest as if struck with a massive coronary and started screaming. A large dark stain bloomed on his shirt and vest. Hot black liquid popped and sizzled as it oozed from the hole. His screaming stopped as if with a mute button as another orifice opened up on his Adam's apple. More dark fluid popped and sizzled like chicken fat on a griddle. Garbled sounds like dog food sliding from a can issued through the butler's throat.

Cain watched the vampire cooking, liquefying from the inside out, his fingers slipping off his hands like flesh-colored gloves. He wanted to look away, but couldn't. His eyes were paralyzed just as sure as his legs. He watched the man's eyes slide like jelly from the sockets, just pools of some black substance spilling onto his cheeks.

Now Claudia was screaming, great shrieks which shook Cain out of his horrified stupor. He inhaled a deep, cleansing breath through his mouth and tasted cooking vampire on his tongue. It made him gag. He could hear Claudia's violent retching.

The other vampires stood and stared as if witnessing a violent murder first-hand for the first time.

Isabella stepped up to the quickly shrinking butler, not much more now than a puddle of dark sparkling stuff and a gray pinstriped three-piece suit. "That's interesting." Her voice sounded as indifferent as if she'd just discovered a burned-out cigarette lying on the step. Pulling Cain to his feet, she hissed, "Into the house."

Eagle cursed under his breath as Cain disappeared from his crosshairs as if he'd been a holograph that'd suddenly been shut off. His curse caught in his throat as he watched the butler melt. It was... mesmerizing. Not until something crossed in front of his scope did he realize the vampires were moving.

"Target compromised," Eagle said into his mike, as calmly as if he'd said he liked mayo on his tuna fish sandwich, as he set his crosshairs on the back of a retreating vampire and pulled the trigger. "Target compromised," he repeated. "Dvanaesti is Oscar Mike. Inside the house. Two vampires neutralized." He watched the second vampire melt in his scope.

Wrench smiled as she stepped on the accelerator. The tires squealed as they tried to find traction with the asphalt. The man with Gabriel chambered a tranquilizing round while Gabriel positioned himself by the side door.

They were approaching the guard shack. Wrench watched as the guard stepped out, arms waving in alarm.

"Now," Rotty yelled.

Gabriel pulled the door open as the other man took aim and fired the tranq round. The guard dropped as they sped by. Gabriel slammed the door shut and huddled back down.

"Two. Engage Target." Rotty shouted into his mic as the tires gripped and the van shot forward.

Gabriel could hear the roar of the outboard engine over the radio as Augustine yelled, "Engaging."

"Hang on," Wrench warned as she slammed on the brakes and turned the wheel, causing the van to go into a spin. The vehicle stopped facing the way it'd just come in front of the Dvanaesti gate. Before Gabriel could get his bearings, the van doors opened. The man in the back with him jumped out, his weapon laying down suppressive fire at and over the fence. Dust and debris spat up at their feet. Someone was firing back.

Rotty smacked a button on the van's ceiling as he jumped out. "Stay with Wrench till I come for you, Hawthorne," Rotty yelled over his shoulder as he picked up a small sack and moved to the gate.

"Compound targets neutralized." Hawk's voice squawked calmly in everyone's ear.

Rotty pressed his talk button. "Good job, Hawk. You and Eagle move to your secondary position."

For his part, Gabriel was feeling fuzzy. He'd been in a shootout once when he'd been a street cop, and he'd had a few scrapes as a private citizen. But this was something new. He'd never been in a firefight. He wasn't feeling scared, just out of his element, and this was one of those things you couldn't take baby steps with. You either got it or you didn't when the time came. If you got it, you might die. You might not. But you could be an asset. If you didn't get it, then you were a liability that got yourself and others killed.

Gabriel wasn't necessarily a spiritual man, but he lifted his eyes skyward and said a quick prayer that, either way, no one on his side of the game would die on account of him. His prayer was cut short. He wasn't gazing upon the van ceiling but upon the heavens. The entire roof was now upright, looking like a large flat-screen television.

He looked at Wrench and saw she was grinning at him. She pointed to the roof. "The vampires are about to become illumined." She laughed at her joke, slipping on her balaclava and gloves and motioning for Gabriel to do the same.

"Fire in the hole," Rotty boomed over the radio. "Flip the switch and watch the cockroaches scatter."

The head of security at the Dvanaesti mansion, a vampire named Jasper, could hear the gunfire before any humans wasted time screaming it into his earpiece. It was almost as irritating to him as the silly girl's screams, which she'd renewed upon watching the second vampire melt, or the sounds of bullets smacking into the front wall, the door, and through the windows, like little mosquitoes buzzing a human's ears then moving just out of reach to be swatted.

Shockwaves rattled the house. Claudia may have heard one large explosion, but Jasper counted four distinct detonations and knew exactly what'd happened: Their adversary had planted C4 on the gate hinge plate assemblies and blown them. The human guard screaming, "The perimeter's been breached," over and over, was superfluous. Jasper made a mental note to kill him if the man survived. He was being both unnecessarily obvious and emotional. Jasper didn't need either on his security detail. It made him look bad in front of Cain Dvanaesti and, more importantly, Isabella. For if Isabella wasn't happy with his performance, Roman wouldn't be either.

At the moment, his performance was woefully inept; he knew. But, in his defense, he reasoned, he had no experience with melting vampires and humans having the upper hand. He noticed Isabella staring at him, waiting for him to do something. Otherwise, she'd relieve him of duty, as well as his life, and assume control. Spotting Billy, a young vampire, he ordered, "Check the gate."

Billy pulled back the curtain.

Bright blue light stormed through the windows as if the day had broken in the middle of the night. Billy screamed in agony, staggering away from the window as if he'd been shot and beating blindly at the air around him.

Claudia threw her hands up to shield her eyes. Vampires uttered surprised grunts as if they'd just touched something hot. Their skin bloomed a deep, angry red, like a bad sunburn, and they retreated into the shadows.

Billy bumped into Claudia. She could see that his face was charred, his eye sockets smoldering. Claudia went into hysterics.

"Someone calm her down," Isabella said with a dead calm, "before I do."

Augustine and his team waited just behind the bright blue UV lights. He stole furtive glances at his team. He couldn't see their faces or eyes behind the thermal motion goggles and balaclavas, but their straightened backs and heads facing the mansion told him they were ready. It was like watching a racehorse in the stall just before the bell. Each man and woman stood poised to explode from their hold positions and take the mansion or die trying.

He felt a rush of pride surge through his body, greater than any adrenaline rush. He wanted to hug each one, tell them it was an honor and a privilege to lead them tonight, to fight alongside them, and to fall among them if that were fate's plan. When this is over, he vowed, we will hug the living and toast the dead.

Rotty's voice, booming with exhilaration, rang out over the radio. "One and Two. Move. Fire teams, light it up."

Augustine watched as his team marched out onto the grounds. Malachi and a female he'd make sure received a name after tonight, whether she lived or died, moved to point. Each had a weapon hanging from a tactical sling on their side. Right now, however, the six-shot M32 grenade launcher was the weapon of choice for the fire teams. They continued to walk as they aimed at the second-floor windows and fired.

Anne had only been a vampire for a decade when she was chosen to be part of the Dvanaesti mansion staff. The fact that Roman Dvanaesti had bestowed such an honor upon an infant was not lost on her. The other vampires named to the Miami home staff were all at least a century old and had risen through the ranks of the Dvanaesti Empire. But as Isabella and others could tell her, Anne's innocence was eclipsed by her viciousness and cunning. Isabella felt that Anne's viciousness and cleverness were second only to hers in the clan.

So she'd gone to work in the mansion five years ago as a maid and had loved every minute of it. The other vampires on staff had openly shared their desire to move to the Dvanaesti mansion outside Rome and serve their master directly, but not Anne. In Miami, she had the honor and the pleasure of serving Roman and Cain. She was a part of her master's plan for the greatest nation in the history of the world. None but Isabella and the Miami mansion staff could claim that honor.

And for that honor, she'd taken up a weapon, a poker from the fireplace in the back bedroom she'd been preparing for Claudia Bennett, the woman who'd produce the next generation of Dvanaesti's she'd proudly serve when the gunfire and explosions had started. She'd picked up the poker not because she needed a weapon to defend herself but because the poker served as a convenient skewer for human kabobs. She'd planned on bursting through the window but had been trapped by the bright blue light. She'd crawled to the window and tugged the curtains closed, but not before being burned. She'd looked into the mirror and watched her skin bubble with blisters, smelled the acrid stench of burnt hair, and felt something she hadn't felt in years. Pain.

Now she could hear Claudia downstairs, screaming hysterically, Billy crying in agony, and, outside, a human ordering to light it up. She had no idea what that meant when something small came crashing through the window, dragging the curtains down. It was a canister, and as if the glass had shredded it open, gas spewed from it like blood from a severed carotid artery. Everything in the room, Anne noticed, including herself and the air itself, was turning into fire.

Pain exploded in her body as she watched her skin blacken, crackle, and peel away from the muscle and then the bone. She felt the marrow in her bones explode and decided her only chance for survival was out the window; the fire had come in. She started running pell-mell and burst through the glass, feeling the shards peel her charred muscles from her bones, and into the bright blue light.

The pain was unfathomable as she felt herself disintegrate into dust.

54

"Get Cain to the safe room." Jasper had to shout to be heard over the screams of Billy rolling on the floor in agony, over Claudia as she tried to press herself through the wall, over the grenade canisters whizzing through the air on all sides, and over the vampires, like the floor, ablaze. Whoever was responsible for this assault had planned well, Jasper thought.

"Claudia," Cain screamed as the vampires surrounded him, grabbed him, and forced his head down as they started to move.

A smoke grenade slammed into the wall next to Claudia's head, sending her into a new round of hysterics and coughing as she sucked a lungful of the gas into her body.

Isabella crossed to Claudia and forced her to the floor. "I've got her," Isabella screamed. "We're right behind you."

The details surrounding Cain moved, and Claudia watched what looked like a film in fast-forward. She screamed, this time from surprise.

"Will you stop doing that?" Isabella hissed in exasperation as she lifted Claudia to her feet. She was about to take off after Cain when an incendiary grenade splintered the hallway Cain had just been pulled through.

Isabella grabbed Claudia and two vampires who'd started screaming as their clothes turned to fire and whisked them all from the room.

This time, Claudia uttered a soft 'oh.' She felt what she could only explain as a newfound understanding of what an astronaut or test pilot meant when he said he was moving so fast it made his liver quiver. She would've sworn she'd moved from the foyer to the door leading to the library in the blink of an eye. Except, she hadn't had time to blink. She watched a blur beating at the flames of two writhing forms. Once the flames were out, Isabella stood where the blur had been.

Isabella pulled a smoking form to his feet by what was left of his shirt. "Guard this hallway and kill anyone who comes this way. Anyone. And tell Jasper I'll find an alternate route to the safe room." She pointed to the other form. "Check the library."

The vampire nodded, and Claudia watched as the vampire vanished. The library door flew open, but she saw nothing else. A voice from inside the library called, "Clear."

Claudia couldn't process what she was seeing. The one standing guard and the other running into the library should be screaming in pain. They should either be writhing or motionless on the floor, not standing guard or running into a room.

Isabella grabbed Claudia and moved into the library.

Rotty watched as flames now engulfed the second floor. He listened to the screaming vampires and couldn't help but think it was one of the sweetest sounds he'd ever heard. He watched shadows in the foyer blur and disappear after one of his grenadiers stumbled as he fired, sending the grenade through the front door. So far, that was the only aspect that hadn't gone to plan. Some might've thought Eagle's failure to kill Cain Dvanaesti, but Rotty had been glad Eagle had missed. He hoped for that honor himself.

He spoke into his mic. "Time to light the torches."

The two nameless soldiers with him each tossed their M32 grenade launchers to the ground without a second thought. One had strapped an M2A1-7 flamethrower to his back. He pulled the hose and nozzle from its holster as the other soldier turned the tank's fuel valve into the 'on' position and slapped the gunner on the shoulder.

The others with him also flipped on the UV lights fixed to the barrels of their weapons.

"Two. Ready to cook?" Rotty asked.

"Ready," Augustine responded.

Rotty looked at the people gathered around him. They each nodded in turn. "Shake and bake."

The flamethrower immediately shot a stream of fire up the steps in front of him before mounting the stairs. Rotty's team fell into position, weapons ready, with Rotty in the rear.

Rotty watched the fire climb the stairs and couldn't help but smile as he thought of the Old Testament story of God leading the Israelites by night in a pillar of fire. He wasn't a particularly spiritual man, but Rotty understood the symbolism. Fire provided light in the dark, warmth in the cold, and safety in the wilderness, a sign of God's presence to his people that no harm should come to them. Israel's enemies fled before the fire or were consumed by it, just as his enemies would.

The flame thrower entered the house and shot a stream of fire up the stairs, then to his left and right as the others followed him and quickly set up a perimeter.

Billy had stopped screaming. Stopped moving. Rotty looked at him, taking in with deep satisfaction the charred and blackened face, the empty eye sockets, and pumped two rounds into Billy. One into his chest, the other into his head.

Rotty stepped back to keep from getting any of the quickly liquefying Billy onto his boots. "Hawthorne, Wrench. You're with me." He nodded at Eagle, Hawk, and the yet-to-be-named man.

Eagle nodded back, then turned. Hawk and the nameless man followed.

Jasper had his hand on the scruff of Cain's neck, keeping him hunched over. "Keep your head down and your feet moving, Sir." Jasper sounded more like a teacher admonishing a class of students than a subordinate addressing his superior. If he'd had the slightest hint of this tone at any other time, Isabella would've ripped his tongue out. But at this moment, Jasper was in charge. It was no different from the Secret Service guarding the President. The President was the most powerful man in the free world until his life was threatened. Then he was a stupid child playing in traffic that needed to be manhandled to safety.

Once they were away from the immediate danger, Jasper slowed down only to find the attack was coming from the front and the back. He could hear the incendiary grenades being fired, hear the screams from vampires on the second floor, smell the cooking of vampire flesh, and the burning of the house. So he decided to move very slowly so he didn't run straight into an ambush. He tightened his grip on Cain's neck as he walked.

Cain quietly complied.

Jasper was just about to sigh with relief, the safe room only a few feet away, when they turned a corner, walking into a flame of fire.

The two vampires at point burst into flame as they screamed.

Jasper tossed Cain to the ground and took off like a shot towards the flamethrower, feeling his skin melt and smelling his brows and hair singe. He slammed into the flamethrower, wrapping his arms tightly around the man and slamming him into the ground. He could feel the tanks collapse under his grip, could smell the petrol.

The blast rocked the house and knocked Wrench off her balance, causing the vampire's strike to miss her head. Instead, he hit her shoulder, dislocating it, forcing her hard into the wall; her head left a hole in the drywall. She groaned as she collapsed to the floor. The vampire might've been able to take advantage of this, but Gabriel and Rotty were also thrown off balance. Their weapons and UV lights swung wildly, the lights cutting across the vampire left burnt flesh in their wake.

The vampire stumbled backward, screaming. Rotty aimed and fired.

Cain pulled himself up onto his feet and swayed. He heard a high-pitched, persistent ringing, and nothing else. He snapped his fingers by his ears, but didn't hear it. The smell of burnt wood, hair, and flesh permeated the air. He'd never been intoxicated, but decided it must look and feel like this. The walls were swaying in the opposite direction he was, and the floor kept threatening to rise and clock him one right on the chin. He thought he heard shouting behind him, but it had to be far away.

He turned to see two intruders, a man and a woman, weapons raised and pointing at him, screaming something to him or someone behind him. Maybe, he thought in his daze, they're beckoning to me, wanting me to come with them. He took a step, his eyes focusing on their trigger fingers, which now, he noticed, were squeezing hard.

Rotty finished popping Wrench's shoulder back into place. She grunted and squeezed Gabriel's fingers hard. She'd instructed him to cross his fingers so that when she squeezed, the bones wouldn't rub on each other. Sure enough, when she did, he felt pressure but no pain.

"Can you hold this?" Rotty offered her the weapon. She took it with no more than a grimace. "Get yourself out of here." He growled.

Wrench stared at him, head shaking in defiance.

Rotty clapped a reassuring hand on her shoulder. She let out an involuntary moan. "You did good tonight," his voice paternal, "I'm proud of you. Now fall back to the van, or I'll kick your keister back there myself."

Her nod was reluctant and weak.

Rotty stood up and gestured down the hall. "Let's go, Hawthorne."

Isabella sat Claudia on the sofa. She rubbed Claudia's neck while making soft shushing sounds. Claudia sat sobbing but beginning to feel a little drowsy.

Isabella could hear a soft crackle above and behind her, smelled the peculiar scent of burning insulation, and knew the fire was eating its way into the room. She turned and watched with a bland curiosity as the paint on the ceiling darkened and then bubbled.

Claudia finally heard the crackling and popping as the ceiling gave way. She screamed as the weight of the fire pushed through like a rushing liquid into the room. The fire hit the floor, splashing onto the books and drapes, igniting them like kindling.

"Be still." Isabella clamped her hand onto Claudia's shoulder as she whipped around to face the door. "Check it," she commanded.

The vampire moved to the door, twisted the knob, and opened it. His body rocked backward as the rounds slammed into its body. Before he could hit the floor, the putrefaction was already more than half finished.

Before Rotty could storm into the room with guns blazing and Gabriel hot on his heels, Isabella had already crossed the room and grabbed each man. Gabriel hit the shelving. Books cascaded down on his head. Rotty slammed into the wall. Isabella grasped Rotty before he could bounce back and hurled him headlong into the fireplace mantle. Bones snapped. His left foot faced the wrong direction. His right hand looked as if it had no bones in it. His skull was flat in the back.

Again, Isabella had a hold of him before he could crumple to the ground, fangs exposed. Rotty looked up into her eyes, black with fury.

"One, One," a voice shouted through Rotty's radio. "Cain Dvanaesti is dead. I repeat. Cain Dvanaesti is dead."

Rotty smiled up at Isabella. Four of his teeth were missing. Blood spilled from the corners of his mouth. He laughed and coughed up blood.

Isabella's eyes grew darker as she sank her teeth into Rotty's throat.

"Quiet," Augustine snapped at the two men who'd started making whooping shouts at the announcement. There were still vampires in the house, and they now had more reason than ever to attack. They might even be more reckless. They were in a dangerous situation. Augustine clicked on his mic. "Okay. Time to settle down. This is still a hostile environment. What is your location?"

What was left of the Alpha team, their only designation since neither had yet to earn a name, stood in the hall. By firelight, they checked their weapons, reloaded magazines, and waited for Augustine to get them. Malachi was dead, which was sad, but the operation was successful. Cain Dvanaesti was dead.

"So what name do you hope to have bestowed upon you?" He asked the woman as he slapped a fresh magazine into his weapon.

"I don't—"

He waited as he chambered a round. "You don't what?"

But she didn't respond.

He turned. "What don't—?"

She was gone. He immediately pulled his weapon into a tactical position and moved forward down the hall, looking right and left.

The fire caused shadows to move. He jerked right and left, up and down, prepared to fire in a second, but they were only shadows. Something struck his knee. Hard.

"Ow. What the—?" His voice caught in his throat as no air would leave his body. It was her head, ripped cleanly from her shoulders. He heard a hiss, like wet breath being sucked through teeth, and looked up. He opened his mouth to scream, but never got the chance.

Isabella felt the last of Rotty's blood ebb weakly over her teeth and onto her tongue. Heard his heart stop. She let what was now nothing more than a bag of dry bones fall from her hands to the floor.

It had been messy. She could feel the thick liquid coating her lips and cheeks, dripping from her chin onto her blouse and matting the silk to her skin. She hadn't fed like that in a long time, with abandon, with pure animal bloodlust. It felt good. Soothing. Intoxicating. Cathartic.

Cain was dead. Thirty-five years of separation from her master, of raising his son...gone. She couldn't say wasted. Nothing Roman asked her to do was a waste of her time. It had only been thirty-five years. What was that to her, Isabella Reese? Isabella Dvanaesti. Isabella Medici. What were thirty-five years to a woman who'd lived more than eight hundred?

She breathed in, inhaling the scents of burning wood, paper, and fabric. And of blood. Blood under a pile of books on the floor. As she turned, she caught sight of Claudia sitting on the sofa, frozen, her face screwed up in an inaudible scream, eyes bulging. Isabella smiled at her, revealing fangs wet and dark with Rotty's blood.

The appearance of the fangs and blood caked on Isabella's face was like a sharp slap across Claudia's face. Now she screamed. Piercing. Blood-chilling.

Isabella's grin grew wider.

Claudia stood, still screaming at Isabella. No. Not Isabella. That wasn't a woman across the room from her. That wasn't human. That was a thing. A—

The thing's hand was around her throat, slamming her head into the wall. The grip was tightening, crushing her windpipe, stifling her scream. Claudia's face was swimming in and out of focus. A rancid metallic tang was in the air. It made her eyes water and her throat feel like she'd swallowed ash.

Then the grip loosened. Her feet found the floor. She hadn't realized she'd been dangling more than a foot above it. Isabella's face sharpened. She was grizzly, but her eyes had softened as if she were looking at a frightened child.

"There, there, Sweet Claudia," Isabella cooed as she stroked Claudia's hair. "It's all right now. It's all right." Her smile was warm like a grandmother's. "It's all right, my little sparrow."

She didn't say anything for a long moment but continued to stroke Claudia's hair, her eyes focused on Claudia's face. "Roman was right about you. You would've made an excellent helpmate for Cain." Isabella leaned in and tenderly kissed Claudia's forehead. "You are beautiful. Charming. And intelligent." The warm smile went a little crooked. "But." Isabella's hand traced Claudia's forehead over the bridge of her nose and lips to her chin, which she cupped and pulled Claudia's face into her own. "None of that matters. Not anymore."

Now the smile twisted.

Claudia pressed herself against the wall as her hands instinctively moved to protect herself.

"This," Isabella let her fangs retract and then spring out like a switchblade, "is going to hurt."

And now Isabella was rising, floating backward as if blasted off her feet by some unseen and unheard explosion. She screamed in surprise.

Claudia heard Isabella's shrieks of surprise as she realized it wasn't an explosion but something that had wrenched Isabella off her feet. She watched as it slammed Isabella's body into the burning bookshelf. Isabella dropped to the floor, consumed in a fiery cascade of books, wall, and ceiling. The thing that had ripped Isabella away and thrown her into the fire turned to face her. She screamed.

55

Cain heard Claudia's scream. A scream of panic. Of horror. Saw her take a step back away from him.

Could her shock be so great that she didn't even recognize him? He took a step towards her.

"Stay away from me," she shrieked.

He watched her arms fly up to protect herself as if he were coming at her, swinging the back of his hand. He stopped and looked at her, puzzled. Why was she behaving like this? Isabella was trying to kill her, and he'd saved her. Why was she staring at him like he was some monster?

It stung. He knew it shouldn't, that she was in shock, but it did. She was cowering from him. *Him.* The man who loved her. Cherished her. Saved her life. He felt a flash of anger and watched her flinch. He cleared his throat and heard the growl. She flinched again. His eyes widened. So his throat was a little rough. With all the smoke and noxious fumes, who wouldn't? He felt anger rise in him. No, he told himself. No. She's just in shock. He must tamp down his anger. He must put aside these feelings. She was raw, that was all, and not herself. He needed to calm her, to soothe her.

"Claudia." He'd spoken her name with tenderness but had been drowned out by some preternatural moan.

Claudia shrank, bursting into tears.

Cain held up his hands in supplication and saw they weren't hands. Not human hands. The fingers were elongated, knobbly-jointed, with long, curved nails that looked more like scythes. They were stained with blood. The skin was a mottled black and grey. Veins the color of ripe plums snaked across the hands and forearms.

He turned and saw a demon watching him through the reflection in the glass curio. There was no other word for it. There could be no other word for it. It had been in the room the whole time. He hadn't seen it. This had been what Claudia had been screaming at. He needed to put distance between himself and this... thing.

He stepped back. The demon stepped back. He raised his hand. So did the demon. It was the same mottled, elongated, scythe-like hand. He felt his knees weaken. He was not looking at a demon.

I'm looking at me.

His brow was high, the skin the same mottling as his hands, veins snaking across his face and neck. His eyes were crimson. He opened his mouth. The jaw opened larger than was humanly possible. Each tooth was sharpened to a point.

As he watched, stunned, he saw himself changing. Metamorphosing back into the human he remembered as Cain Dvanaesti.

He collapsed to his hands and knees, oblivious to the searing heat and thickening smoke. Who was he now, he wondered. What was he now? What had made him this way? Was it his father's blood? Did his father know about this? Did he know this might happen? Had he planned it? Did he care? Was Cain no more than a pawn? Just a puppet? And what about Claudia? What did she think now? Did she still love him? Or did she abhor him now?

A chill passed through his veins. He felt fear, loathing, embarrassment, and hatred. He didn't think he could take it. He thought his heart would explode. He was sure that's what he wanted. His vision blurred. Hot tears ran down his cheeks.

Claudia stood there, still pressed into the wall, watching the thing that'd become Cain, on hands and knees, crying. Was it Cain? How could it be? Cain was a human being, and that thing hadn't been human. It looked like Cain now, and Cain was crying. Sobbing. His whole body was heaving.

She opened her mouth to say his name, but her throat was too dry. Not even a hoarse whisper escaped her lips. She cleared her throat, trying to breathe, but the air was hot. "Cain," she said again in a crackle. She took a step. "Is that you, Cain?"

She desperately wanted it to be. Willed it to be. She didn't know whether to laugh or cry. If this were Cain sobbing on the floor, he was also that monster. That demon thing that had saved her life and killed Isabella. But not her.

Claudia took another hesitant step. She reached out like a frightened child at a petting zoo, wanting desperately to feel Cain, afraid she would place her hand on something else. She pulled back. Steeling herself, she rested a hand on his shoulder.

He felt the coolness of her skin on his shoulder. Now it was his turn to flinch. His turn to fear her. What would he see in her eyes? Fear? Disgust? Hatred? Love? Forgiveness? He didn't know which would be worse. Again, he wished his heart would cease beating. Just stop. Cease to be.

But it didn't stop. He didn't cease to be. He turned.

Her eyes were rounded with fear, but they also shimmered. The shimmering wasn't tears. He watched as her eyes searched his. She bit her bottom lip. "Cain?"

Cain nodded weakly. "I'm here, My Love."

She saw what she was looking for, that glimmer in his eyes. The glimmer that no other person on the planet had. Could have. She didn't know how or why, but she knew. This was Cain. He was back. Back? No. The other. The beast. That was Cain, too. But it wasn't a beast. It'd been a physical manifestation of the darkness that dwelt in every soul. Terrifying. Disturbing. But as she now realized, it was oddly comforting on some level. Cain had been both horrible and vulnerable at the same time. A thin smile spread across her face. "Cain." She said again, satisfied this time.

Cain stood and took her hands into his. "Are you all right?"

She nodded. "What happened? Are you all right?"

He pulled her into him. "I am now."

Her warmth washed over him, and he felt the heat of the fire. He finally noticed the room. It was burning all around them. If they didn't leave and fast, the fire would consume them just as surely as it had consumed everything else.

"We need to go." He took her hand and moved towards the window.

"We can't." Claudia's voice was strong now. More confident. "We've got to get Gabriel out, too." She started looking around. "He's here somewhere."

By an unexplained instinct, Cain closed his eyes, remembered Gabriel, and inhaled. His eyes popped open and riveted on a pile of books just beginning to ignite. He pointed at it. "There."

Cain moved to the burning pile and ripped book after heavy book away.

Gabriel lay unconscious on the floor. Blood dribbled from his nose and ear.

Cain grabbed Gabriel by the collar and yanked him to his feet. "Now," he shouted over the din of exploding wood and roaring flames. He offered his arm. Claudia grabbed Cain's free hand. "Close your eyes and hang on." He commanded.

Cain hugged Gabriel and Claudia to him, and quicker than any other human, though not as quick as when he was the demon, he burst through the window and into the fresh night air.

"One," Augustine said into his mic as he stood in the backyard watching the mansion burn. "One. What is your position?" He uttered a solitary curse. "I hope you're out of the house." It had been a long time since Augustine had felt this helpless.

He glanced down at the two team members with him, lying on the grass, catching their breath. "I hope you're all out of the house."

Wrench pulled herself up into the van. Her shoulder screamed with pain. She'd heard Augustine's call for One and had waited for Rotty's response, silently voicing the same wish as Augustine. "I hope you're out of the house."

She was scanning the burning mansion when she saw it.

"Two. We have movement. Three figures just burst through a window on the east side of the house," she shouted into her mic as she pulled herself out of the van. "Repeat. Three figures just busted through a window on the east side of the house. Checking it out."

"Copy, Wrench." Augustine's voice crackled in her ear. "We'll rendezvous with you there."

"Gabe? Gabe, can you hear me?"

Gabriel swam through the fog of unconsciousness toward the voice saying his name.

"Gabe? You need to wake up now."

I'm trying.

"Are you sure he's okay?"

"I'm no doctor, my Love."

It was a man's voice. It was calling the pretty woman's voice, my Love. Gabriel started swimming faster. "But I don't see or feel any serious injuries."

Gabriel felt himself breaking through, waking up. He wanted to tell the pretty woman's voice that he was okay. He was there to rescue her, but all he managed to say was, "humnah."

"I'm sorry?" The male voice asked.

"I think he's coming around."

"Humnah," Gabriel repeated. Though he still couldn't speak, he could open his eyes. He did and found the male smiling with amusement and the pretty female looking with compassion. He blinked to bring them into focus. It was Cain Dvanaesti and Claudia. He smiled. "Hum..." he stopped and cleared his throat. "I'm...here." He wanted to keep speaking, but his throat felt parched.

"Yes, you are," said Cain, now grinning.

"I'm...here...to...rescue you." His voice was a haggard whisper.

"Rescue me from what?" Cain looked confused now.

Gabriel shook his head as he pointed at Claudia. "You. I'm here to rescue you."

Now it was Claudia's turn to look bemused. "From what? Who? Cain? No. I don't need rescuing from Cain."

"Need...to...get...you away...from here." Gabriel tried to reach out and take her hand or stroke her cheek. Instead, he waved it weakly in her face and let it drop to his side. He felt drugged.

Cain knelt beside Gabriel. "Look, Mr. Hawthorne. Gabriel. I love Claudia. Do you understand that? I don't know who," his mind flashed back to the memory of his reflection in the mirror moments ago, "or what you think I am. But I'm not those things. I love Claudia. And Claudia loves me." He took Gabriel's hand. "I know you love Claudia. But not like I do. You fear for her safety, Gabriel. But I can keep her safe. I'm the only one at the moment who can."

Gabriel shook his head again. "In...danger."

"But not from me." Cain held Gabriel's gaze.

As he looked into those eyes, he knew Cain was telling him the truth. Knew Cain could and would keep her safe. He needed to let them go. Together. It was the right thing to do. He nodded to Cain.

Cain smiled and nodded back. "Thank you." He released Gabriel's hand and gaze, stood up, and looked around. "We need to go, Claudia. Now."

Claudia nodded and looked at Gabriel. "Goodbye, Gabe." She stood up. Cain placed his hands around her waist and looked both ways...

And they were gone.

Wrench stopped short. She'd seen three people on the side of the house. One supine person, and two people on their knees beside. Before she could take another step, the people kneeling stood and disappeared.

She dropped to one knee and pulled her weapon into tactical position as Hawk and Eagle ran up behind her, weapons drawn. "Mr. Hawthorne? Is that you?"

"Wrench," Eagle shouted. "Where's Rotty?" He and Hawk scanned the perimeter in opposite directions.

"Yeah," Gabriel replied.

"Who was with you?" Wrench tried to remain calm, but her voice trembled.

"Huh?" Gabriel answered after a minute. "Oh, Cain Dvanaesti and Claudia."

"Cain Dvanaesti?" Hawk asked over his shoulder, continuing to peer into the tree line.

"That's impossible." Wrench eyed Gabriel.

Augustine and the others reached Gabriel and Wrench, weapons drawn. "Wrench. Hawk. Eagle. Hawthorne. Anyone else?"

Wrench dropped her weapon and stood up. "No, Sir. We must be it." She rubbed her aching shoulder. "Cain Dvanaesti's alive."

"But we had a report—" Augustine listened to the approaching sirens. "Is the van clean?"

Wrench pulled out a small black box from her cargo pants pocket. She inserted a key, twisted it to the left, and then back. The van disintegrated.

"It is now," Wrench responded.

Augustine nodded. "Let's get to the boat then." He nodded towards the flashing lights. "They'll be here soon. We can figure this out on the way back."

Wrench watched the house burning on the horizon as Augustine maneuvered the boat out to sea. "So what happened to Rotty?"

Everyone on the boat looked at Wrench.

Gabriel's gaze dropped to the floor of the boat.

"Where's Rotty?" Wrench's voice was filled with cool accusation.

Gabriel didn't say anything because he didn't know. The last thing he remembered, Rotty had shot whoever had opened the door. Then he was outside the house. He had a splitting headache, maybe a cracked rib; his skin felt like he had a bad sunburn, but he couldn't tell anybody how or why.

Wrench shoved her weapon into Gabriel's face. "I asked you a question." Her voice was a dead, cold fury.

Augustine's sidearm was out of the holster and at Wrench's temple in less than a beat. "Okay, Wrench. Settle down."

"Not until this waste of space tells me what happened to Rotty. He was with him."

"Shoulder that weapon now, Wrench. Or I will use deadly force."

Wrench didn't move but stared down at Gabriel, eyes wild.

"Wrench." Augustine's voice remained calm. "If anyone understood what tonight was about and the possible ramifications, it was Rotty. He knew that he, you, me, even Mr. Hawthorne here might not make it out alive. He knew it and was willing to accept that. You accepted that as well when you agreed to come with him. Don't let Rotty's death be in vain. Do him proud and shoulder that weapon."

Nobody moved.

Gabriel was sure Wrench would pull the trigger, and Augustine would pull his trigger a half second later.

"Wrench," Gabriel finally said. "I honestly don't know what happened to Rotty. We were in the library. Some woman attacked us. The next thing I knew, I woke up outside the house with Cain and Claudia." Then he added, "I don't know what happened, but I know I owe him my life."

The explanation sounded weak and maybe even somewhat melodramatic to Gabriel's ears. He hoped it didn't resonate the same with Wrench.

Wrench stared hard at Gabriel for a long beat before finally nodding and dropping her weapon.

Augustine holstered his sidearm. "We lost five people tonight. Five. I don't know how many of them we killed. We know that Cain Dvanaesti survived." Augustine looked at Gabriel. "What I want to know, Mr. Hawthorne, is what happened to Cain Dvanaesti and Isabella Reese."

Gabriel looked nonplussed at Augustine. "I don't know who Isabella Reese is, and I don't know what happened to Cain Dvanaesti." He shrugged. "Or Claudia."

Wrench and the others made noises of disgust or sarcasm.

Gabriel thought of telling them of the conversation he'd had with Cain and Claudia right before they'd disappeared, but he could already hear the snickering of the gathered Illuminati. Hear his defense.

Well, why else would the guy save my life? Why's it so hard to believe Claudia would ask him to save me? He told me outside that no one could love or protect her like him. Why wouldn't he do something like that if she asked?

Gabriel heard Augustine's response in his head.

Why indeed.

Gabriel said nothing.

Augustine stared into the water as if contemplating his last statement. Finally, he looked up at Wrench. "Let's get back to the warehouse. We need to let Caiaphas know what happened."

56

Cain cursed as he realized he'd punched the wrong number again into the pay phone keypad. His hands shook from a chill not carried on the night air but emanating from deep inside him. He depressed the hook switch and tried again, only to push the wrong number on the first attempt. He slammed the receiver onto the cradle.

This is insanity, he told himself, rubbing his hands together and blowing over them as if to warm them. Ten minutes ago, he'd been beside Claudia as she knelt, talking to Gabriel Hawthorne. Now he was standing outside a little convenience store in Weston on Vista Park Boulevard.

Ten minutes ago, he'd told Claudia it was time to go, had scooped her into his arms, and started running. He'd run down the street, across the bridge separating the private island from the mainland. Homeless people sleeping on sidewalks never noticed as he passed. Joggers and late-night strollers commented on the sudden breeze, and drivers of emergency vehicles dismissed the blurred streak as a trick of their lights. He'd run over thirty-six miles in ten minutes. Run.

He had no idea how he'd done it, only that he had. He wasn't in running shoes and wasn't wearing workout clothes. He was in dress shoes and a suit. Or at least, he looked at the burned and bloodied tatters of fabric clinging to him, what was left of a suit. He'd only wanted to get Claudia away as fast as he could and had. Now he couldn't dial a number. Of course, now that he felt he had Claudia safely away from the mansion, he also had time to think about what had happened to him, what he'd become, what he'd done to his assailants, and what he'd done to his assailant, Isabella.

Isabella.

The name blew through his brain like the first winds of an approaching Atlantic storm. He rubbed his temples hard. He'd killed Isabella. Again, he had no idea how he'd done it, only that he'd wanted to stop her from harming Claudia, and he'd stopped her.

He felt Claudia place a hand on his shoulder. "Let me try." Her voice was small but strong. Cain's eyes swept over her face. Her hair was windswept like she'd been riding in a convertible or perhaps a motorcycle with no helmet at speed. Her smooth face was smudged with soot and dirt and what smelled pleasantly of blood.

Cain recoiled.

Claudia's eyes widened with shock. "I'm...I'm sorry. I didn't mean to touch you."

"No. It's not that." Cain forced his lips into a smile. "I just..." He stopped. He didn't know what to say. Someone else's blood was smeared across his fiancée's face, and he could smell it. It smelled better than any fragrance she'd ever worn. It excited him. Exactly how did you explain that to your fiancé? The answer was you didn't. "I'm just a little jumpy. This is all new for me."

That was true. Claudia wasn't the only one experiencing previously unknown facts about the world. Claudia was learning the truth about vampires, and Cain was learning he'd become one. Somehow, he'd turned into a vampire. Something more than a vampire.

He'd seen vampires "change" but never into what he'd seen in the mirror. It was just their countenance, their demeanor. Fangs were the only physical sign. All the rest was part of the myth vampires had created. Vampires' heads elongate as their hairline recedes. Their eyes change color. Maybe they even grow a snout so that they resemble some demonic feline. Everybody knows that from the movies. Vampires were the ultimate PR gods.

Then there was the reflection in the glass. Him. That reflection was not human, and that scared him. What did that mean? Would he no longer be able to walk in the sunlight? Would he begin to crave blood as his only source of nutrition? Worse were the questions regarding Roman. Did his father know or suspect this would happen?

This made him shiver again. He'd always thought his father was a strong, stoic man doing what needed to be done. Roman came from a time when fathers didn't show affection, but he was still loving and caring. But now. What kind of uncaring, insensitive man was his father?

Claudia's smile was loaded with wariness, almost ruefulness, and Cain thought he could see her visibly age ten years with that smile.

"I understand," she said. She turned to the phone, plucked the receiver from the cradle, and asked, a finger paused over the keypad, "What number are you trying to enter?"

Cain stared in amazement. Her hands, despite what she'd been through tonight, were steady. It had to be that journalist training, he mused to himself. Always cool, calm, and collected. The rock amidst the torrent.

Cain mumbled the numbers, and Claudia punched the pad, holding the phone to her ear and only relinquishing it when she heard the ring.

Cain heard the phone's pop as it was answered and the man's light continental accent. "Salve."

"Father."

"Son." Roman's sigh was heavy with relief.

Cain thought he could hear the man slump back in his chair.

"Are you all right?" Roman asked.

Cain's voice quavered. "Yes." He'd never heard such anguish and relief in his father's voice.

"And Claudia?" Roman's voice sounded like a fresh wave of anguish was passing over it. "Is she safe?"

"Yes, Father. She's here with me."

Cain looked at Claudia, who waved a hand at the phone.

"She says Hi."

There was a moment of silence before Cain heard his father utter something unintelligible in Italian.

"I'm sorry, Father, but…"

"But what?" Roman asked, dismissing the apology. "You are okay. Claudia is with you. What is this 'but'?"

"The mansion…it's destroyed. The guards…" Cain's voice faltered. If he finished this sentence, it would lead to the inevitable question, 'How did Isabella die?' Cain was sure that whatever love and compassion Roman felt towards his son would evaporate with that question.

"The mansion is only a thing. And things eventually wear out and must be replaced. The lives lost are…regrettable but not unexpected. The guards died doing what they lived to do. Protect you. And you, my son, you are not replaceable."

"But the scandal. What will that do to my chances in the Senate? You were expecting me to win."

"You are a good son, Cain. A very good son," Roman soothed. "But the Senate is like the mansion, only a thing which will one day wear out. It is temporary. Here today and gone tomorrow."

"And the scandal?" Cain pressed.

"Who cares about such things? You and Claudia are safe. That's all that matters."

"But...what do I do? I have no guards left. Isab-...I don't know whom I can trust. I don't know how the people who attacked us tonight did it, how they defeated your guards. I don't know what to do. Where to go."

"Cain. Don't worry about anything. I'm not. Do you hear any worry in my voice? No. Do you know why? Because I have you, and you have Claudia. Yours and Claudia's safety is the only thing that matters to me. Now. This is what I want you to do. Get yourself and Claudia to the airport, but move slowly. Do not attract any attention to yourselves. I will have the jet prepared to bring you and Claudia to me. Don't worry about anything else. Just deliver yourself and Claudia safely to the airport. Call me when you are on the plane."

"Okay." Cain felt stronger. There was a plan. He had something to do, something to follow. Cain only just now realized his father hadn't asked about Isabella and wasn't bothered by the loss of the mansion, Senate seat, or the lives of his faithful servants. His only concern was his son's life and well-being, and his son's return to him.

"Cain?" Roman interrupted Cain's musings.

"Yes, Father?"

"I love you."

Cain's eyes burned with hot saline. "I love you too."

"Be safe."

Cain heard the click as Roman hung up. He set the receiver back in its cradle and turned to face Claudia.

Claudia's eyes searched his. "What did he say? What does he want us to do?"

Cain reached up and caressed her cheek, noticing his hand was no longer shaking. He smiled at her. "To come home."

57

Marcus and Caiaphas sat in the parlor, drinking tea and reflecting on their comrades-in-arms who'd died that night. Caiaphas had been pleased with Augustine's news that the Phase Two munitions were highly successful. The report, however, that half of the strike team, including Rotty, had been killed in action, dampened any excitement or elation at this news.

Caiaphas considered the entire mission a loss upon hearing that Cain Dvanaesti had survived.

Yet Caiaphas had to admit that Cain Dvanaesti had rescued Gabriel Hawthorne from the burning mansion without engaging any other members of the Illuminati, which meant the mission was not a complete failure. They had learned of Cain Dvanaesti's humanity in that action. Perhaps, Caiaphas thought, Cain was the chink in Roman Dvanaesti's armor. And Claudia was the chink in Cain's armor.

Marcus's phone chimed with a text message. He pulled the phone from his pocket and read it.

"Message from the Miami Airport. Roman D filed flight plan MIA to ITA, immediate departure, two passengers." He looked at Caiaphas, who was smiling. "What do you make of it?"

He thought for a moment. "Where is Augustine?"

"Still at the warehouse in Miami."

Caiaphas's smile broadened. "Get him on the phone, please. I want him at that airport."

Marcus dialed Augustine's number. "What are you thinking, Caiaphas?"

Caiaphas did not immediately answer but waited for Marcus to tell Augustine to hold. "Rotty's audacity may have afforded us an opportunity, Marcus. Cain Dvanaesti will not be guarded."

58

Benecio DeSanto, the Commissario of the Polizia Municipale, directed his Alfa Romeo 159 around the larger-than-life fountain of Christ on the cross and stopped. He looked at the hulking mansion. It seemed to know his mood and was sulking right along with him. DeSanto cut the engine as his phone rang. He looked at the ID and sighed. It was his assistant. He punched the Accept button.

"Salve," DeSanto said in a tired tone.

"Commissario," the young man said and then burst into a tirade as if his boss would be easier on him if the message were delivered in a machine gun barrage of words.

DeSanto didn't understand every word his assistant said, but he got the gist. He rolled his eyes and punched the dashboard. "Are you sure?" His tone was accusatory, and the young official took it personally.

"I'm only the messenger, Commissario—"

"That's enough," DeSanto cut across him. He was in no mood for his assistant's self-absorbed martyrdom speeches. He stepped from the car. "Very well, then. Keep me informed."

He thumbed the End button without waiting for a response and pocketed the phone. Steeling himself, he walked up the stairs to the front door. He knocked, wishing he could delegate this aspect of his job to someone else. Even if he could, he wouldn't. Not when Roman Dvanaesti was concerned. The man was too good for the community. Even as a boy, DeSanto remembered his parents requesting special favor for Dvanaesti when they blessed supper.

As Dvanaesti opened the door, DeSanto marveled at how much the man still looked the same, like he hadn't aged a day.

Dvanaesti smiled. "And to what do I owe the pleasure of this visit, Commissario DeSanto?

DeSanto took a deep breath. "I'm sorry, but I am the bearer of bad news today, Signore Dvanaesti. There's been an accident."

Dvanaesti waited, the smile not wavering. "I don't understand."

DeSanto shifted from foot to foot. "Your son's airplane crashed into the Atlantic.

The smile slipped from Dvanaesti's face. "What?"

"Your son's airplane went down. He's feared dead."

Dvanaesti's eyes narrowed. "What do you mean, 'feared dead?'"

DeSanto felt Dvanaesti's eyes boring into him and now wished he could jump from the balcony and seek cover. "His body is yet to be recovered. The bodies of the pilot and a female, whom we assume to be his fiancée, Ms. Claudia Bennett, were found in the wreckage."

Dvanaesti stared through the man.

DeSanto was afraid Dvanaesti might drop from a heart attack. "Is there anything I can do for you, Signore Dvanaesti?"

"No." Dvanaesti shook his head as if trying to shake loose a memory. "Thank you, Commissario. Please keep me informed." He closed the door in what DeSanto could only attribute to a stunned and broken heart. He walked back to his car, wishing he'd sent his assistant.

In the mansion, Dvanaesti walked with an unhurried step to the library. He picked up the phone and dialed a number.

"Yes, Mr. Dvanaesti."

"Why was I just informed by the Commissario of an accident involving my son?"

"I'm sorry, Mr. Dvanaesti?" The man at the end of the line sounded confused.

"You are in charge of his plane, are you not?"

"Yes, Sir."

"The plane went down."

"Yes, Sir."

"But you did not inform me, but by the local police commissioner, who'd received word from the Italian Air Authority."

Now the voice got the point. "Yes, Sir. I was waiting for confirmation regarding Cain's body, Sir. We followed your instructions to the letter, Mr. Dvanaesti. Any investigation will state it was a mechanical failure." There was a moment of silence before the man blurted out in haste. "Don't worry, Mr. Dvanaesti. I'm sure he's dead."

"If my instructions had been followed to the letter, I would've been informed of four fatalities. I would not have been informed of three fatalities and one missing body."

"No human could've survived that crash."

"And yet it appears at least one has."

"I'm sure his body will surface in a day or two."

"You willing to bet your life on it?"

The man at the end was silent for a long beat. "N-no no, Sir."

"Then you should assume he's alive until the body's recovered. Understood? Now find the body." Dvanaesti hung up.

59

"Further tragedy for the First Family of Florida this morning." The radio personality read the news script with crisp precision. "Last night, Governor Dvanaesti's private residence in Miami burned to the ground. Though the governor was not there, none of the staff who lived in the home survived. Authorities have determined that an electrical short in the kitchen caused the blaze.

"This morning, the Italian Air Authority reports that Cain Dvanaesti's private jet, a Bombardier Global 5000, reported smoke in the cockpit and within minutes disappeared from radar. The aircraft was over international waters on its way to Italy. Search and rescue operations are underway. The bodies of the pilot, co-pilot, and an unidentified female, believed to be the governor's fiancée, were recovered. However, Cain Dvanaesti's body is still missing."

A Coast Guard spokeswoman's voice began to drone about the square miles of ocean being searched and the number of air and watercraft being utilized, but Gabriel didn't pay attention. He stared at the radio from the backseat without seeing it. His stomach flooded with what felt like a gallon of acid. He was sure that if he looked down, he'd see a hand digging its way into his chest and wrapping cold fingers around his heart.

Wrench shot a furtive glance at Gabriel's reflection in the rearview mirror. She hadn't slept in thirty-six hours, but didn't think a sleeping pill and a fifth of bourbon would knock her out. She knew what Gabriel was thinking. She might not know what he was feeling, or maybe she did. She'd lost not only her mentor last night but the one man she ever loved. No one knew that, not even Rotty. Especially Rotty. She wondered if Augustine didn't suspect now, after her outburst at Gabriel on the boat the night before. She'd been thanking God she'd never let him or anyone else know her feelings.

Caiaphas had ordered Augustine to the airport, and Augustine had ordered them to a private hangar. Gabriel hadn't said anything after her altercation with him on the boat. He hadn't slept on the Cessna either. She was sure he might open up or nod off once she'd piloted the Cessna to cruising altitude, but he hadn't. He'd just been a zombie.

He still looked like a zombie, but Wrench knew that with a guy like Gabriel Hawthorne, looks could be deceiving. She reached up and turned the radio off. The driver shot her a glance, but she pointed a silent finger at the road.

Gabriel heard the radio snap off and felt the silence engulf him. Since Cain and Claudia's vanishing act, Gabriel had never given up hope that he'd find a way to save Claudia from Cain. He'd find her and convince her she needed to leave Cain. He'd gone over it in his mind again and again. Different scenarios. Different locations. Different words. Always the same outcome. Claudia left Cain. She lived happily ever after. Single or with someone else. It didn't matter. She lived.

This wasn't about him. Gabriel didn't want her to choose him over Cain. He didn't want her to choose him at all. He didn't want her in his life like that anymore. He loved his life, and a wonderful woman with an impeccable reputation and an aspiring career would only get in the way. She'd pester him night and day to do the right thing until he killed her in her sleep. So anybody. Except for Cain Dvanaesti and him.

He might've had that chance as well if not for Caiaphas.

Caiaphas.

Gabriel cursed the man in his head. He'd heard the Illuminati's policy regarding those knowingly associating with vampires. Guilty by association. Not exempt from the same fate as the vampires. But Caiaphas had seemed different. He seemed a man ready to allow someone another last chance. Yet now, Caiaphas had proven no different from the rest.

He looked up and was surprised to see the car slowing for the dirt road, which the Illuminati had spared no expense to maintain, pockmarked and potholed.

Caiaphas was standing on the porch, waiting for them, and as the car pulled to a stop in front of the house, he slowly came down the steps.

Wrench thought he looked tired. Old. Like he'd aged twenty or thirty years since they left. She heard the back door open and saw Gabriel Hawthorne hurtling toward Caiaphas.

The driver cursed as he jumped from the car, or would've jumped had he not forgotten his seatbelt was still fastened. He tugged at the latch as Wrench jumped from the car and sped to Caiaphas' rescue.

Wrench could see blood pouring from Caiaphas's nose. Gabriel had one hand around Caiaphas's throat and the other poised to pummel him. Caiaphas was making no effort to defend himself.

"That's enough, Mr. Hawthorne." Wrench hooked an arm around Gabriel's raised fist and used her body weight to drag Gabriel backward off Caiaphas.

The driver finally extricated himself from the vehicle and grabbed Gabriel as he tried to stand back up, locking him in a half-nelson and forcing Gabriel to his knees.

Wrench helped Caiaphas to his feet. His suit was torn and filthy, now spotted with crimson. He held on to Wrench's shoulder to steady himself. "Thank you, Wrench." He looked at her as he pulled a white cotton handkerchief from his pocket. "I'm sorry for your loss. I know what Rotty meant to you." His hand grazed her cheek. She blushed, knowing he did, but said nothing.

Gabriel looked up at Caiaphas, panting, feeling his neck and shoulder on the cusp of exploding. Satisfaction swelled in his chest as he watched the white handkerchief turn red. He felt the bloom of fresh pain in his neck as the driver noticed the stained cloth too.

Caiaphas waved a hand at the driver. "Please release Mr. Hawthorne."

The driver opened his mouth to protest, but Caiaphas cut him off. "Release him." His voice was quiet, his tone grandfatherly.

The driver's jaw muscles rippled as if clamping down to keep the vomit from exploding out of his mouth. He let go of Gabriel, shoving him as he did.

Gabriel fell forward onto his hands.

Caiaphas ignored the shove. "Thank you." He stepped forward and offered his hand to Gabriel.

Wrench stepped forward.

"That will not be necessary, Wrench. Mr. Hawthorne only acted as I'm sure you would if you were confronting someone you felt responsible for a loved one's demise." His eyes were fixed on Wrench. They were not accusatory but knowing. Understanding. Sympathetic.

Wrench's gaze dropped to her feet. Her nod was almost imperceptible.

Caiaphas fixed Gabriel with the same knowing, understanding, sympathetic gaze. "Please come with me, Mr. Hawthorne."

Gabriel followed Caiaphas into the dilapidated mansion. Though he'd been here before, Gabriel marveled at just how condemned the structure's exterior looked and how state-of-the-art the interior was. The Illuminati had some deep pockets. He could hear the driver on his heel, and Wrench only a step behind him.

Caiaphas walked through the foyer and into a hall. He stopped before a door at the end of the hall, opened the door, and stepped aside.

Gabriel took a hesitant step through.

The room looked straight out of a Hollywood summer popcorn thriller. It was cold, dark, and filled with electronic equipment. Against a wall were what looked to Gabriel like computer servers. Facing the doorway was a rack of computer monitors and flat-screen televisions surrounding one large flat-screen. The monitors showed different data streams. The televisions were tuned to CNN, Fox News, BBC, Al Jazeera, and local Russian, Chinese, and Korean programming. Two men sat at computer terminals, each. They wore headsets and didn't acknowledge the intrusion.

The image on the large flatscreen was Augustine. Marcus stood in the middle of the room, talking to Augustine.

"We appear to have a visitor," Augustine said as his image pointed to Gabriel. "And what the—" but Augustine's next set of expletives were drowned out as everyone in the room turned and saw Caiaphas's suit.

"I fell." Caiaphas gestured for Augustine to continue whatever he was saying as he entered.

Augustine blinked away the distraction and finally regained his composure. "I was telling Marcus we're having trouble stabilizing him."

"Him?" It was out of Gabriel's mouth before he realized it.

Augustine's eyes narrowed but softened as he realized who'd interrupted him. "Yes, Mr. Hawthorne. Him. I'm sorry, but Miss Bennett didn't make it."

Silence surrounded each person in the room like a coffin. Finally, Caiaphas spoke. "What seems to be the trouble?"

"Huh? Oh." Augustine looked embarrassed. "Blood tests have been...inconclusive."

Quizzical glances bounced around the room like a racquetball.

Caiaphas was unfazed. "Explain, please, Augustine."

"Well...his blood is neither human nor any known animal species. The computers don't recognize it. Not even as a synthetic. It makes partial matches; that's about it."

"Partial matches with what?" Marcus asked.

"Human. But only partial."

"Does it identify it as his blood?" Caiaphas asked.

"No."

Caiaphas nodded as if he expected these answers. "Could you please relate to Mr. Hawthorne my instructions to you last night?"

Augustine blinked. "Sir?"

Caiaphas repeated. "My instructions to you last night. Please tell Mr. Hawthorne what they were."

Augustine didn't take his eyes off Caiaphas. "You instructed me to head to Miami International Airport, where Cain Dvanaesti's private jet was preparing to leave for Italy. Dvanaesti would be unprotected, so it might be easier to speak with him. I was asked to appeal to his humanity." His expressions were like a child's answering a parent's demand to have their orders repeated so that the words Italy and humanity sounded more like questions.

Caiaphas continued. "And did you?"

"No." Augustine appeared relieved. "I'd missed him. His plane was taxiing when we arrived.

"So what did you do?"

"I ordered our jet to pursue."

"Were you on that jet?"

Augustine nodded, looking more like a defendant on the witness stand, looking for the trap in the question.

"What methods did you employ?"

"I'm sorry?" Augustine now looked between Caiaphas and Marcus.

For his part, Marcus had no idea where any of this was going except to prove Augustine's proficiency at his job and Rotty's rightful heir. The information being discussed was irrelevant, so far as he could tell. But

Caiaphas had his madness in his methods. So Marcus only stared back at Augustine.

"What methods to ensure a successful pursuit did you employ?" Caiaphas asked, as if he were asking him, what beverage he preferred with his meal.

"We secured a homing device to the Dvanaesti aircraft before its departure, and we knew its filed flight plan. We followed that flight plan at a lower altitude to avoid detection from both radar and Dvanaesti's jet."

"Did you witness what happened to his jet?" Caiaphas prompted.

"Not directly. As his plane crossed into international waters, we intercepted radio traffic from Miami reporting smoke in the cockpit. We watched as the plane banked and hit the water nose-first."

Everyone in the room, except Caiaphas, was riveted to the screen. Without realizing it, Gabriel had moved closer to Augustine's image.

"What did you do?"

"I ordered the pilot to drop down to a safe jumping altitude and circle the homing signal. It was still operational. I then parachuted from the plane into the water and swam approximately two hundred yards to Mr. Dvanaesti's aircraft."

"It was floating?"

Augustine nodded. "But I could tell it would submerge within a few minutes. There were several large holes in the fuselage."

"Did you enter the aircraft?" Caiaphas' voice was easy.

Augustine nodded.

"And what did you see?"

Augustine swallowed audibly, then licked his lips and glanced between Gabriel and Caiaphas."

Caiaphas nodded for him to continue.

"The cockpit was destroyed. The pilot was missing. Cain Dvanaesti was covered in blood but breathing. Very shallow but breathing. And he had a very faint heartbeat. His face was horribly swollen. I couldn't believe he was still alive."

"And Miss Bennett?" Caiaphas probed.

Augustine pursed his lips but said nothing.

"Miss Bennett?" Caiaphas repeated.

Another moment passed before Augustine finally spoke. "Miss Bennett...had not been belted into a seat prior...to...impact."

The man's face told the rest of the story. No one in that room wanted to know what he'd seen; what speed, altitude, the violence of a movable force striking an immovable object looked like. It was like some sick algebra word problem where the outcome was known, but no one wanted to solve the equation.

Gabriel felt his knees buckle.

"And so..." Caiaphas prompted Augustine.

"I called for our rescue chopper, ordered the plane to continue circling the site until it arrived, and pulled Cain's body from the wreckage. I was treading water, holding Cain Dvanaesti when it sank."

"And where is Cain Dvanaesti now?" Caiaphas asked quietly.

Augustine's shoulders lifted, grateful at the change of subject. "With me in Orlando." He then reached up, grabbed the device capturing his image, and rotated it till it showed Cain Dvanaesti lying unconscious in a hospital bed. The face was swollen and slightly elongated. The eyes were closed and a deep plum purple. The body's skin tone seemed to move, to crawl, undulating between human flesh tone and a mottled gray and white and black.

"What the—?" Gabriel's voice broke off as Cain sighed heavily, his body shuddering as the skin tone rippled inky black to cadaverous gray and back to inky black before resuming a human flesh tone.

So that was that, Gabriel thought. Cain Dvanaesti was this... thing on the screen that had survived an airplane crash. Gabriel had been right. Cain Dvanaesti had been the death of Claudia Bennett. Gabriel wanted to laugh, cry, and vomit all at once.

Gabriel felt his knees buckle. The room wasn't spinning, but it was off-kilter. Sweat bloomed on his forehead.

"Are you all right, Mr. Hawthorne?" Someone was asking him from a thousand yards away. He wanted to respond, *no, I think I'm going to throw up and pass out.* But he couldn't. He was afraid to open his mouth. His eyes darted for something to grab hold of, to latch onto to keep standing. But there wasn't anything. So he let his body stagger backward until his back collided with the wall.

"Are you all right?" A female voice was asking from somewhere in the distance. Not as far as the first voice, still far enough in the ether to concern Gabriel.

He mopped his forehead and nodded. "I'm going to be sick." He pushed himself out of the room. Finding a large vase with a beautiful flower arrangement, Gabriel pulled the flowers out, cast them aside, dumped the water onto the carpet, and vomited into the vase.

60

Caiaphas poured tea into a cup in front of Gabriel. "Lady Grey. It may not sound as masculine as Earl Grey," he filled his cup, "but the Lady is much more exciting." He set the teapot down.

After Gabriel had finished vomiting, Caiaphas led Gabriel to the small parlor. He'd set him at the table and bustled about making tea. He loved making tea. It was not just a passion but a purpose. It was the one ordered thing Caiaphas could count on in an increasingly unordered world.

Tea preparation was both an art and a science to Caiaphas. Different tea leaves require different brewing, temperature, and steeping times. That was the science. The art came in choosing the tea to match the drinker's mood. There was also a bit of philosophy to tea, Caiaphas mused, as he remembered an old Japanese proverb, 'If a man has no tea in him, he is incapable of understanding truth and beauty.'

He looked at the younger man sitting beside him at the parlor table. Gabriel needed the art, science, and philosophy of tea at this moment. Lady Grey, Caiaphas knew tea enthusiasts would ask with a raised eyebrow at this moment. Well, he was a bit of a British tea snob. And it was already on the table.

"Drink." He sipped and gestured at the cup in front of Gabriel. "It will help."

Gabriel continued to stare through the table to some space only he could see. "She's gone." His eyes filled, but no tears fell.

"Yes, Mr. Hawthorne. She is." He sipped again, leaving the silence alone until Gabriel was ready to fill it.

Finally, Gabriel spoke. "If I hadn't let her leave with him, she'd probably still be alive."

"You would never have been able to convince her, Mr. Hawthorne. She was in love with Cain Dvanaesti, and Roman Dvanaesti would never have allowed her to leave Cain's side."

"Like he could've stopped her," Gabriel said with proud defiance.

"He could. And probably did." Caiaphas sipped.

"What do you mean? *Probably* did?"

"Mr. Hawthorne, of all the myths, one is correct. Vampires can 'charm' humans to exert a certain amount of mental and emotional control over us."

"Claudia would never have fallen for some vampire mojo."

"Miss Bennett probably never even realized it was occurring, Mr. Hawthorne."

"Yeah, well. We see where the mind control got him, huh?" Gabriel picked up the cup and gulped down the tea. "Plane still went down. I guess there are some things even Roman and Cain Dvanaesti can't control."

Caiaphas refilled Gabriel's cup. "You're a smart man. Surely your intelligence is not failing you now."

Gabriel blinked at him. "What?"

Caiaphas refilled his cup. "Cain Dvanaesti owned a Bombardier Global 5000 jet. It was a gift from his father, Roman Dvanaesti. The aircraft was kept in a state-of-the-art hangar. The crew of mechanics maintaining it were vampires. What are the odds that that plane could suffer some catastrophic malfunction which would cause it to crash?"

Gabriel swirled a spoon around in his tea. "You think the mechanics crashed the plane?"

"Mr. Hawthorne. Cain Dvanaesti had to have been becoming a headache for his father. He proposed on television, neglected or tried to neglect his gubernatorial duties, and whisked his fiancée off to meet his father without his father's permission."

"How do you know all that?" Gabriel demanded.

Caiaphas shrugged. "We have a member of the Illuminati working in Cain's office. Of course, that is neither here nor there anymore, as the saying goes."

"Why?"

"Because Cain Dvanaesti is no longer the Governor of Florida."

"He's still alive—"

"There's something that's still alive, but that something is no longer human."

Gabriel pondered what Caiaphas was telling him. It just didn't make any sense. Lots of kids were headaches for their folks. *He'd* brought his mother to tears and his father to the point of throwing his hands up in disgust when he was a teenager. But that didn't mean his parents arranged to knock him off. That couldn't be what Caiaphas was saying. He had to be blaming the mechanics. "So the mechanics, what, overhear Roman Dvanaesti whining about his kid and decide to make Roman's life easier by killing him?"

Caiaphas's smile was a weary one as he considered Gabriel's question. "I believe those mechanics, like all vampires working for him, would never do anything to anyone without Roman Dvanaesti's authorization."

"So you *are* saying Roman Dvanaesti told his mechanics to sabotage the plane."

"Roman Dvanaesti made two phone calls to the Miami International Airport, Mr. Hawthorne. The first was to file the flight plan. The second was to the hangar." He took a long breath and let it out slowly. "There's no other way to say this. Roman Dvanaesti ordered the murder of Claudia Bennett and Cain Dvanaesti, but to make it look like an accident."

Gabriel picked up his cup and hurled it across the room. It slammed against the wall and splintered, staining the wallpaper. "Where is he?"

Caiaphas frowned as the stain inched its way down the floral print. He never cared for the wallpaper, but he disapproved of wasting tea. The British tea snob again. "I am not going to try to stop you, Mr. Hawthorne. We each have a path we must tread in this life. Nor will I refuse you any assistance if you ask for it. Even for what I believe will be an exercise in futility.

"There are only two things I ask of you. First, before you take any action, let your mind subdue your emotions. They can be the death of a man. Second." Caiaphas opened a manila envelope and slid a photo across the table to Gabriel. "Do you recognize this woman?"

Gabriel looked at the photograph and shrugged. "Nope."

Caiaphas didn't seem surprised. "Perhaps you've heard her name? Isabella Reese?"

"Yeah. Rotty and Augustine were talking about her before we left for the Dvanaesti mansion. Augustine asked if I'd seen her in the mansion during the operation." Gabriel slid the picture back to Caiaphas. "Who is she?"

"She's listed as Governor Dvanaesti's assistant. More likely, she's his bodyguard. Before that," Caiaphas shrugged, "she was his surrogate mother. Before his birth, she worked for Roman Dvanaesti as a personal assistant. And before that, she was Isabella Dvanaesti."

"She was married to Roman Dvanaesti?" His voice rose with incredulity. "What was she? Ten?"

Caiaphas answered. "Miss Isabella Reese has been, what's the phrase? Thirty and holding. For a very long time."

Gabriel shot Caiaphas a skeptical glance. "How long?"

Caiaphas pursed his lips, but not out of annoyance. He seemed genuinely interested in answering, but not in deciding how much to divulge; rather, in deciding how much information Gabriel could handle. Finally, he said. "How familiar are you with the Medici family, Mr. Hawthorne?"

Gabriel shrugged. "They're a big Italian family out of Florence? Very rich. Powerful. All but died off?" Gabriel leaned forward. "Are you trying to tell me this Isabella chick was a member of the Medici family?"

"No, Mr. Hawthorne, I'm not. We believe she is the Matriarch of the Medici family."

Gabriel gaped at Caiaphas.

"The Medici family came out of the Mugello region of Italy, north of Florence, sometime during the beginning of the Thirteenth century. The actual Patriarch and Matriarch of the family are not known. Conveniently, this was a time when not all marriages, births, and family trees were necessarily recorded for anyone other than wealthy families. Also, this was a time when literacy among the impoverished was at best scant.

"The name Medici is ambiguously powerful. What I mean is that the exact meaning of the name is unknown. Medici is the plural of medico, meaning medical doctors. But the name has a nice ring and is easy to pronounce. It sounds strong. Elegant. Royal.

"Our scholars have uncovered documents from the Mugello region of Italy. These documents include legal papers, personal letters, and diaries. While none of these documents mention Roman Dvanaesti by name, they describe a country doctor bearing striking similarities to Roman Dvanaesti. This country doctor was a good friend of a local farmer with a daughter named Isabella."

Caiaphas paused to let Gabriel absorb what he'd just said. When he saw that it had, Caiaphas continued. "This farmer became gravely ill. But with the ministrations of this country doctor, he made what was then considered a miracle recovery. People remarked in diaries and letters how he danced at his daughter's wedding.

"But something happened to the farmer at his daughter's wedding. Nothing physical. It was spiritual. Psychological. Again, this is in letters and diaries of friends, family, and associates. He sent the good country doctor away, and his health deteriorated almost immediately. He was dead within three months. Soon after, Isabella and her husband emigrated to Florence. The good country doctor not only advised them to go but also accompanied them. There were, of course, already family members there. The good doctor became a good friend, confidant, and advisor to many of the family, including Giovanni Medici, founder of the Medici Bank. We find this last relationship significant."

"But why would he do that? Why would he *need* to do that? You said he's been a vampire for at least a thousand years. Probably more. Wouldn't he already be rich? Powerful?"

"And do you remember our conversation about *Chess*, Mr. Hawthorne?"

Gabriel thought about that for a moment. "So you're saying he maneuvered himself into the confidences of the Medici family and helped create the Medici bank as some kind of *Chess* move?"

Caiaphas folded his fingers in front of him. "Well. The Medici family produced four Popes of the Catholic Church, rose to the Duchy and then the Grand Duchy of Tuscany. And founded the Medici Bank, revolutionizing banking with double-entry bookkeeping to track credits and debits. Incidentally, accountants for the Medici family were the first to use this system."

"He wanted to get in on the ground floor of banking?"

"I'm saying, Mr. Hawthorne, that Roman Dvanaesti created banking as we know it today."

Caiaphas let Gabriel gnaw on that for a minute. "So, to answer your question about the age of Miss Reese, I would be safe to say she's thirty and holding and has been holding for over six hundred years.

"I would also be safe in saying that Roman has been playing this game of manipulation for more than a thousand years. He has a precedent. A modus operandi, if you will."

Gabriel thought about this. "So why are you telling me all this?"

"Because I believe the more you know about an enemy's past, the better you may predict his future. Especially if you plan on ending that future."

Gabriel mulled this over for a long moment. "So you want me to have my chance? Even though you think it's fruitless."

Caiaphas nodded.

"So what will you do for me?"

"What would you like?"

Gabriel thought about it for a moment. "Transport to Italy and a magazine of Phase Twos for my Beretta."

Caiaphas smiled. "I can do that."

61

It was a gorgeous day, with not a cloud in a sapphire-blue sky. It reminded Gabriel of the day six weeks ago as he walked out of Senator Weathers's office. He'd just finished telling them, not that it mattered, that there was no dirt to be found on Cain or Roman Dvanaesti. Cain was JFK on crack, just like they feared. But he was dead now. He'll be sainted in Florida, but his impact on politics will extend no further.

That last part was Caiaphas's idea. Well, the whole thing was Caiaphas's idea. He thought it best to let a little time pass. Tie up all the loose ends of the case and his life, and then confront Roman with a clear conscience.

So here he was. All the loose ends had been tied up. People in D.C. were told he was taking some well-deserved time off. Travel. Europe. Italy. He had a full magazine of Phase Two rounds locked and loaded, safety off, in his Beretta, snug in the shoulder holster under his jacket. He walked up the long drive leading to Roman Dvanaesti's home and thought about what had brought him to this point. *Who* had brought him to this point.

Weathers and Lemay.

If it hadn't been for them, he would never have lost Stefan Owusu. Claudia would still be alive, making the world a better place. He would never have met Caiaphas or known of the Illuminati as anything other than that group in that movie about the Vatican getting blown up. Those were the days. Ignorance had indeed been bliss.

Maybe when I'm finished with Roman Dvanaesti, he thought, I'll off Weathers and Lemay. Or frame them for something. Let the vampires show up at their doors. That made him smile. Until the image of Stefan popped into his mind, and he frowned. Now, he thought of all the people who'd died because they'd crossed the path of one man. One thing, Gabriel corrected himself. Roman Dvanaesti. A vampire among vampires. Well, Gabriel thought to himself, that would end today.

"Salve," a voice called out.

Gabriel looked up to see an old gentleman heading towards him from the building to the right of the villa. Gabriel had been lost in thought and hadn't realized he'd sat down at the large fountain. He looked at the fountain.

Christ on the cross, the water flowing from his hands, feet, eyes, and side. It made him shiver.

"Salve," the old man repeated. He was tall and lean, wearing brown work boots, tan pants, and a long-sleeved shirt. He took off his worn and tattered hat and dropped his gloves into it. He smiled broadly.

"Salve." Gabriel held up a hand and waved.

The old gentleman laughed with delight and began speaking Italian very quickly.

"No, no, no, no." Gabriel held up his hands in supplication. "I don't speak Italian. That's all I know. I'm looking for Signore Dvanaesti."

"Signore Dvanaesti?"

"Yes. Si. Signore Dvanaesti."

"Si. Signore Dvanaesti." The older man swatted Gabriel's shoulder this time as if rewarding him for speaking Italian fluently. He nodded, picked up Gabriel's duffel bag, and motioned for Gabriel to follow.

Gabriel followed him up the stairs and into the villa. He was fascinated by the fresco but wasn't allowed the time to look at it. The old Italian kept beckoning him to follow. He came to a door, opened it, and stepped aside. It reminded Gabriel of Caiaphas. The day when he learned Cain was alive and something other than human. This time, however, Gabriel didn't step through the doorway with hesitation but marched into a grand study.

Gabriel's first reaction was, 'It's bigger than my entire house.' The walls were covered in tapestries and paintings. Plinths stood every eight feet, supporting statues and other artifacts. Everything in the room, including the carpet and drapes, looked ancient. Gabriel wondered if he'd stepped through some wormhole into a museum.

Gabriel's eye was caught by a portrait at the far end of the room of a young man and woman dressed in what looked like Greek or Roman togas. The woman was beautiful. The man was familiar.

Wandering around, Gabriel found an easel with a canvas covered with cloth. Gabriel couldn't help himself. He lifted the fabric and gasped. Claudia Bennett stared at him, lips curled in a satisfied grin, a glass of red wine in her hand, standing on a veranda overlooking...what was that, Gabriel wondered as he moved closer to the portrait, the entire landscape on fire?

"It was meant to be a wedding present." The soft voice boomed throughout the room.

Gabriel jumped and spun around to see the old gentleman standing in the doorway. Only he didn't look old anymore. And he was better dressed in a suit and tie. Gabriel stepped backward, knocking over the easel.

The old Italian caught the easel and painting before they could hit the floor. Gabriel looked from the door to the easel. It had to be thirty yards, at least.

"It is a pleasure to meet you, Gabriel Hawthorne." The man righted the easel and placed the painting back on it.

Gabriel looked back at the door and then at the man. Thirty yards.

"Permit me to introduce myself." He offered Gabriel his hand. "Roman Dvanaesti."

Roman's ice-cold flesh worked like a cold shower on Gabriel's senses. Dead flesh, he thought to himself. Only dead flesh in a freezer should feel that cold. He released Roman's hand and looked the man, the vampire, over. A twenty-five-hundred-dollar gray Armani pinstripe suit hung perfectly on his frame.

Roman looked to be in his late fifties, with short, curly gray hair, tanned skin radiating vigor and vitality, and hazel eyes that shone brightly. He was smiling. And Gabriel couldn't stifle the shiver that ran up his spine. There was something dangerous in that smile, like a raptor eyeing its next juicy meal.

"Forgive me for misleading you. It is not polite to receive guests in work attire. I needed to change into something more suitable to the occasion."

Now the only thing cold Gabriel wanted to feel in his hands was the grip of his Beretta. He could feel the one tucked into the shoulder holster. Or did he? He had a moment ago. He pressed his arm into his side and felt an empty holster. Panic swept across Gabriel's face.

Roman smiled at the look of panic. "I took the liberty of relieving you of your burden." He motioned to a small table by the door, where Gabriel saw the Beretta. "The Phase Two rounds would not have worked on me."

"Because—" Gabriel's voice had come out as a squeak. He cleared his throat. "Because you're an ancient vampire?"

"I am." Roman moved to what looked like an eighteenth-century sofa and sat down. "You would never get a chance to fire them." He motioned for Gabriel to sit down in a chair across from him.

"You were admiring the portrait of my wife and me."

"That's you?" Gabriel hated that he sounded like a pubescent kid finding out the girl he was dating was in the first porn film he'd ever seen.

Roman, however, didn't seem to mind. "Yes. When I was mortal."

"Your wife was-...is very beautiful."

"Was. She has been dead for as many years as I have. I painted that portrait from memory."

Gabriel looked at the painting. Roman and his wife were dressed as if it were...Roman Empire? It was on canvas and had a distinctly Renaissance look. He looked back at Roman. "It's beautiful. It's got so much detail it looks like a photograph."

Roman smiled with appreciation. "Thank you. I've had many lifetimes to perfect my style."

Gabriel looked at the portrait. "What was your wife's name?"

"Claudia." Roman gazed at the portrait. "She was the smartest, most intelligent, strongest person I knew."

"Claudia," Gabriel repeated.

"Claudia Bennett reminded me of her. It was a shame."

"A shame you had to kill her?" Gabriel spat.

Roman's eyes flicked from the portrait to Gabriel. He thought the gaze would slice his flesh wide open. "Do not mock me, Mr. Hawthorne."

Gabriel decided to change the subject. "Who were you in that portrait? That memory?"

Roman laughed. "Why is it that when people claim to be reincarnated, they always say they were Marie Antoinette? Or Prince Charming? Why was no one Prince Charming's chamber pot boy?" He leaned forward. "That is what I wish. I could have been Prince Charming's chamber pot boy."

"I'm sorry, I'm not following." Gabriel pushed himself back in his chair, wanting to put distance between himself and Roman.

Roman leaned back and sighed. "Should I give you a hint? Would you know who I am if I told you I washed my hands of him? If I sat on my human throne while the King of the Jews stood silently before me? If I told you my wife warned me to let him go, but I did not listen? And how many times over the centuries I wish I had obeyed her."

Gabriel looked at the man, his mouth falling open. Was he claiming to be? Was he out of his mind? And yet what was more insane? To claim to be an ancient vampire or to be...

"Pontius Pilate?" Gabriel's voice was incredulous.

Roman closed his eyes. "I have not been called by that name in a very long time."

"But...then...how...?" Gabriel couldn't find the words.

Roman took a deep breath. "Even before the Morning Star was cast from heaven, he knew of God's plan of salvation. And so, after the fall, he decided he would copy that plan to mock it. Spoil it. He decided he would offer immortality to the first person to commit murder. "And Cain killed his brother Abel. Lucifer went to Cain at night and offered to be his father. Convinced him to drink his blood, and he would become immortal. Mighty. Cain was greedy. He was angry with God. He drank Lucifer's blood and became the first Akhkharu.

"Then Lucifer commissioned Cain to call twelve unto him. He gave Cain the power to make them Akhkharu. And those twelve would have the power to make others. I was the twelfth Akhkharu Cain called."

"Twelve?" Gabriel wanted to stand up, run, and not stop. Not until he reached his home, crawled into his bed, and pulled the covers over his head. Instead, he sat there, white-knuckling the armrests.

"I am what you call the baby of the family. I am the youngest and least powerful of the Ancients." Roman crossed his legs. "So. Was this attempt for reciprocity yours or Caiaphas's idea?" He looked at Gabriel's stunned face. "Yes, Mr. Hawthorne. I know about Caiaphas and the Illuminati." He smiled. "I created them. They were my idea."

Gabriel's mind was swimming. "Why would you create an organization whose sole purpose is to destroy you?"

"Have you noticed how much Caiaphas likes to reference Chess? How I place and move my pieces? What Caiaphas fails to realize is that he is also playing Chess. As a piece on my board." Roman ran his tongue over his teeth as if savoring a tasty morsel. "Caiaphas is my queen, the most powerful and useful piece on my board. But even the queen has to have a mind working behind her. She moves or stays based on that mind's wants and needs. All the pieces do. The reason why Miami happened was not that a pawn went rogue. It happened because I wanted it to."

Gabriel felt a thrill of horror slide cold from his chest into his stomach. "You knew we were coming. And why."

Roman nodded.

"You were willing to sacrifice your people, your son. How could you do that?"

"The Illuminati needed a victory. They needed to see the potency of the Phase Two munitions. I wanted Miami closed and my son removed from the board."

"You're a monster." Gabriel hissed.

"A monster," Roman repeated, frowning. He was quiet for a moment. "I have walked this earth for over two millennia, watching man's inhumanity to his brother and sister. I have watched Humankind justify its cruelty in the name of God. Political ideology. Race. Ethnicity. Man rapes, murders, and subjugates for no other reason than entertainment." His chuckle was soured by contempt. "And you call me a monster."

Gabriel blinked and saw that the place where Roman had been sitting was empty. His head snapped to the right at the sound of Roman's voice.

"You look like a bourbon man to me." Roman stood across the room with his back to Gabriel, pouring a dark liquid from a crystal decanter into glasses.

Gabriel blinked again and found Roman standing beside him, offering him a glass. "This is from the late seventeenth century."

Gabriel took the glass from Roman, trying not to tremble as he held it.

Roman gestured for Gabriel to take a sip. He smiled as Gabriel tried to stop the look of delight that was forming on his face. He held his glass up to his nose and closed his eyes in pleasure as he inhaled the scent of the liquor deep into his lungs.

Sipping the bourbon, Gabriel reveled in its smoothness. He could almost forget Roman sat across from him. Almost.

"You and I have something in common, Mr. Hawthorne. Neither of us was worthy of the Claudias in our lives."

"You murdered my Claudia," Gabriel spat. "I never touched yours. I think that puts me ahead of you in the worthiness department."

"Do not presume you can judge me, Mr. Hawthorne." Roman stood and walked to a plinth carrying a statue of Saturn. Crossing his hands behind his back, he stared at the god of time. "You can never understand. Your lifespan is too brief. Your attention span is too short. The decisions you make today are for tomorrow. Most humans can only plan next year's vacanza. Fewer can plan even five years ahead. The decisions I make today may not bear fruit for centuries. It is like a bovaro reasoning with a toro. Humans will never be more than a food source. Nothing more than cattle."

"Why are you telling me this?" Gabriel asked.

"You're an intelligent man, Gabriel Hawthorne. You already know."

"Because you don't plan on letting me leave this room alive." Gabriel's throat made a dry click when he tried to swallow. He willed himself to look into Roman's eyes. He knew Roman wouldn't charm him, wouldn't put any mojo on him. "Go ahead then." Gabriel spat in defiance. "Kill me."

"Oh, Mr. Hawthorne. There are worse fates than death." Roman smiled. His fangs extended.

EPILOGUE

The boardroom of Darby, Langley, and Luna bustled with paralegals and interns fetching coffee and water in hopes of catching the eye of one of the partners. For some, the years spent as a waitress or waiter to pay for school were paying off. Others would make better wait staff than they would ever make as attorneys.

Harold Darby, the only one of the founders of the prestigious law firm still alive, waved away a pretty young intern with an irritated hand. She'd just tried, again, to place her body within his view under the misguided impression that the ninety-one-year-old attorney would enjoy the sights she had to offer.

If she'd researched the old partner as well as she'd researched law schools, she would have discovered Darby had never married, never had a girlfriend in his entire life. Not even a high school sweetheart. If the intern had checked the proverbial belt, she would've found Darby's notch-free. And even if he'd been fifty years younger, he would still have given his secretary the same gesture he'd given her just now: He wanted that female intern gone from the firm before lunch.

He had eyes only for the law. Lady Justice was his mistress. The company of any other female held no interest for him unless, of course, that woman felt the same way about the law. Sandra Day O'Connor was a woman whose company he enjoyed. On those occasions when he went to lunch with her, Barbara, his executive assistant, would jokingly tell anyone who called on him that he was off having an affair.

Darby's mind was still keen. His body was still relatively healthy. But most of the other partners and junior partners thought he might be succumbing to senility. During these marathon board meetings, which were long on the business of the firm and short on law, Darby's mind would ponder a question he wanted to ask Sandra the next time they had lunch or a particular case he'd enjoyed. When he ran out of questions and cases, he would nap rather than fire everyone in the room.

Today was no different.

They had reviewed attorneys ready for a junior partnership, junior partners ready for a partnership, and partners ready for a senior partnership; had an exhaustive review of the quarterly and year-to-date expenses and profits; and were taking a quick break for bladders to be emptied and cups to be filled before they started with the interview of Jacquelyn Dvanaesti for a possible spot as the junior partner under the tutelage of the firm's current star senior partner and reigning jackass, William Howard.

Darby looked around the table at the partners, junior partners, and board members taking their seats around the table and other staff taking their seats around the periphery, and wondered how he'd let the firm get this big. Perhaps he should fire everyone, shut down the firm, and open a little practice in some strip mall. Just him and Barbara. He'd have more time for lunch with Sandra. That idea put a smile on his face, which was just as quickly wiped away when William Howard leaned forward and started to speak.

"I have won more cases singlehandedly than the other partners in the room combined," Howard announced. He nodded towards Darby. "I have done more to put this law firm on the map than our distinguished founders, with all due respect, regarding the clientele I have brought in. I have made more money for this firm than anyone else. Ever."

Howard looked around the room and felt no shame in meeting each person's eye.

"In short, I have made this firm what it is today. I have done that without anyone's assistance. So I am at a loss as to why I am now being forced to coddle and hand-hold a junior partner, which I have noticed no other senior partner has ever had to do. I don't care that she graduated Suma Cum Laude and number one in her class at Harvard. I don't care that her commencement speech is considered one of the finest ever delivered at Harvard."

"What do you care about?" Morgan, a sixty-five-year-old partner who'd considered retiring from the firm and becoming a judge, asked.

"How about the fact she's been with this firm for six minutes?" Howard glared at Morgan. "How about the fact that we have junior partners and attorneys with an actual track record in the courtroom?" Howard made a point of staring hard at several of his fellow partners. "Partners coddle and handhold. Not the senior partners." Howard looked at Darby. "And we have never fast-tracked anyone in the entire history of this firm."

"Fast-tracked for what exactly?" Marino, the firm's first female senior partner, asked.

Howard smirked. "Isn't that obvious? Even to you?"

Marino knew what this last question meant, and she opened her mouth to respond as the room broke out in murmurs. It was no secret that Howard was a sexist. He believed a woman's place in a firm was as a paralegal or a courtroom stenographer. Marino had won more cases than Howard, but Howard had discounted her wins because he'd decided she must have traded sexual favors for legal ones. This was very different from his monetary favors.

Marino said, "She does have a track record. If you look at percentages, Howard, she's at a hundred percent. Which is twice as good as you did in your first six minutes with the firm."

Howard opened his mouth, but Darby held up a hand. "Let's just bring Ms. Dvanaesti in," he said as he thought, before I report your monetary favors to the bar, William.

An intern nodded and opened the door. He gestured to someone outside the room to enter, then stepped aside to allow Jacquelyn Dvanaesti to enter. He let his eye wander over her professionally and conservatively dressed body as she passed him.

Jacquelyn entered the room with grace and confidence as if she'd been entering this room for years. She met every person's gaze with a genuine smile that reached her eyes. A chair had been placed for her at the end of the table, and she sat down without waiting to be offered the seat.

Her self-confidence was not lost on Darby or anyone else in the room. Confidence, Darby noted. Not overconfidence. Not a sense of grandiose self-importance like Howard. Darby also noted her attire, which signaled to him that she respected the law and herself. He liked this young attorney. He was intrigued by this young attorney who was beautiful without knowing it, brilliant without flaunting it. He leaned forward. "May I call you Jacquelyn?" Darby asked.

The room went silent. Darby never addressed anyone by first name. That was unprofessional, in his opinion. The only person they knew him to call by their first name was Sandra Day O'Connor.

Jacquelyn blushed but nodded.

Darby nodded as well. "What drew you to the law, Jacquelyn?"

Jacquelyn stared at Darby as if the answer was obvious. As if everyone in the room shared the same answer. "Because I love the law. The law is humanity in its purest and sincerest form. The law doesn't allow itself to be governed by the heart or popular opinion. It is the essence of not what is right but what is just. When practiced honestly, the law is blind to wealth and poverty. It cares for nothing more than what is best for society."

Darby smiled.

Howard rolled his eyes and opened his mouth to rip apart the kiss-up answer she'd provided when a phone started ringing.

Everyone looked around the room aghast. Phones never rang in this room because no phones were allowed. Not even Howard dared to bring his cell phone into one of these meetings. Still, a phone rang.

Jacquelyn reached into the breast pocket of her suit and withdrew her ringing cell phone.

Howard opened his mouth to speak, but Jacquelyn held up one finger to silence him. She looked at Darby. "I have to take this call. It's my father letting me know about my mother. She was seriously injured in a fire two months ago."

Jacquelyn stood up, turned, and left the room.

As the door closed, the room burst into upheaval. Some marveled at the young attorney's intestinal fortitude. Others voiced their anger at her audacity.

Darby didn't hear any of it. Instead, he smiled and leaned back in his chair. Finally, he thought to himself, there is hope for the future. He wasn't thinking of the firm but of the law.

THE END